KILL or be KILLED

IMAGE COMICS, INC.

Robert Kirkman — **Chief Operating Officer**
Erik Larsen — **Chief Financial Officer**
Todd McFarlane — **President**
Marc Silvestri — **Chief Executive Officer**
Jim Valentino — **Vice President**
Eric Stephenson — **Publisher / Chief Creative Officer**
Corey Hart — **Director of Sales**
Jeff Boison — **Director of Publishing Planning & Book Trade Sales**
Chris Ross — **Director of Digital Sales**
Jeff Stang — **Director of Specialty Sales**
Kat Salazar — **Director of PR & Marketing**
Drew Gill — **Art Director**
Heather Doornink — **Production Director**
Nicole Lapalme — **Controller**

Standard Cover, ISBN: 978-1-5343-0651-6
Forbidden Planet/Big Bang Comics Variant, ISBN: 978-1-5343-1101-5

IMAGECOMICS.COM

 Publication design by Sean Phillips

Volume Four

KILL or be KILLED

Ed Brubaker
Sean Phillips
Elizabeth Breitweiser

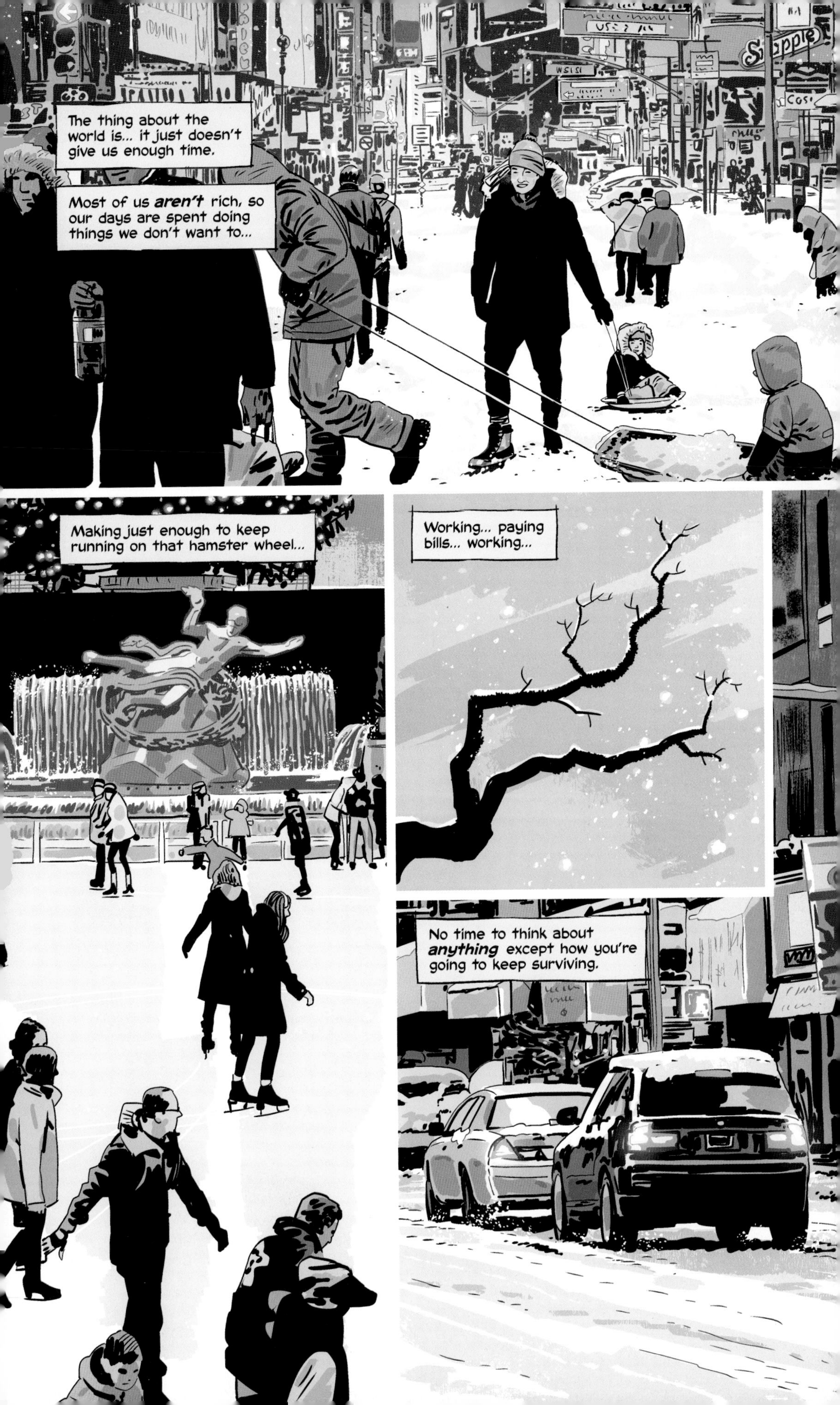

The thing about the world is... it just doesn't give us enough time.
Most of us ***aren't*** rich, so our days are spent doing things we don't want to...
Making just enough to keep running on that hamster wheel...
Working... paying bills... working...
No time to think about ***anything*** except how you're going to keep surviving.
Snapple

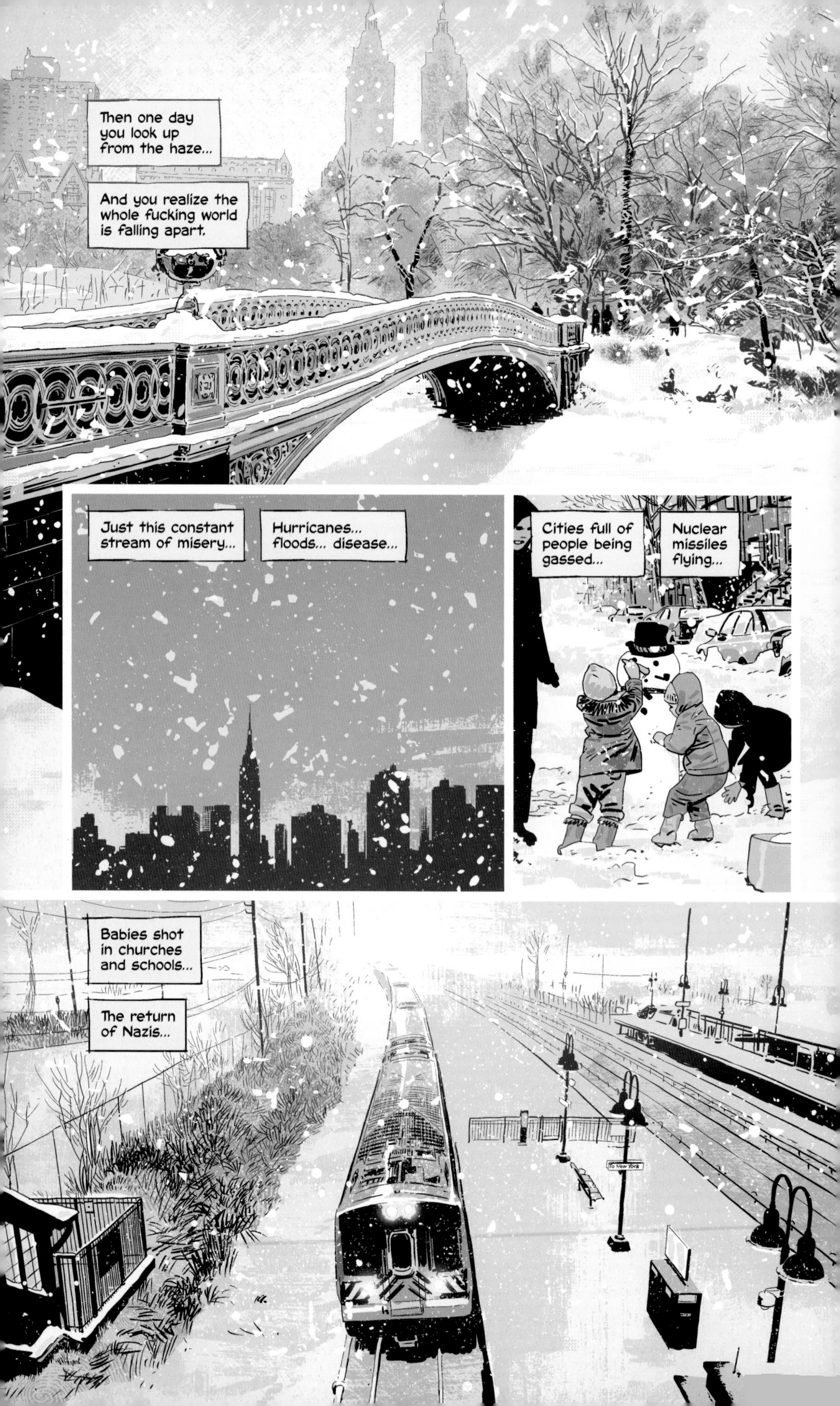
Then one day you look up from the haze...
And you realize the whole fucking world is falling apart.
Just this constant stream of misery...
Hurricanes... floods... disease...
Cities full of people being gassed...
Nuclear missiles flying...
Babies shot in churches and schools...
The return of Nazis...
To New York

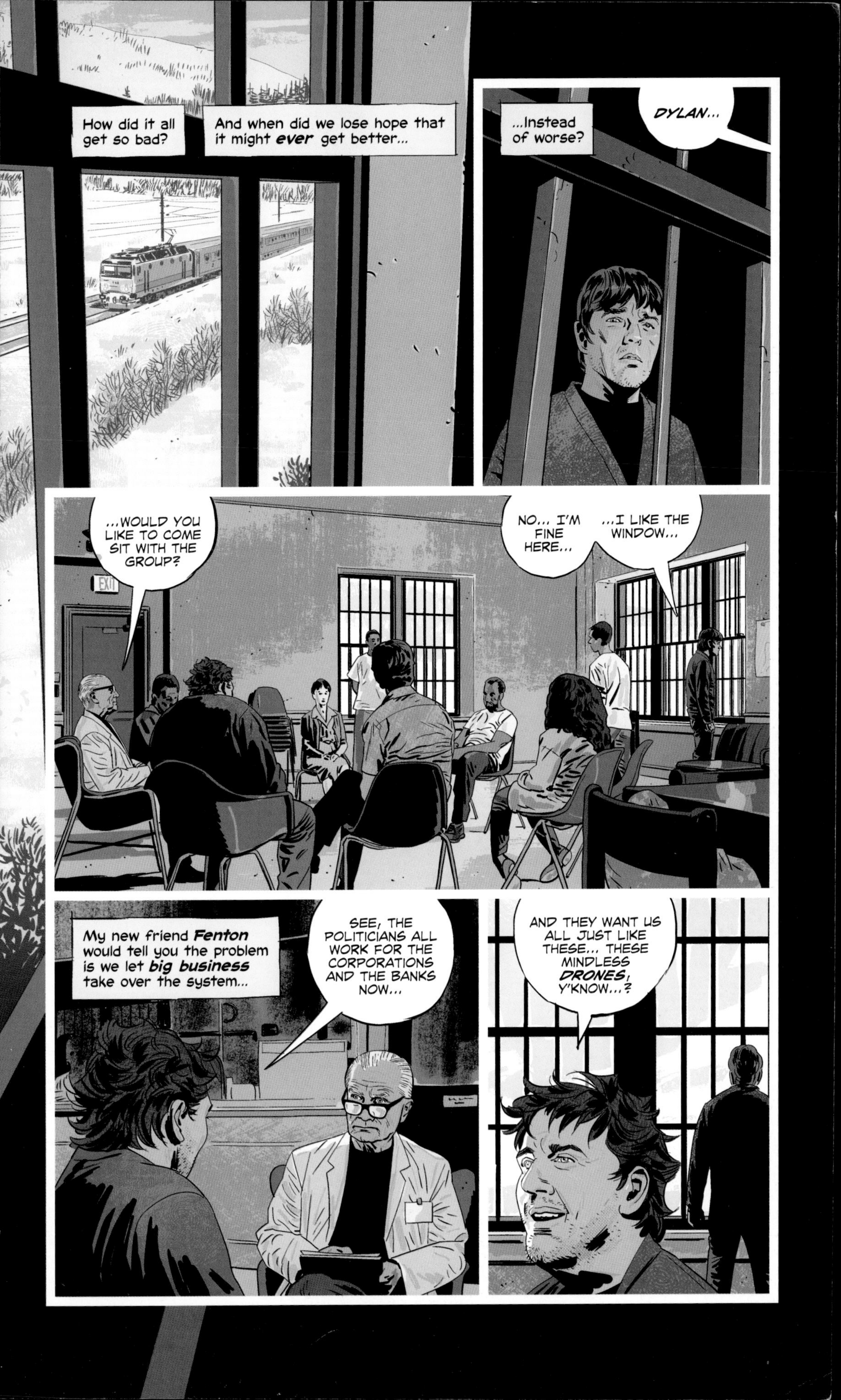
How did it all get so bad?
And when did we lose hope that it might *ever* get better...
...Instead of worse?
DYLAN...
...WOULD YOU LIKE TO COME SIT WITH THE GROUP?
EXIT
NO... I'M FINE HERE...
...I LIKE THE WINDOW...
My new friend **Fenton** would tell you the problem is we let ***big business*** take over the system...
SEE, THE POLITICIANS ALL WORK FOR THE CORPORATIONS AND THE BANKS NOW...
AND THEY WANT US ALL JUST LIKE THESE... THESE MINDLESS ***DRONES***, Y'KNOW...?

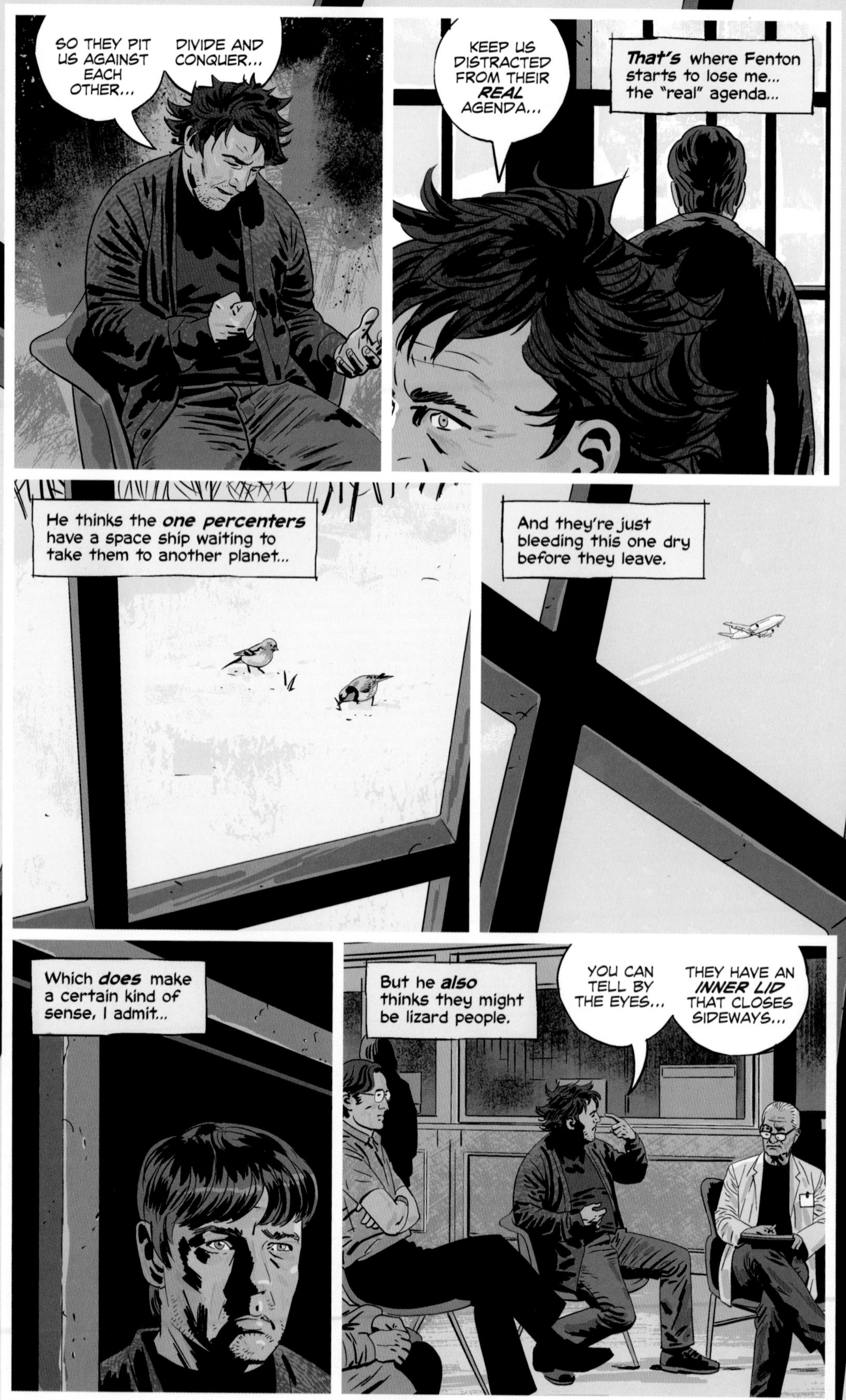
SO THEY PIT US AGAINST EACH OTHER...
DIVIDE AND CONQUER...
KEEP US DISTRACTED FROM THEIR REAL AGENDA...
That's where Fenton starts to lose me... the "real" agenda...
He thinks the one percenters have a space ship waiting to take them to another planet...
And they're just bleeding this one dry before they leave.
Which does make a certain kind of sense, I admit...
But he also thinks they might be lizard people.
YOU CAN TELL BY THE EYES...
THEY HAVE AN INNER LID THAT CLOSES SIDEWAYS...

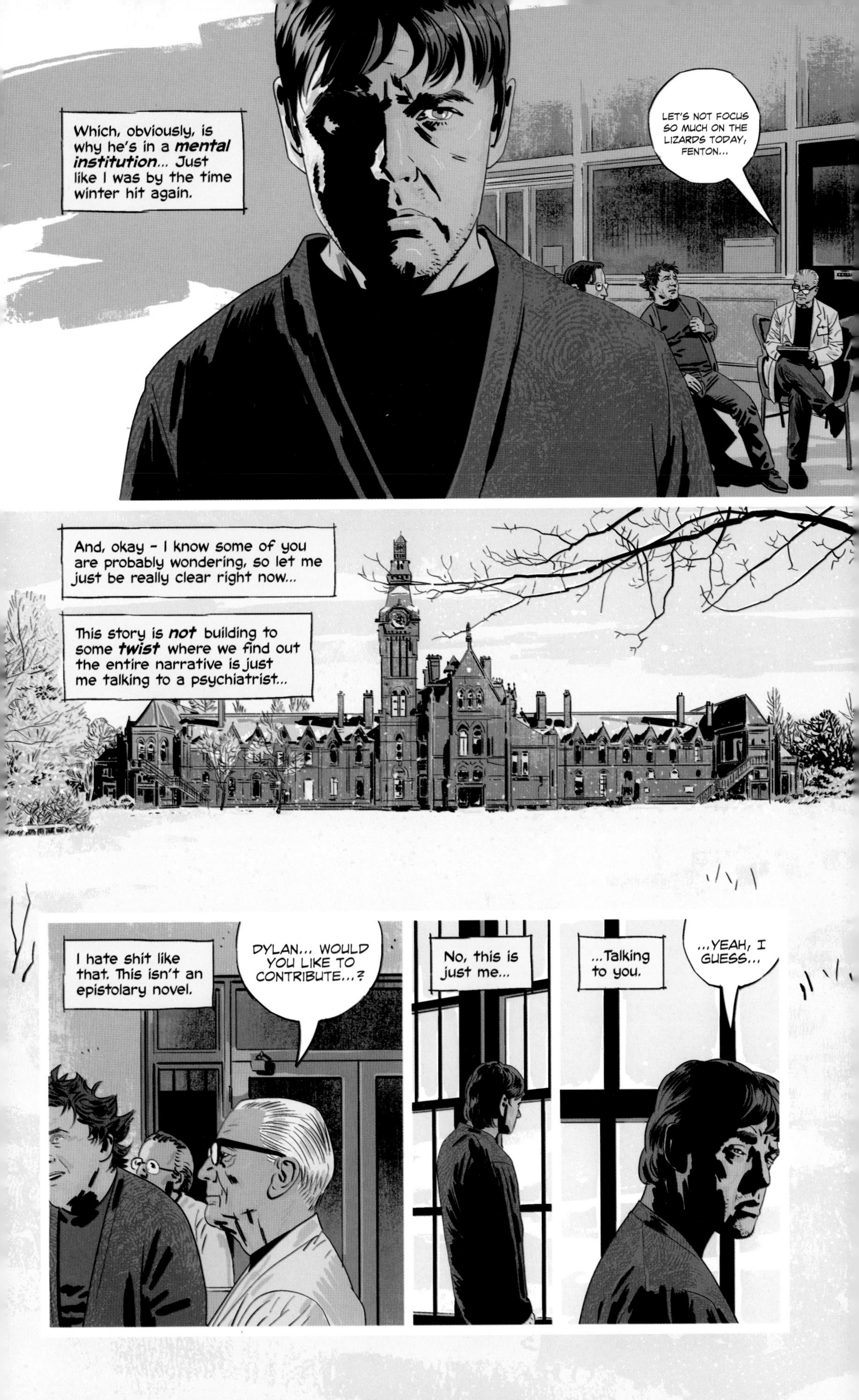
Which, obviously, is why he's in a ***mental institution***... Just like I was by the time winter hit again.
LET'S NOT FOCUS SO MUCH ON THE LIZARDS TODAY, FENTON...
And, okay – I know some of you are probably wondering, so let me just be really clear right now...
This story is ***not*** building to some ***twist*** where we find out the entire narrative is just me talking to a psychiatrist...
I hate shit like that. This isn't an epistolary novel.
DYLAN... WOULD YOU LIKE TO CONTRIBUTE...?
No, this is just me...
...Talking to you.
...YEAH, I GUESS...

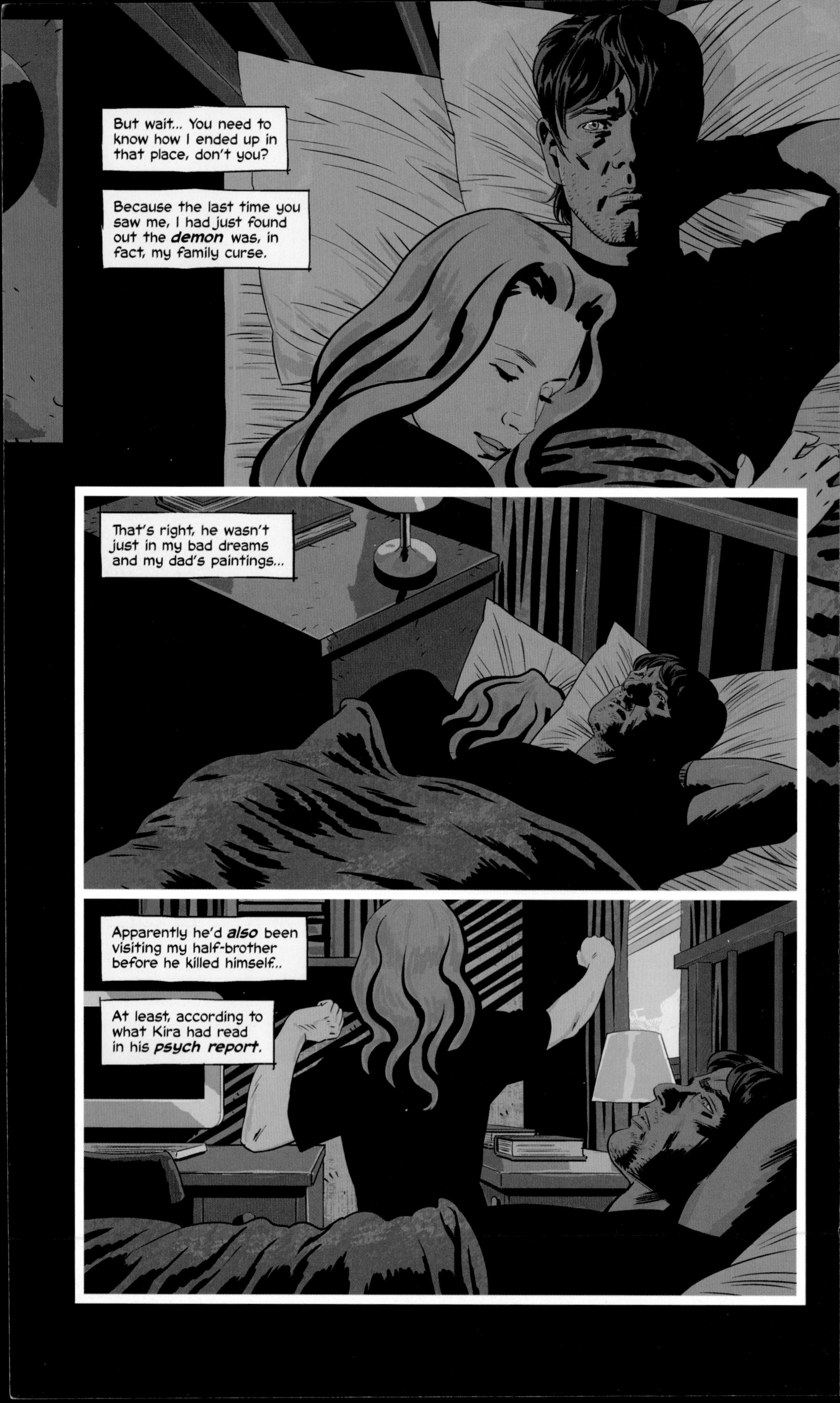
But wait... You need to know how I ended up in that place, don't you?
Because the last time you saw me, I had just found out the **demon** was, in fact, my family curse.
That's right, he wasn't just in my bad dreams and my dad's paintings...
Apparently he'd **also** been visiting my half-brother before he killed himself...
At least, according to what Kira had read in his **psych report**.

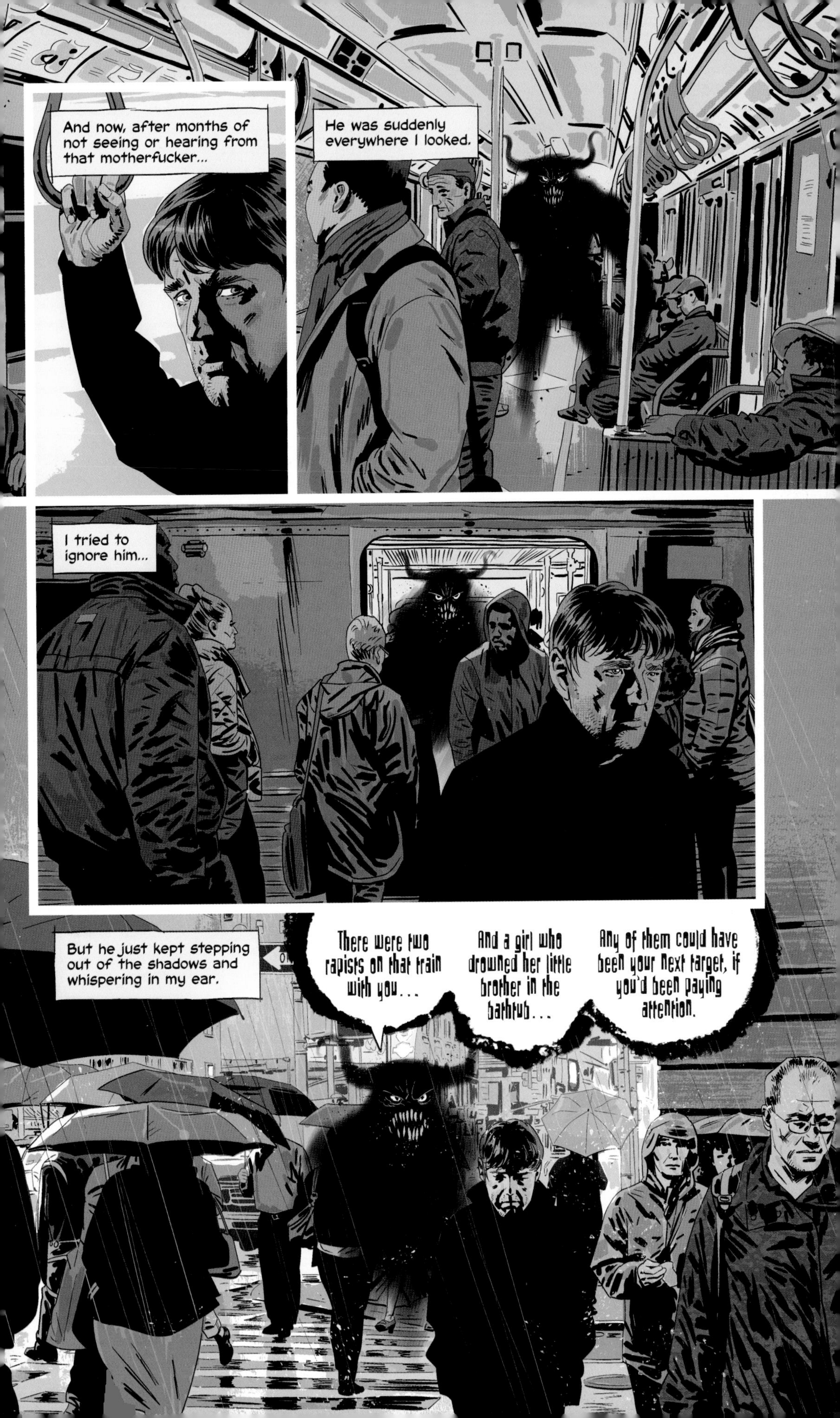
And now, after months of not seeing or hearing from that motherfucker...
He was suddenly everywhere I looked.
I tried to ignore him...
But he just kept stepping out of the shadows and whispering in my ear.
There were two rapists on that train with you...
And a girl who drowned her little brother in the bathtub...
Any of them could have been your next target, if you'd been paying attention.

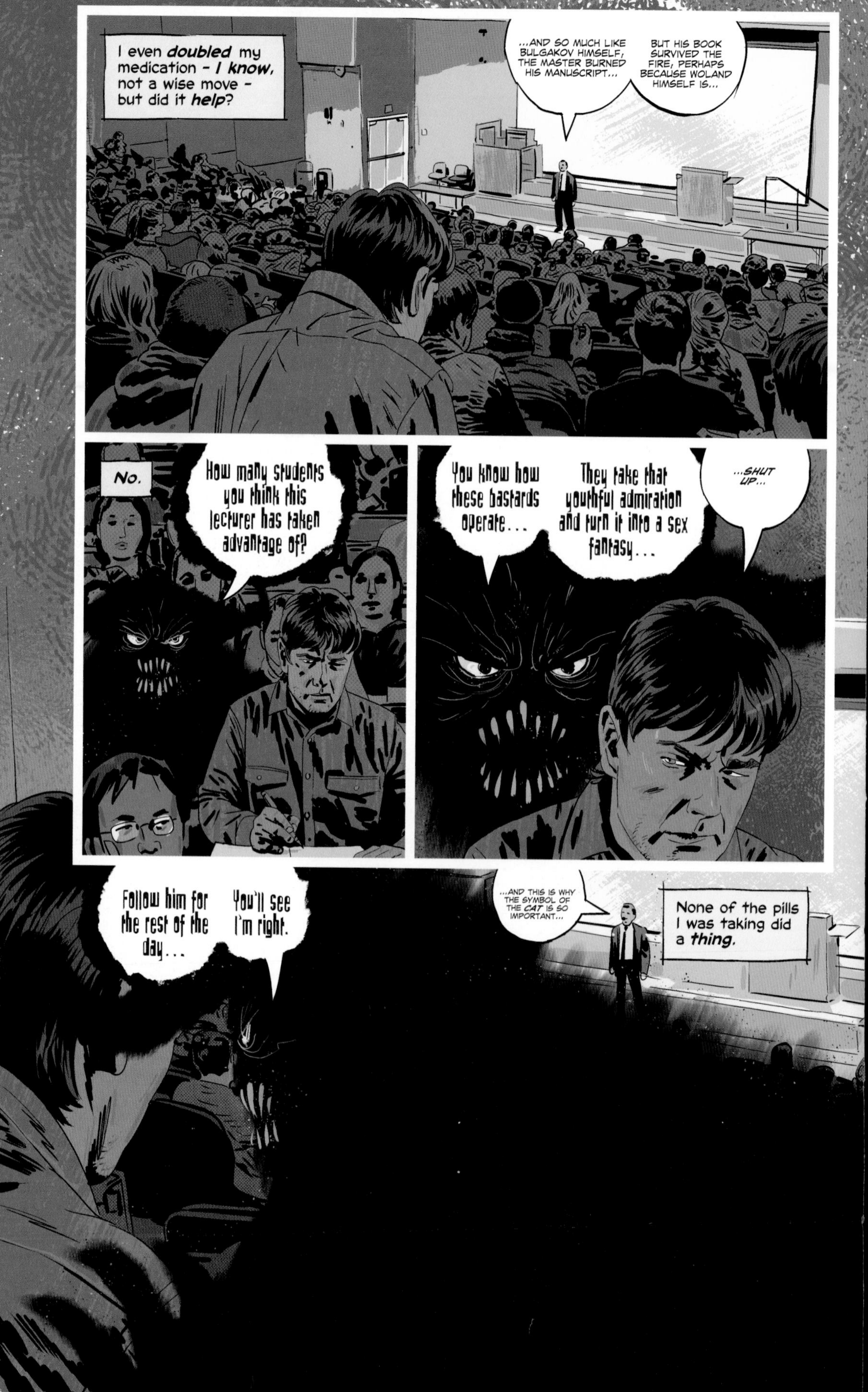

I even *doubled* my medication - *I know*, not a wise move - but did it *help*?
...AND SO MUCH LIKE BULGAKOV HIMSELF, THE MASTER BURNED HIS MANUSCRIPT...
BUT HIS BOOK SURVIVED THE FIRE, PERHAPS BECAUSE WOLAND HIMSELF IS...
No.
How many students you think this lecturer has taken advantage of?
You know how these bastards operate...
They take that youthful admiration and turn it into a sex fantasy...
...SHUT UP...
Follow him for the rest of the day...
You'll see I'm right.
...AND THIS IS WHY THE SYMBOL OF THE *CAT* IS SO IMPORTANT...
None of the pills I was taking did a *thing*.

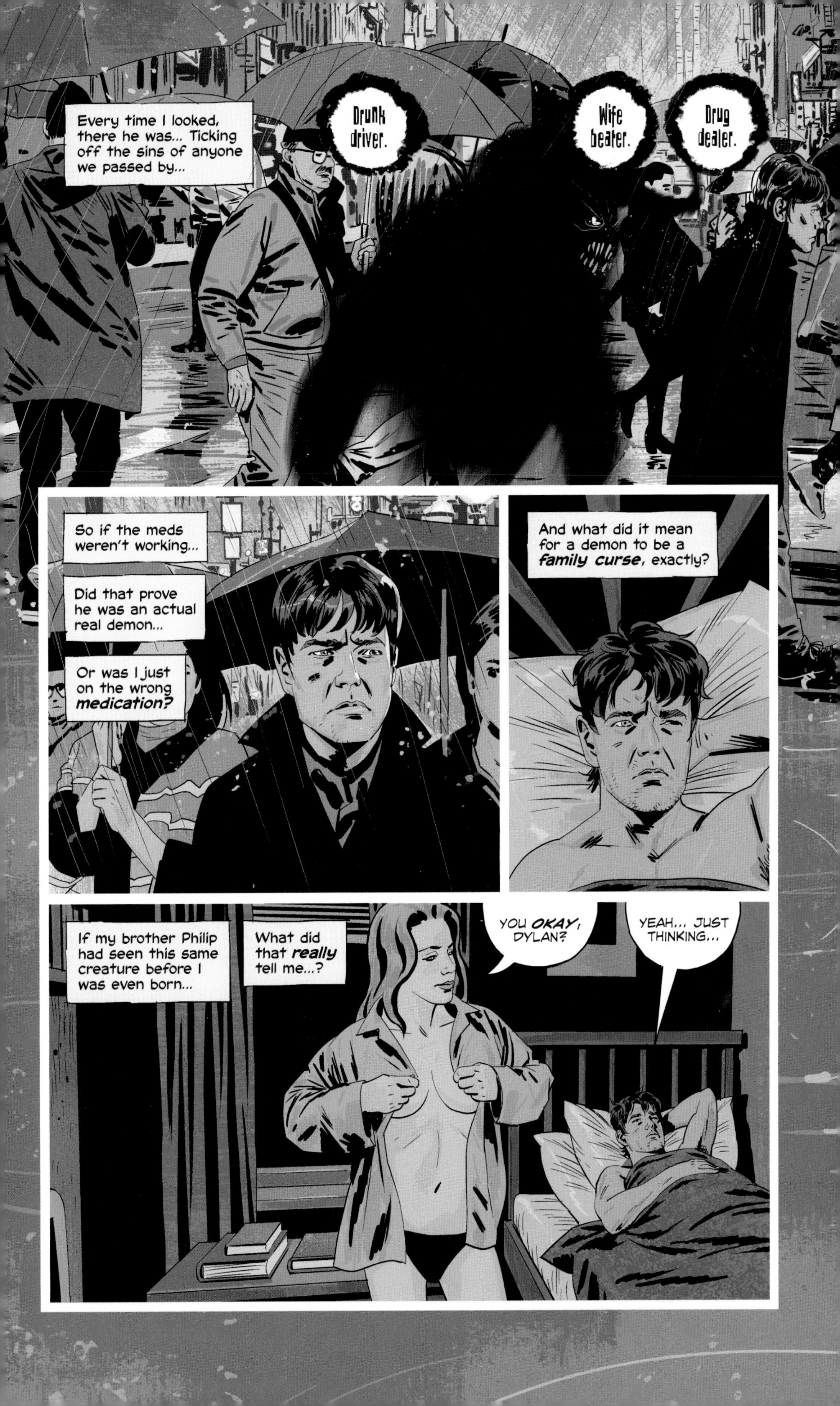

Every time I looked, there he was... Ticking off the sins of anyone we passed by...
Drunk driver.
Wife beater.
Drug dealer.
So if the meds weren't working...
Did that prove he was an actual real demon...
Or was I just on the wrong *medication?*
And what did it mean for a demon to be a *family curse*, exactly?
If my brother Philip had seen this same creature before I was even born...
What did that *really* tell me...?
YOU *OKAY*, DYLAN?
YEAH... JUST THINKING...

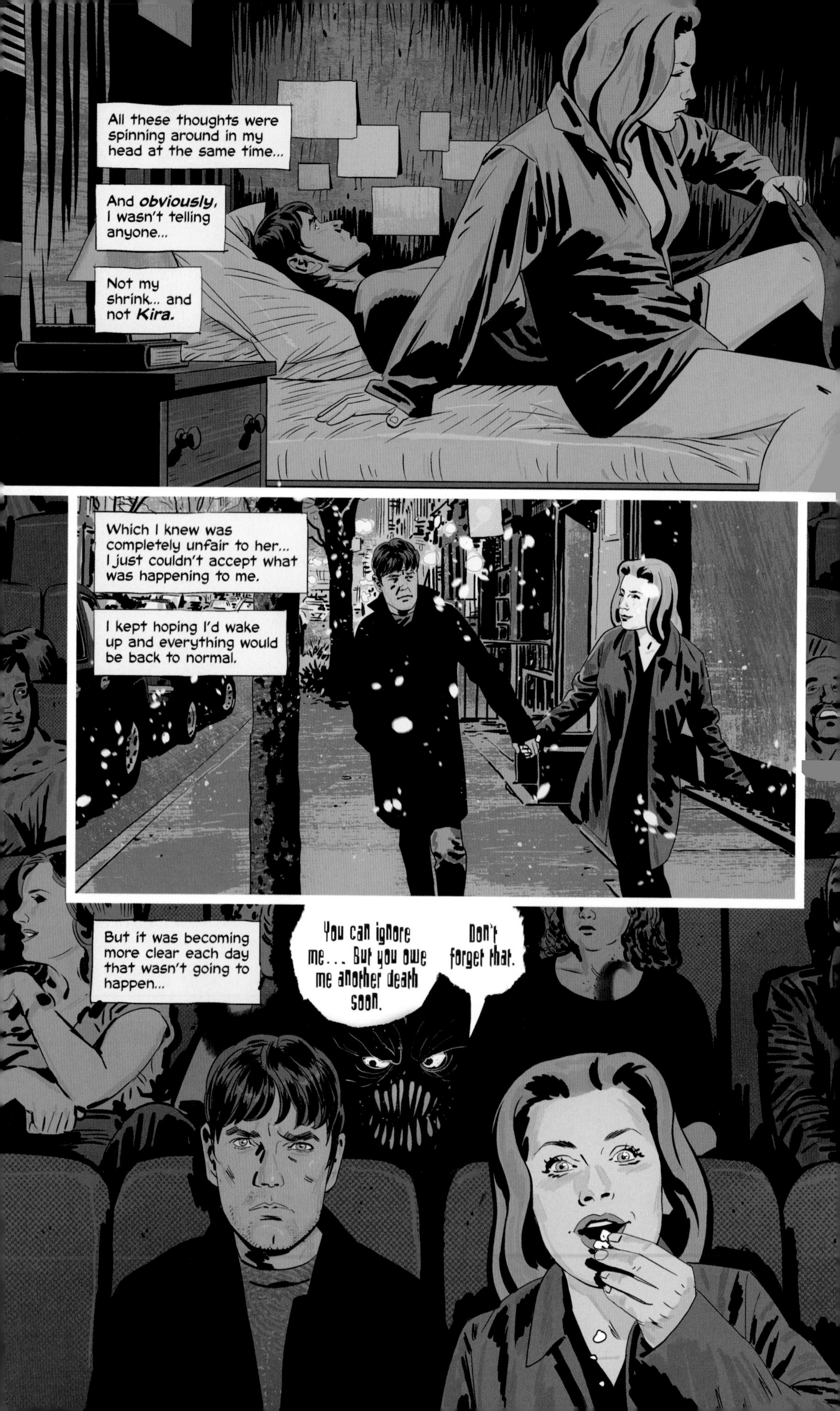
All these thoughts were spinning around in my head at the same time...
And *obviously*, I wasn't telling anyone...
Not my shrink... and not *Kira.*
Which I knew was completely unfair to her... I just couldn't accept what was happening to me.
I kept hoping I'd wake up and everything would be back to normal.
But it was becoming more clear each day that wasn't going to happen...
You can ignore me... But you owe me another death soon.
Don't forget that.

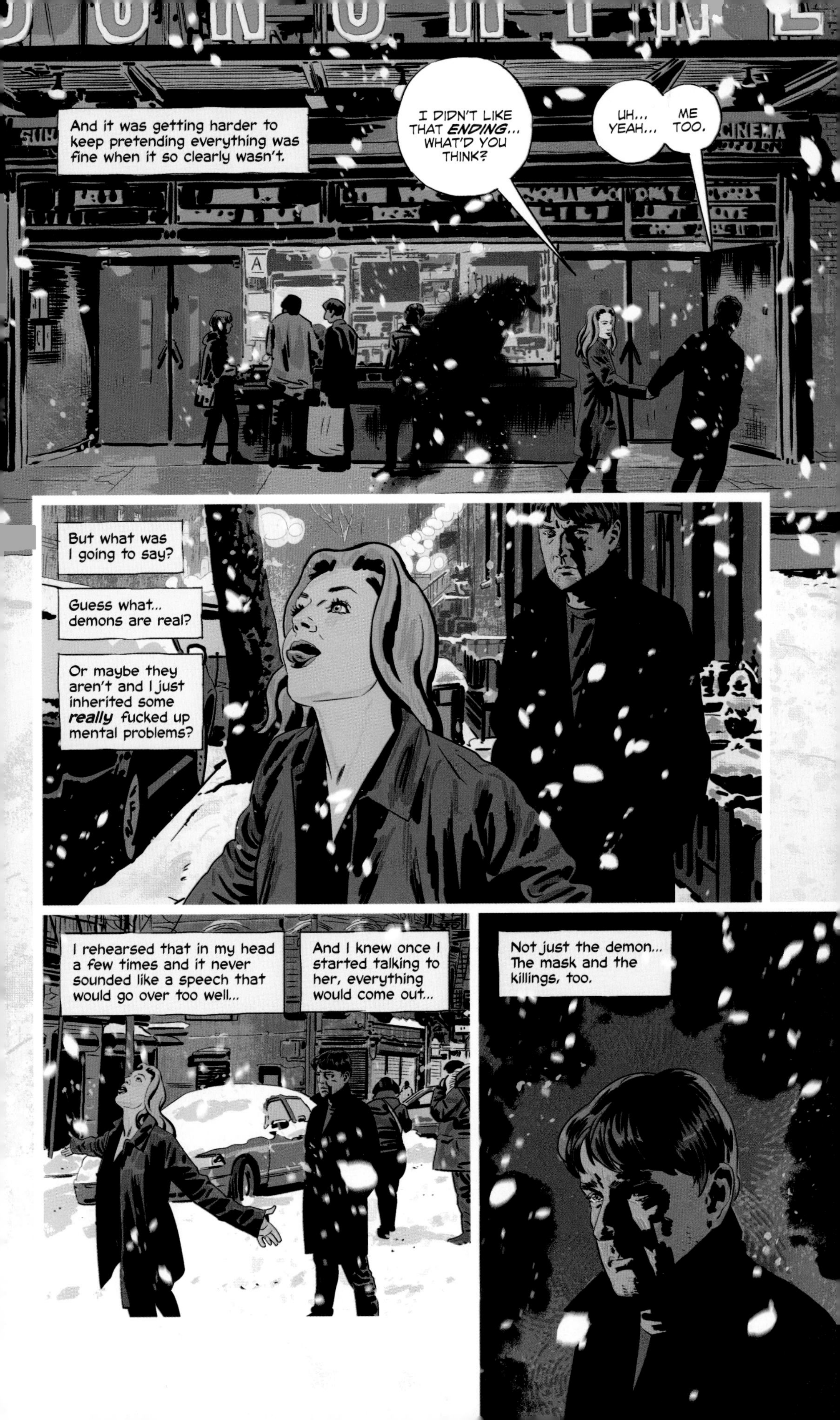
And it was getting harder to keep pretending everything was fine when it so clearly wasn't.
I DIDN'T LIKE THAT *ENDING*... WHAT'D YOU THINK?
UH... YEAH...
ME TOO.
CINEMA
But what was I going to say?
Guess what... demons are real?
Or maybe they aren't and I just inherited some ***really*** fucked up mental problems?
I rehearsed that in my head a few times and it never sounded like a speech that would go over too well...
And I knew once I started talking to her, everything would come out...
Not just the demon... The mask and the killings, too.

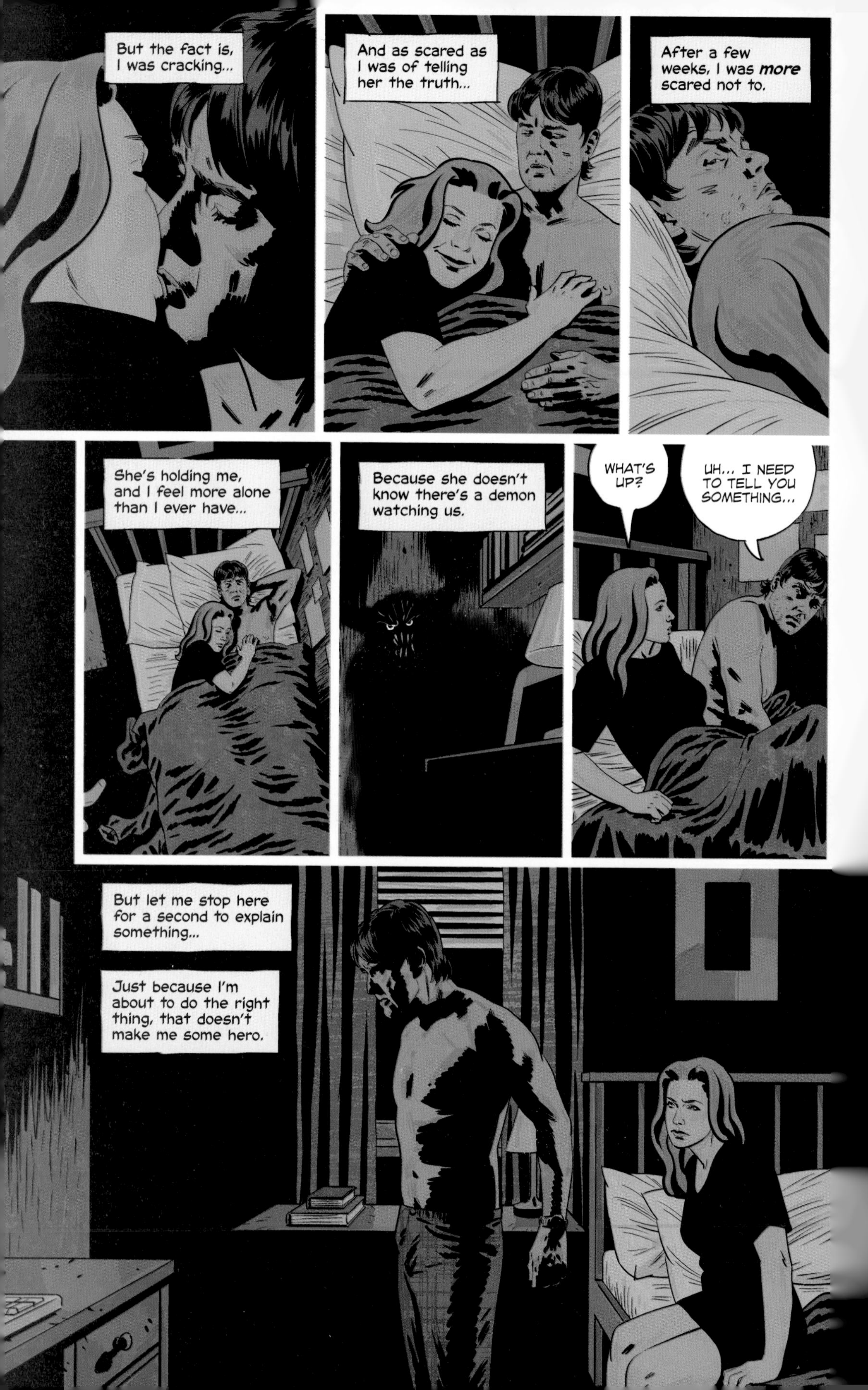

But the fact is, I was cracking...
And as scared as I was of telling her the truth...
After a few weeks, I was *more* scared not to.
She's holding me, and I feel more alone than I ever have...
Because she doesn't know there's a demon watching us.
WHAT'S UP?
UH... I NEED TO TELL YOU SOMETHING...
But let me stop here for a second to explain something...
Just because I'm about to do the right thing, that doesn't make me some hero.

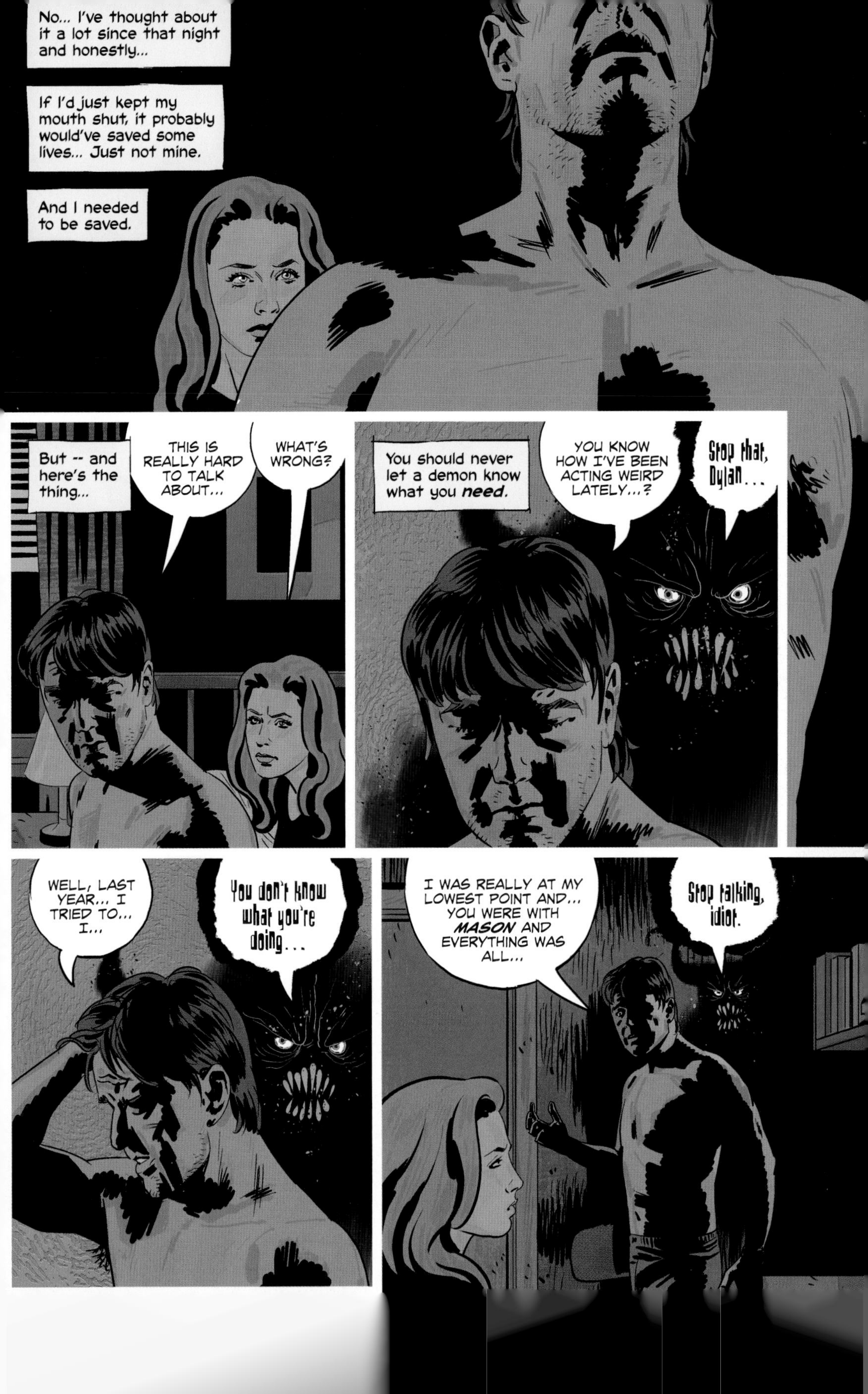
No... I've thought about it a lot since that night and honestly...
If I'd just kept my mouth shut, it probably would've saved some lives... Just not mine.
And I needed to be saved.
But -- and here's the thing...
THIS IS REALLY HARD TO TALK ABOUT...
WHAT'S WRONG?
You should never let a demon know what you **need**.
YOU KNOW HOW I'VE BEEN ACTING WEIRD LATELY...?
Stop that, Dylan...
WELL, LAST YEAR... I TRIED TO... I...
You don't know what you're doing...
I WAS REALLY AT MY LOWEST POINT AND... YOU WERE WITH **MASON** AND EVERYTHING WAS ALL...
Stop talking, idiot.

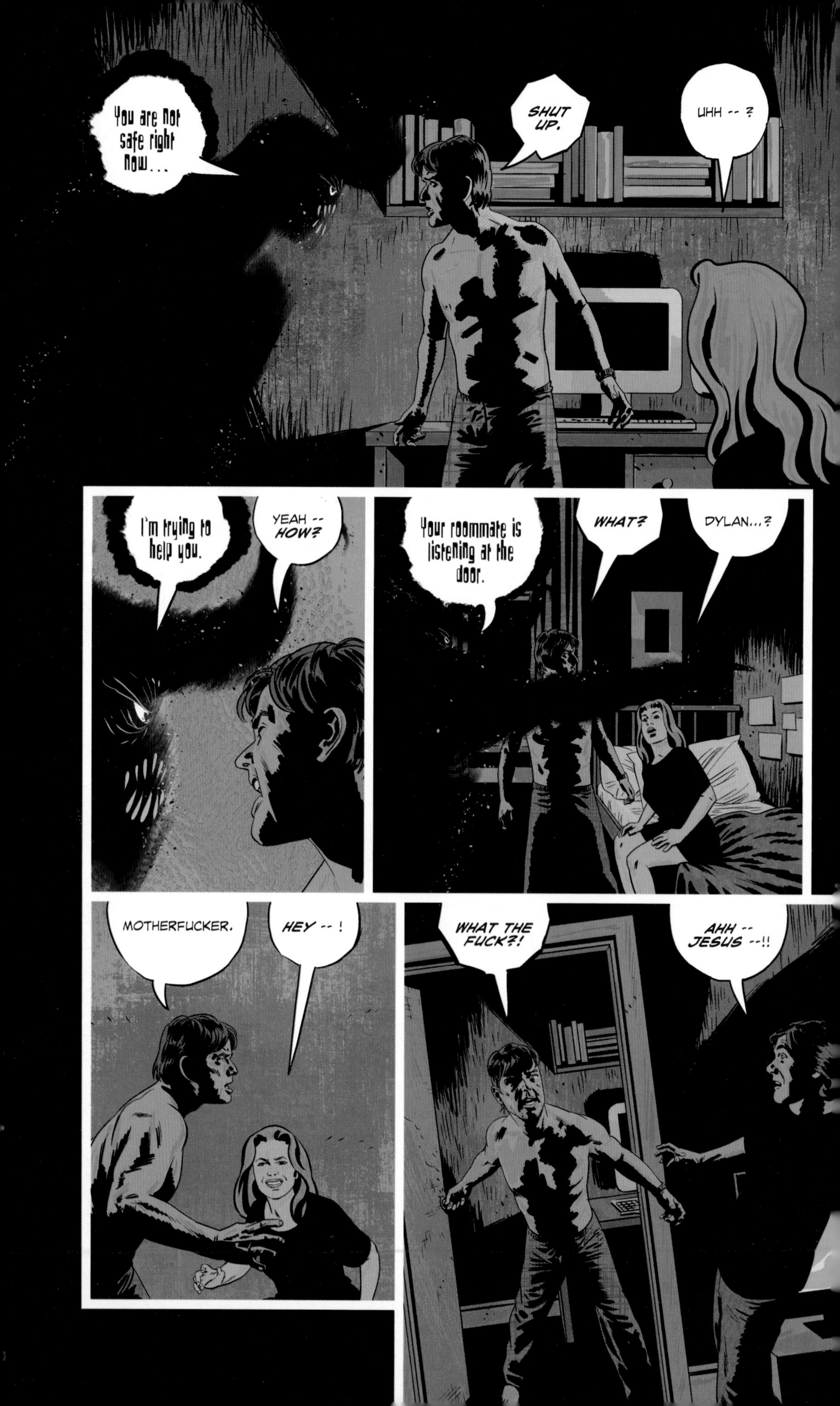
You are not safe right now...
SHUT UP.
UHH -- ?
I'm trying to help you.
YEAH -- HOW?
Your roommate is listening at the door.
WHAT?
DYLAN...?
MOTHERFUCKER.
HEY -- !
WHAT THE FUCK?!
AHH -- JESUS --!!

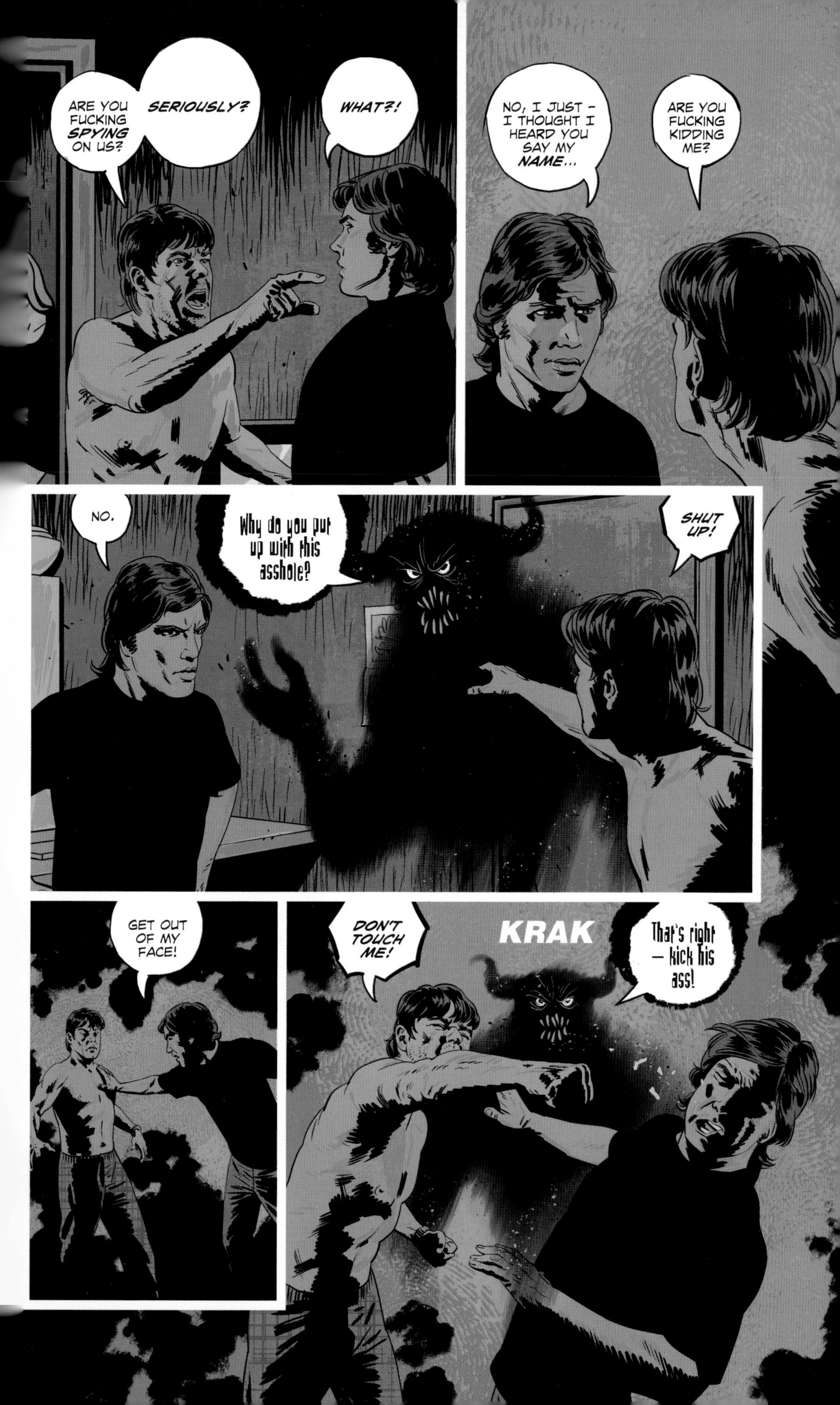
ARE YOU FUCKING SPYING ON US?
SERIOUSLY?
WHAT?!
NO, I JUST – I THOUGHT I HEARD YOU SAY MY NAME...
ARE YOU FUCKING KIDDING ME?
NO.
Why do you put up with this asshole?
SHUT UP!
GET OUT OF MY FACE!
DON'T TOUCH ME!
KRAK
That's right – kick his ass!

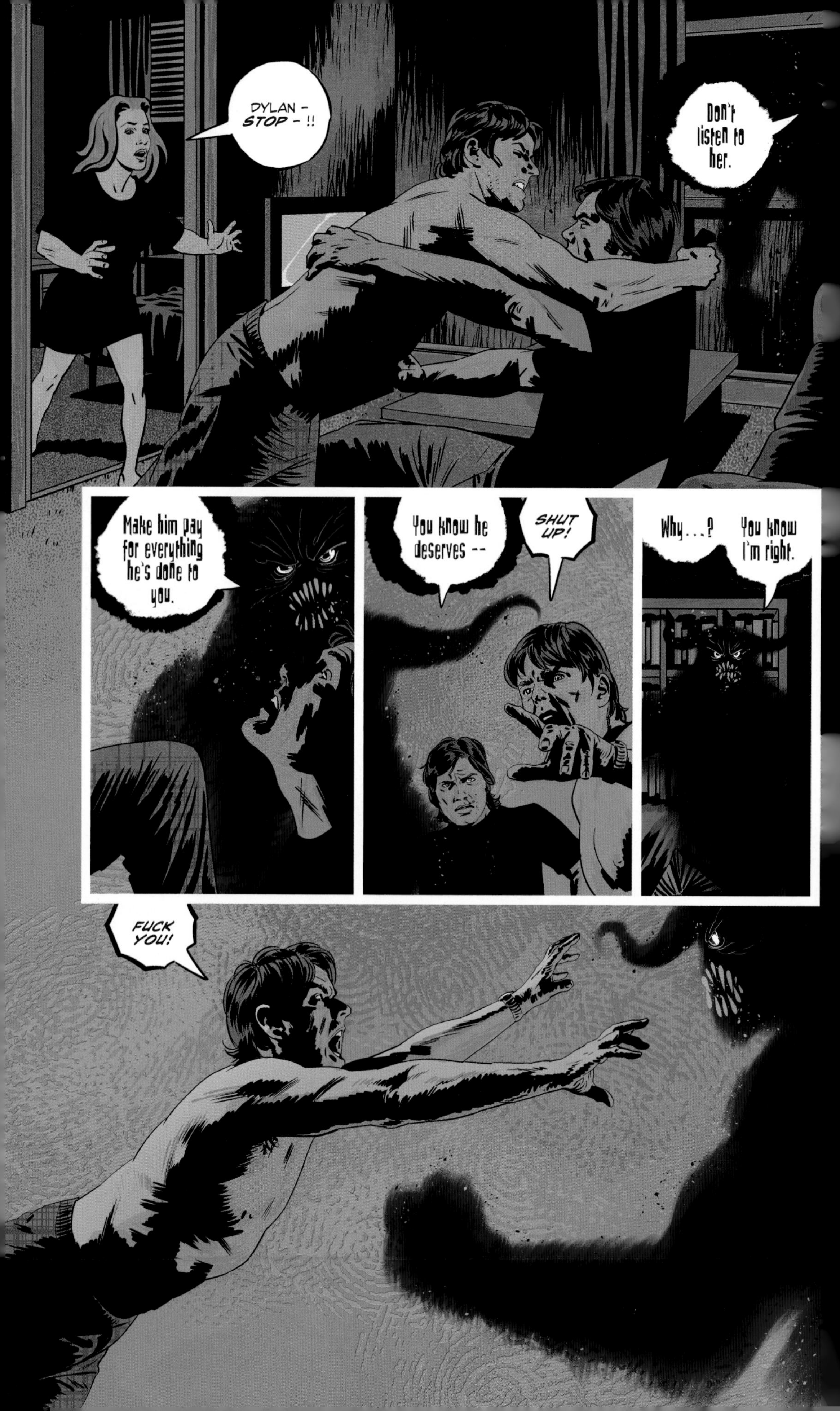
DYLAN -
STOP - !!
Don't listen to her.
Make him pay for everything he's done to you.
You know he deserves --
SHUT UP!
Why...?
You know I'm right.
FUCK YOU!

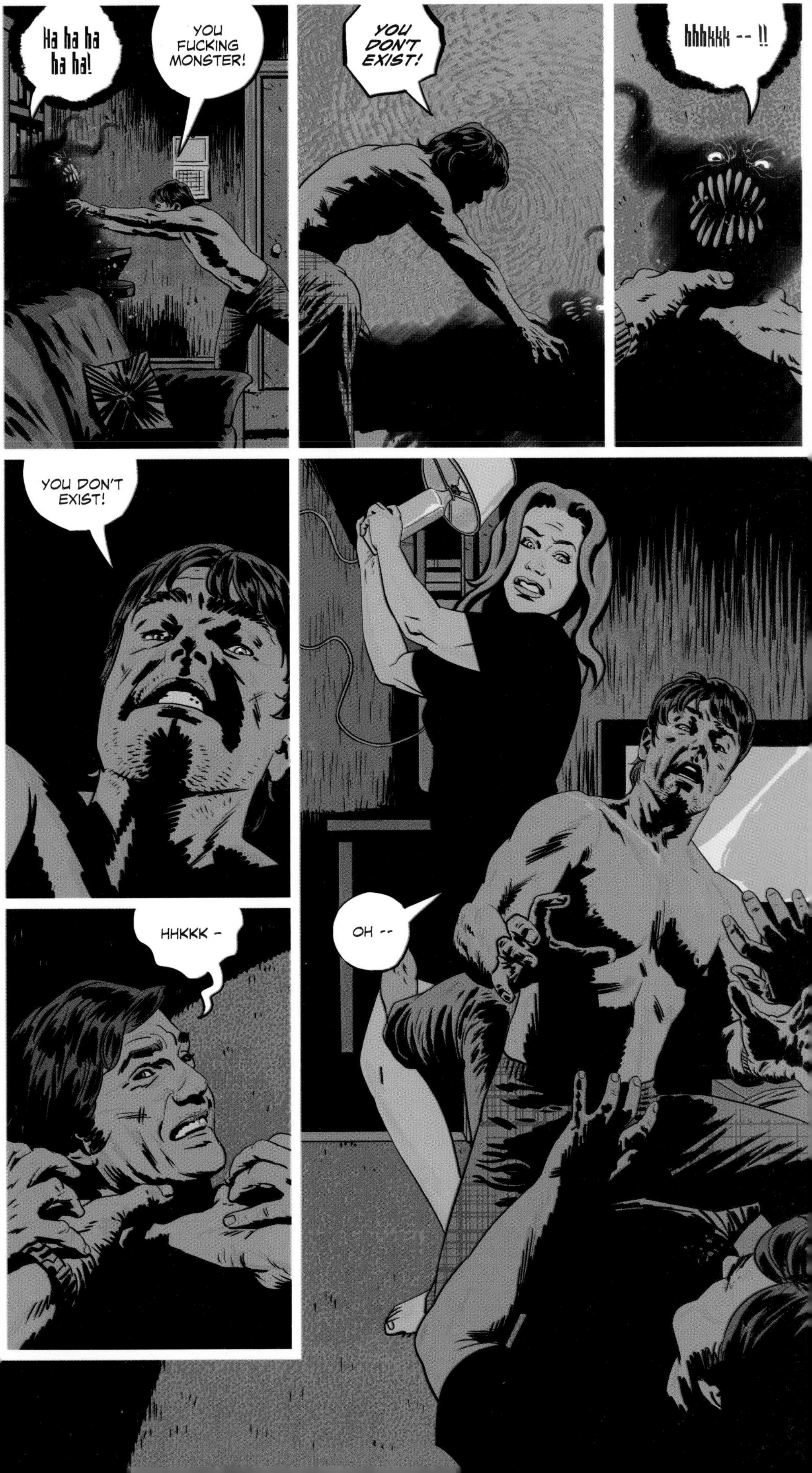
Ha ha ha ha ha!
YOU FUCKING MONSTER!
YOU DON'T EXIST!
hhhkkk -- !!
YOU DON'T EXIST!
HHKKK -
OH --

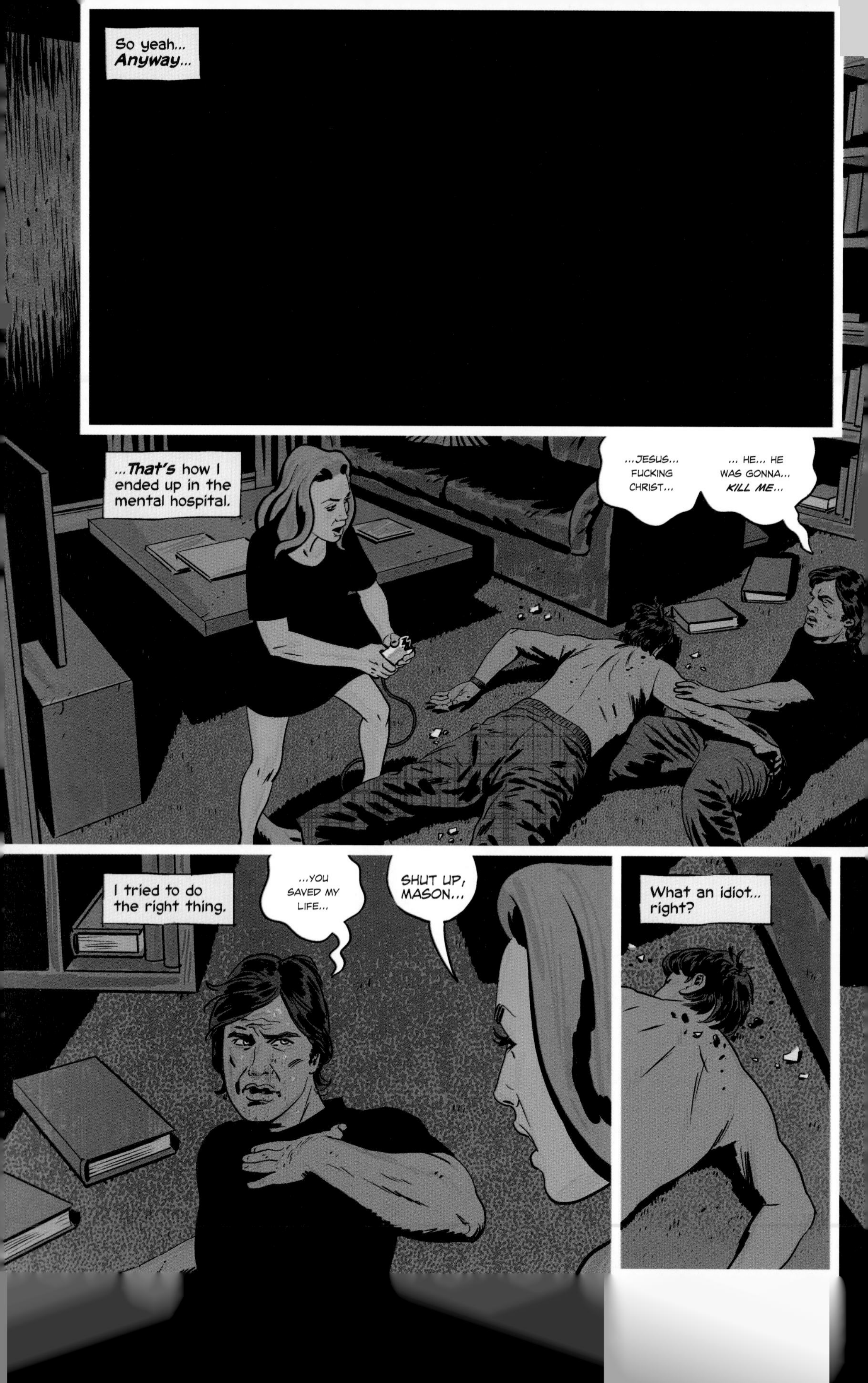

So yeah... Anyway...
...That's how I ended up in the mental hospital.
...JESUS... FUCKING CHRIST...
... HE... HE WAS GONNA... KILL ME...
I tried to do the right thing.
...YOU SAVED MY LIFE...
SHUT UP, MASON...
What an idiot... right?

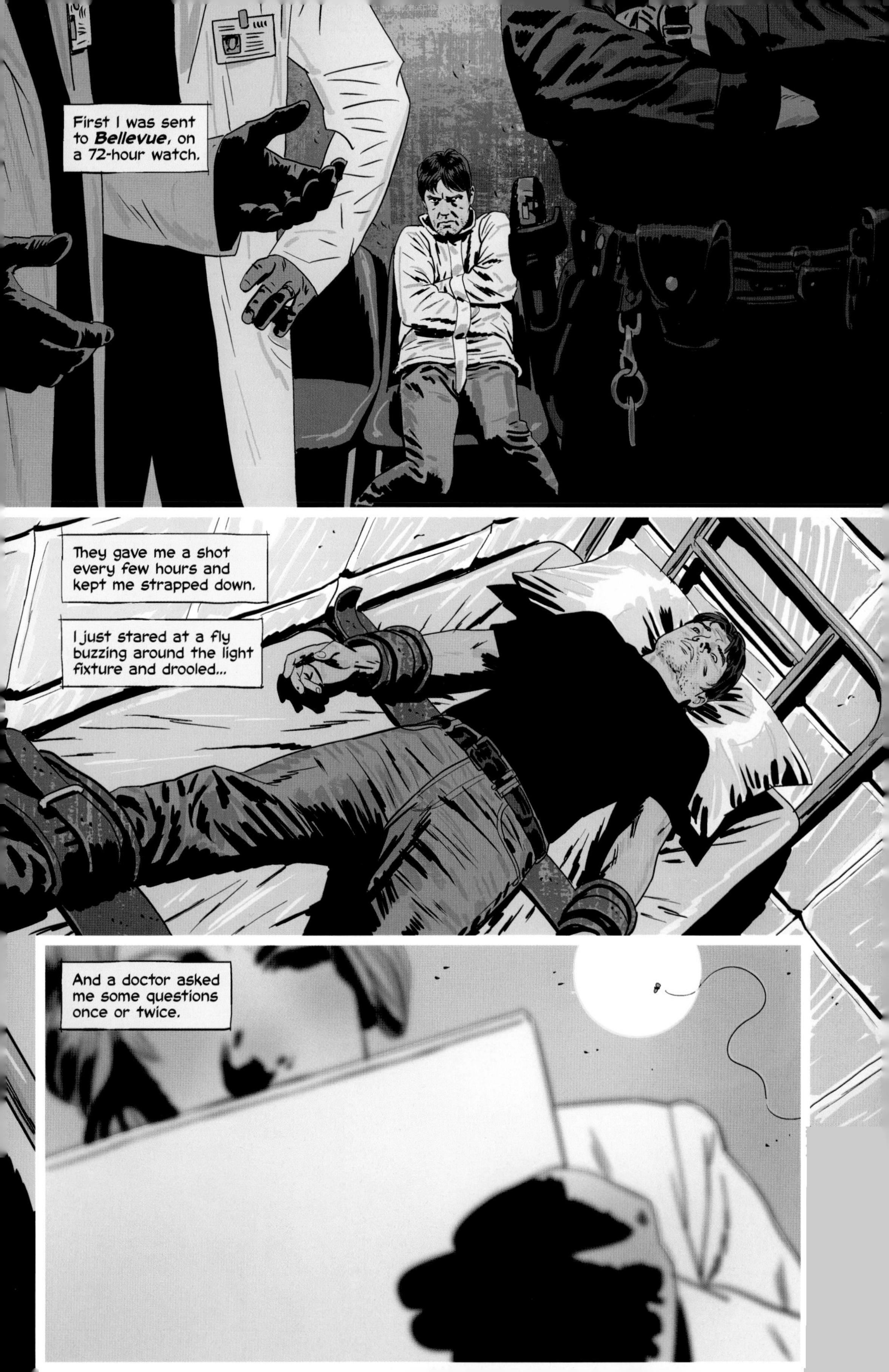
First I was sent to ***Bellevue***, on a 72-hour watch.
They gave me a shot every few hours and kept me strapped down.
I just stared at a fly buzzing around the light fixture and drooled...
And a doctor asked me some questions once or twice.

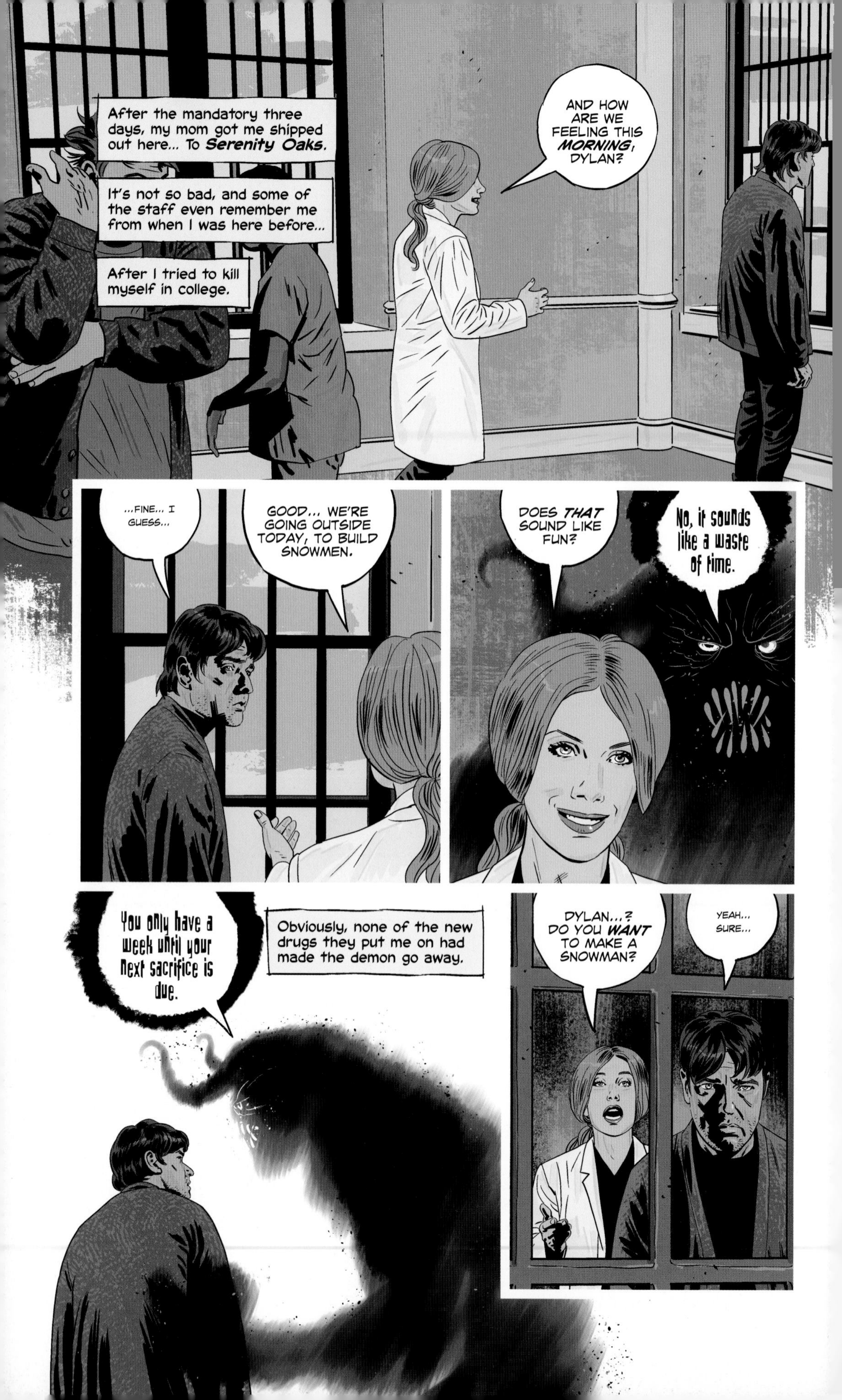

After the mandatory three days, my mom got me shipped out here... To *Serenity Oaks*.
It's not so bad, and some of the staff even remember me from when I was here before...
After I tried to kill myself in college.
AND HOW ARE WE FEELING THIS *MORNING*, DYLAN?
...FINE... I GUESS...
GOOD... WE'RE GOING OUTSIDE TODAY, TO BUILD SNOWMEN.
DOES *THAT* SOUND LIKE FUN?
No, it sounds like a waste of time.
You only have a week until your next sacrifice is due.
Obviously, none of the new drugs they put me on had made the demon go away.
DYLAN...? DO YOU *WANT* TO MAKE A SNOWMAN?
YEAH... SURE...

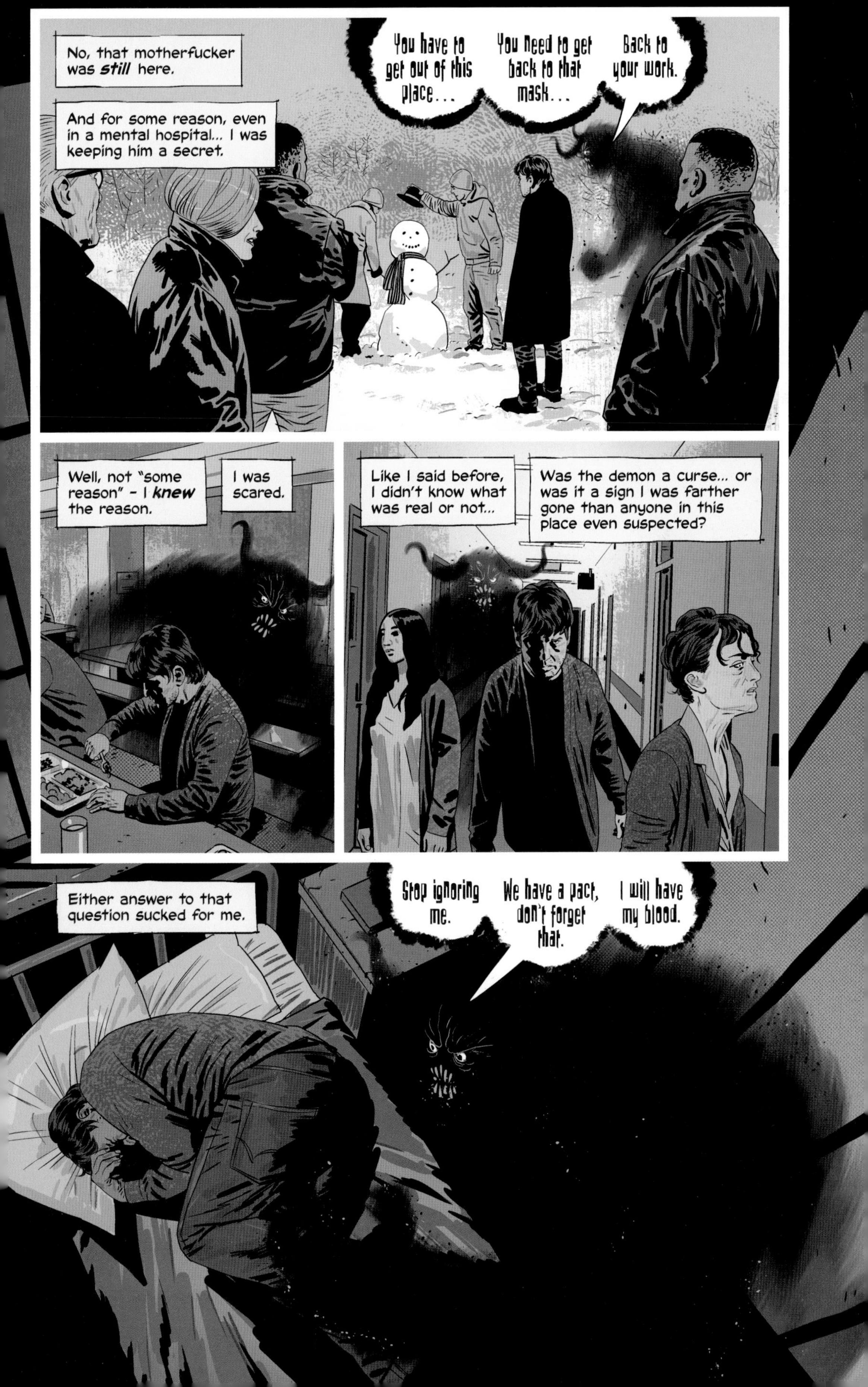

No, that motherfucker was *still* here.
And for some reason, even in a mental hospital... I was keeping him a secret.
You have to get out of this place...
You need to get back to that mask...
Back to your work.
Well, not "some reason" - I *knew* the reason.
I was scared.
Like I said before, I didn't know what was real or not...
Was the demon a curse... or was it a sign I was farther gone than anyone in this place even suspected?
Either answer to that question sucked for me.
Stop ignoring me.
We have a pact, don't forget that.
I will have my blood.

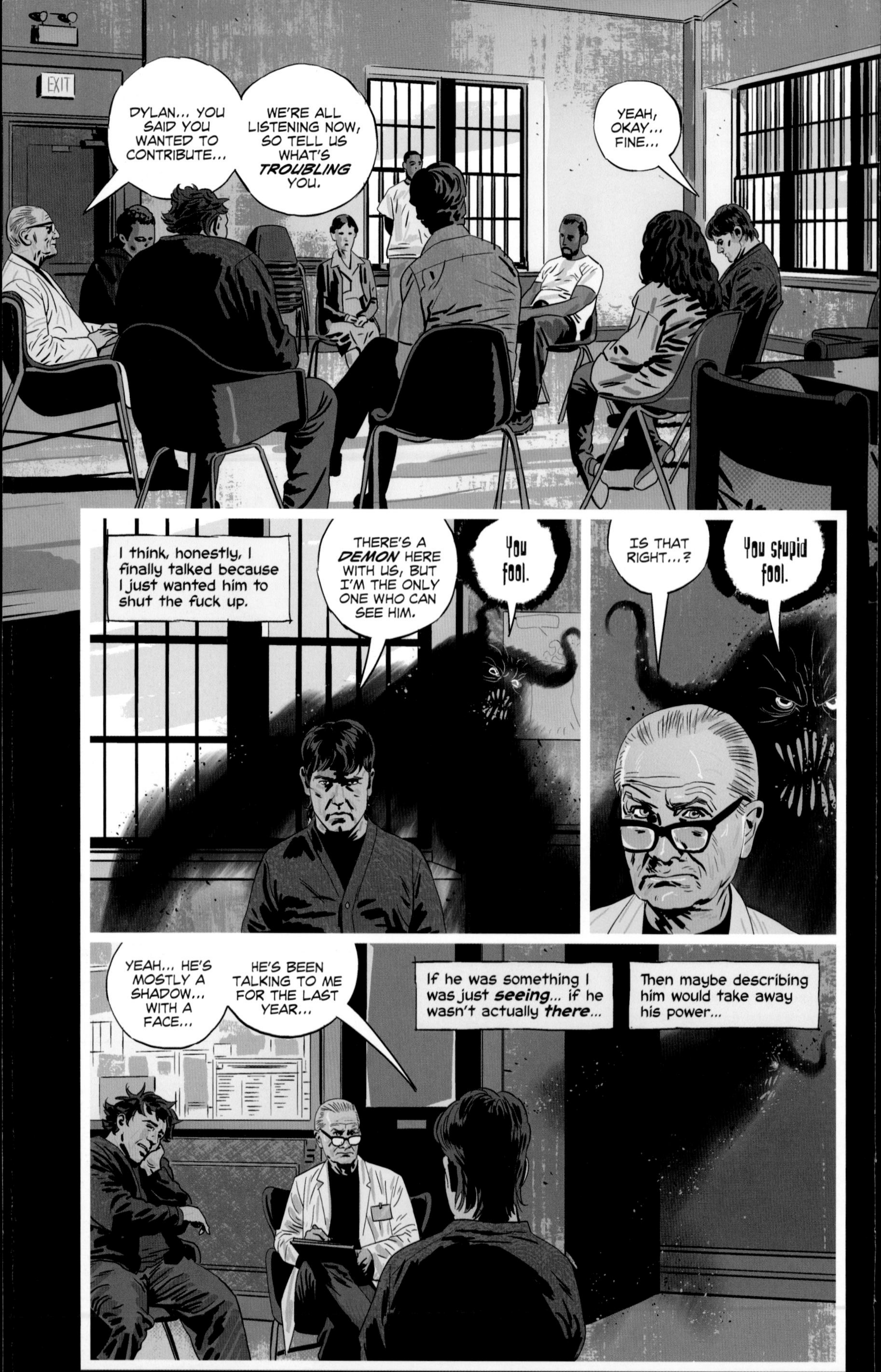
EXIT
DYLAN... YOU SAID YOU WANTED TO CONTRIBUTE...
WE'RE ALL LISTENING NOW, SO TELL US WHAT'S *TROUBLING* YOU.
YEAH, OKAY... FINE...
I think, honestly, I finally talked because I just wanted him to shut the fuck up.
THERE'S A *DEMON* HERE WITH US, BUT I'M THE ONLY ONE WHO CAN SEE HIM.
You fool.
IS THAT RIGHT...?
You stupid fool.
YEAH... HE'S MOSTLY A SHADOW... WITH A FACE...
HE'S BEEN TALKING TO ME FOR THE LAST YEAR...
If he was something I was just *seeing*... if he wasn't actually *there*...
Then maybe describing him would take away his power...

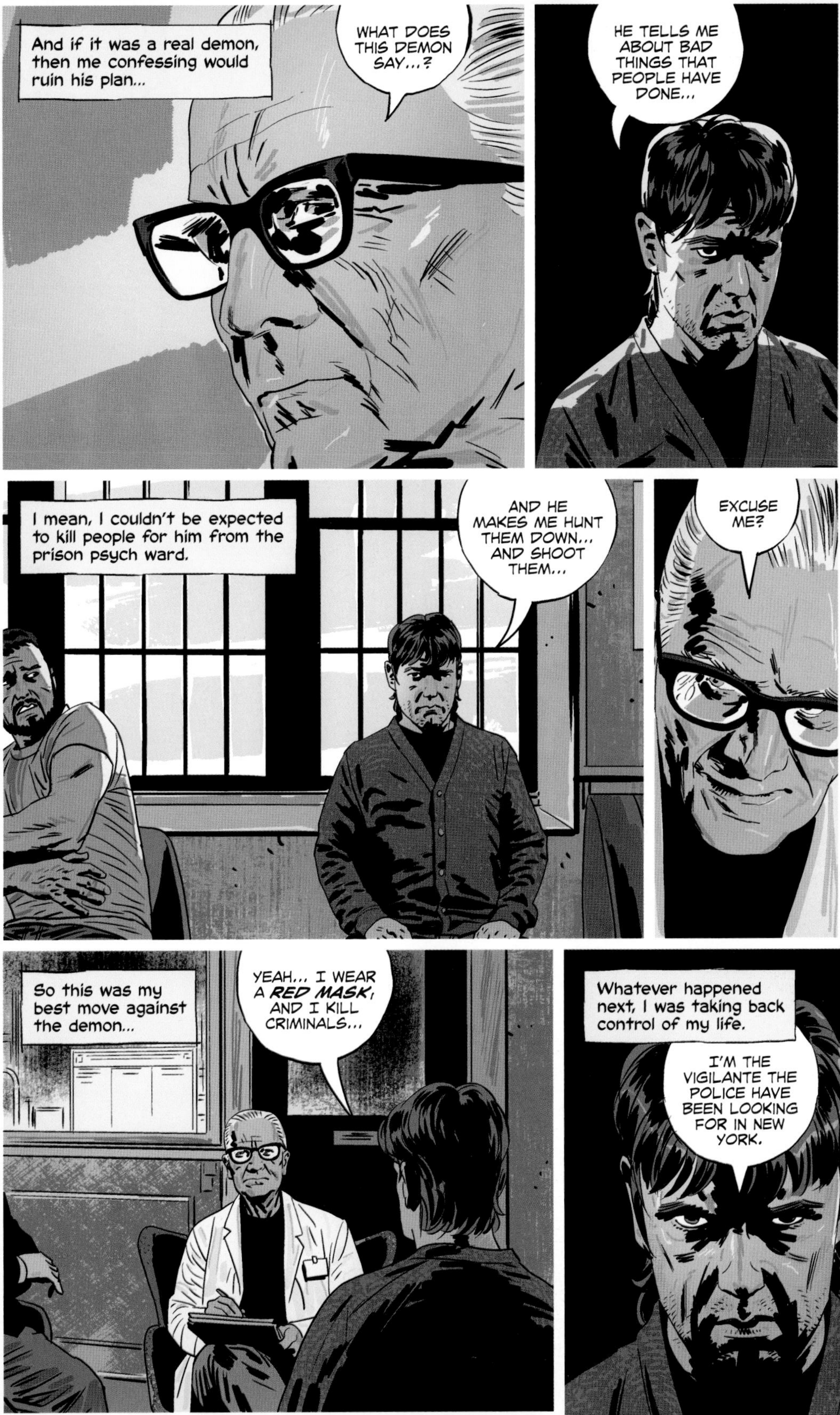
And if it was a real demon, then me confessing would ruin his plan...
WHAT DOES THIS DEMON SAY...?
HE TELLS ME ABOUT BAD THINGS THAT PEOPLE HAVE DONE...
I mean, I couldn't be expected to kill people for him from the prison psych ward.
AND HE MAKES ME HUNT THEM DOWN... AND SHOOT THEM...
EXCUSE ME?
So this was my best move against the demon...
YEAH... I WEAR A RED MASK, AND I KILL CRIMINALS...
Whatever happened next, I was taking back control of my life.
I'M THE VIGILANTE THE POLICE HAVE BEEN LOOKING FOR IN NEW YORK.

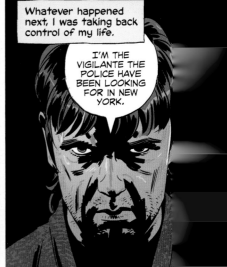

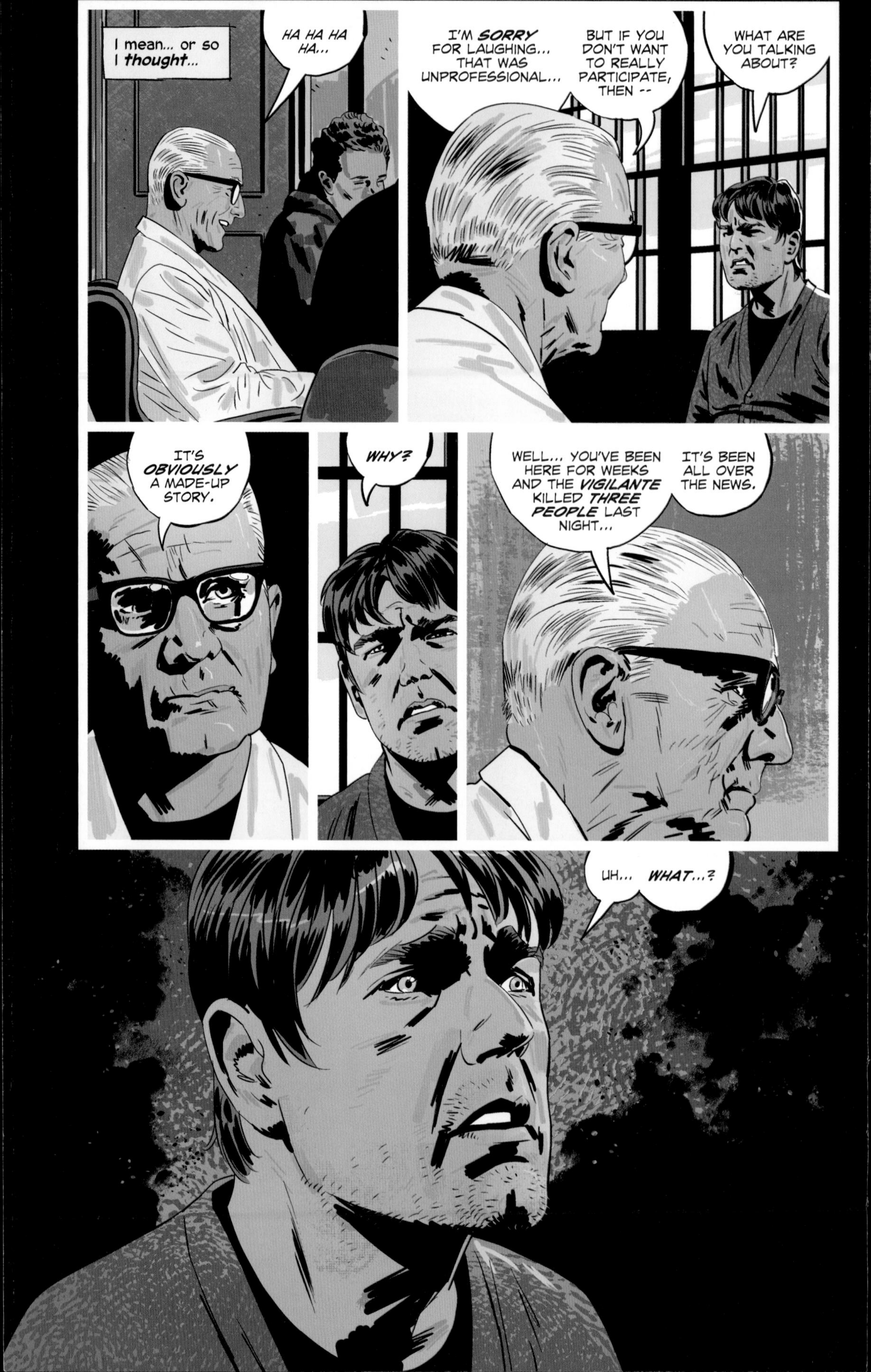
I mean... or so I **thought**...
HA HA HA HA...
I'M SORRY FOR LAUGHING... THAT WAS UNPROFESSIONAL...
BUT IF YOU DON'T WANT TO REALLY PARTICIPATE, THEN --
WHAT ARE YOU TALKING ABOUT?
IT'S OBVIOUSLY A MADE-UP STORY.
WHY?
WELL... YOU'VE BEEN HERE FOR WEEKS AND THE VIGILANTE KILLED THREE PEOPLE LAST NIGHT...
IT'S BEEN ALL OVER THE NEWS.
UH... WHAT...?

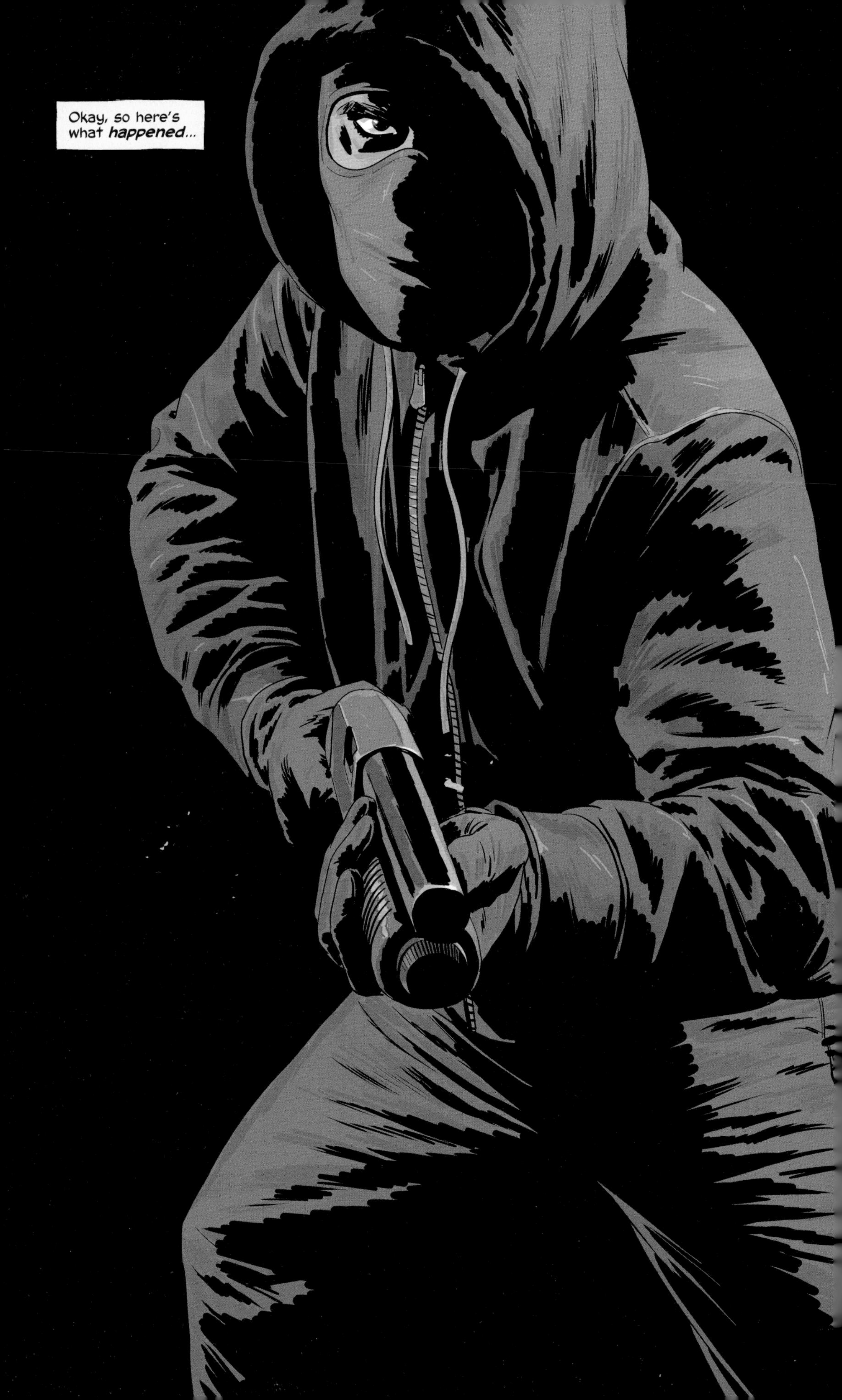
Okay, so here's what *happened*...

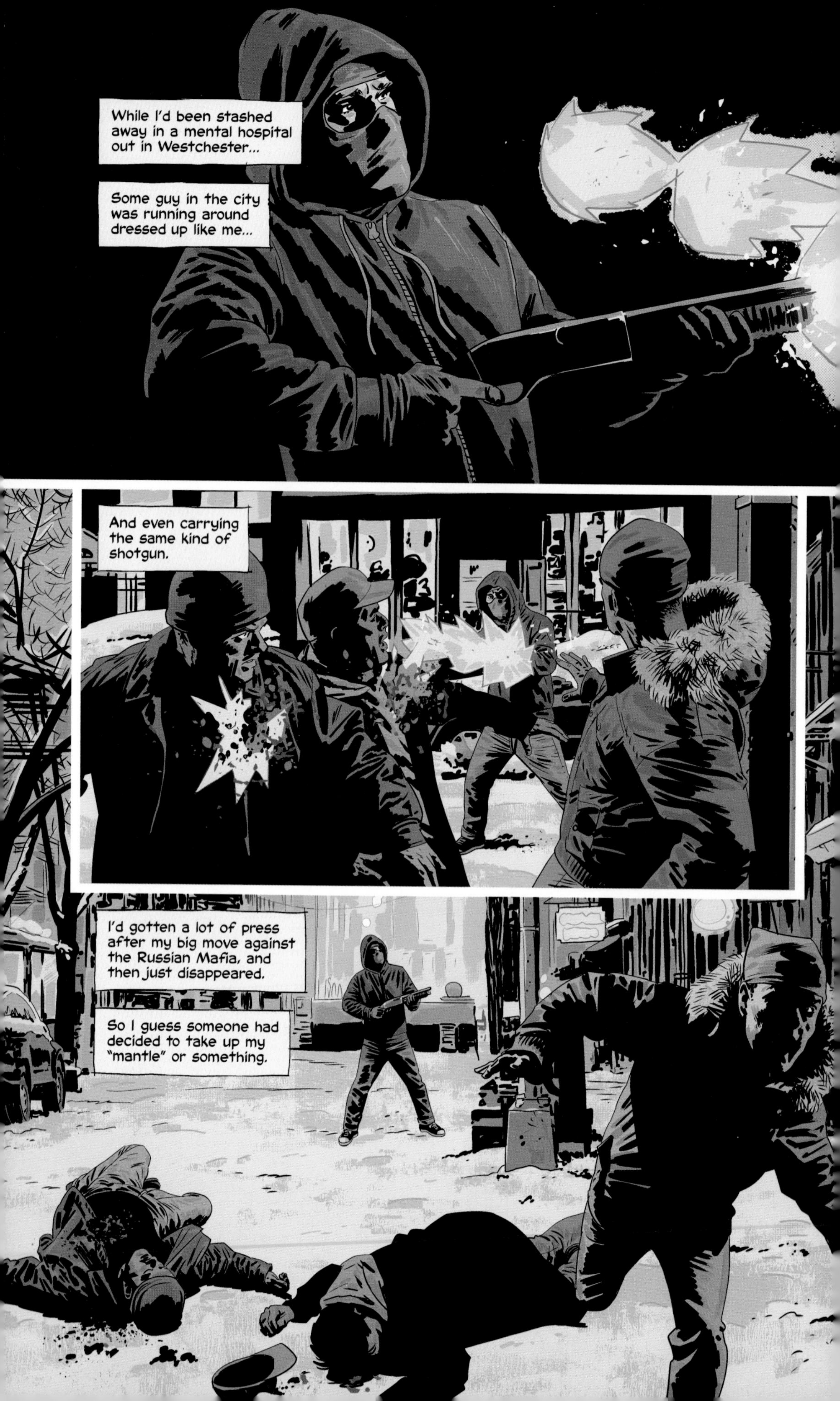
While I'd been stashed away in a mental hospital out in Westchester...
Some guy in the city was running around dressed up like me...
And even carrying the same kind of shotgun.
I'd gotten a lot of press after my big move against the Russian Mafia, and then just disappeared.
So I guess someone had decided to take up my "mantle" or something.

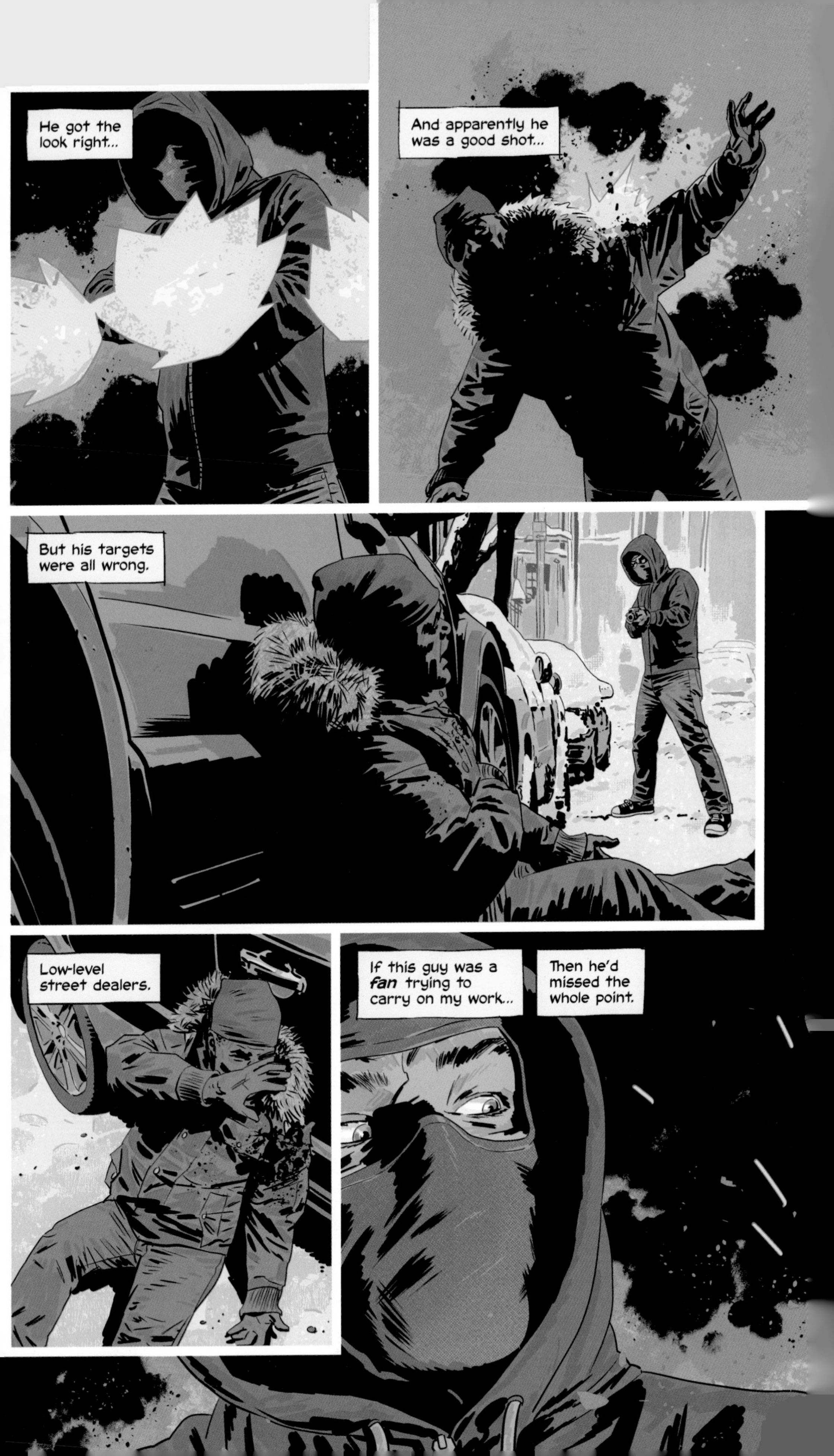
He got the look right...
And apparently he was a good shot...
But his targets were all wrong.
Low-level street dealers.
If this guy was a *fan* trying to carry on my work...
Then he'd missed the whole point.

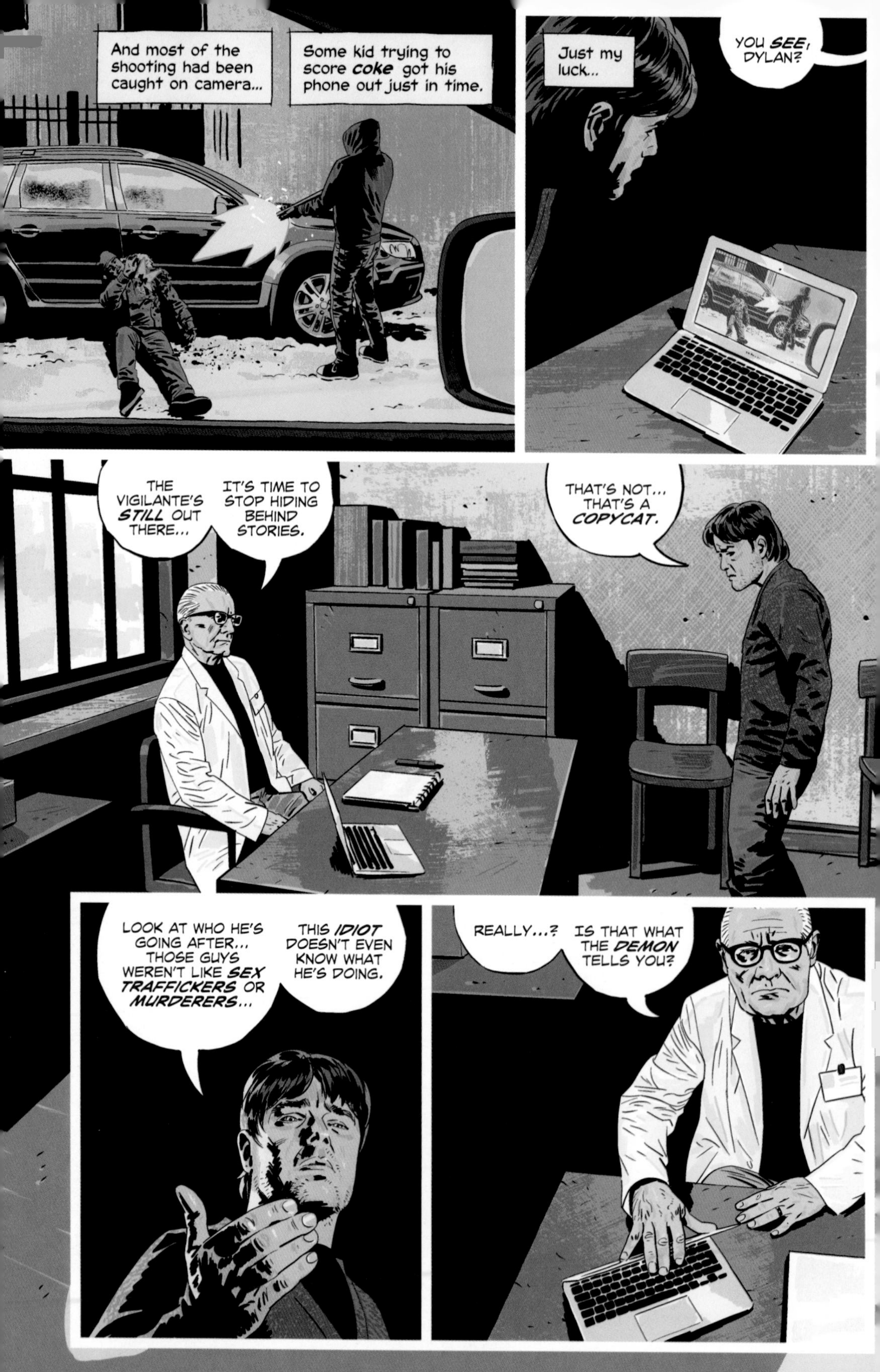
And most of the shooting had been caught on camera...
Some kid trying to score *coke* got his phone out just in time.
Just my luck...
YOU *SEE*, DYLAN?
THE VIGILANTE'S *STILL* OUT THERE...
IT'S TIME TO STOP HIDING BEHIND STORIES.
THAT'S NOT... THAT'S A *COPYCAT*.
LOOK AT WHO HE'S GOING AFTER... THOSE GUYS WEREN'T LIKE *SEX TRAFFICKERS* OR *MURDERERS*...
THIS *IDIOT* DOESN'T EVEN KNOW WHAT HE'S DOING.
REALLY...?
IS THAT WHAT THE *DEMON* TELLS YOU?

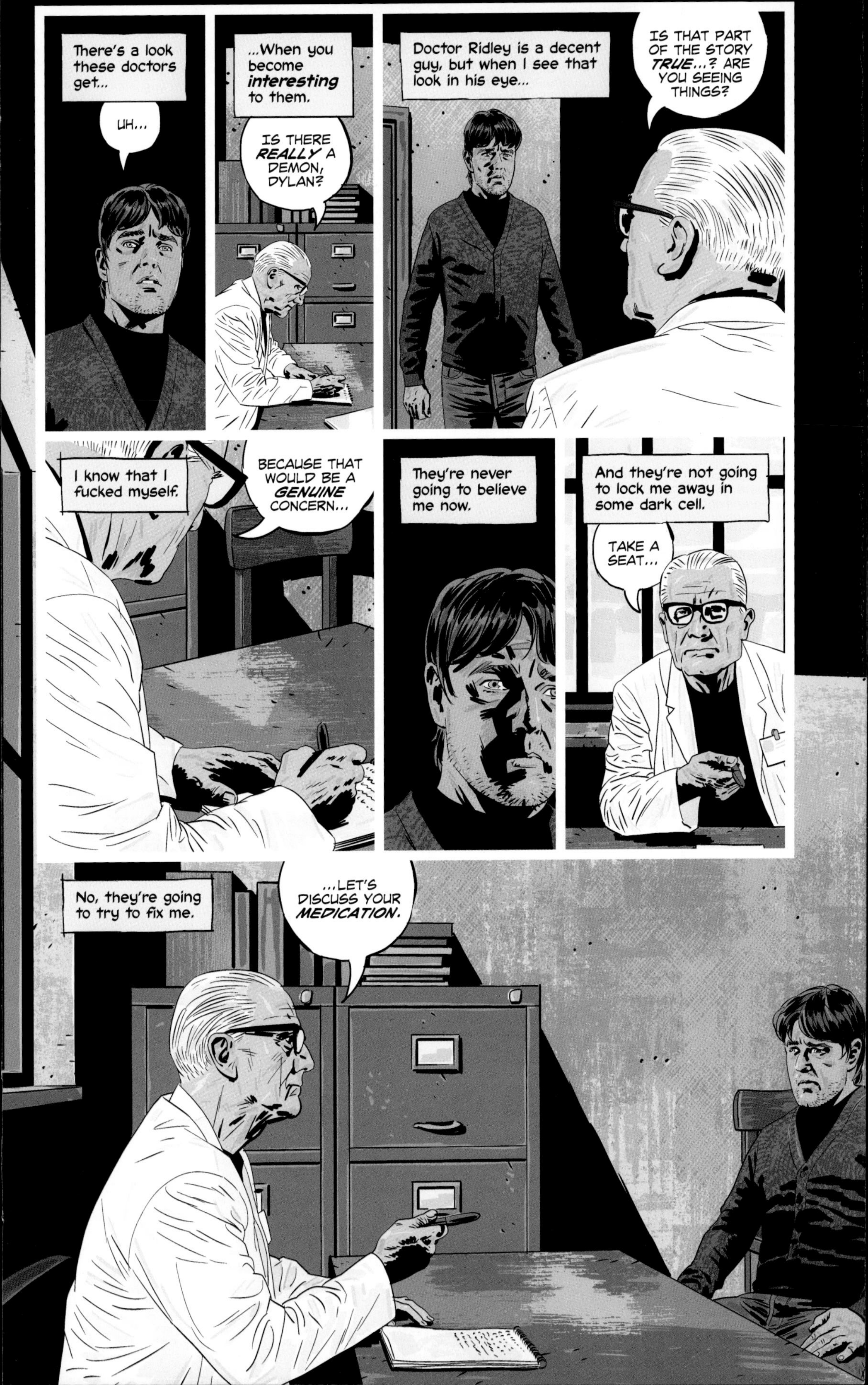
There's a look these doctors get...
UH...
...When you become interesting to them.
IS THERE REALLY A DEMON, DYLAN?
Doctor Ridley is a decent guy, but when I see that look in his eye...
IS THAT PART OF THE STORY TRUE...? ARE YOU SEEING THINGS?
I know that I fucked myself.
BECAUSE THAT WOULD BE A GENUINE CONCERN...
They're never going to believe me now.
And they're not going to lock me away in some dark cell.
TAKE A SEAT...
No, they're going to try to fix me.
...LET'S DISCUSS YOUR MEDICATION.

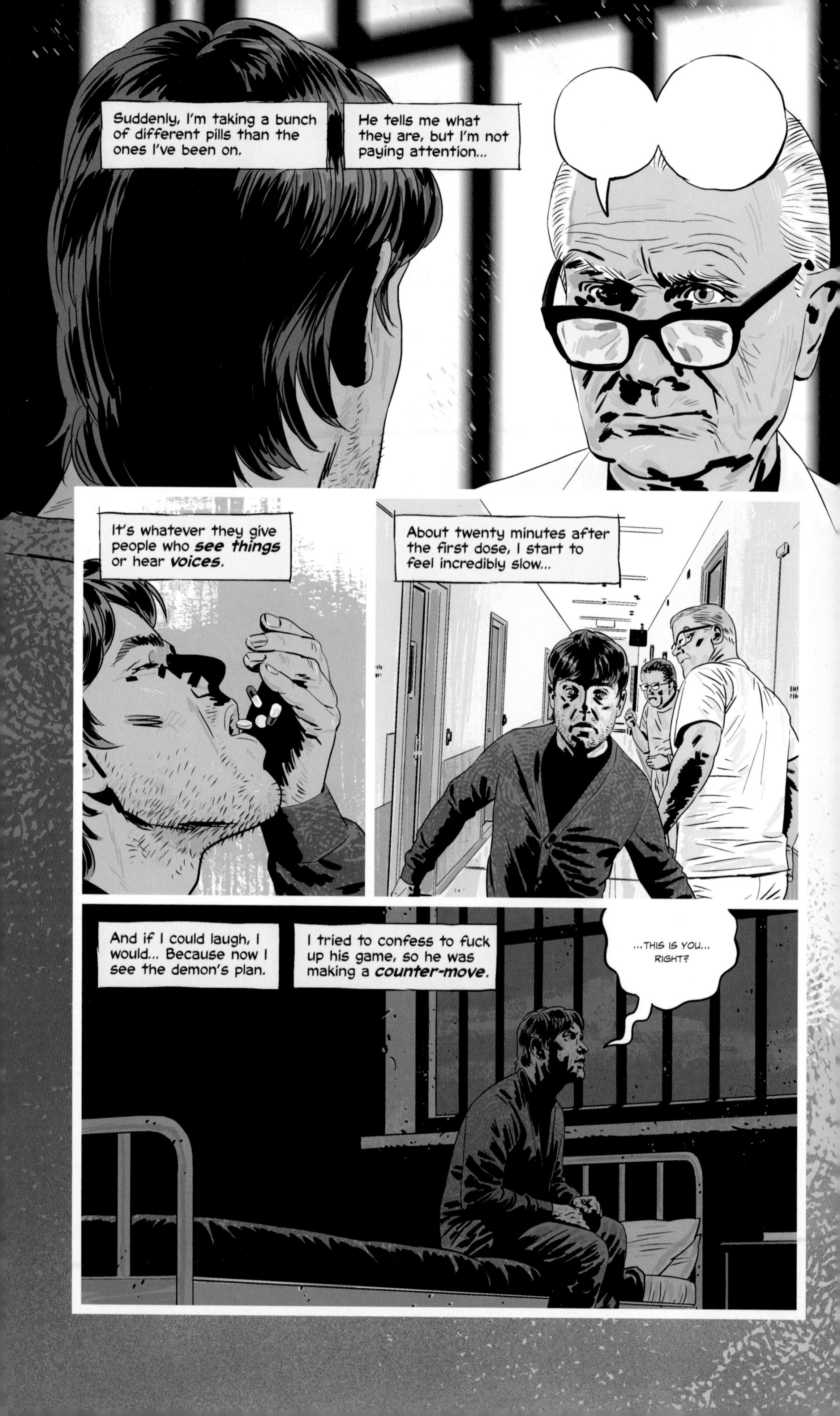
Suddenly, I'm taking a bunch of different pills than the ones I've been on.
He tells me what they are, but I'm not paying attention...
It's whatever they give people who *see things* or hear *voices*.
About twenty minutes after the first dose, I start to feel incredibly slow...
And if I could laugh, I would... Because now I see the demon's plan.
I tried to confess to fuck up his game, so he was making a *counter-move*.
...THIS IS YOU... RIGHT?

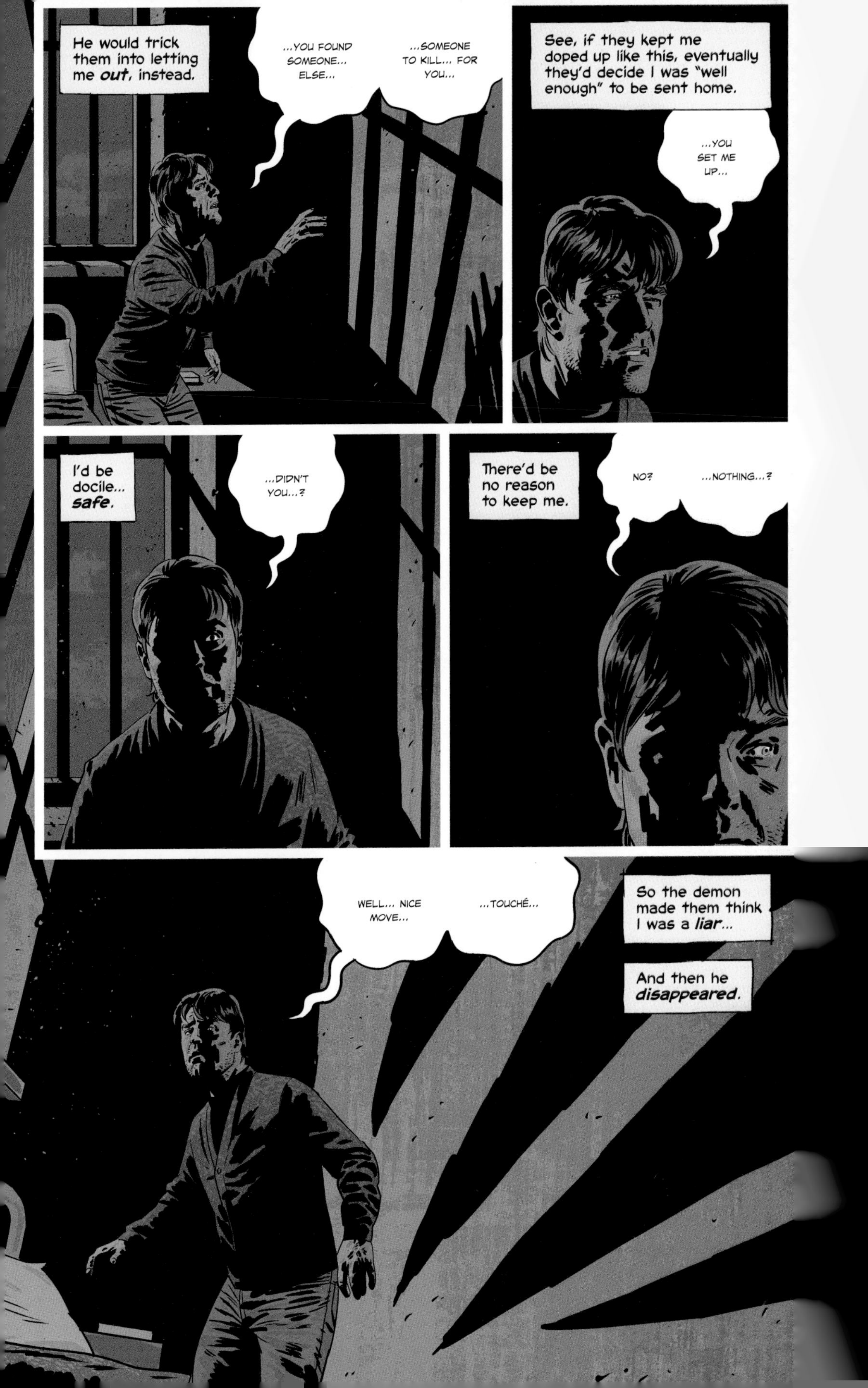

He would trick them into letting me *out*, instead.
...YOU FOUND SOMEONE... ELSE...
...SOMEONE TO KILL... FOR YOU...
See, if they kept me doped up like this, eventually they'd decide I was "well enough" to be sent home.
...YOU SET ME UP...
I'd be docile... ***safe***.
...DIDN'T YOU...?
There'd be no reason to keep me.
NO?
...NOTHING...?
WELL... NICE MOVE...
...TOUCHÉ...
So the demon made them think I was a *liar*...
And then he ***disappeared***.

I could feel my brain getting heavier in my skull as I lay there that night...

Whatever they had me on, it was some serious shit.

I knew after a few weeks like this... maybe a month...

I'd start to doubt I'd ever seen a demon in the first place...

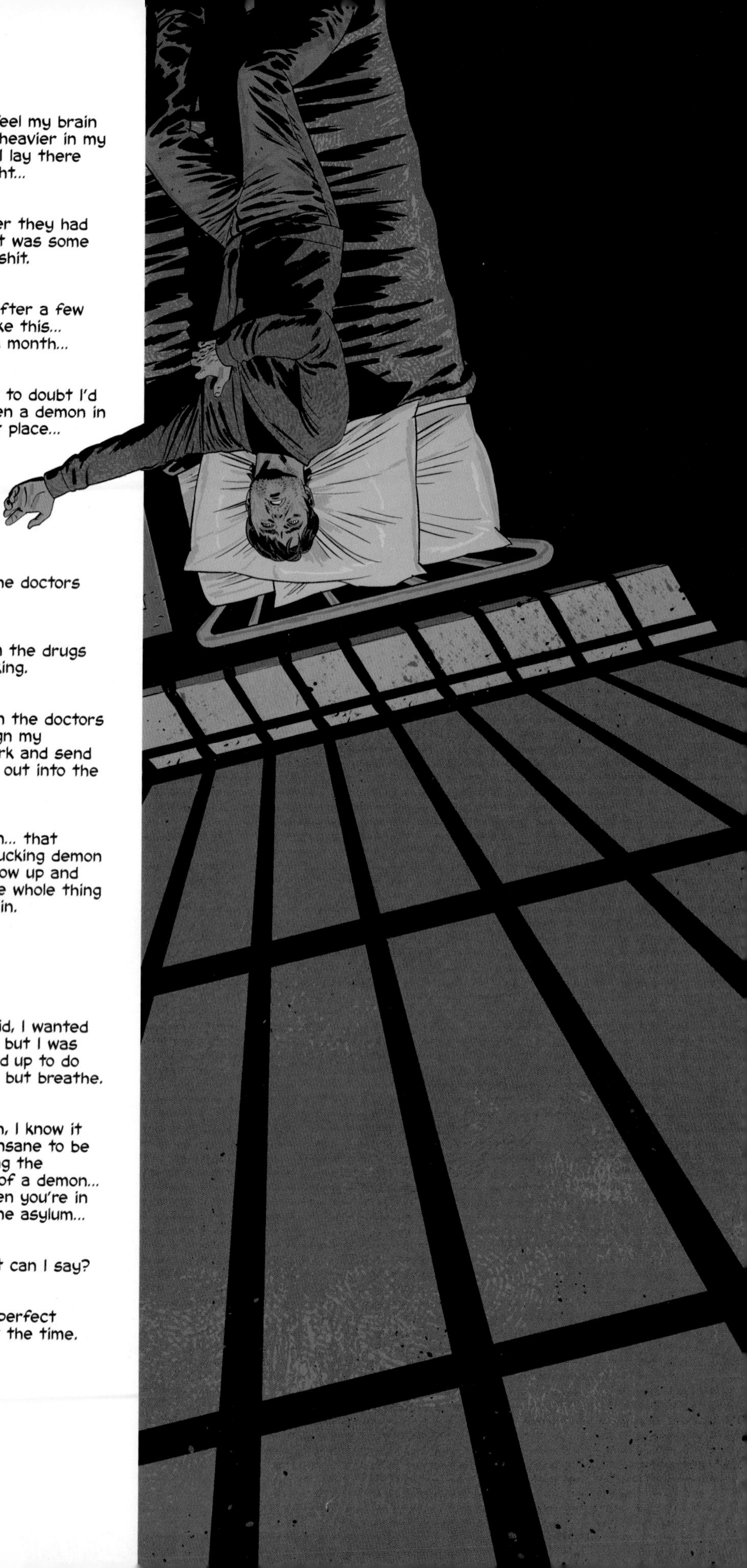

I'd tell the doctors that.

Tell them the drugs are working.

And then the doctors would sign my paperwork and send me back out into the world...

And then... that motherfucking demon would show up and start the whole thing over again.

Like I said, I wanted to laugh, but I was too doped up to do anything but breathe.

And yeah, I know it sounds insane to be dissecting the motives of a demon... even when you're in the insane asylum...

But what can I say?

It made perfect sense at the time.

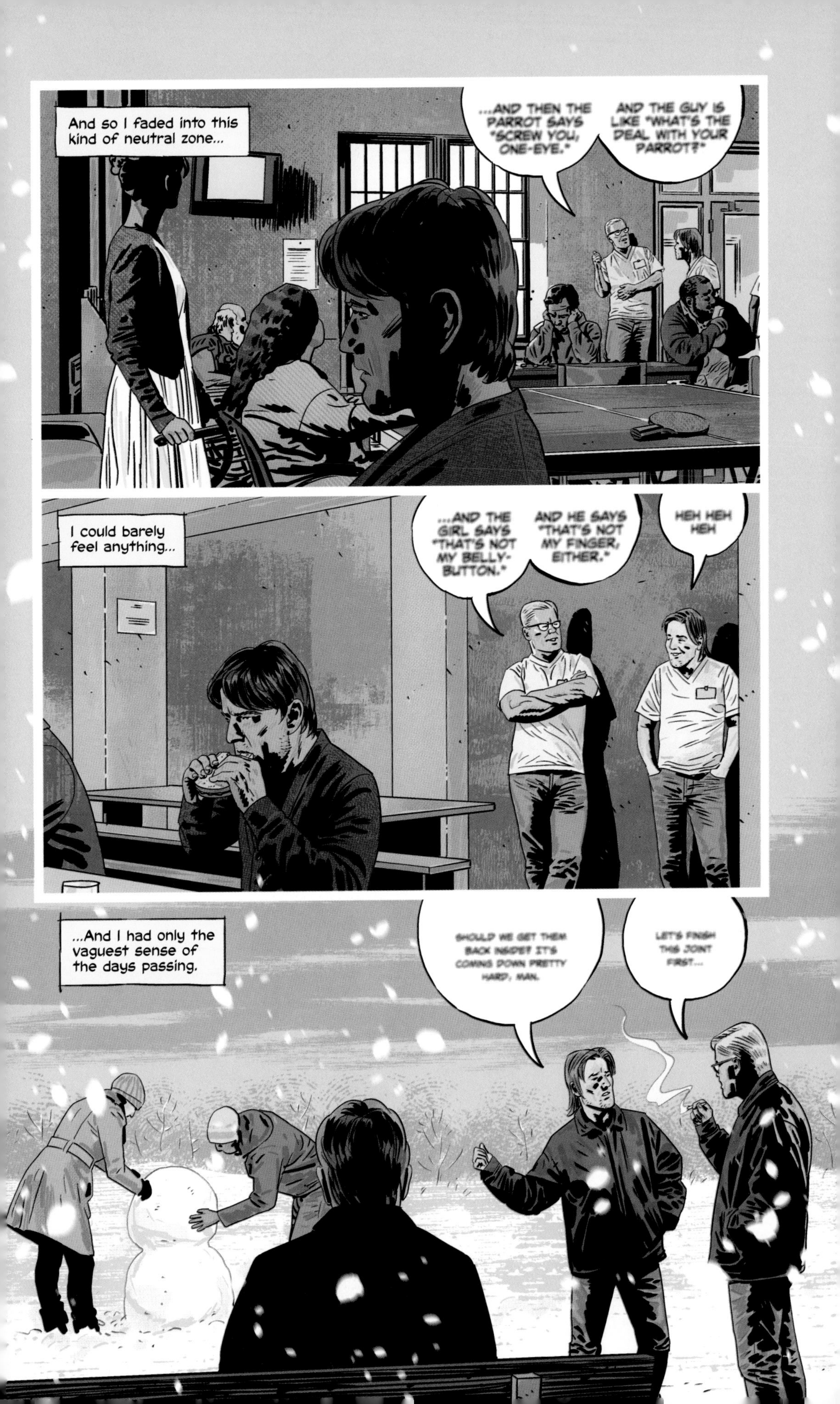

And so I faded into this kind of neutral zone...
...AND THEN THE PARROT SAYS "SCREW YOU, ONE-EYE."
AND THE GUY IS LIKE "WHAT'S THE DEAL WITH YOUR PARROT?"
I could barely feel anything...
...AND THE GIRL SAYS "THAT'S NOT MY BELLY-BUTTON."
AND HE SAYS "THAT'S NOT MY FINGER, EITHER."
HEH HEH HEH
...And I had only the vaguest sense of the days passing.
SHOULD WE GET THEM BACK INSIDE? IT'S COMING DOWN PRETTY HARD, MAN.
LET'S FINISH THIS JOINT FIRST...

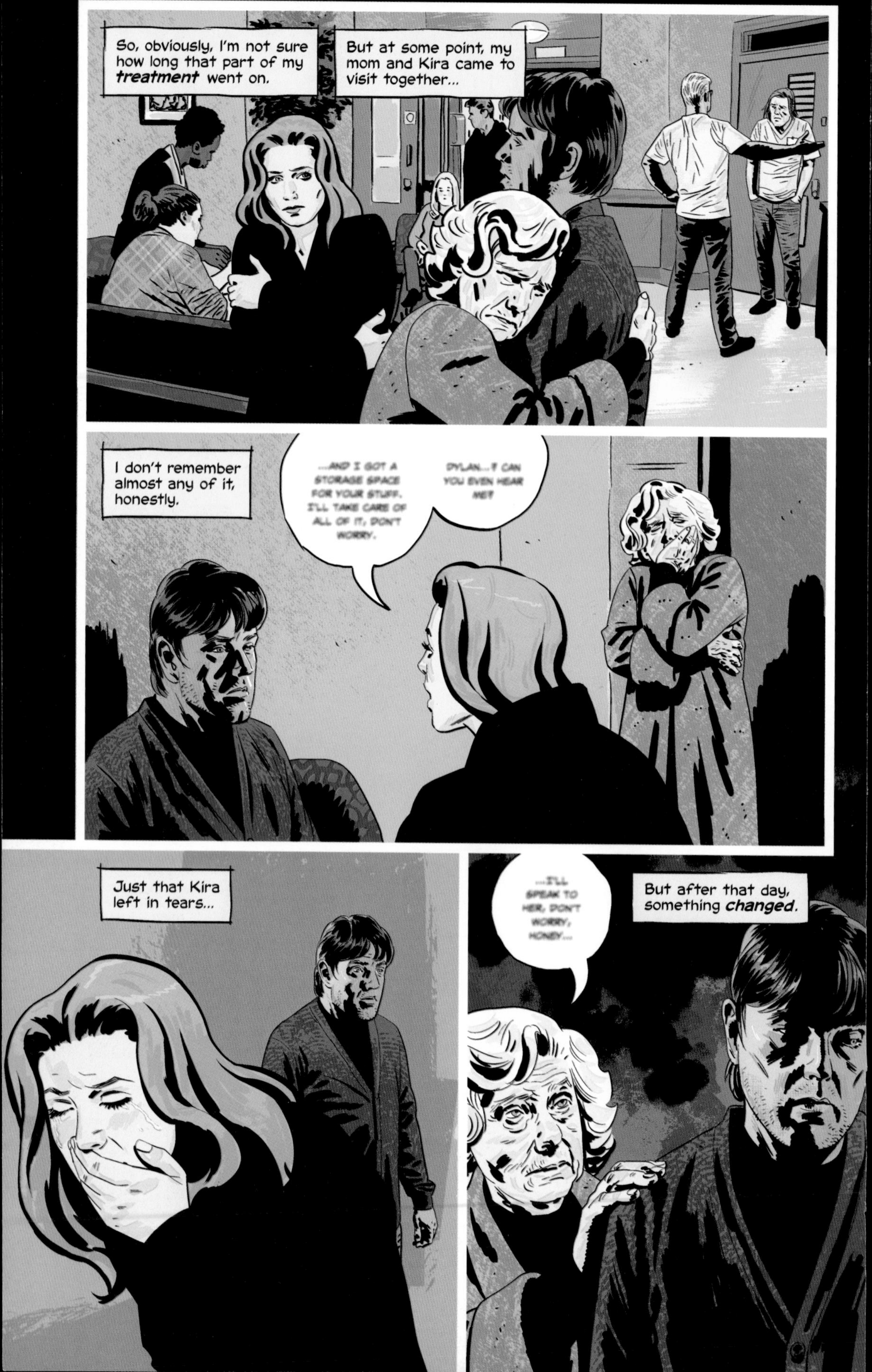

So, obviously, I'm not sure how long that part of my *treatment* went on.
But at some point, my mom and Kira came to visit together...
I don't remember almost any of it, honestly.
...AND I GOT A STORAGE SPACE FOR YOUR STUFF. I'LL TAKE CARE OF ALL OF IT, DON'T WORRY.
DYLAN...? CAN YOU EVEN HEAR ME?
Just that Kira left in tears...
...I'LL SPEAK TO HER, DON'T WORRY, HONEY...
But after that day, something *changed*.

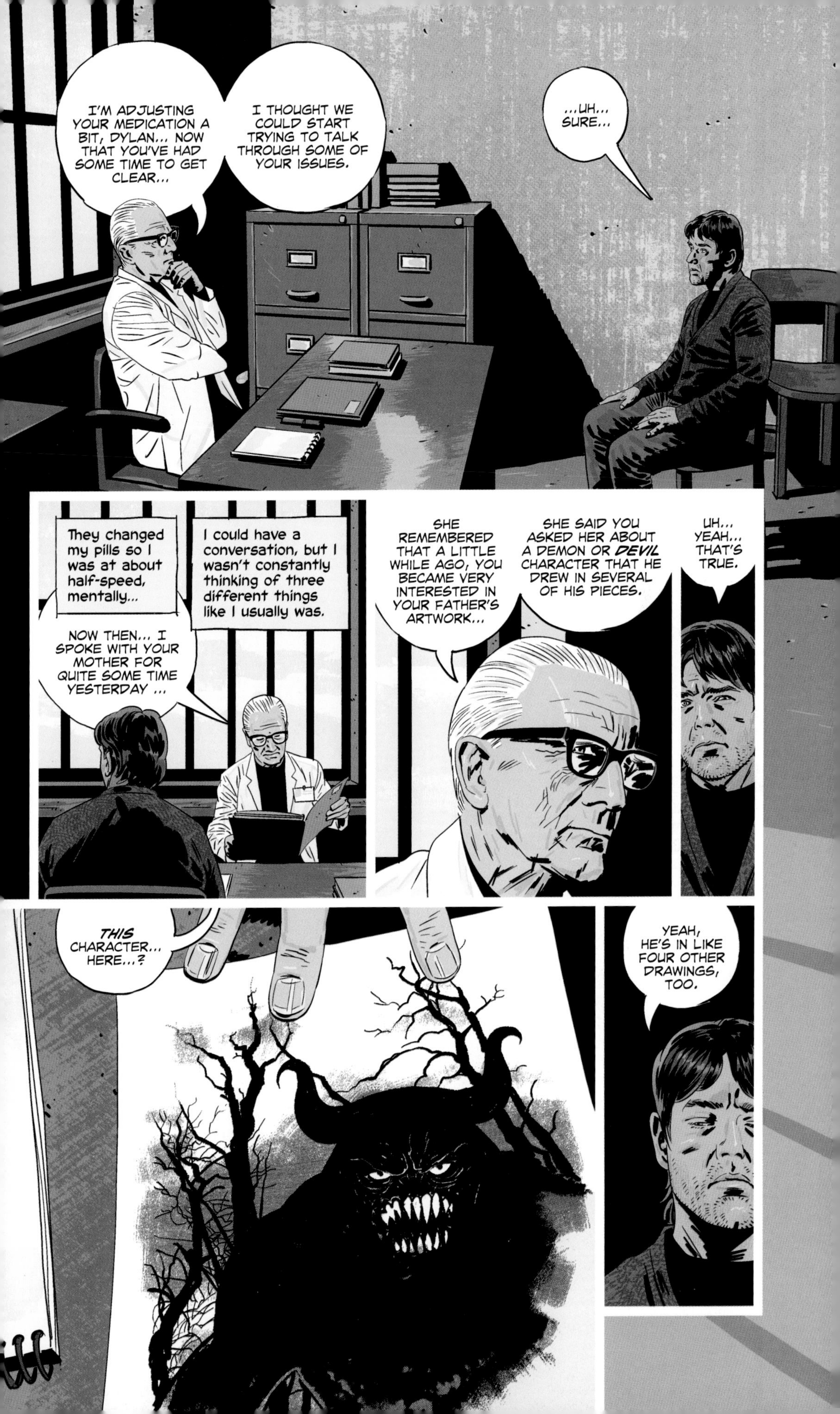
I'M ADJUSTING YOUR MEDICATION A BIT, DYLAN... NOW THAT YOU'VE HAD SOME TIME TO GET CLEAR...
I THOUGHT WE COULD START TRYING TO TALK THROUGH SOME OF YOUR ISSUES.
...UH... SURE...
They changed my pills so I was at about half-speed, mentally...
I could have a conversation, but I wasn't constantly thinking of three different things like I usually was.
NOW THEN... I SPOKE WITH YOUR MOTHER FOR QUITE SOME TIME YESTERDAY ...
SHE REMEMBERED THAT A LITTLE WHILE AGO, YOU BECAME VERY INTERESTED IN YOUR FATHER'S ARTWORK...
SHE SAID YOU ASKED HER ABOUT A DEMON OR DEVIL CHARACTER THAT HE DREW IN SEVERAL OF HIS PIECES.
UH... YEAH... THAT'S TRUE.
THIS CHARACTER... HERE...?
YEAH, HE'S IN LIKE FOUR OTHER DRAWINGS, TOO.

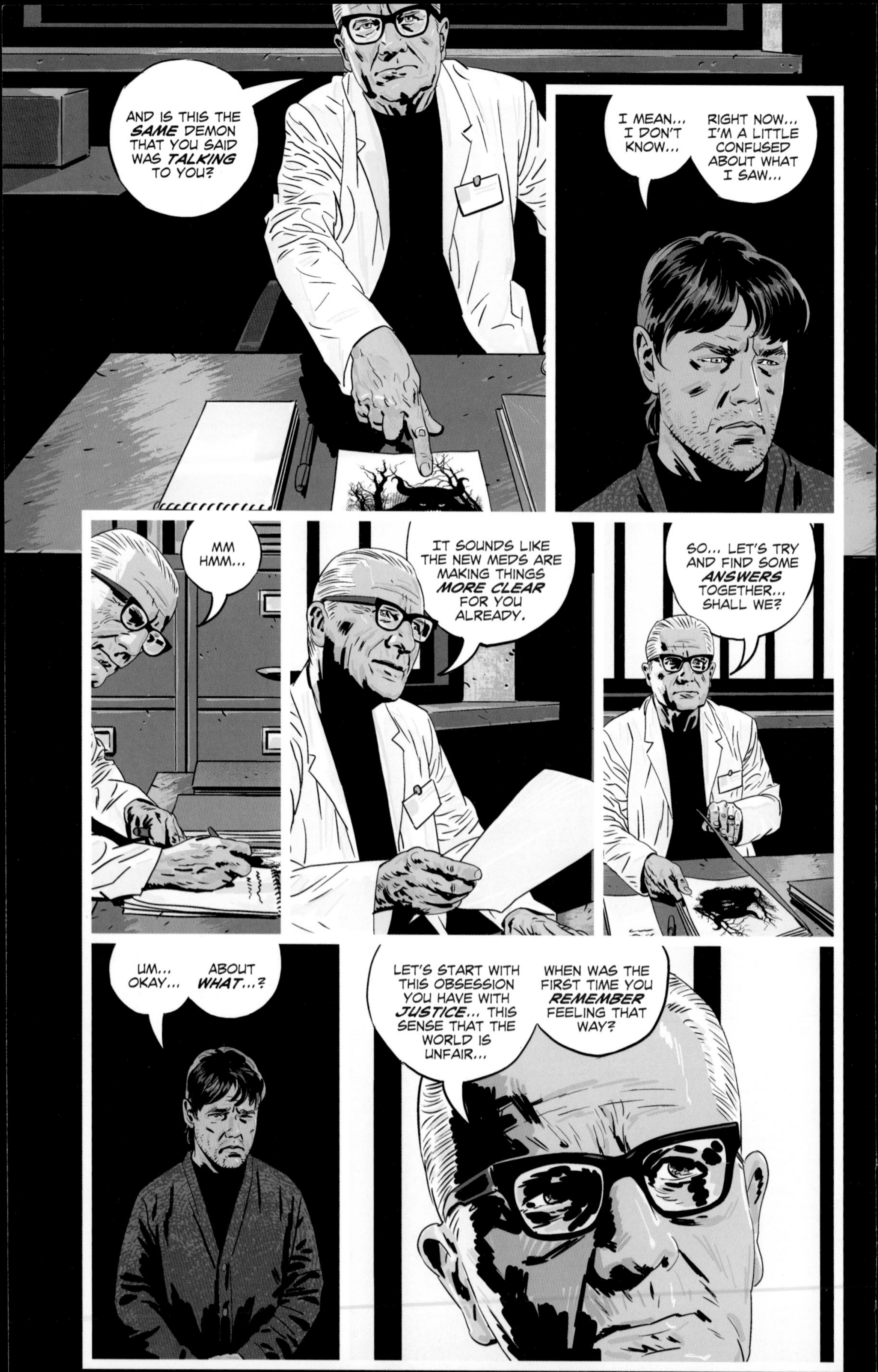
AND IS THIS THE SAME DEMON THAT YOU SAID WAS TALKING TO YOU?
I MEAN... I DON'T KNOW...
RIGHT NOW... I'M A LITTLE CONFUSED ABOUT WHAT I SAW...
MM HMM...
IT SOUNDS LIKE THE NEW MEDS ARE MAKING THINGS MORE CLEAR FOR YOU ALREADY.
SO... LET'S TRY AND FIND SOME ANSWERS TOGETHER... SHALL WE?
UM... OKAY...
ABOUT WHAT...?
LET'S START WITH THIS OBSESSION YOU HAVE WITH JUSTICE... THIS SENSE THAT THE WORLD IS UNFAIR...
WHEN WAS THE FIRST TIME YOU REMEMBER FEELING THAT WAY?

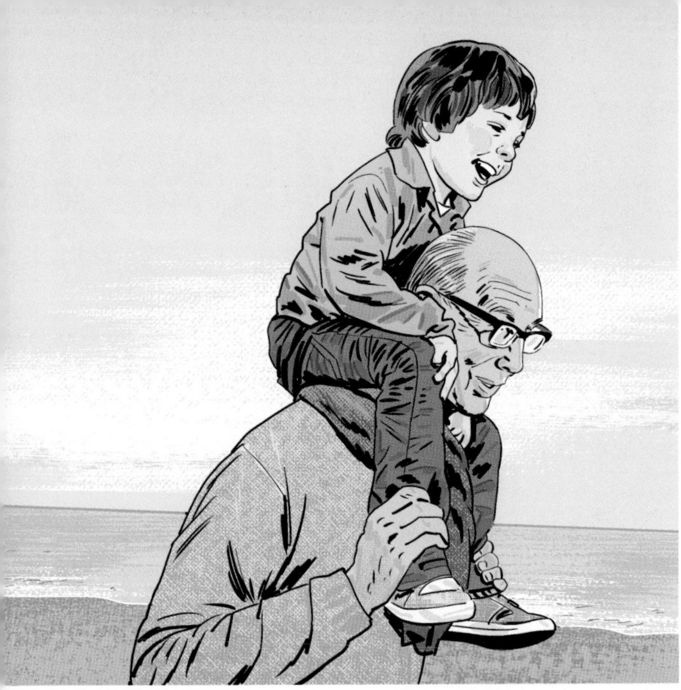

That shouldn't be a hard question to answer... But think about it for a second.

When did ***you*** first look around and realize nothing was the way they taught us it should be?

When did you realize the bad guys had already won... And that was just the way of the world...?

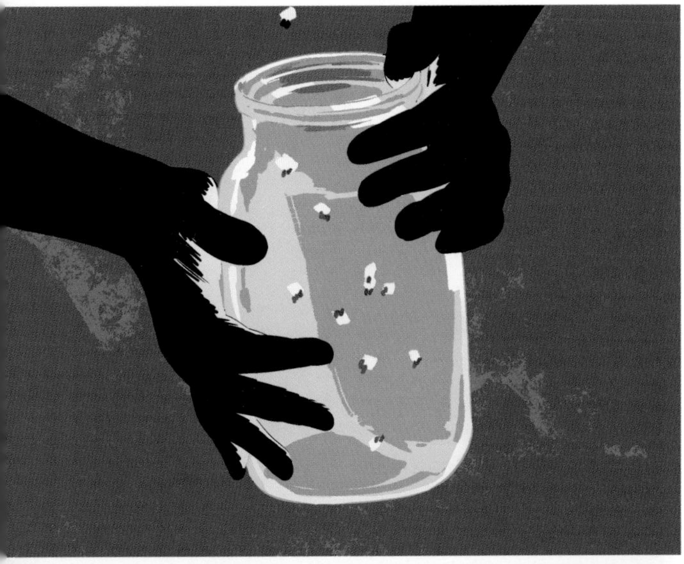

It was easier to go back further, to try to find memories before that... Pure memories.

I remembered a summer night when I was four... When my cousin Elizabeth and I caught fireflies in glass jars.

And I remembered staying up late the first time, when the darkness outside felt comforting and safe...

Like a blanket over the whole town.

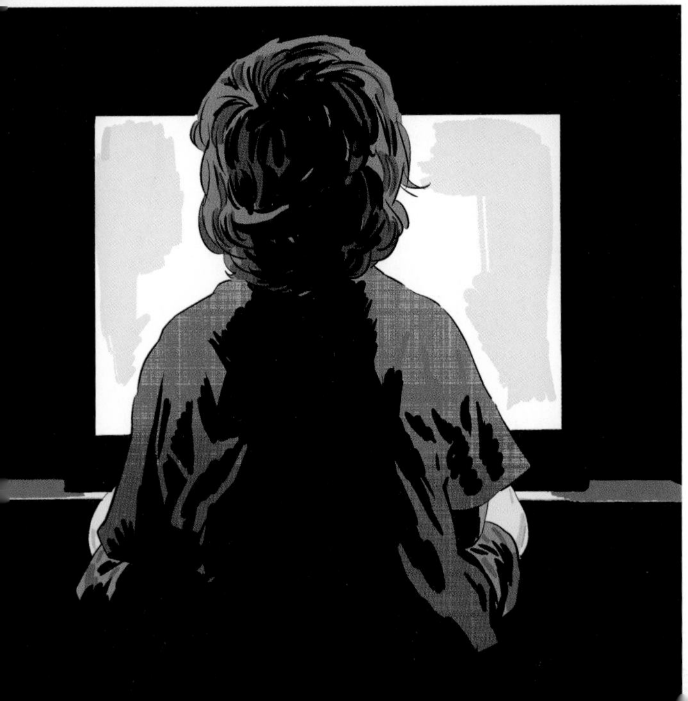

But I couldn't remember when that pure part of childhood had ended... and real life had begun.

Was it when Mom told me about Philip... the brother who'd died nearly twenty years before I was born?

Or was it when I noticed that my father carried an immense sadness inside him all the time?

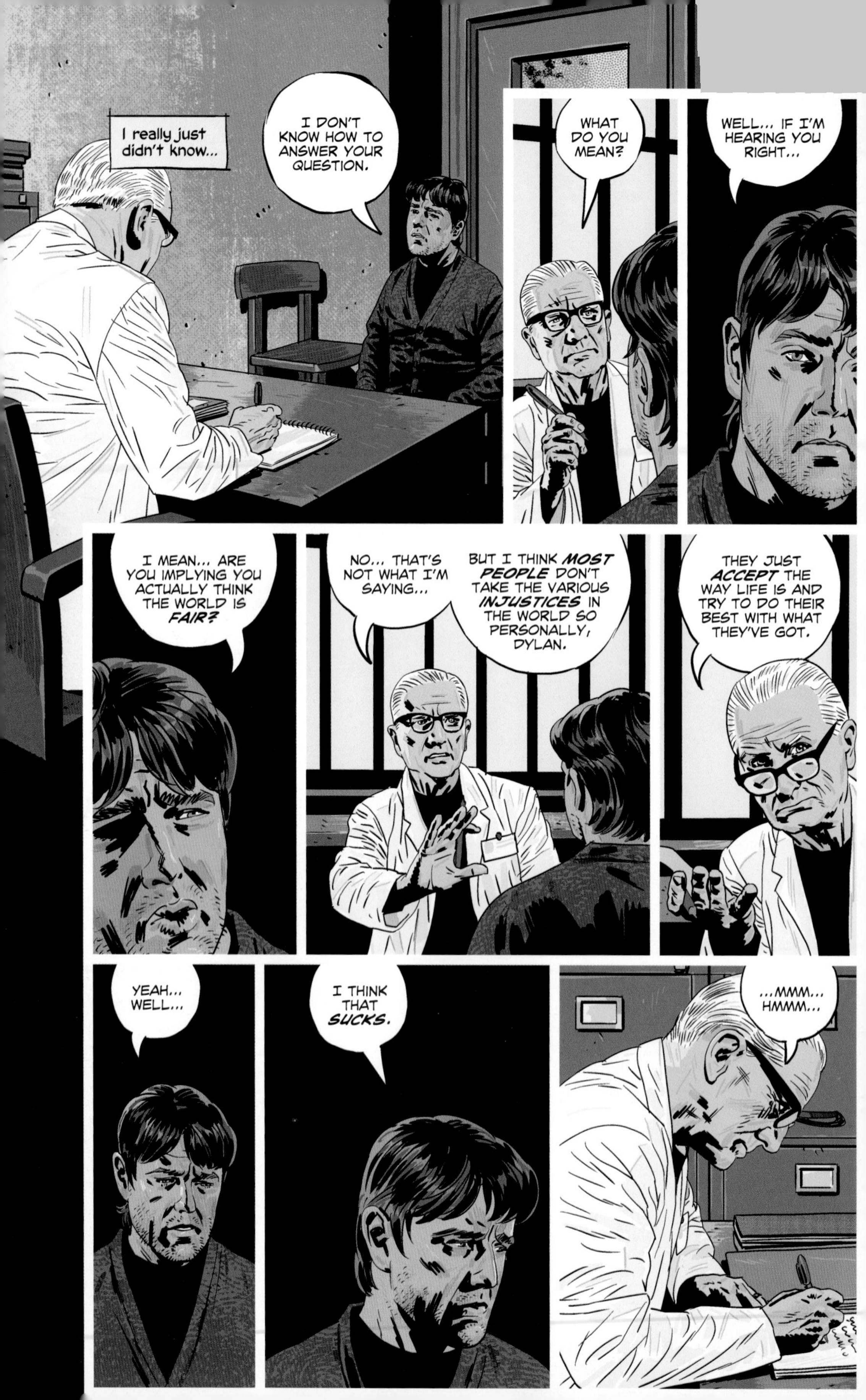
I really just didn't know...
I DON'T KNOW HOW TO ANSWER YOUR QUESTION.
WHAT DO YOU MEAN?
WELL... IF I'M HEARING YOU RIGHT...
I MEAN... ARE YOU IMPLYING YOU ACTUALLY THINK THE WORLD IS FAIR?
NO... THAT'S NOT WHAT I'M SAYING...
BUT I THINK MOST PEOPLE DON'T TAKE THE VARIOUS INJUSTICES IN THE WORLD SO PERSONALLY, DYLAN.
THEY JUST ACCEPT THE WAY LIFE IS AND TRY TO DO THEIR BEST WITH WHAT THEY'VE GOT.
YEAH... WELL...
I THINK THAT SUCKS.
...MMM... HMMM...

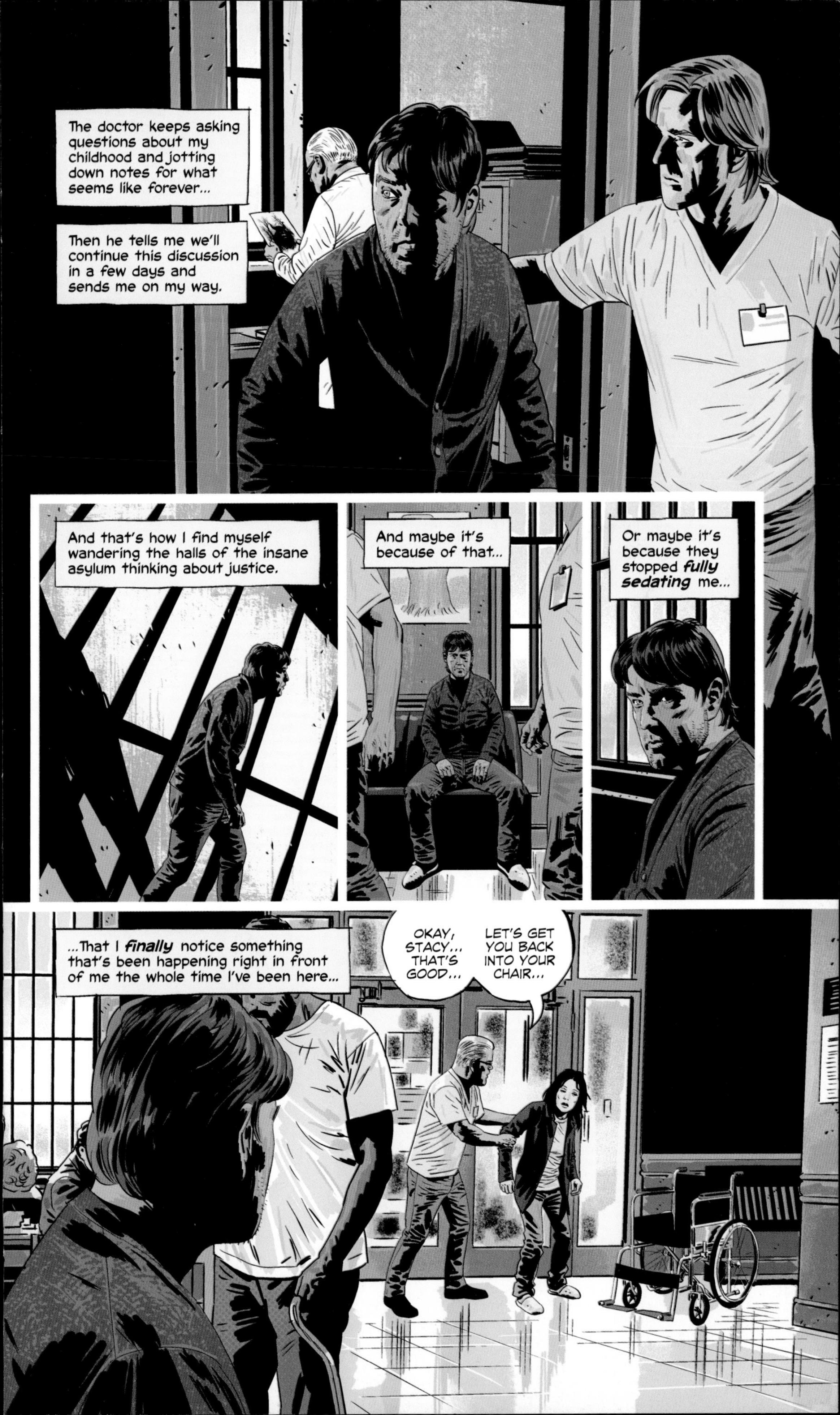
The doctor keeps asking questions about my childhood and jotting down notes for what seems like forever...
Then he tells me we'll continue this discussion in a few days and sends me on my way.
And that's how I find myself wandering the halls of the insane asylum thinking about justice.
And maybe it's because of that...
Or maybe it's because they stopped **fully sedating** me...
...That I **finally** notice something that's been happening right in front of me the whole time I've been here...
OKAY, STACY... THAT'S GOOD...
LET'S GET YOU BACK INTO YOUR CHAIR...

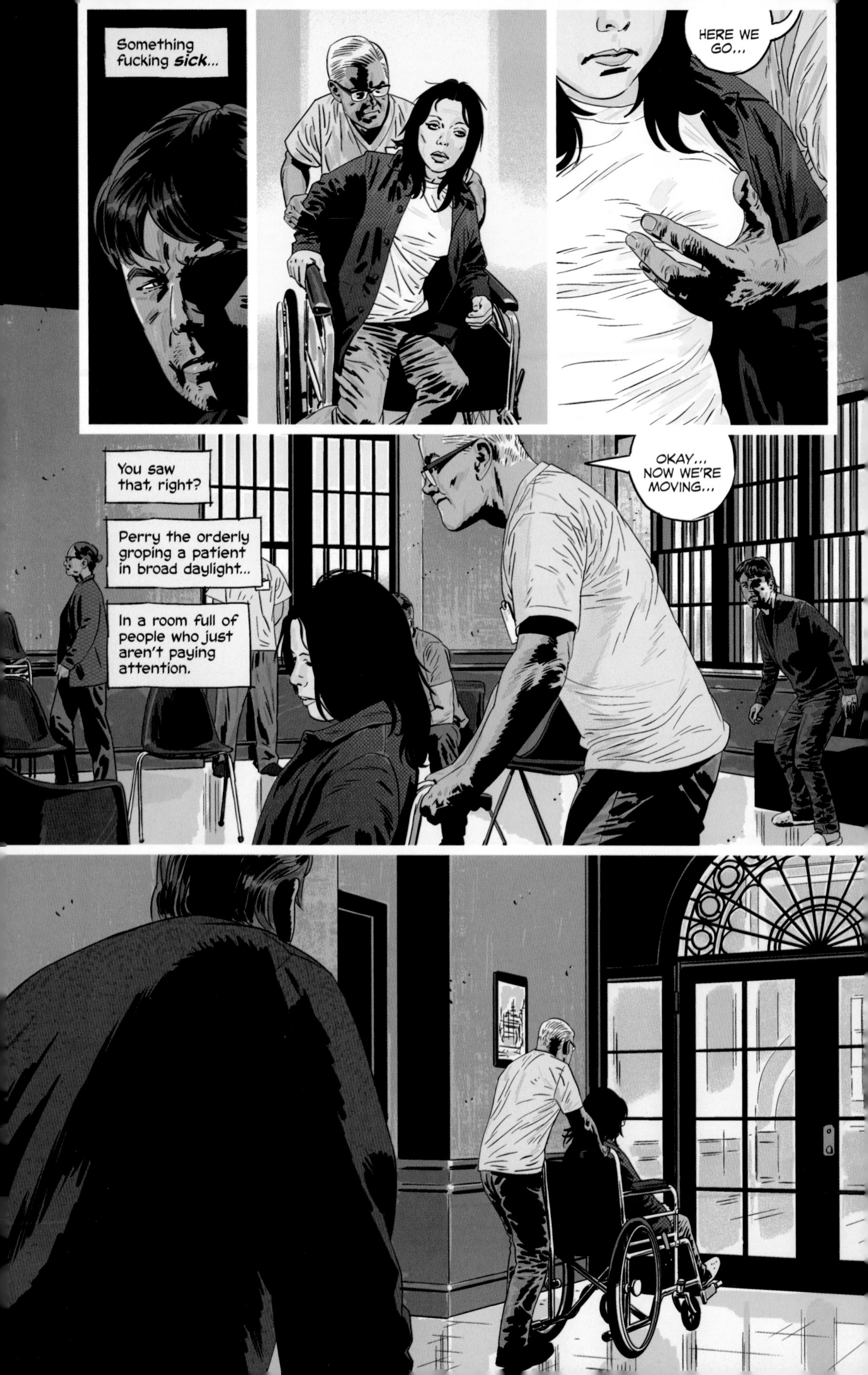
Something fucking *sick*...
HERE WE GO...
You saw that, right?
Perry the orderly groping a patient in broad daylight...
In a room full of people who just aren't paying attention.
OKAY... NOW WE'RE MOVING...

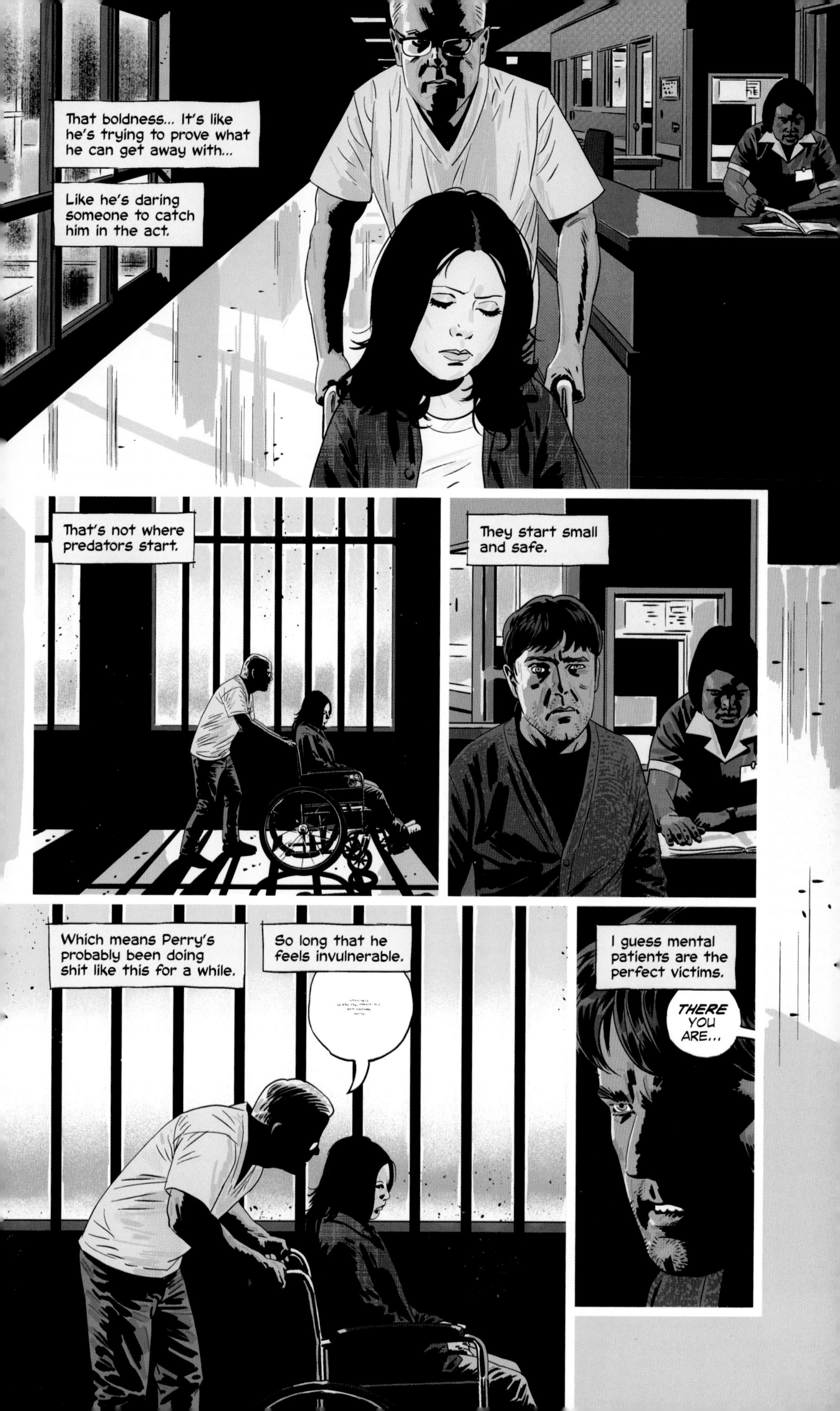
That boldness... It's like he's trying to prove what he can get away with...
Like he's daring someone to catch him in the act.
That's not where predators start.
They start small and safe.
Which means Perry's probably been doing shit like this for a while.
So long that he feels invulnerable.
I guess mental patients are the perfect victims.
THERE YOU ARE...

...I'VE BEEN LOOKING FOR YOU.

HI, NURSE JUDY.

C'MON, LET'S GET YOU BACK TO YOUR ROOM, IT'S GETTING LATE.

OH... UH...

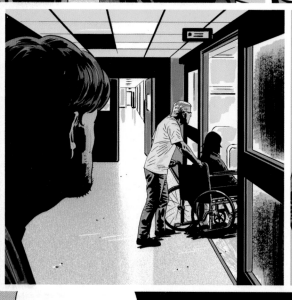

OKAY, I GUESS WE CAN GO...

IS EVERYTHING ALL RIGHT, DYLAN?

NO... NOT REALLY.

BUT IT WILL BE.

OH?

WELL... THAT'S NICE TO HEAR.

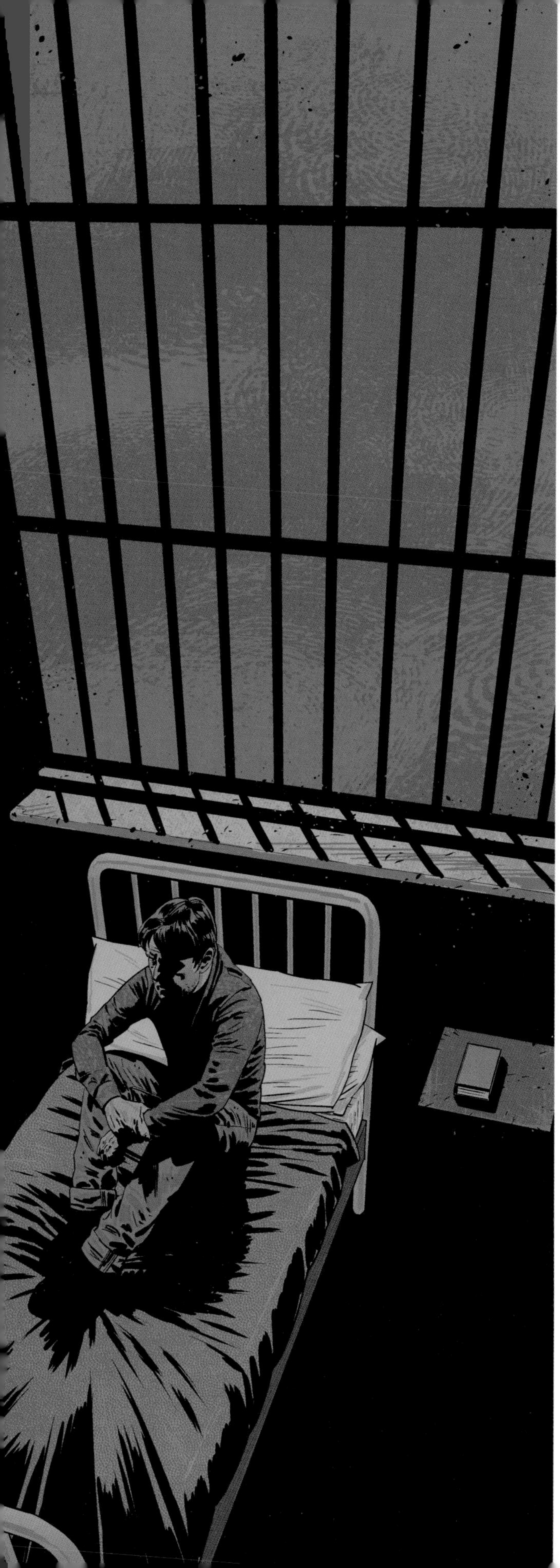

I know what you're thinking... Why didn't I tell Nurse Judy what I saw?

But you should already know the answer to that question, I mean, assuming you've been paying any attention up to this point...

I didn't tell her because I'd decided to kill Perry.

Well, "decide" isn't exactly the right word... It was more like I just ***knew*** it was something that I was going to do.

How many patients had this guy fondled or raped or did who-knows-what to over the years?

And if I tell Nurse Judy, then what happens?

They probably don't believe me, for one thing...

But even if they do, there'd probably be no real evidence against the guy...

So at best, he gets fired and in a few months, he finds someone else to victimize.

No, he has to die... And I don't need a demon to tell me that.

I almost laugh when I think that...

And for a second... I actually feel free...

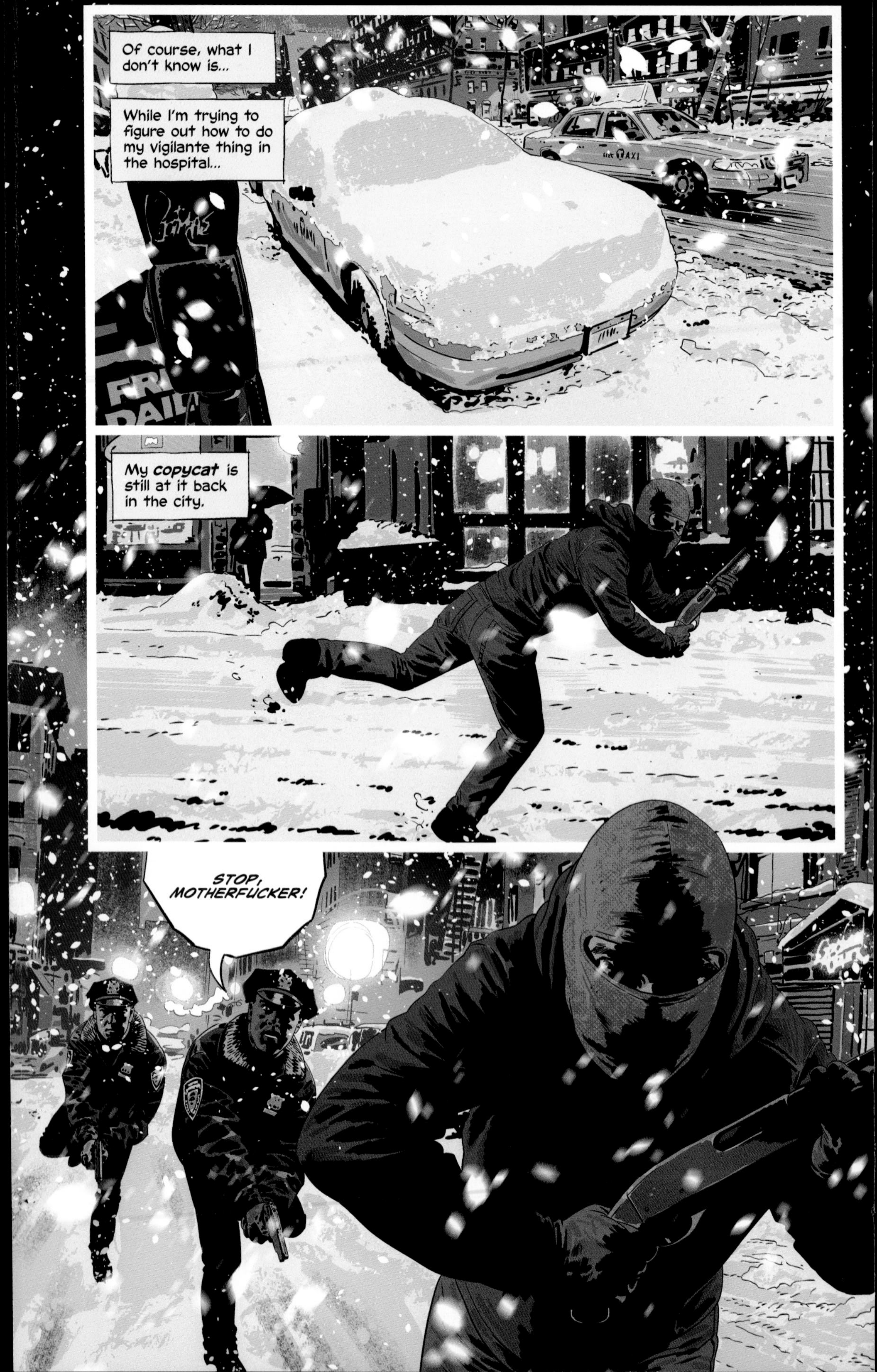
Of course, what I don't know is...
While I'm trying to figure out how to do my vigilante thing in the hospital...
My copycat is still at it back in the city.
STOP, MOTHERFUCKER!

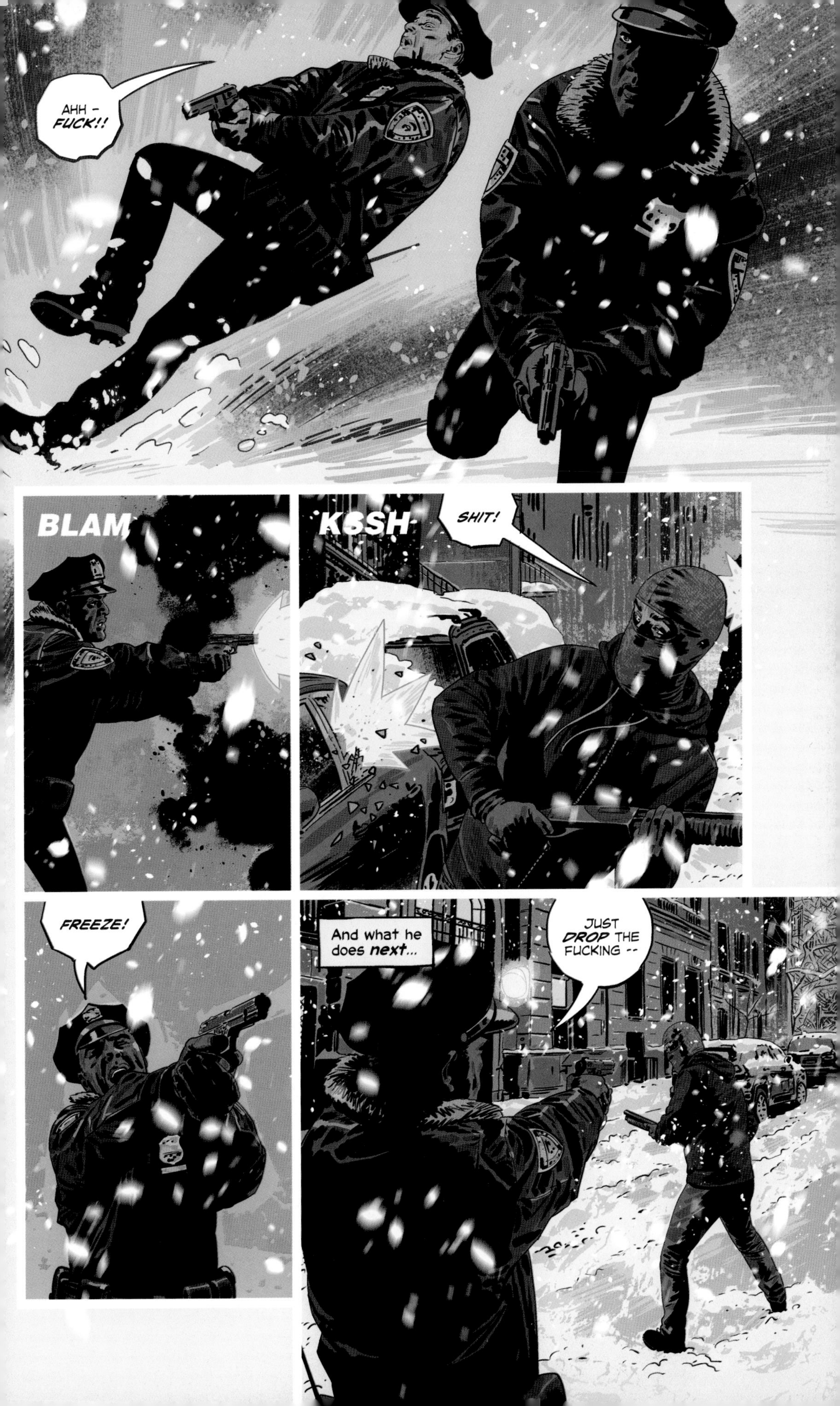
AHH -- FUCK!!
BLAM
KSSH
SHIT!
FREEZE!
And what he does next...
JUST DROP THE FUCKING --

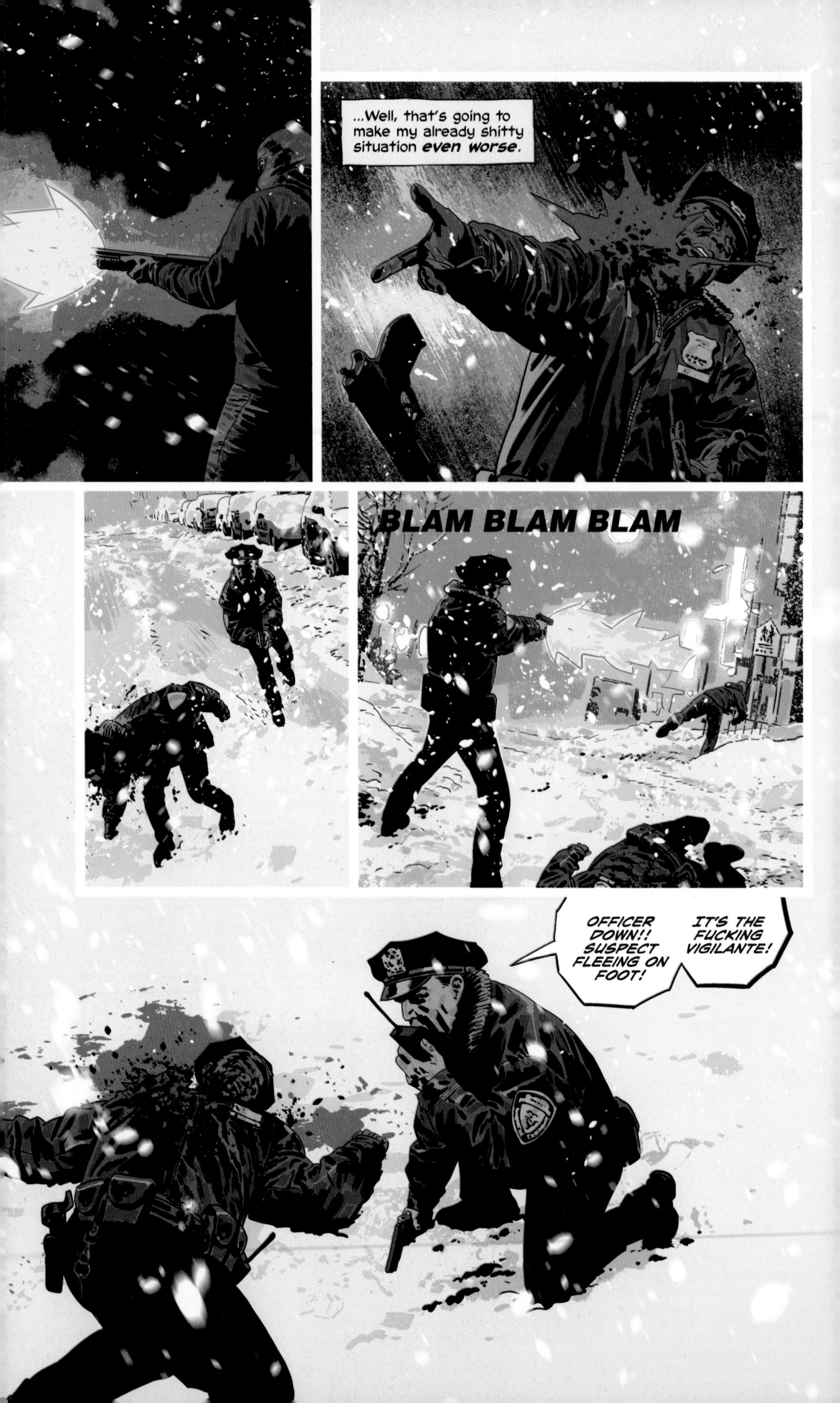

...Well, that's going to make my already shitty situation even worse.
BLAM BLAM BLAM
OFFICER DOWN!! SUSPECT FLEEING ON FOOT!
IT'S THE FUCKING VIGILANTE!

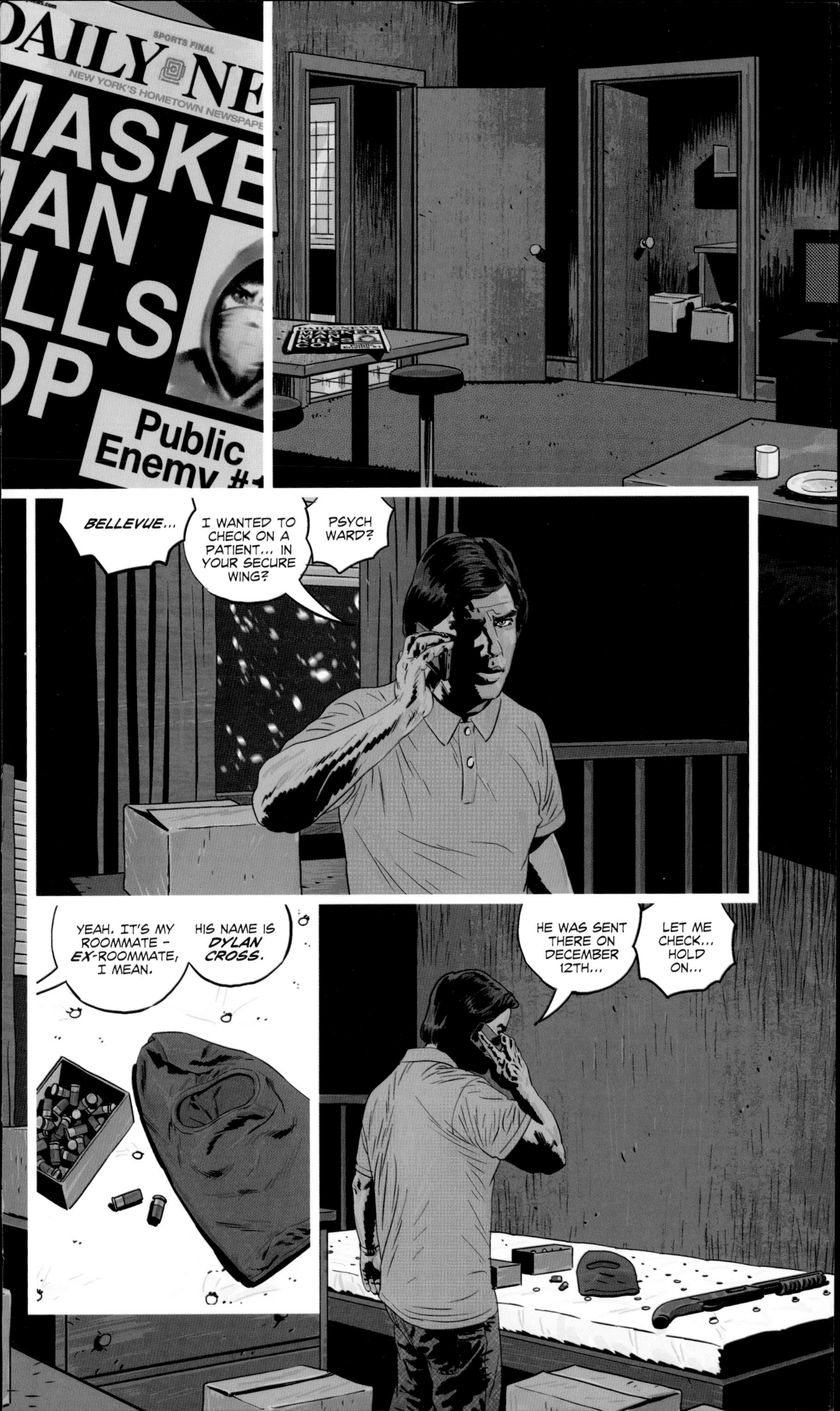
DAILY NEWS
SPORTS FINAL
NEW YORK'S HOMETOWN NEWSPAPER
MASKED MAN KILLS COP
Public Enemy #1
BELLEVUE...
I WANTED TO CHECK ON A PATIENT... IN YOUR SECURE WING?
PSYCH WARD?
YEAH. IT'S MY ROOMMATE - EX-ROOMMATE, I MEAN.
HIS NAME IS DYLAN CROSS.
HE WAS SENT THERE ON DECEMBER 12TH...
LET ME CHECK... HOLD ON...

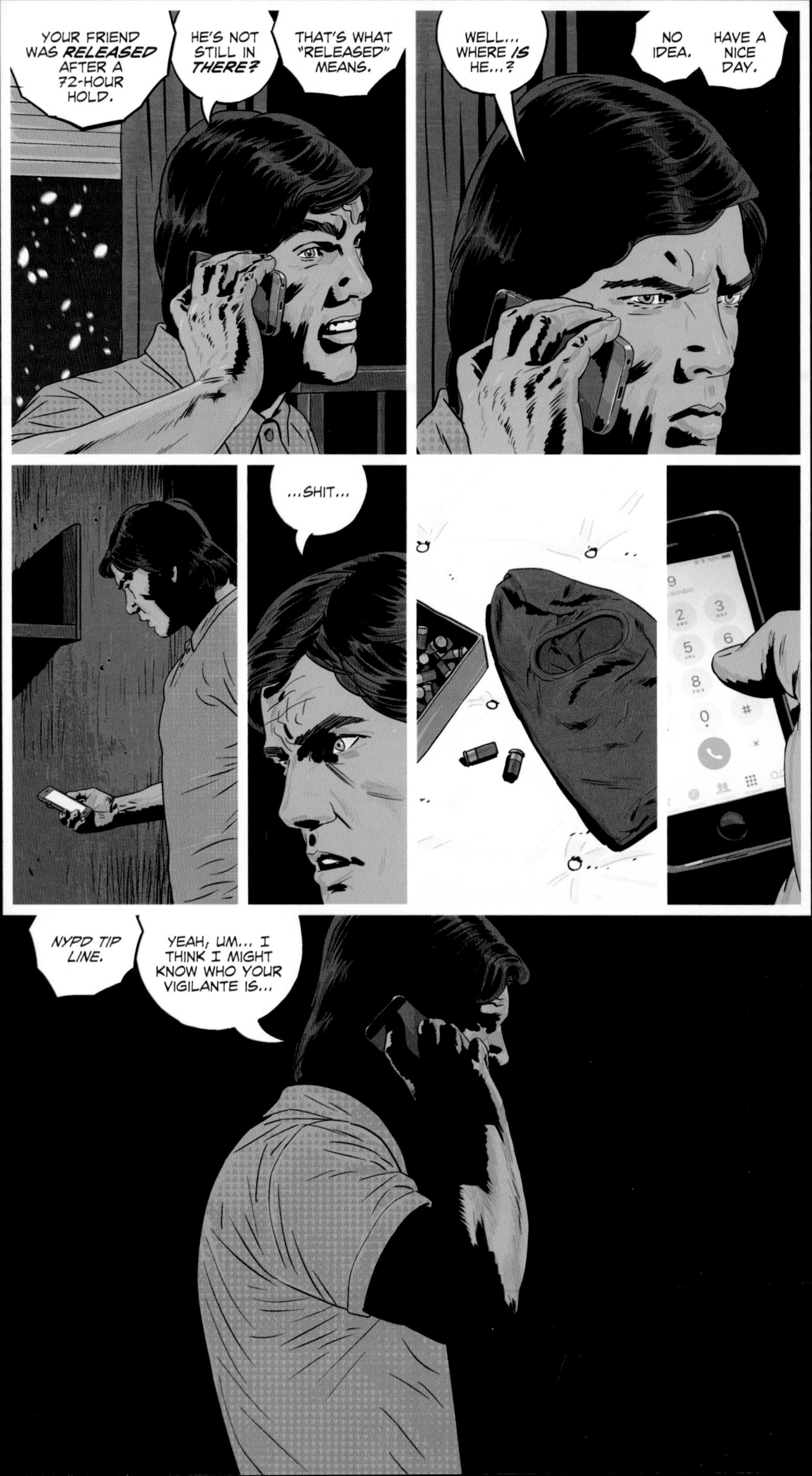
YOUR FRIEND WAS RELEASED AFTER A 72-HOUR HOLD.
HE'S NOT STILL IN THERE?
THAT'S WHAT "RELEASED" MEANS.
WELL... WHERE IS HE...?
NO IDEA.
HAVE A NICE DAY.
...SHIT...
NYPD TIP LINE.
YEAH, UM... I THINK I MIGHT KNOW WHO YOUR VIGILANTE IS...

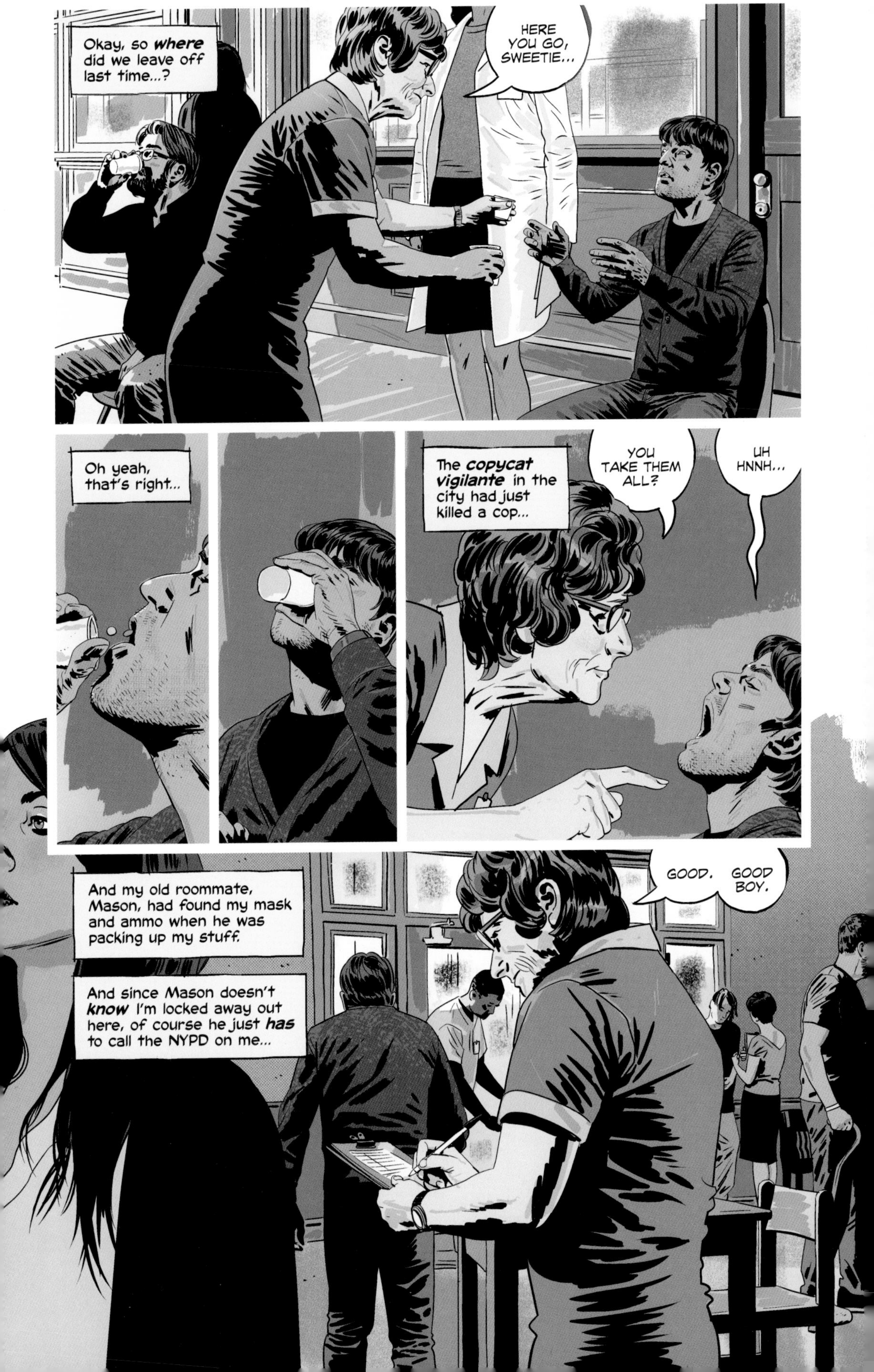

Okay, so *where* did we leave off last time...?
HERE YOU GO, SWEETIE...
Oh yeah, that's right...
The *copycat vigilante* in the city had just killed a cop...
YOU TAKE THEM ALL?
UH HNNH...
And my old roommate, Mason, had found my mask and ammo when he was packing up my stuff.
And since Mason doesn't *know* I'm locked away out here, of course he just *has* to call the NYPD on me...
GOOD. GOOD BOY.

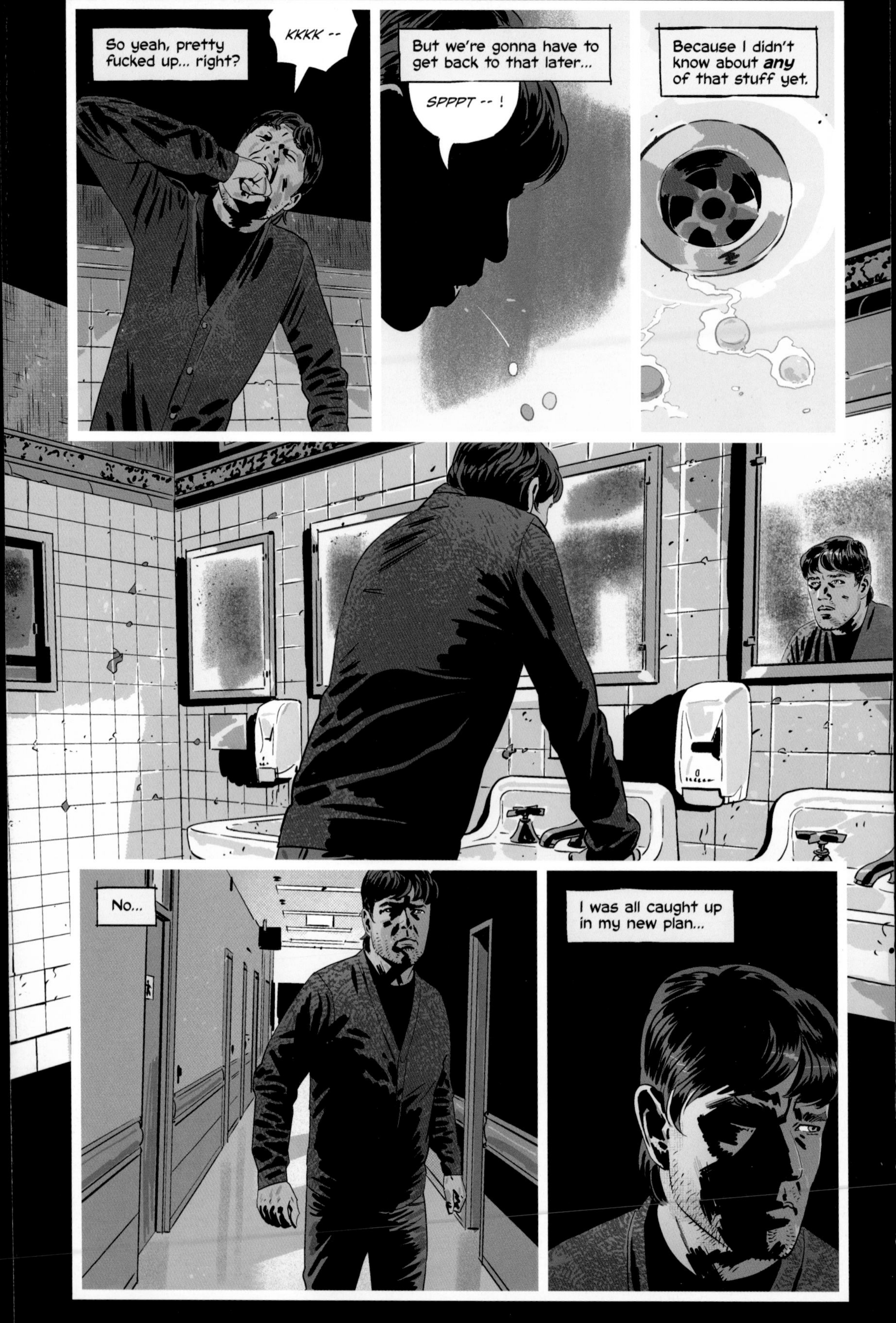

So yeah, pretty fucked up... right?
KKKK --
But we're gonna have to get back to that later...
SPPPT -- !
Because I didn't know about ***any*** of that stuff yet.
No...
I was all caught up in my new plan...

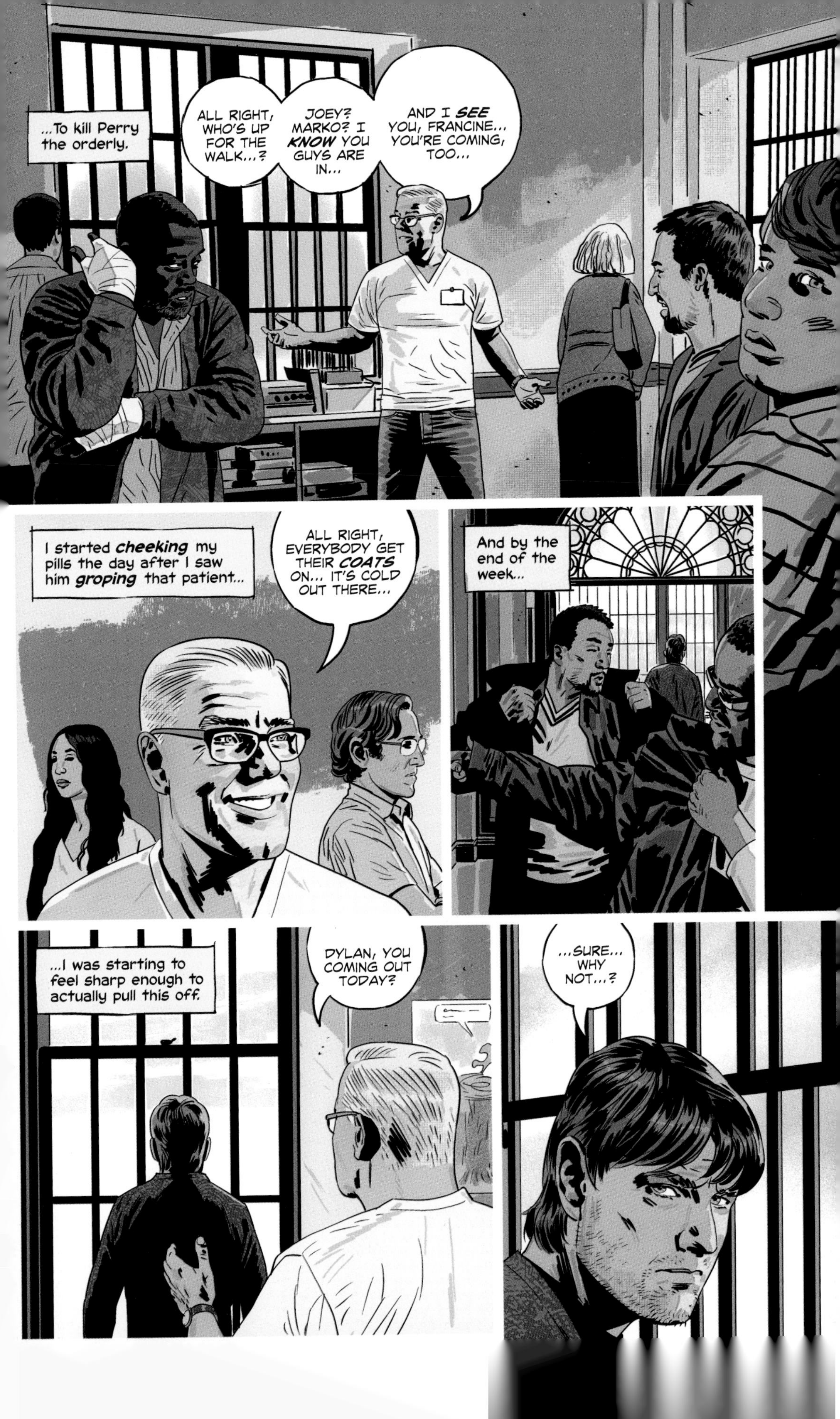
...To kill Perry the orderly.
ALL RIGHT, WHO'S UP FOR THE WALK...?
JOEY? MARKO? I KNOW YOU GUYS ARE IN...
AND I SEE YOU, FRANCINE... YOU'RE COMING, TOO...
I started cheeking my pills the day after I saw him groping that patient...
ALL RIGHT, EVERYBODY GET THEIR COATS ON... IT'S COLD OUT THERE...
And by the end of the week...
...I was starting to feel sharp enough to actually pull this off.
DYLAN, YOU COMING OUT TODAY?
...SURE... WHY NOT...?

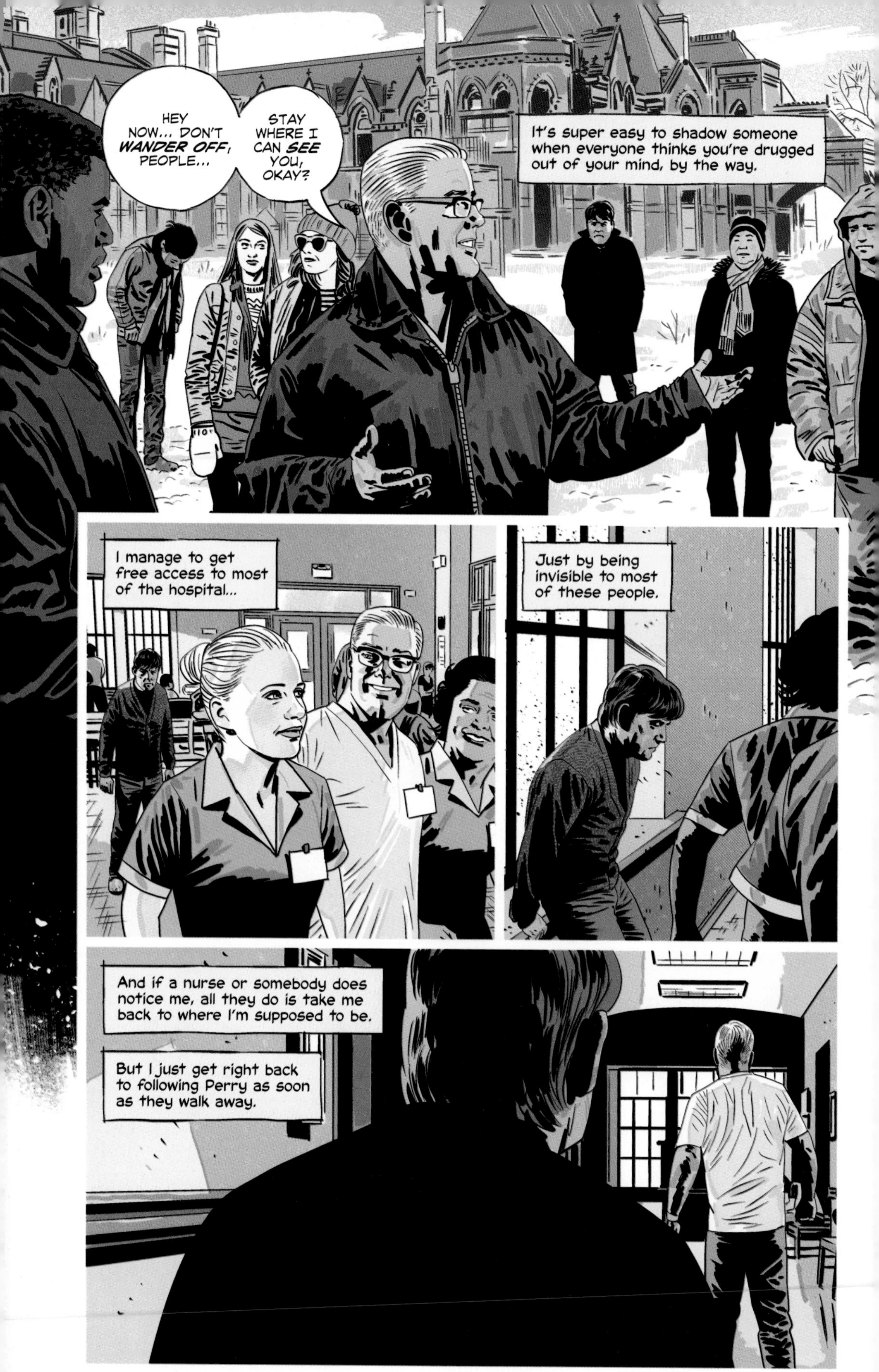
HEY NOW... DON'T WANDER OFF, PEOPLE...
STAY WHERE I CAN SEE YOU, OKAY?
It's super easy to shadow someone when everyone thinks you're drugged out of your mind, by the way.
I manage to get free access to most of the hospital...
Just by being invisible to most of these people.
And if a nurse or somebody does notice me, all they do is take me back to where I'm supposed to be.
But I just get right back to following Perry as soon as they walk away.

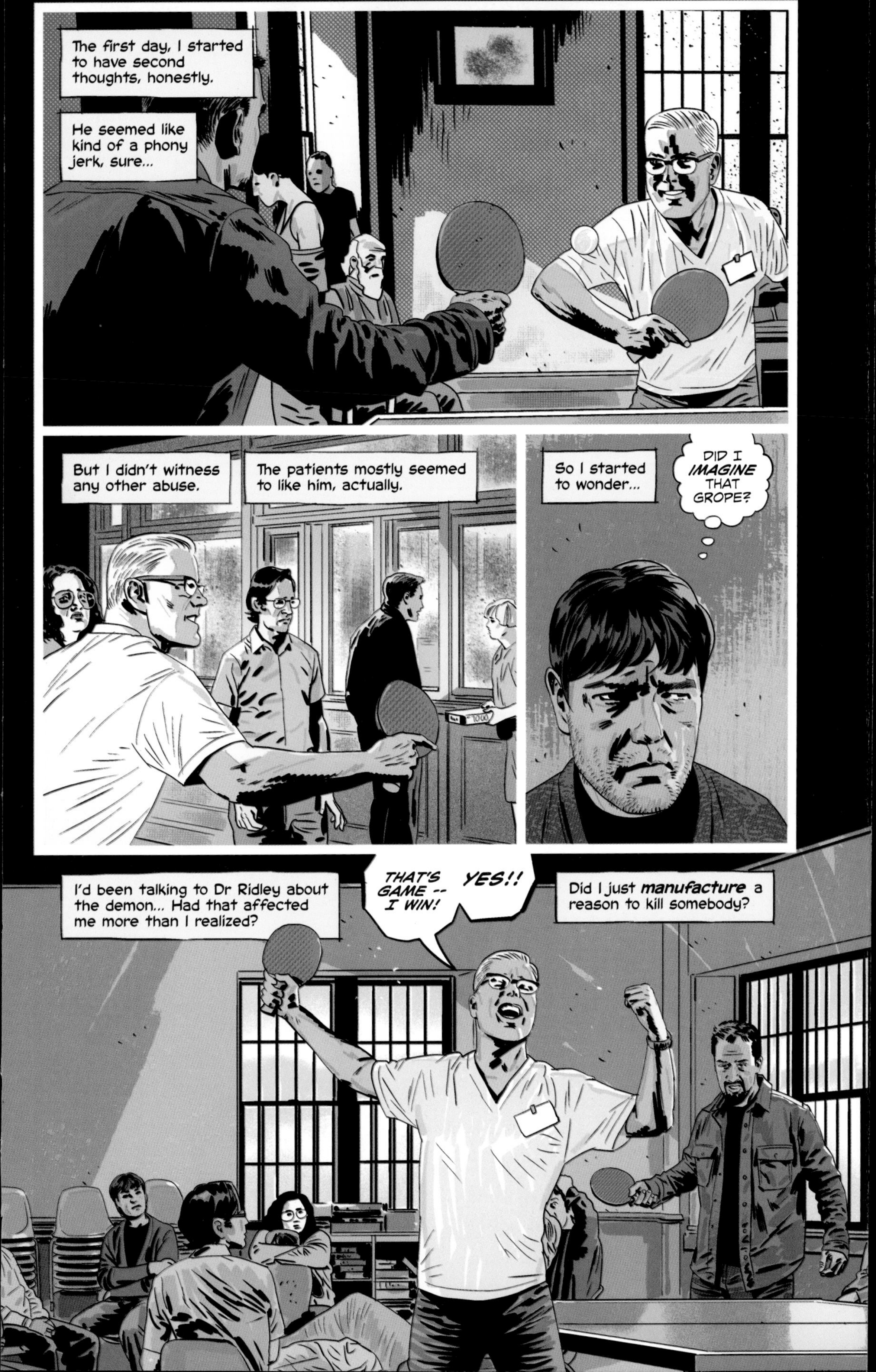
The first day, I started to have second thoughts, honestly.
He seemed like kind of a phony jerk, sure...
But I didn't witness any other abuse.
The patients mostly seemed to like him, actually.
So I started to wonder...
DID I *IMAGINE* THAT GROPE?
I'd been talking to Dr Ridley about the demon... Had that affected me more than I realized?
THAT'S GAME -- I WIN!
YES!!
Did I just ***manufacture*** a reason to kill somebody?

But don't worry -- before I went too far down that rabbit hole, Perry showed his true self again...

There's a woman here, Renata, she must be in her early 40s.

She had a breakdown after her son was killed in a car accident, and now she's on heavy sedation most of the time.

She smiles a lot, but it's a sad smile, y'know?

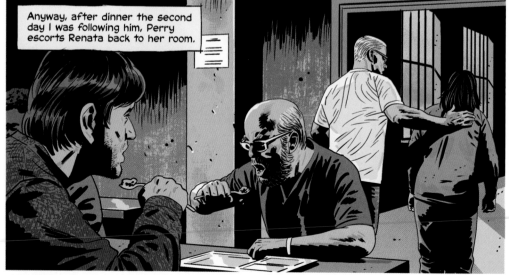

Anyway, after dinner the second day I was following him, Perry escorts Renata back to her room.

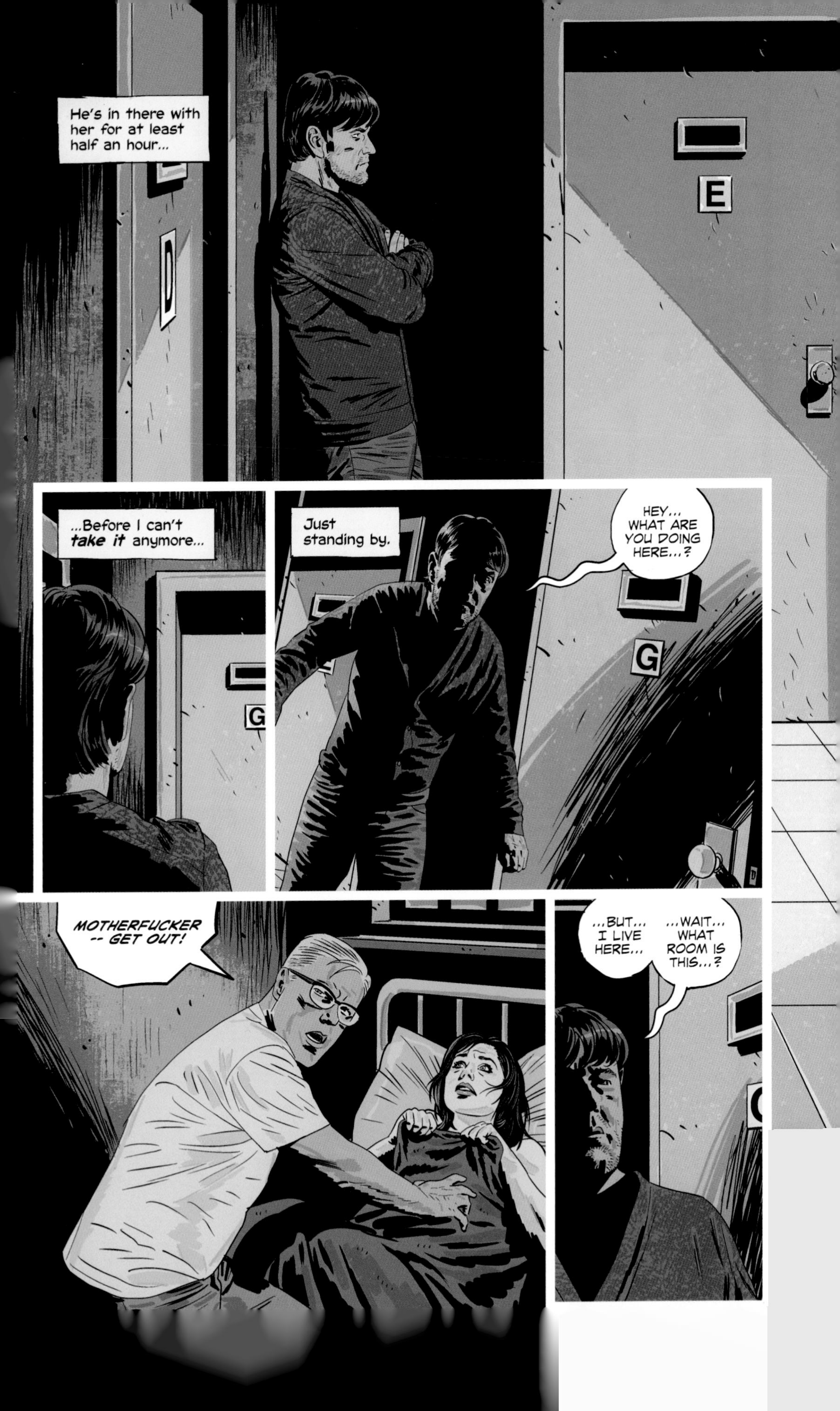
He's in there with her for at least half an hour...
...Before I can't *take it* anymore...
Just standing by.
HEY... WHAT ARE YOU DOING HERE...?
MOTHERFUCKER -- GET OUT!
...BUT... I LIVE HERE...
...WAIT... WHAT ROOM IS THIS...?

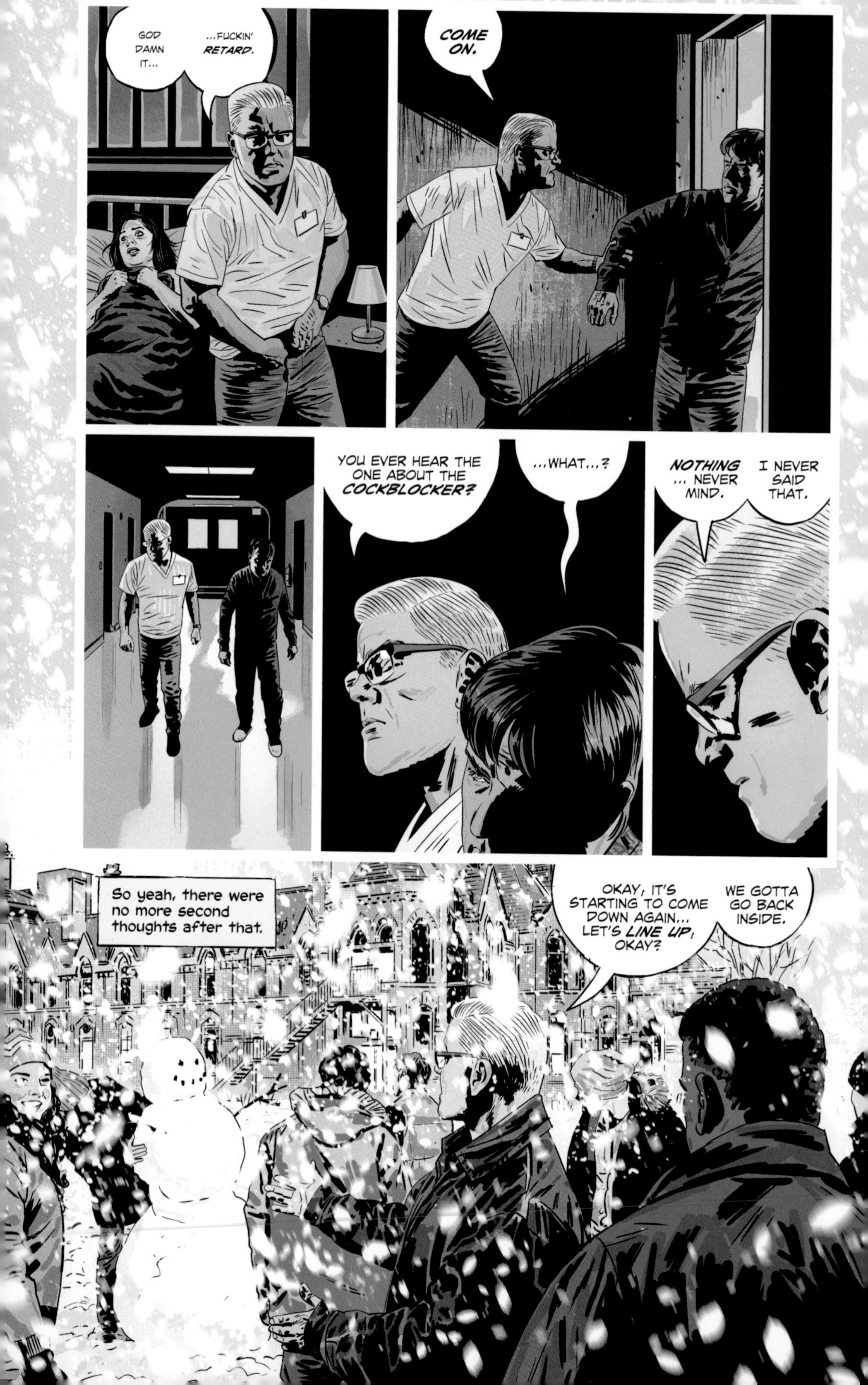
GOD DAMN IT...
...FUCKIN' RETARD.
COME ON.
YOU EVER HEAR THE ONE ABOUT THE COCKBLOCKER?
...WHAT...?
NOTHING ... NEVER MIND.
I NEVER SAID THAT.
So yeah, there were no more second thoughts after that.
OKAY, IT'S STARTING TO COME DOWN AGAIN... LET'S LINE UP, OKAY?
WE GOTTA GO BACK INSIDE.

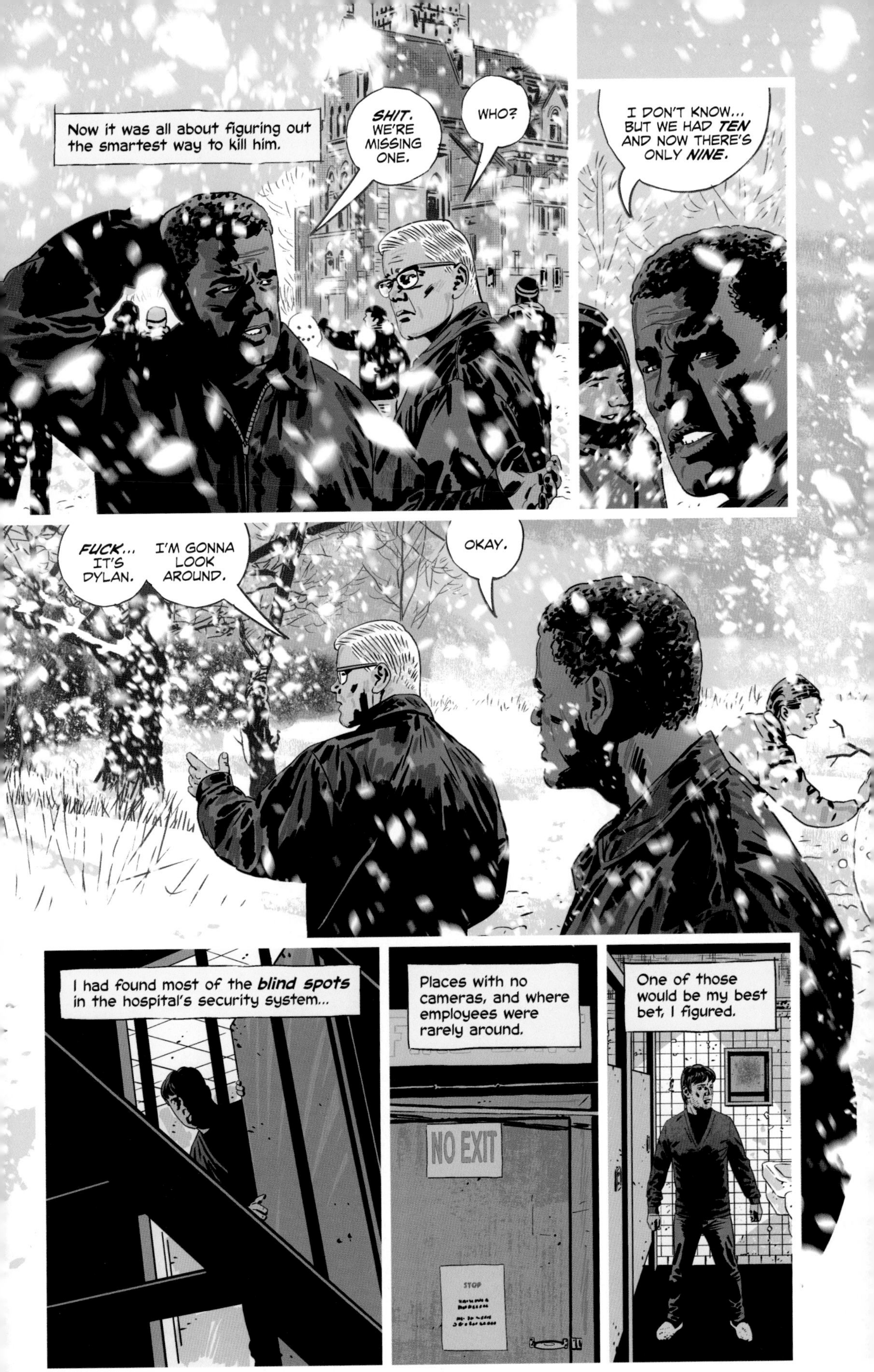
Now it was all about figuring out the smartest way to kill him.
SHIT. WE'RE MISSING ONE.
WHO?
I DON'T KNOW... BUT WE HAD TEN AND NOW THERE'S ONLY NINE.
FUCK... IT'S DYLAN.
I'M GONNA LOOK AROUND.
OKAY.
I had found most of the blind spots in the hospital's security system...
Places with no cameras, and where employees were rarely around.
NO EXIT
STOP
One of those would be my best bet, I figured.

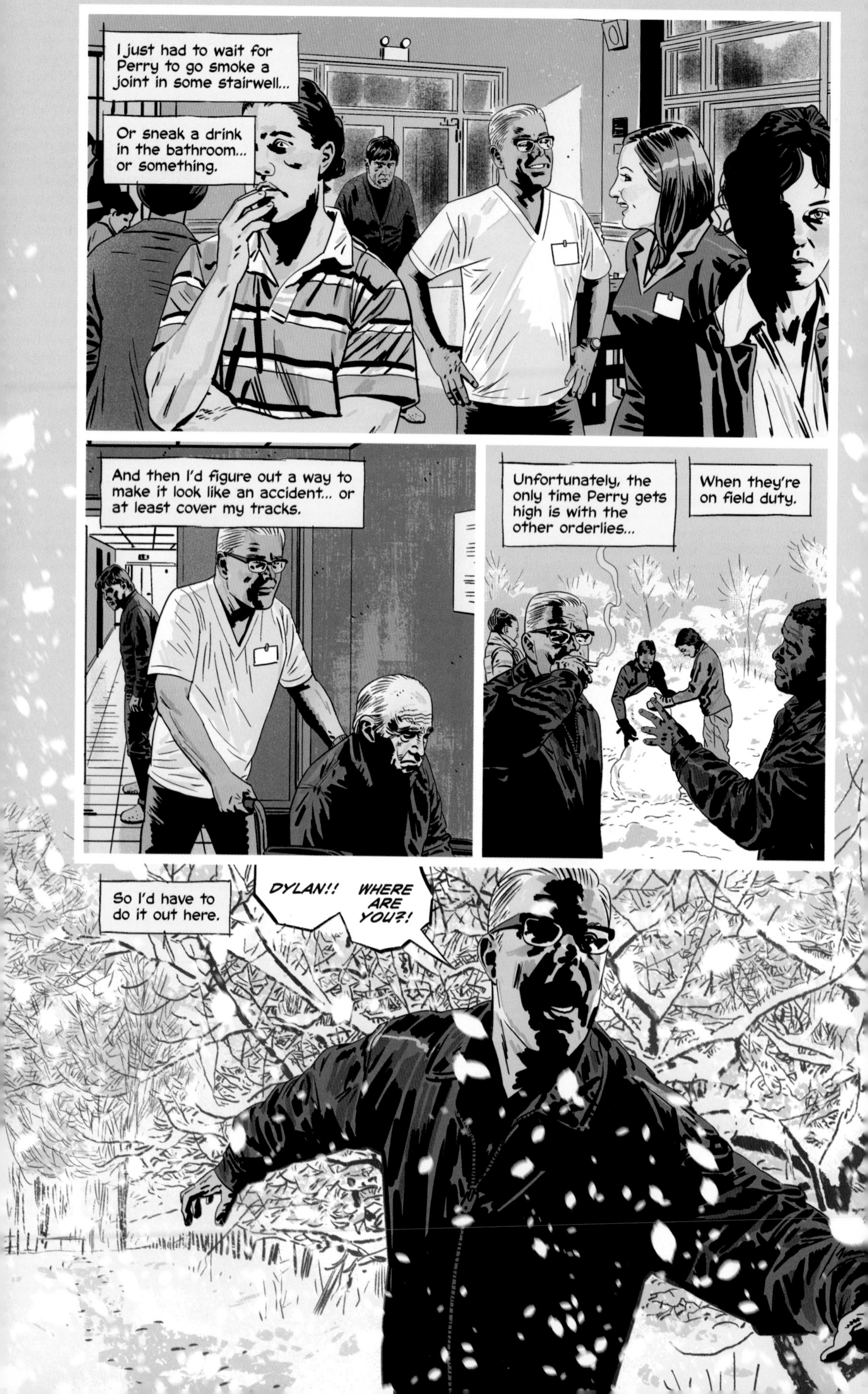
I just had to wait for Perry to go smoke a joint in some stairwell...
Or sneak a drink in the bathroom... or something.
And then I'd figure out a way to make it look like an accident... or at least cover my tracks.
Unfortunately, the only time Perry gets high is with the other orderlies...
When they're on field duty.
So I'd have to do it out here.
DYLAN!! WHERE ARE YOU?!

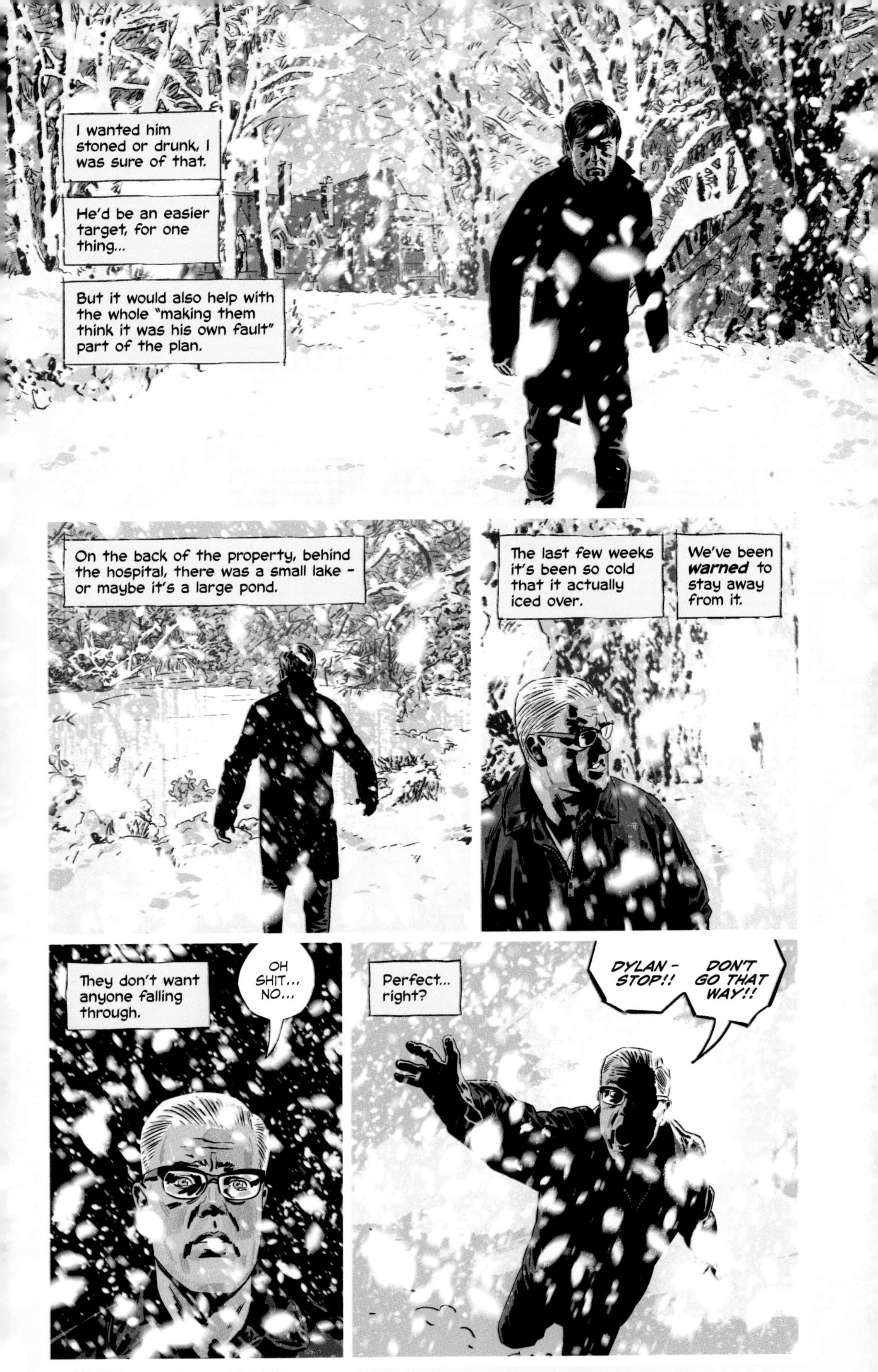
I wanted him stoned or drunk, I was sure of that.
He'd be an easier target, for one thing...
But it would also help with the whole "making them think it was his own fault" part of the plan.
On the back of the property, behind the hospital, there was a small lake - or maybe it's a large pond.
The last few weeks it's been so cold that it actually iced over.
We've been *warned* to stay away from it.
They don't want anyone falling through.
OH SHIT... NO...
Perfect... right?
DYLAN - STOP!!
DON'T GO THAT WAY!!

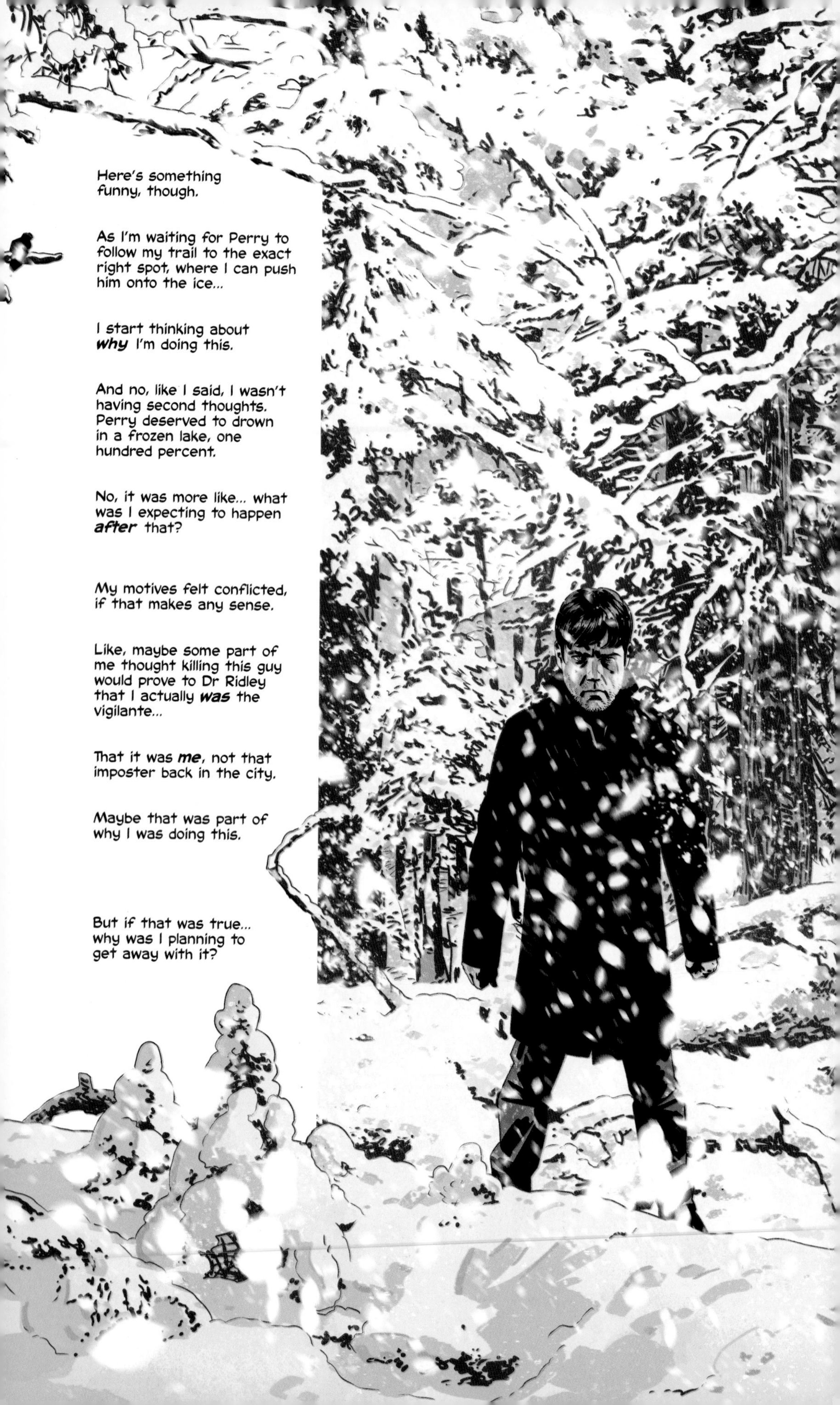
Here's something funny, though.
As I'm waiting for Perry to follow my trail to the exact right spot, where I can push him onto the ice...
I start thinking about ***why*** I'm doing this.
And no, like I said, I wasn't having second thoughts. Perry deserved to drown in a frozen lake, one hundred percent.
No, it was more like... what was I expecting to happen ***after*** that?
My motives felt conflicted, if that makes any sense.
Like, maybe some part of me thought killing this guy would prove to Dr Ridley that I actually ***was*** the vigilante...
That it was ***me***, not that imposter back in the city.
Maybe that was part of why I was doing this.
But if that was true... why was I planning to get away with it?

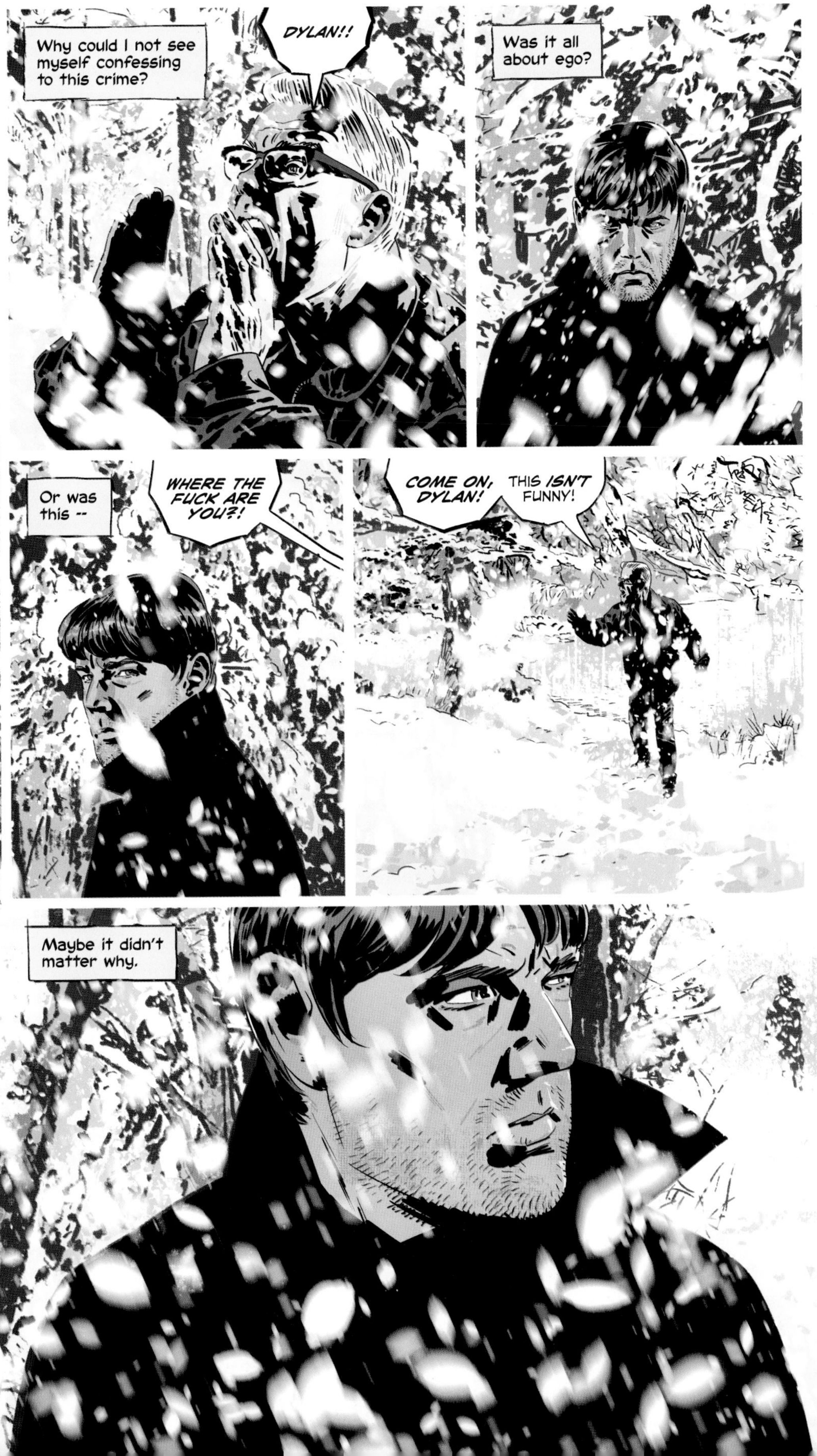
Why could I not see myself confessing to this crime?
DYLAN!!
Was it all about ego?
Or was this --
WHERE THE FUCK ARE YOU?!
COME ON, DYLAN!
THIS ISN'T FUNNY!
Maybe it didn't matter why.

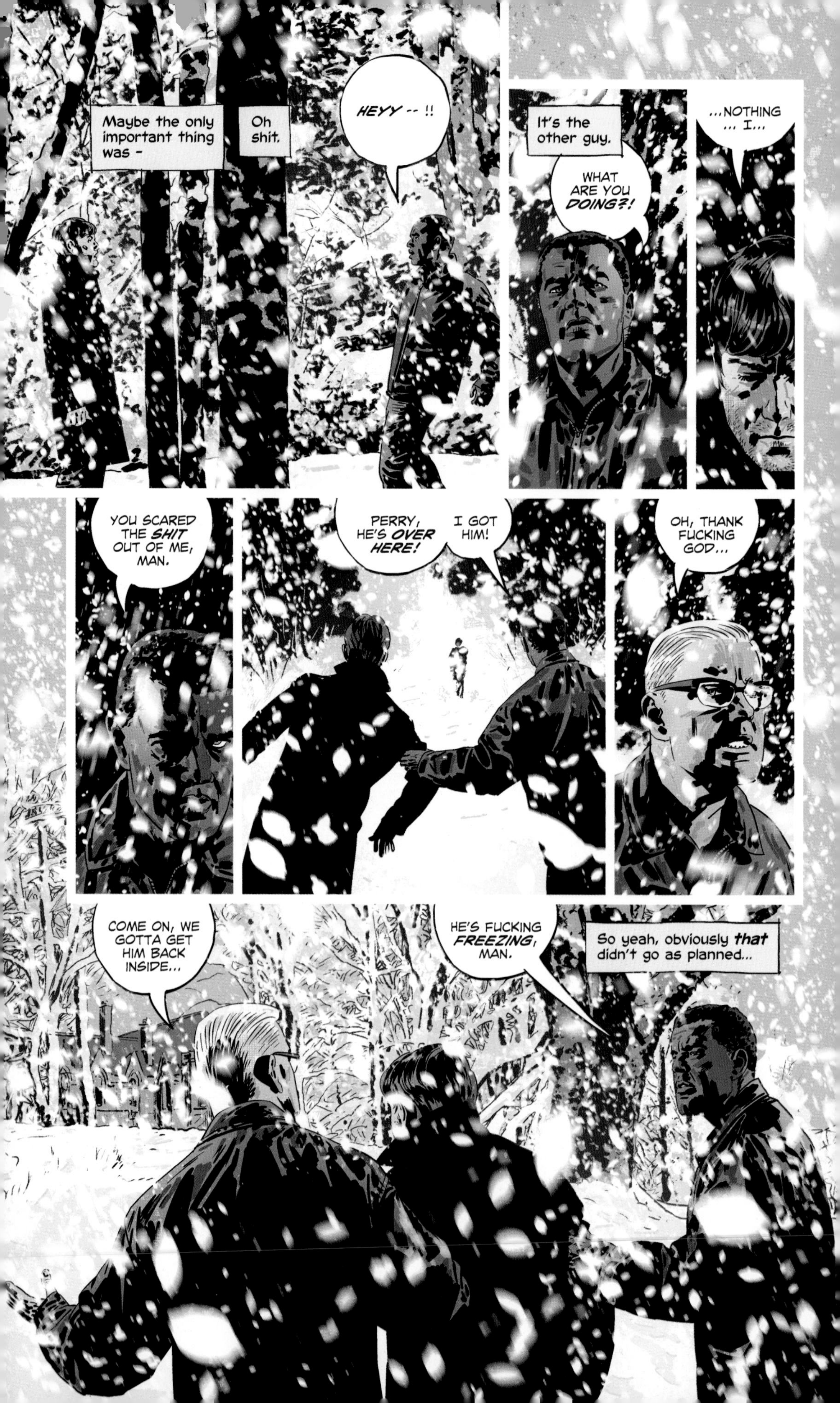

Maybe the only important thing was -
Oh shit.
HEYY -- !!
It's the other guy.
WHAT ARE YOU DOING?!
...NOTHING ... I...
YOU SCARED THE SHIT OUT OF ME, MAN.
PERRY, HE'S OVER HERE!
I GOT HIM!
OH, THANK FUCKING GOD...
COME ON, WE GOTTA GET HIM BACK INSIDE...
HE'S FUCKING FREEZING, MAN.
So yeah, obviously that didn't go as planned...

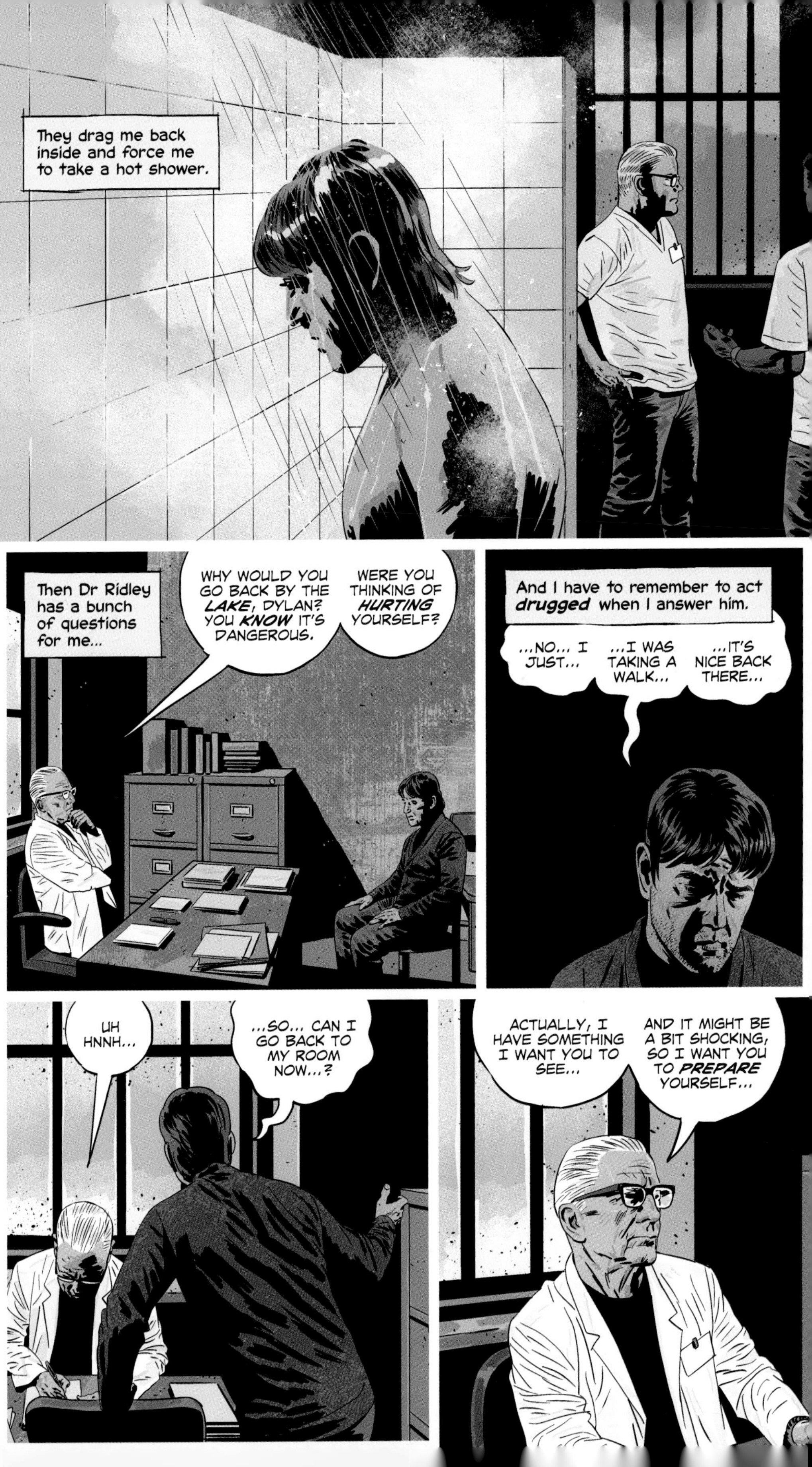
They drag me back inside and force me to take a hot shower.
Then Dr Ridley has a bunch of questions for me...
WHY WOULD YOU GO BACK BY THE LAKE, DYLAN? YOU KNOW IT'S DANGEROUS.
WERE YOU THINKING OF HURTING YOURSELF?
And I have to remember to act drugged when I answer him.
...NO... I JUST...
...I WAS TAKING A WALK...
...IT'S NICE BACK THERE...
UH HNNH...
...SO... CAN I GO BACK TO MY ROOM NOW...?
ACTUALLY, I HAVE SOMETHING I WANT YOU TO SEE...
AND IT MIGHT BE A BIT SHOCKING, SO I WANT YOU TO PREPARE YOURSELF...

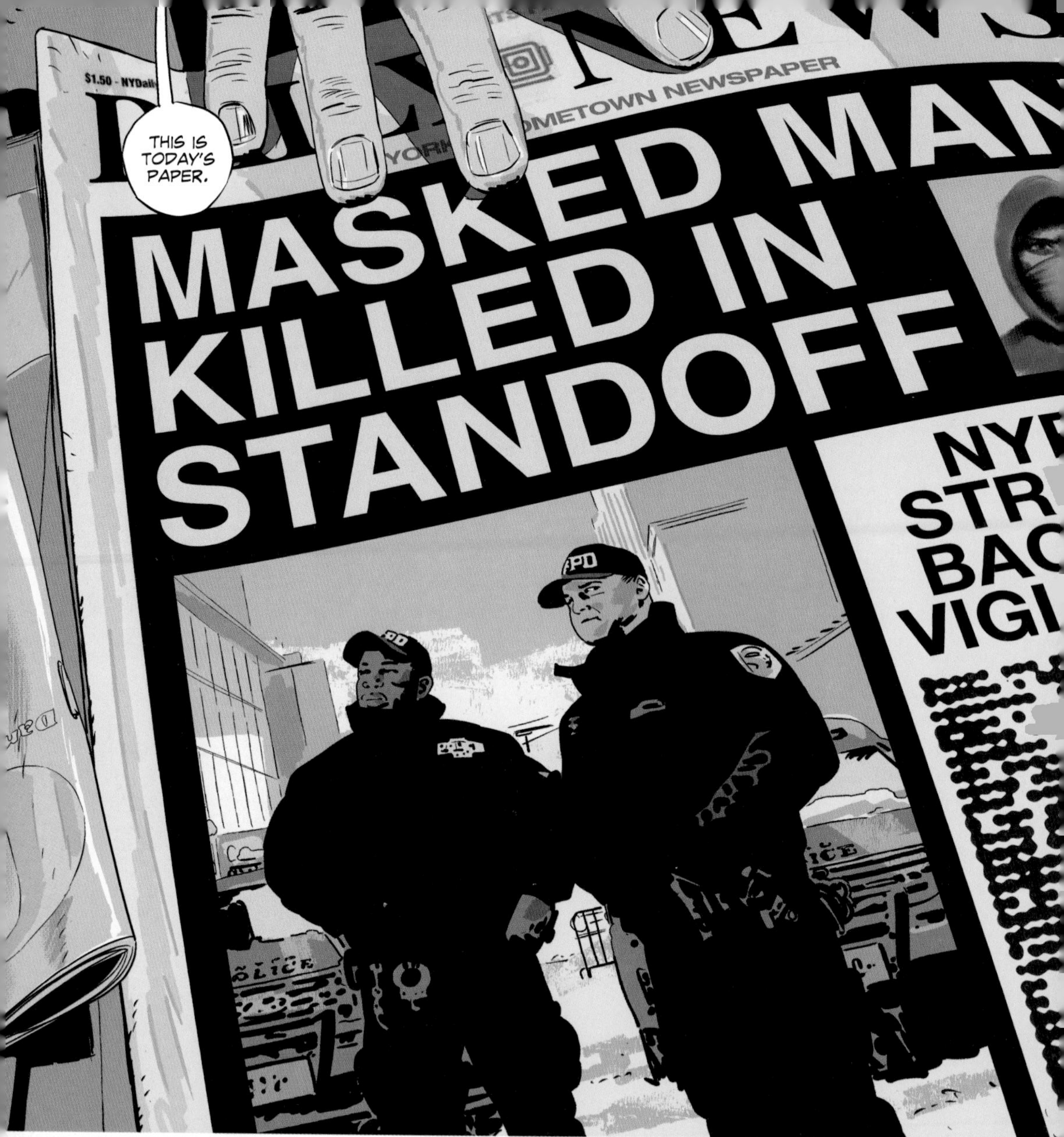
THIS IS TODAY'S PAPER.
$1.50 - NYDaily
HOMETOWN NEWSPAPER
MASKED MAN KILLED IN STANDOFF

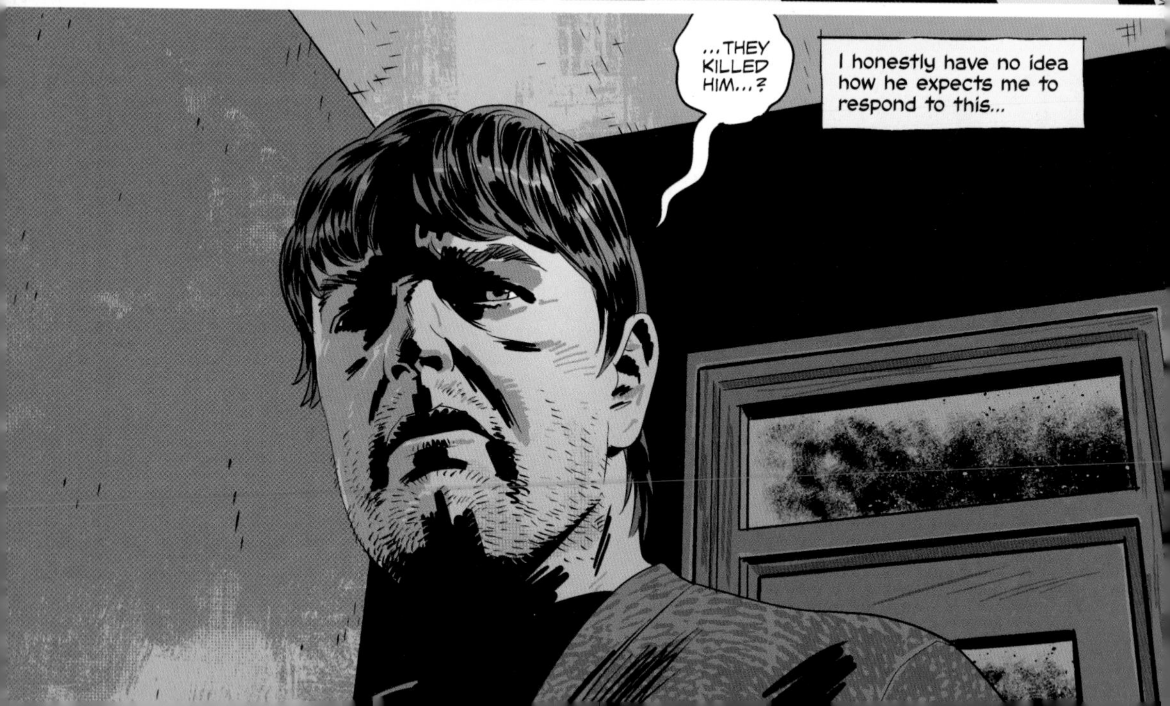
...THEY KILLED HIM...?
I honestly have no idea how he expects me to respond to this...

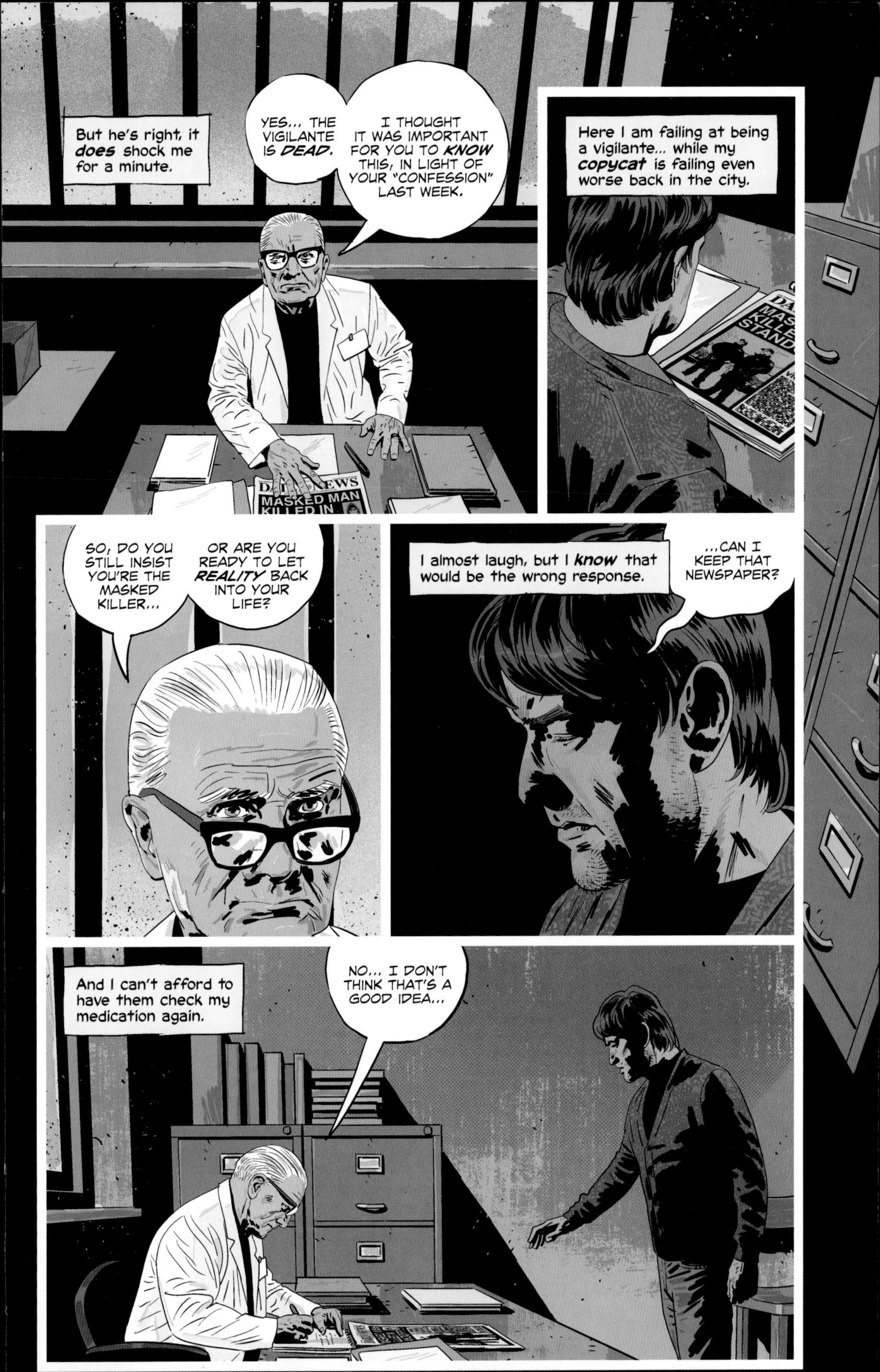

But he's right, it *does* shock me for a minute.
YES... THE VIGILANTE IS *DEAD.*
I THOUGHT IT WAS IMPORTANT FOR YOU TO *KNOW* THIS, IN LIGHT OF YOUR "CONFESSION" LAST WEEK.
DAILY NEWS
MASKED MAN KILLED IN...
Here I am failing at being a vigilante... while my *copycat* is failing even worse back in the city.
SO, DO YOU STILL INSIST YOU'RE THE MASKED KILLER...
OR ARE YOU READY TO LET *REALITY* BACK INTO YOUR LIFE?
I almost laugh, but I *know* that would be the wrong response.
...CAN I KEEP THAT NEWSPAPER?
And I can't afford to have them check my medication again.
NO... I DON'T THINK THAT'S A GOOD IDEA...

It was that night that I realized exactly how much I hated being in this hospital.

I thought I belonged here at first... And maybe I did.

I needed a place to hide and clean out my brain.

Someplace safe, where the people wanted to help me.

But now... Now it just felt like I was trapped.

I couldn't even read a paper or look at the internet.

And I didn't want to hide anymore.

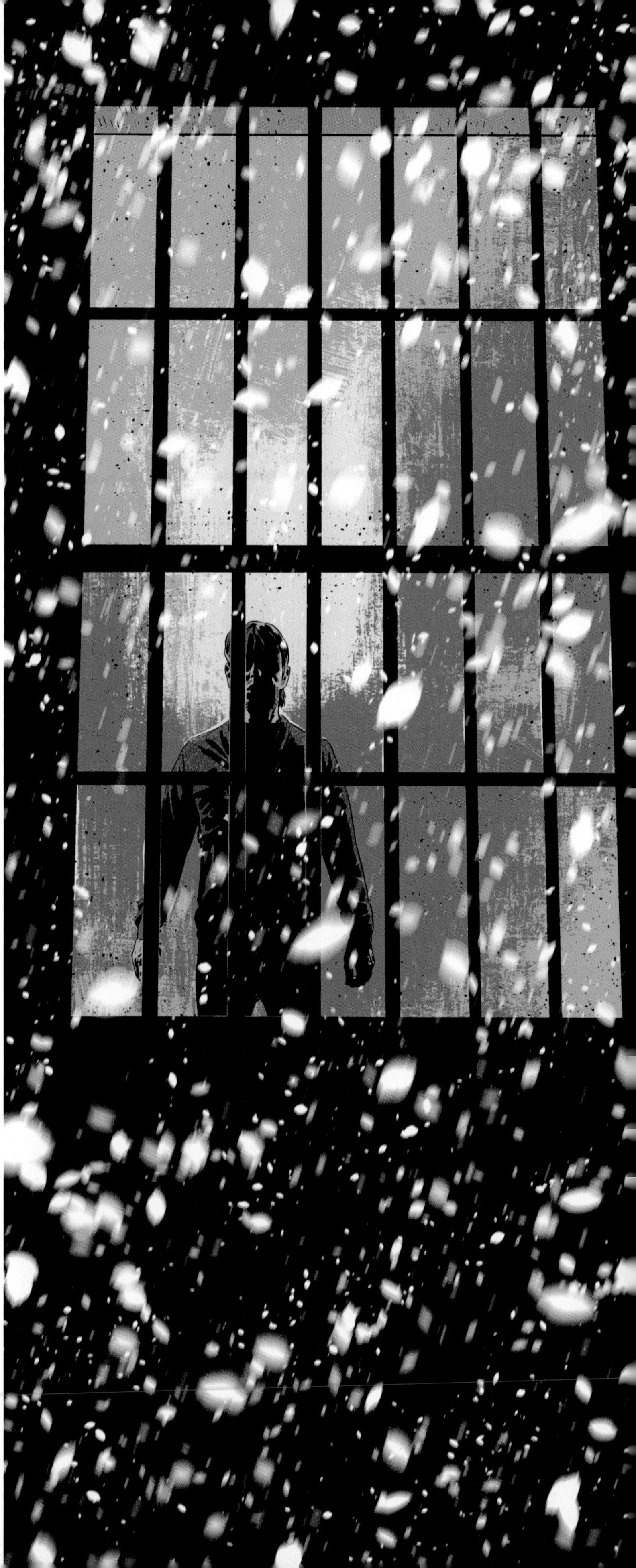

Remember that thing I was talking about before, about my conflicted motives?

Well, suddenly they weren't so conflicted. Suddenly I knew why I'd been planning to get away with it...

And it didn't have anything to do with that copycat who had gotten himself killed.

See... The demon was gone.

But the evil he'd revealed to me... ***that*** hadn't gone anywhere.

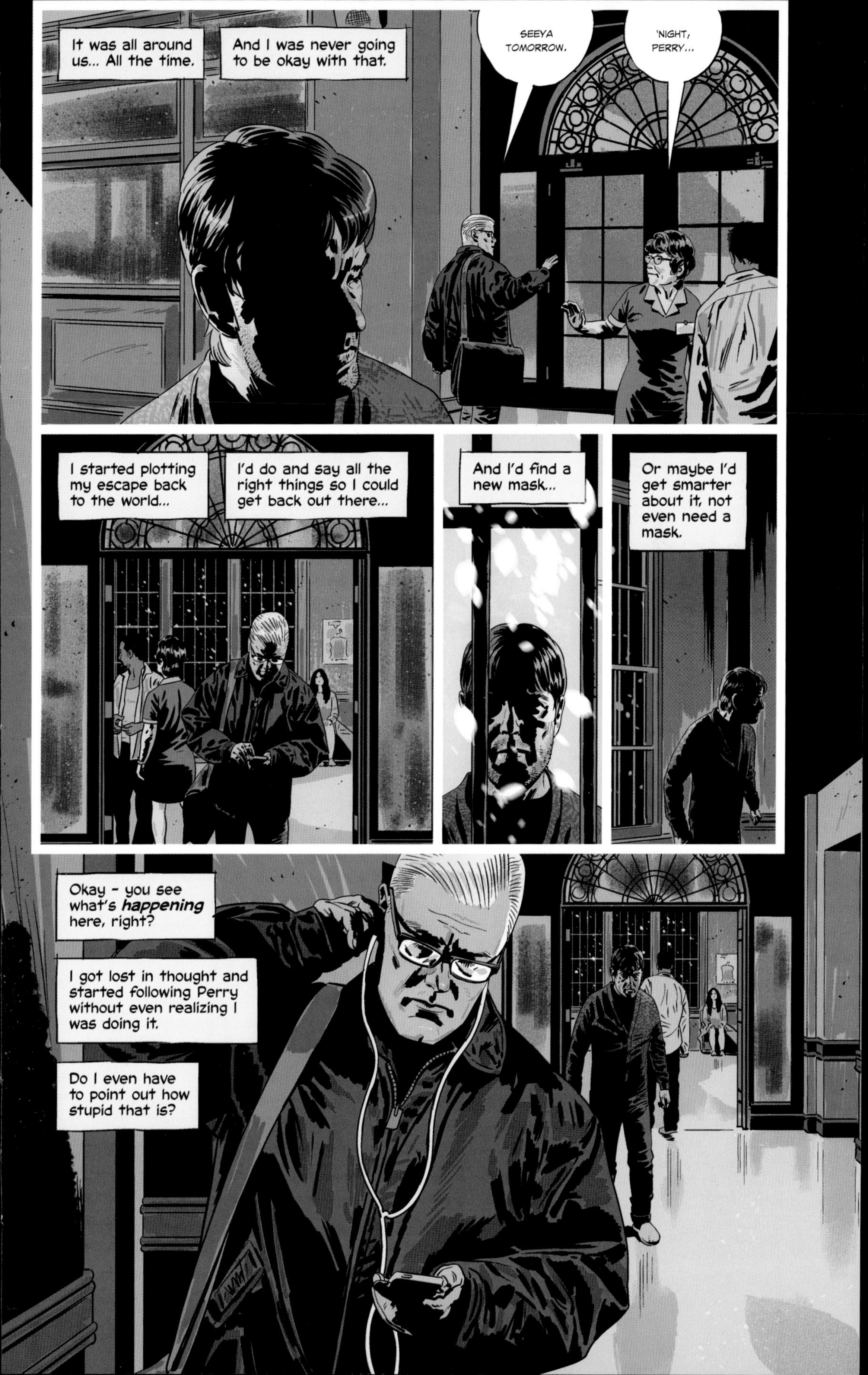
It was all around us... All the time.
And I was never going to be okay with that.
SEEYA TOMORROW.
'NIGHT, PERRY...
I started plotting my escape back to the world...
I'd do and say all the right things so I could get back out there...
And I'd find a new mask...
Or maybe I'd get smarter about it, not even need a mask.
Okay - you see what's ***happening*** here, right?
I got lost in thought and started following Perry without even realizing I was doing it.
Do I even have to point out how stupid that is?

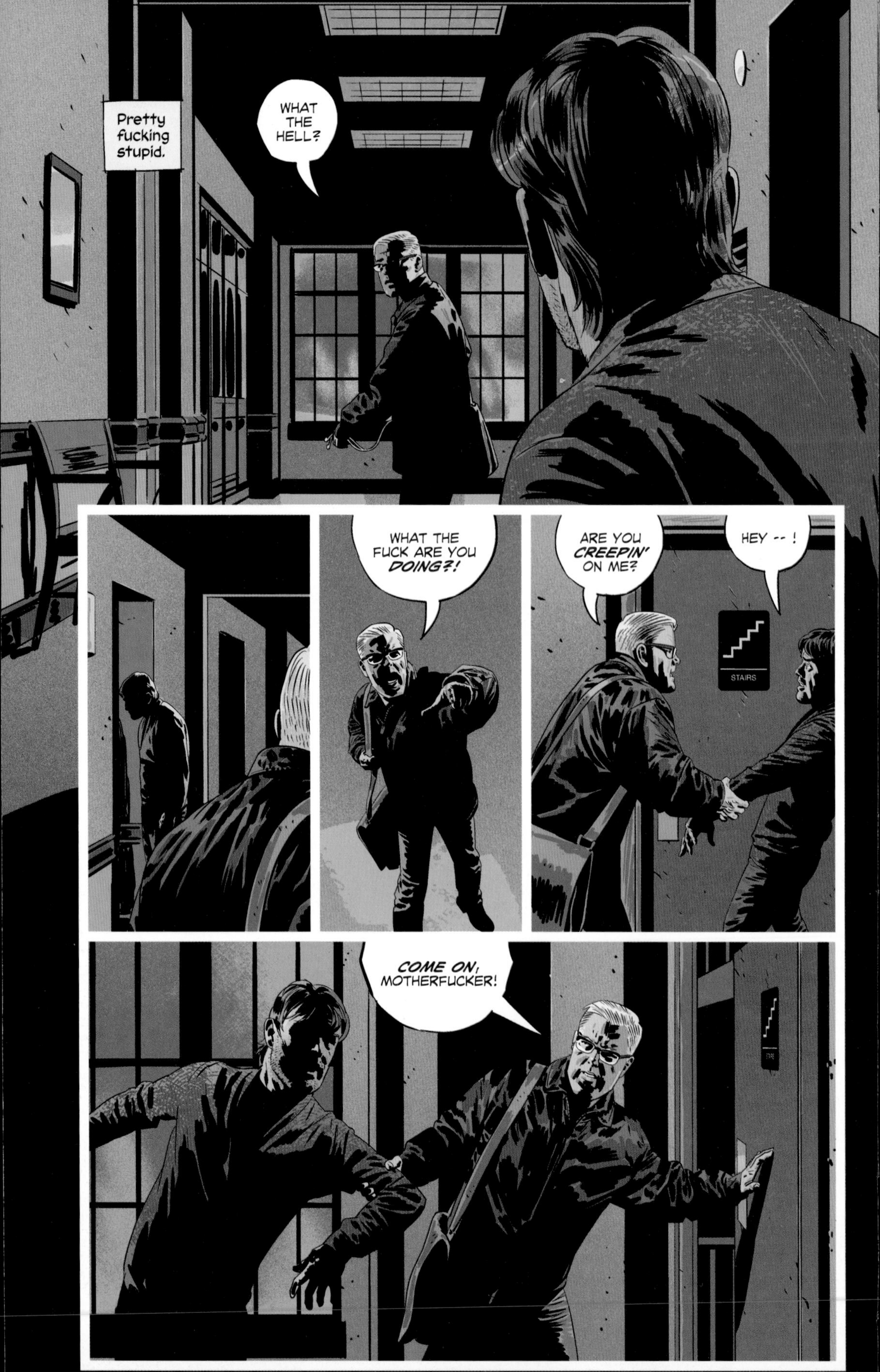
Pretty fucking stupid.
WHAT THE HELL?
WHAT THE FUCK ARE YOU DOING?!
ARE YOU CREEPIN' ON ME?
HEY -- !
STAIRS
COME ON, MOTHERFUCKER!

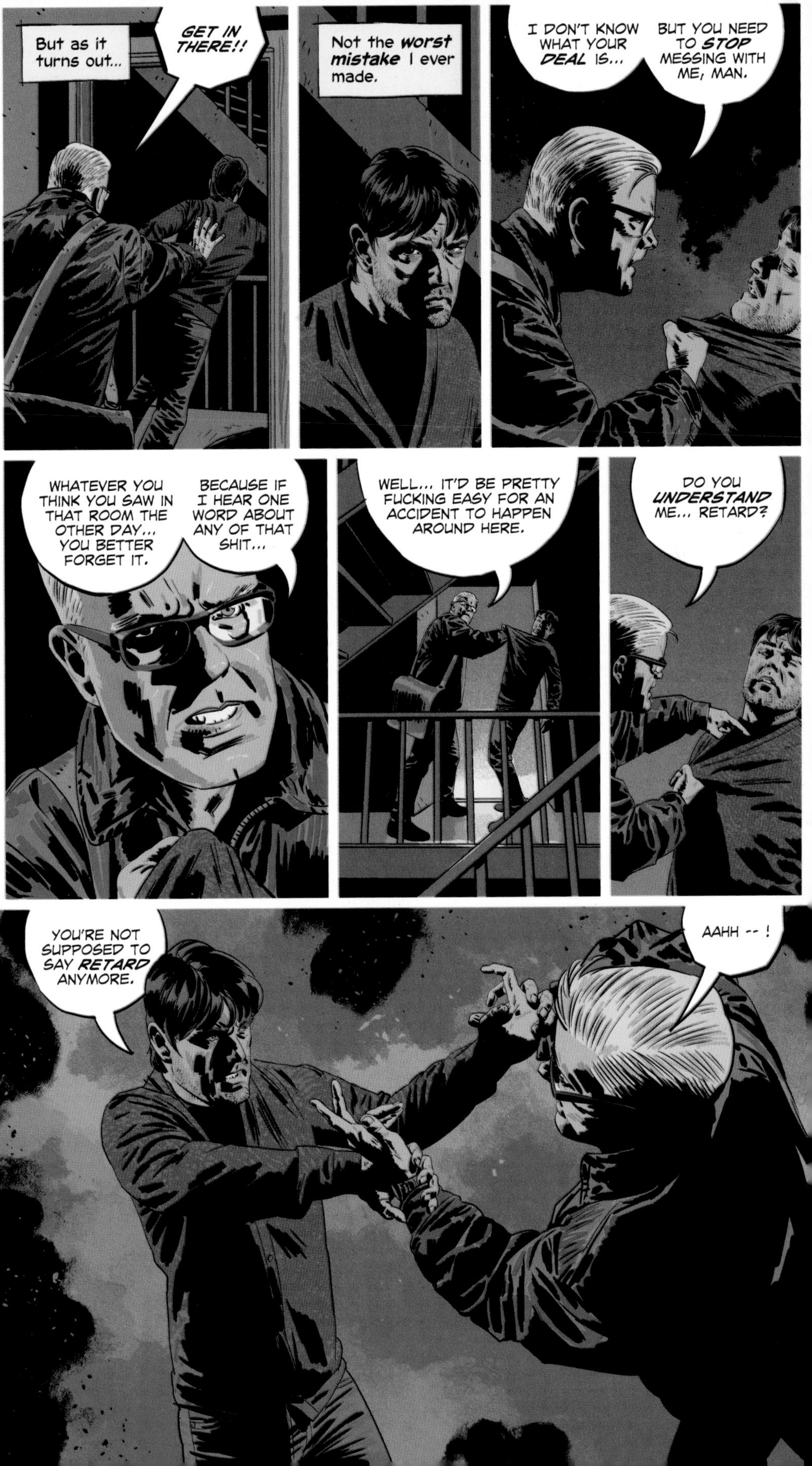
But as it turns out...
GET IN THERE!!
Not the worst mistake I ever made.
I DON'T KNOW WHAT YOUR DEAL IS...
BUT YOU NEED TO STOP MESSING WITH ME, MAN.
WHATEVER YOU THINK YOU SAW IN THAT ROOM THE OTHER DAY... YOU BETTER FORGET IT.
BECAUSE IF I HEAR ONE WORD ABOUT ANY OF THAT SHIT...
WELL... IT'D BE PRETTY FUCKING EASY FOR AN ACCIDENT TO HAPPEN AROUND HERE.
DO YOU UNDERSTAND ME... RETARD?
YOU'RE NOT SUPPOSED TO SAY RETARD ANYMORE.
AAHH -- !

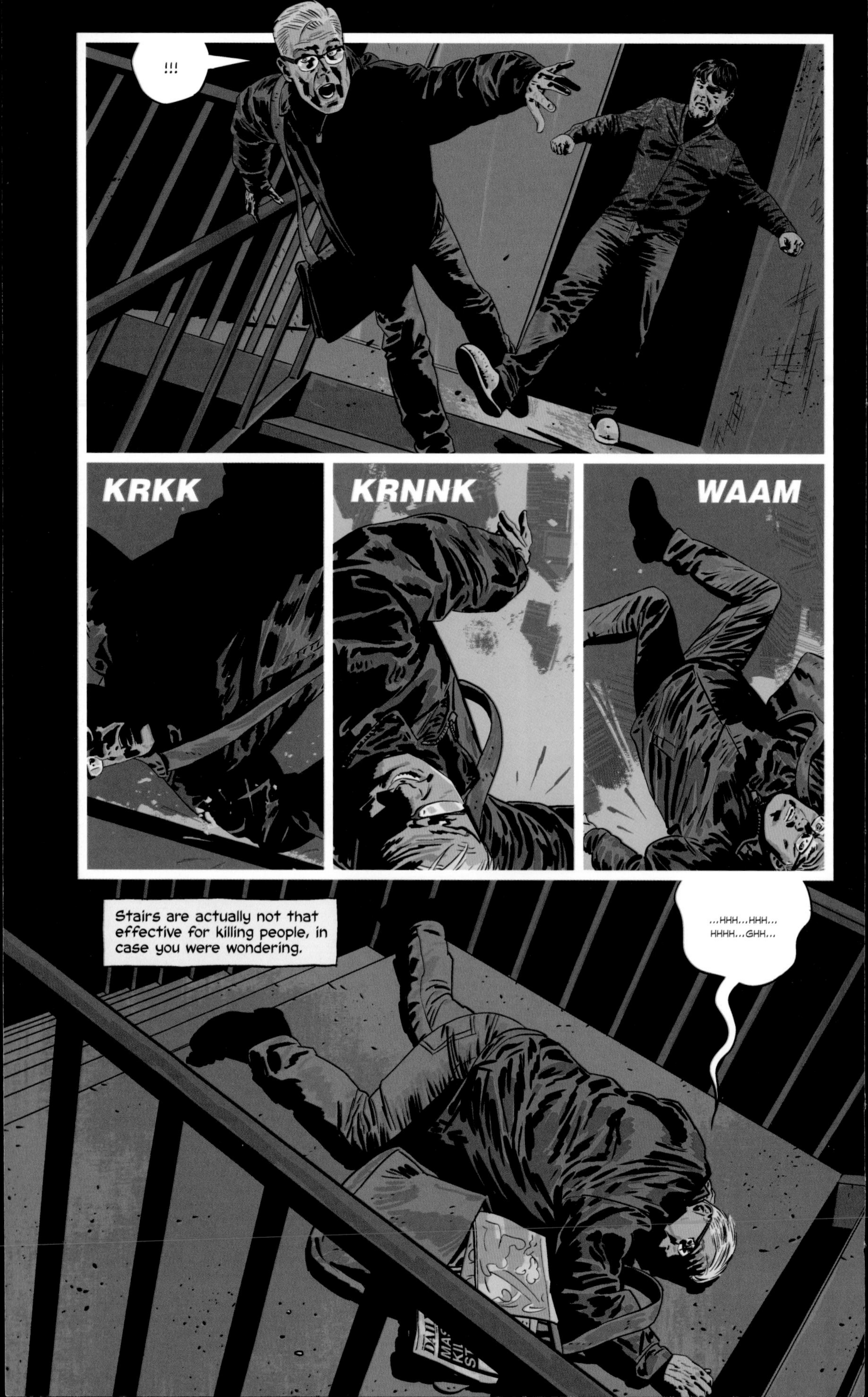
!!!
KRKK
KRNNK
WAAM
Stairs are actually not that effective for killing people, in case you were wondering.
...HHH...HHH...
HHHH...GHH...

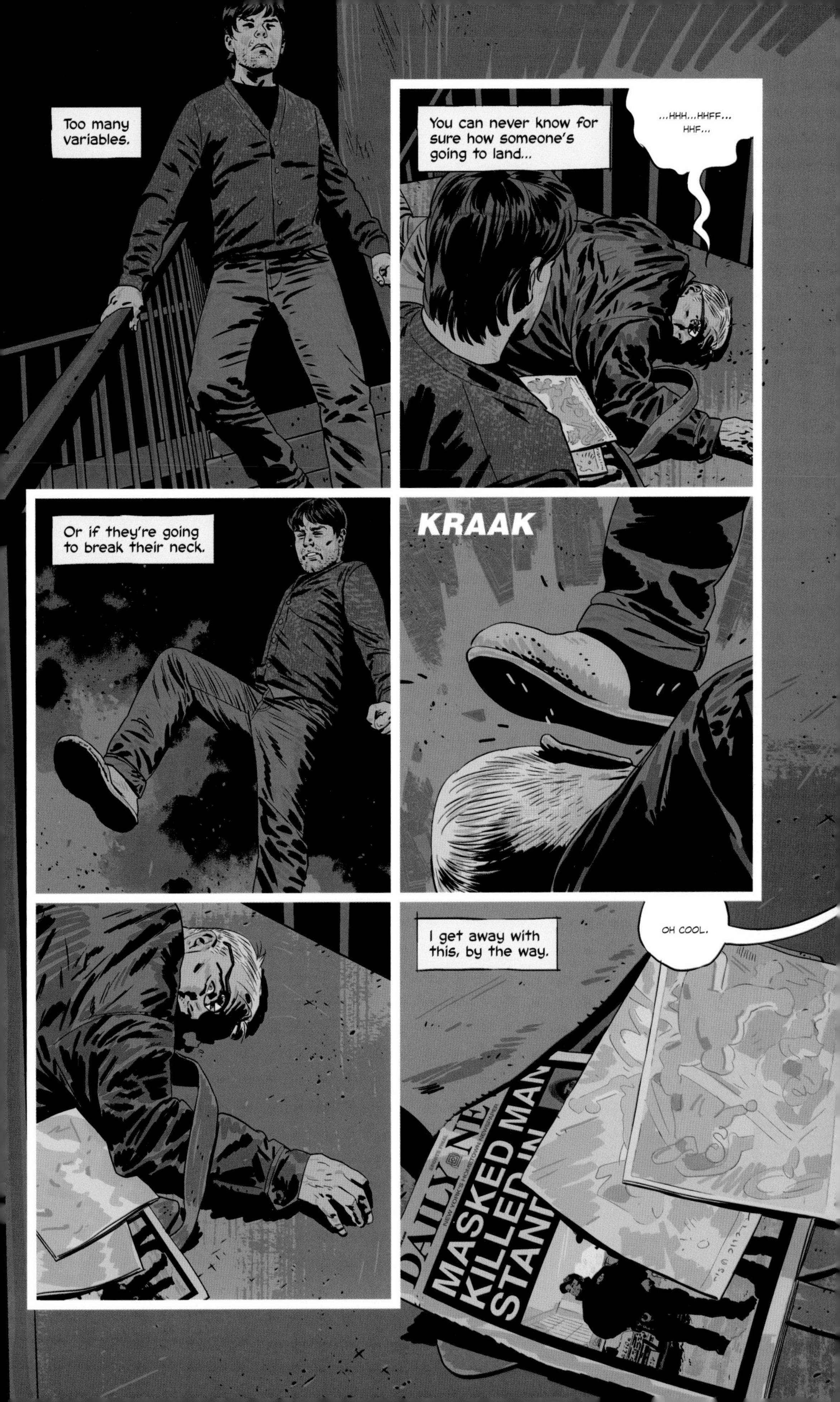
Too many variables.
You can never know for sure how someone's going to land...
...HHH...HHFF... HHF...
Or if they're going to break their neck.
KRAAK
I get away with this, by the way.
OH COOL.
DAILY NE
NEW YORK'S HOMETOWN NEWSPAPER
MASKED MAN KILLED IN STAN

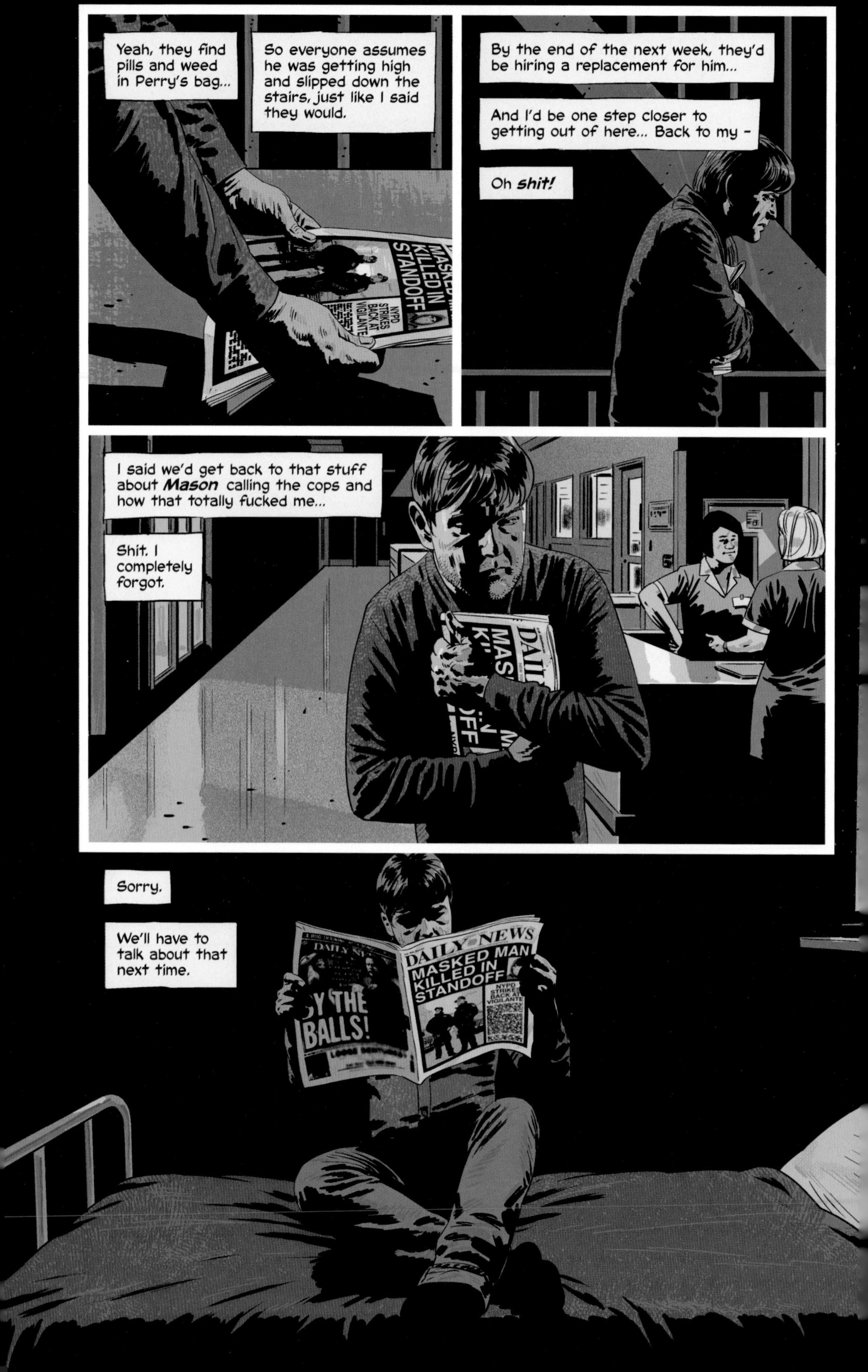

Yeah, they find pills and weed in Perry's bag...
So everyone assumes he was getting high and slipped down the stairs, just like I said they would.
MASKED MAN KILLED IN STANDOFF
NYPD STRIKES BACK AT VIGILANTE
By the end of the next week, they'd be hiring a replacement for him...
And I'd be one step closer to getting out of here... Back to my -
Oh *shit!*
I said we'd get back to that stuff about *Mason* calling the cops and how that totally fucked me...
Shit. I completely forgot.
Sorry.
We'll have to talk about that next time.
DAILY NEWS
MASKED MAN KILLED IN STANDOFF
NYPD STRIKES BACK AT VIGILANTE
BALLS!

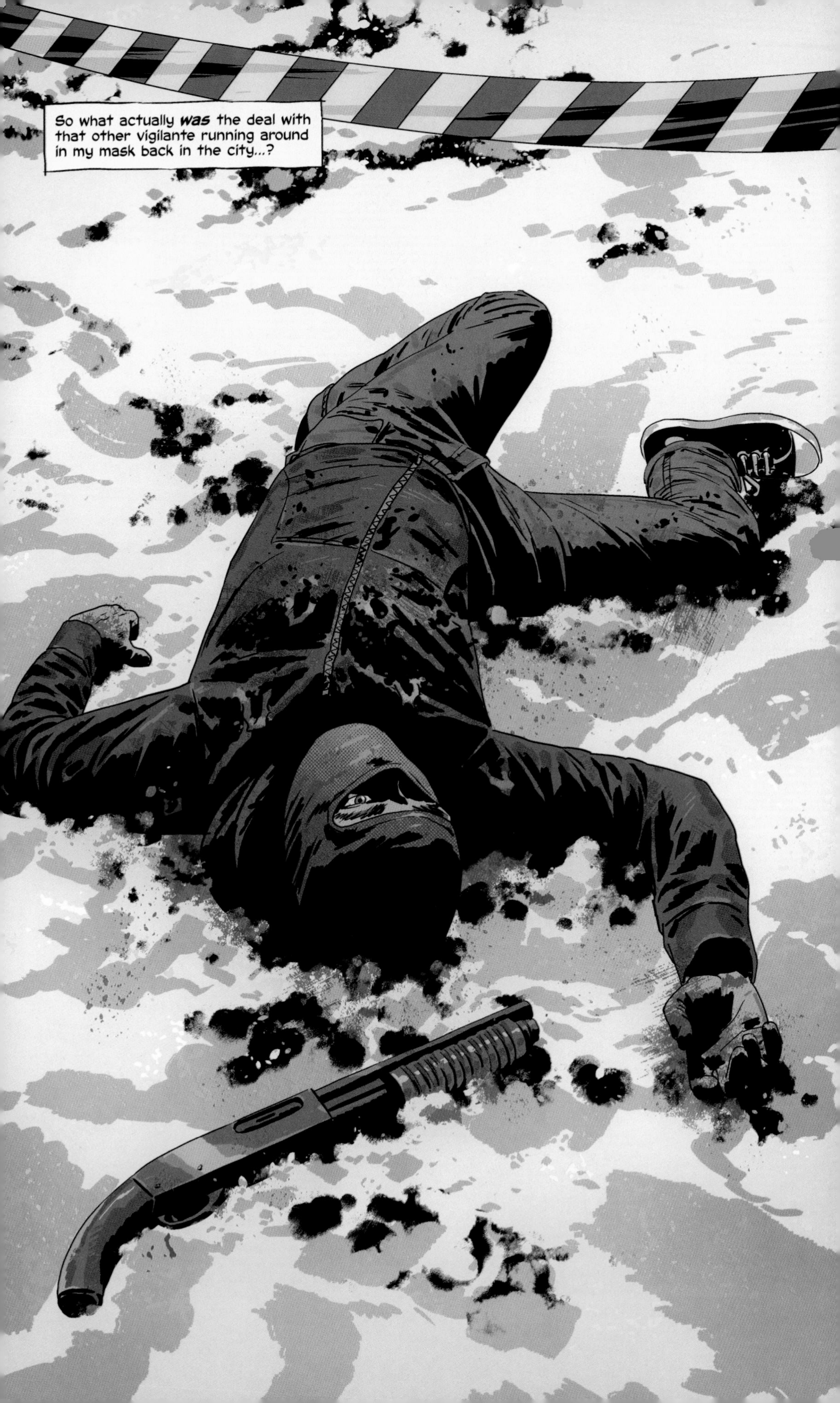
So what actually *was* the deal with that other vigilante running around in my mask back in the city...?

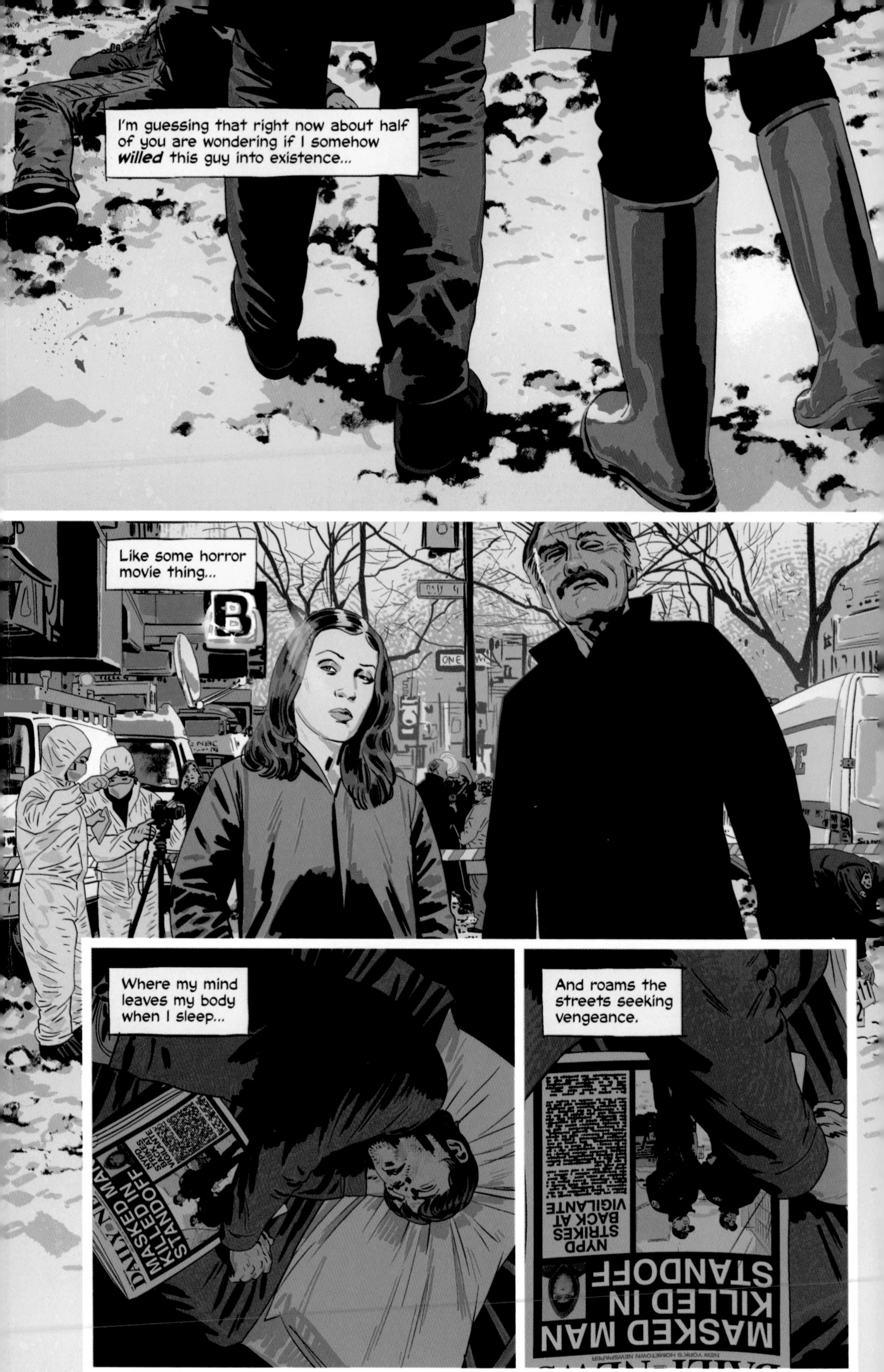
I'm guessing that right now about half of you are wondering if I somehow *willed* this guy into existence...
Like some horror movie thing...
Where my mind leaves my body when I sleep...
And roams the streets seeking vengeance.
MASKED MAN KILLED IN STANDOFF
NYPD STRIKES BACK AT VIGILANTE
NEW YORK'S HOMETOWN NEWSPAPER

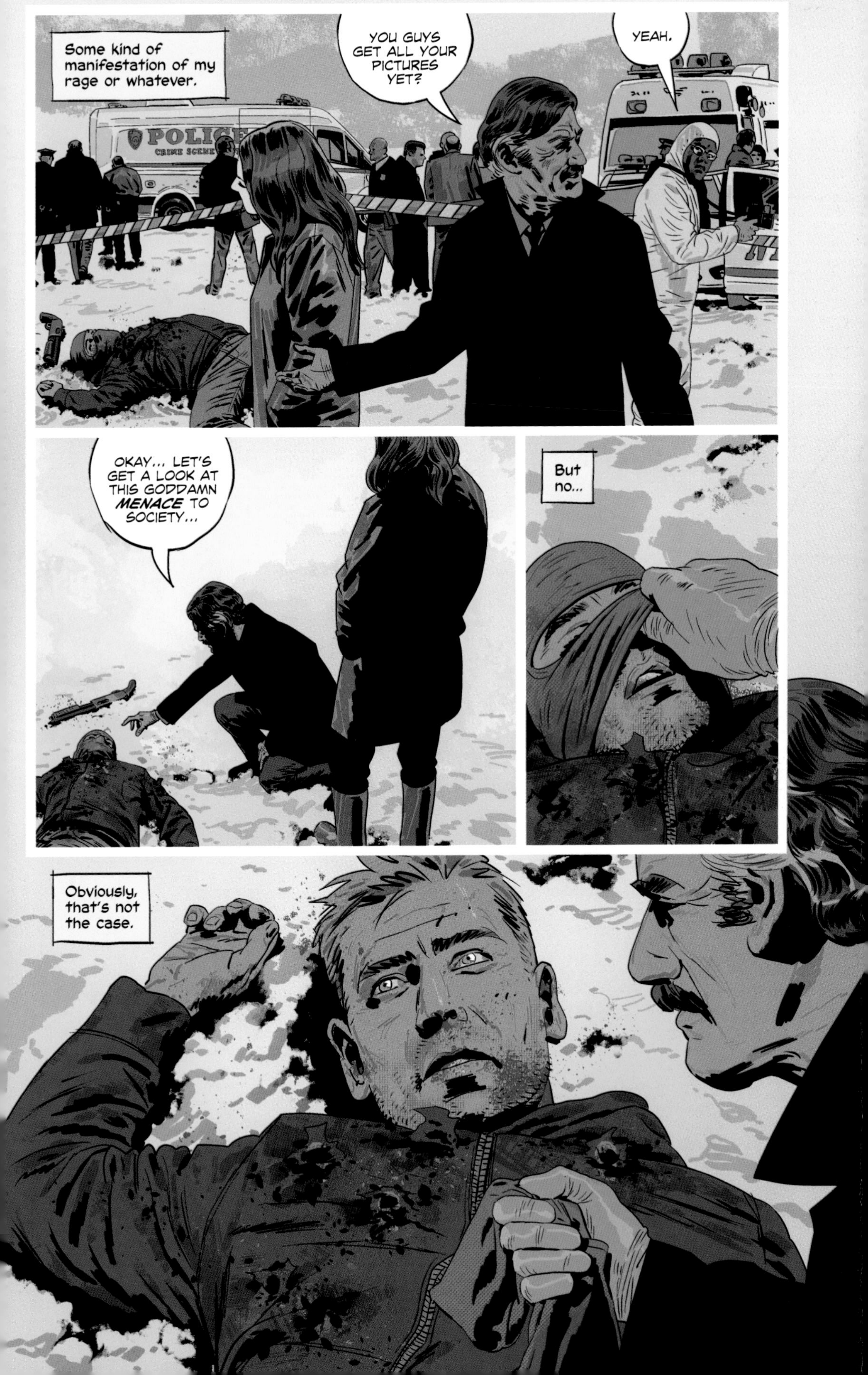
Some kind of manifestation of my rage or whatever.
YOU GUYS GET ALL YOUR PICTURES YET?
YEAH.
POLICE
CRIME SCENE
OKAY... LET'S GET A LOOK AT THIS GODDAMN MENACE TO SOCIETY...
But no...
Obviously, that's not the case.

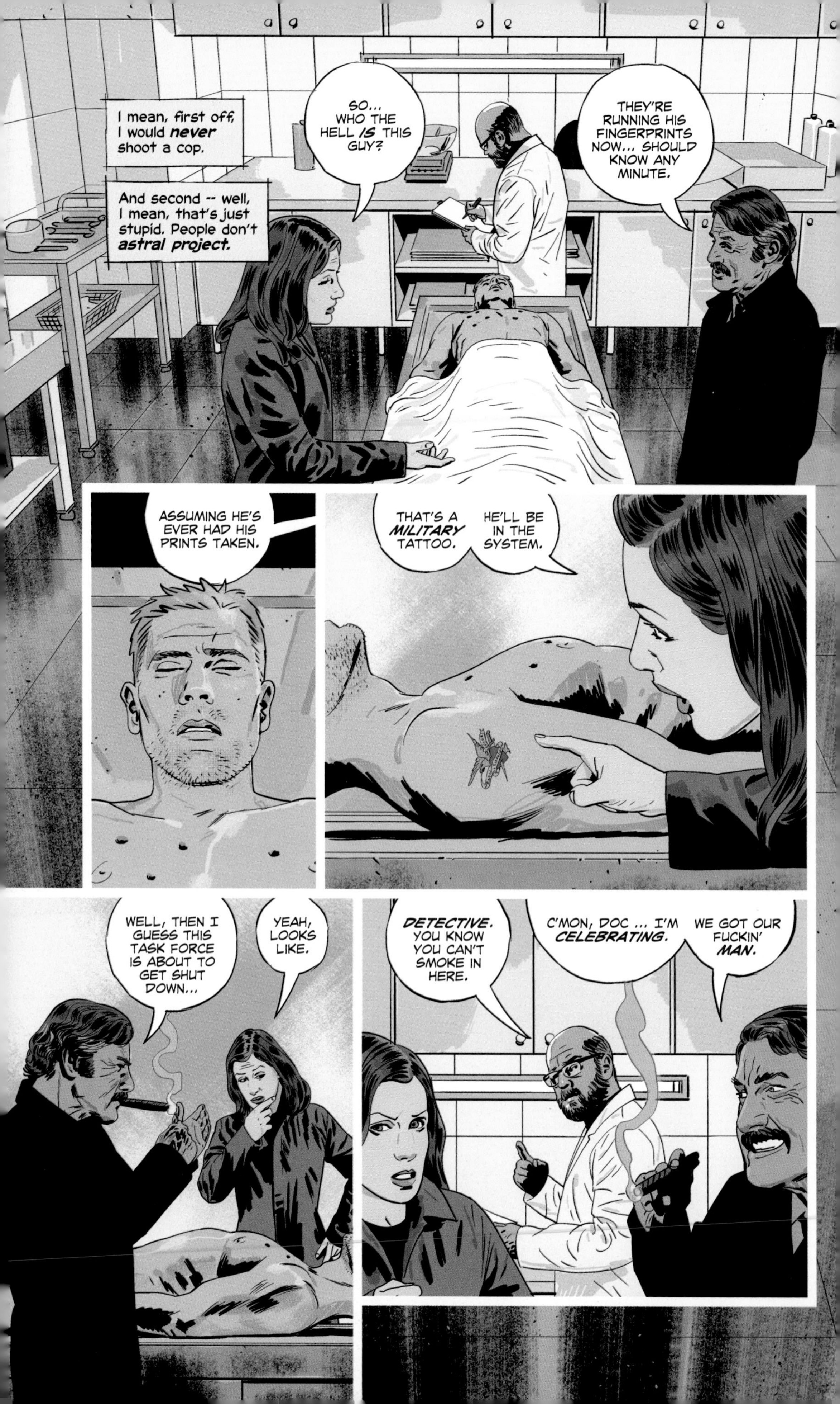
I mean, first off, I would never shoot a cop.
And second -- well, I mean, that's just stupid. People don't astral project.
SO... WHO THE HELL IS THIS GUY?
THEY'RE RUNNING HIS FINGERPRINTS NOW... SHOULD KNOW ANY MINUTE.
ASSUMING HE'S EVER HAD HIS PRINTS TAKEN.
THAT'S A MILITARY TATTOO.
HE'LL BE IN THE SYSTEM.
WELL, THEN I GUESS THIS TASK FORCE IS ABOUT TO GET SHUT DOWN...
YEAH, LOOKS LIKE.
DETECTIVE. YOU KNOW YOU CAN'T SMOKE IN HERE.
C'MON, DOC ... I'M CELEBRATING.
WE GOT OUR FUCKIN' MAN.

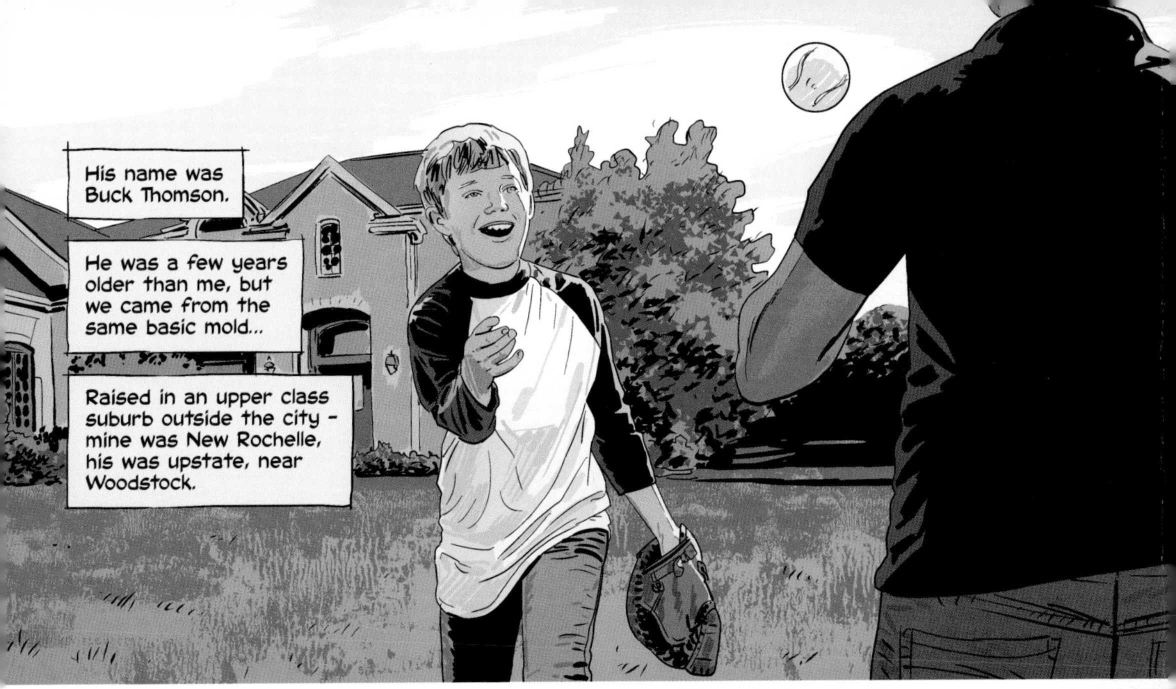
His name was Buck Thomson.
He was a few years older than me, but we came from the same basic mold...
Raised in an upper class suburb outside the city - mine was New Rochelle, his was upstate, near Woodstock.

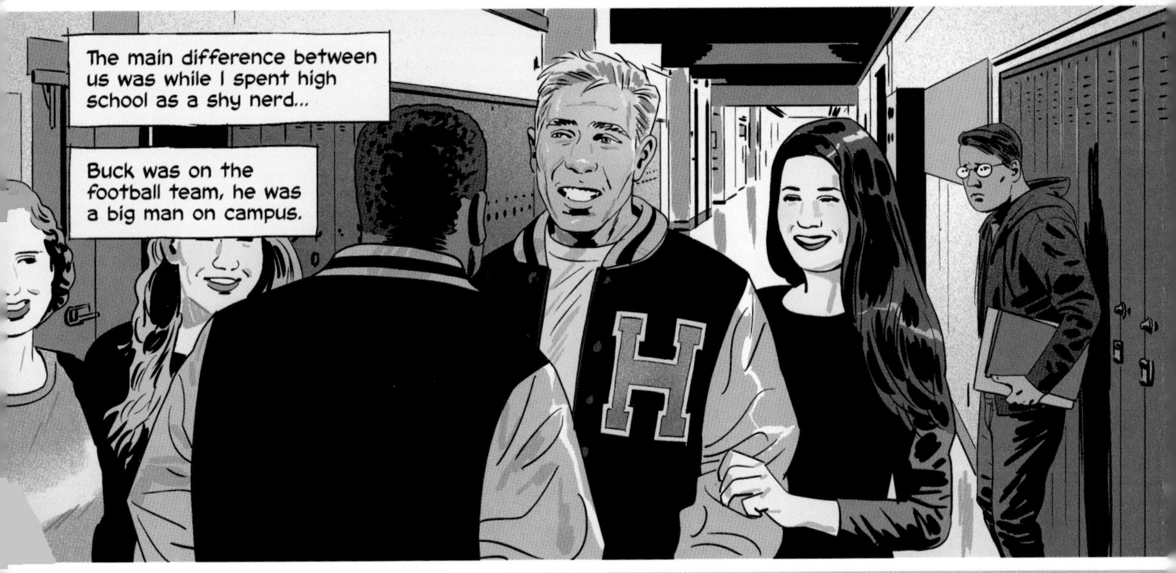
The main difference between us was while I spent high school as a shy nerd...
Buck was on the football team, he was a big man on campus.
H

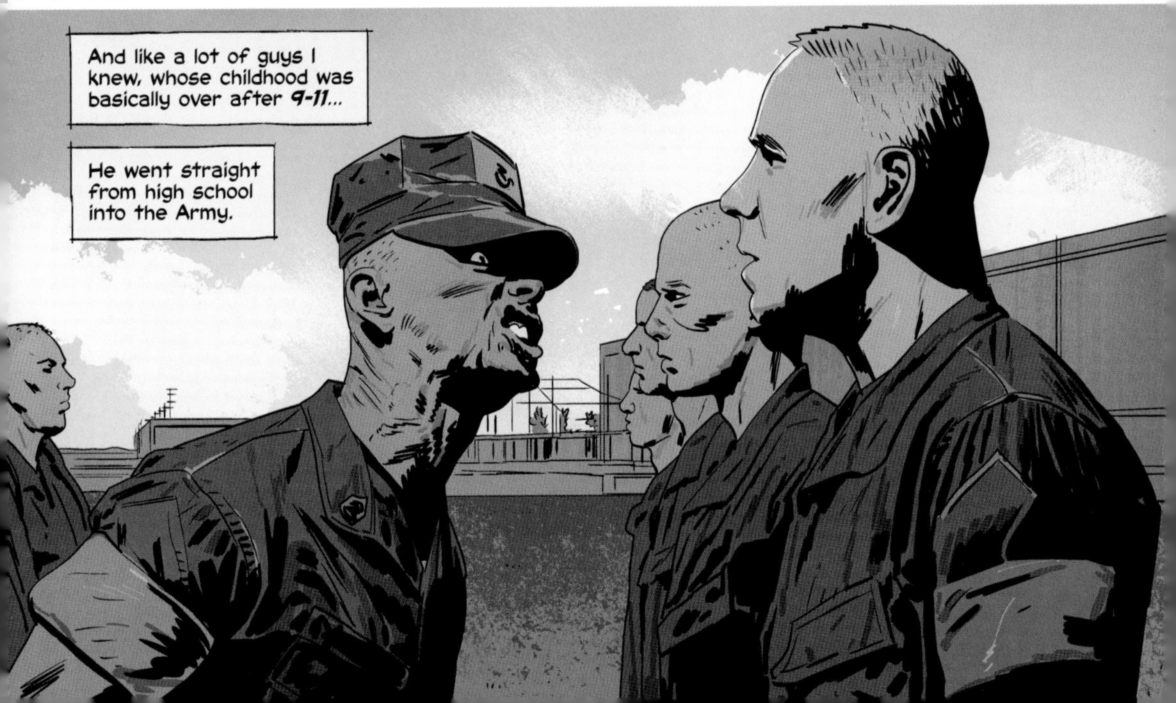
And like a lot of guys I knew, whose childhood was basically over after 9-11...
He went straight from high school into the Army.

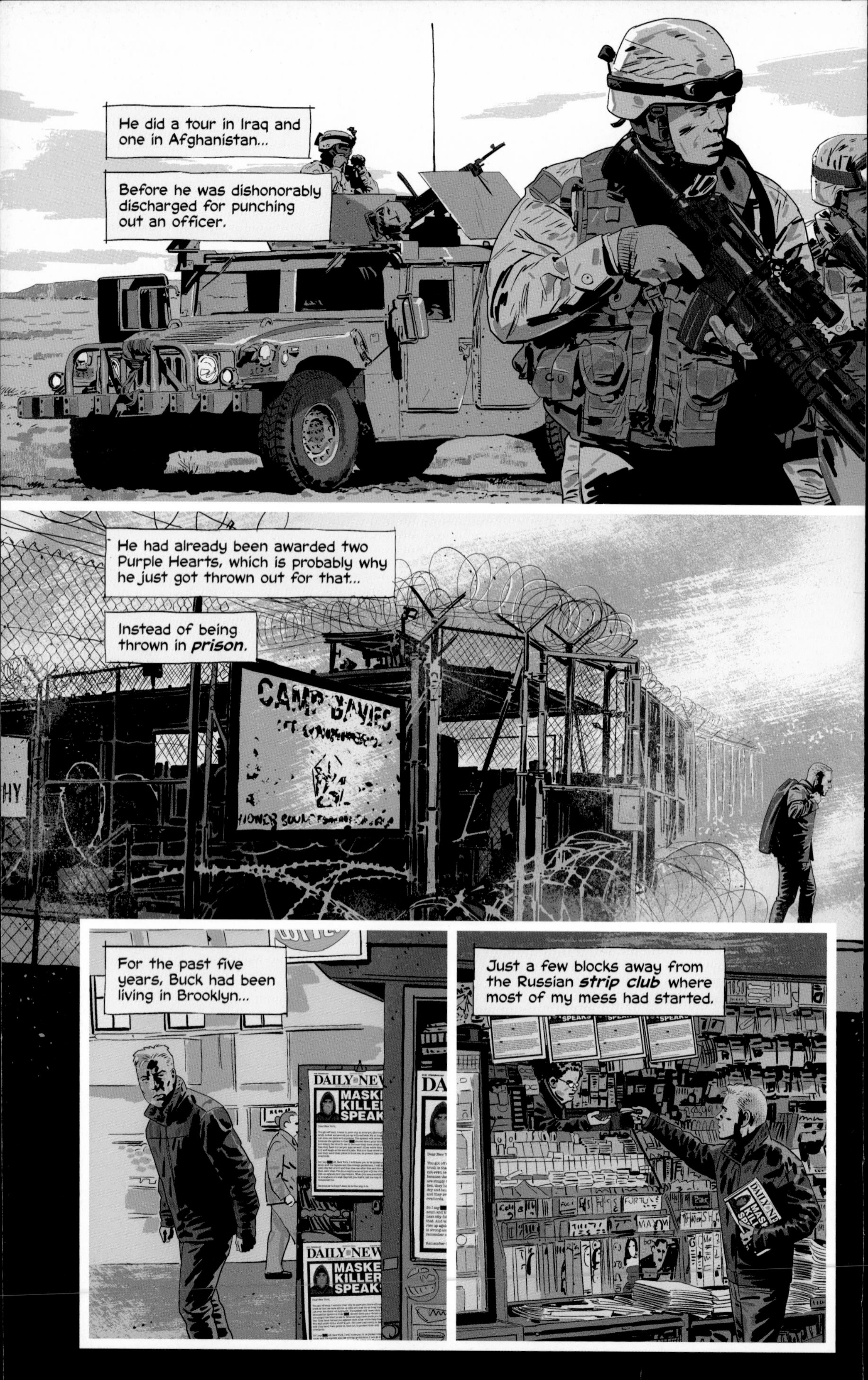
He did a tour in Iraq and one in Afghanistan...
Before he was dishonorably discharged for punching out an officer.
He had already been awarded two Purple Hearts, which is probably why he just got thrown out for that...
Instead of being thrown in *prison*.
CAMP BAYIES
For the past five years, Buck had been living in Brooklyn...
DAILY NEW
MASKE KILLER SPEAK
Just a few blocks away from the Russian *strip club* where most of my mess had started.
SPEAKS

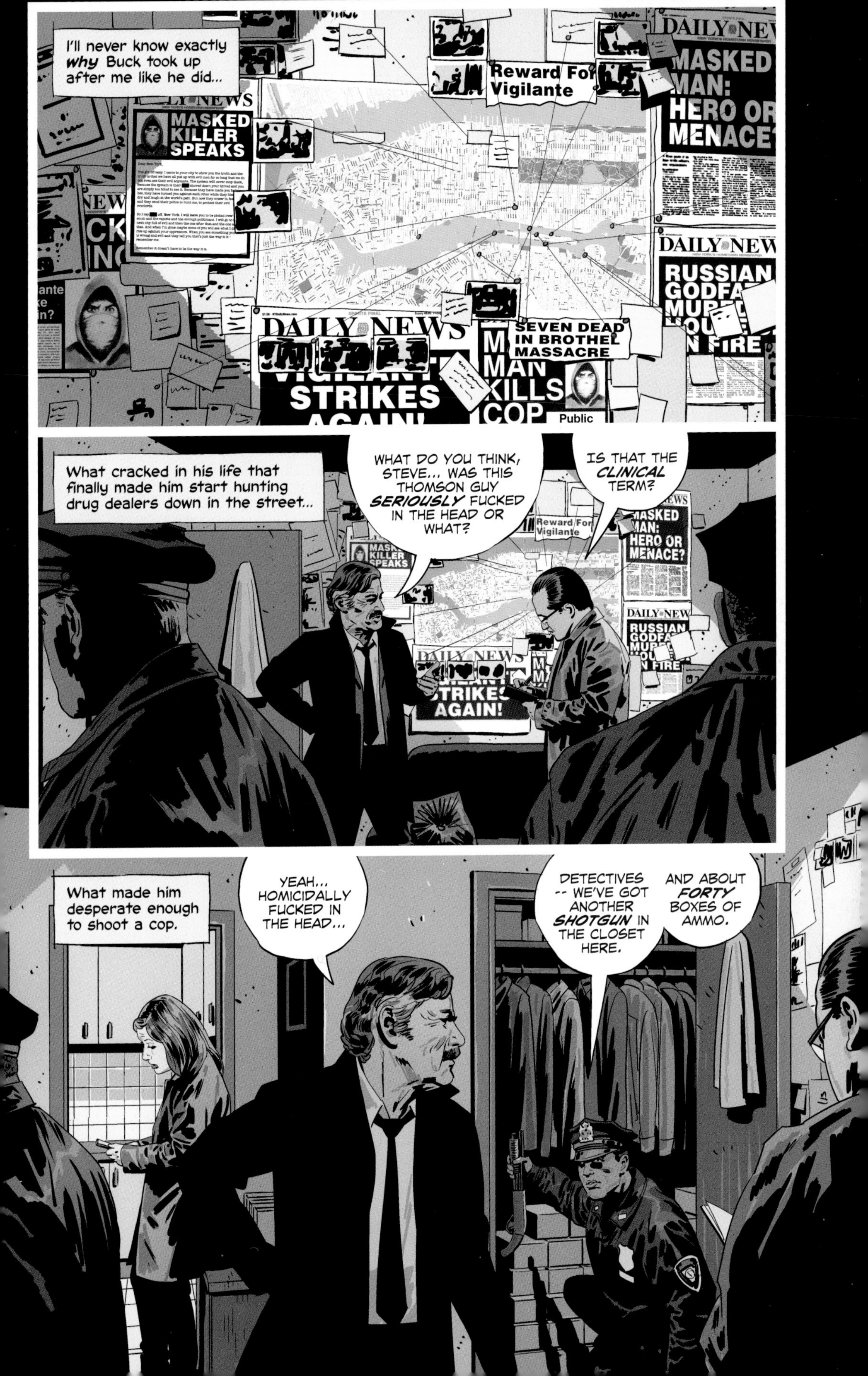
I'll never know exactly *why* Buck took up after me like he did...
DAILY NEWS
MASKED MAN: HERO OR MENACE?
Reward For Vigilante
MASKED KILLER SPEAKS
RUSSIAN GODFA MURD HOU N FIRE
SEVEN DEAD IN BROTHEL MASSACRE
DAILY NEWS
STRIKES AGAIN!
M MAN KILLS COP
Public
What cracked in his life that finally made him start hunting drug dealers down in the street...
WHAT DO YOU THINK, STEVE... WAS THIS THOMSON GUY *SERIOUSLY* FUCKED IN THE HEAD OR WHAT?
IS THAT THE *CLINICAL* TERM?
What made him desperate enough to shoot a cop.
YEAH... HOMICIDALLY FUCKED IN THE HEAD...
DETECTIVES -- WE'VE GOT ANOTHER *SHOTGUN* IN THE CLOSET HERE.
AND ABOUT *FORTY* BOXES OF AMMO.

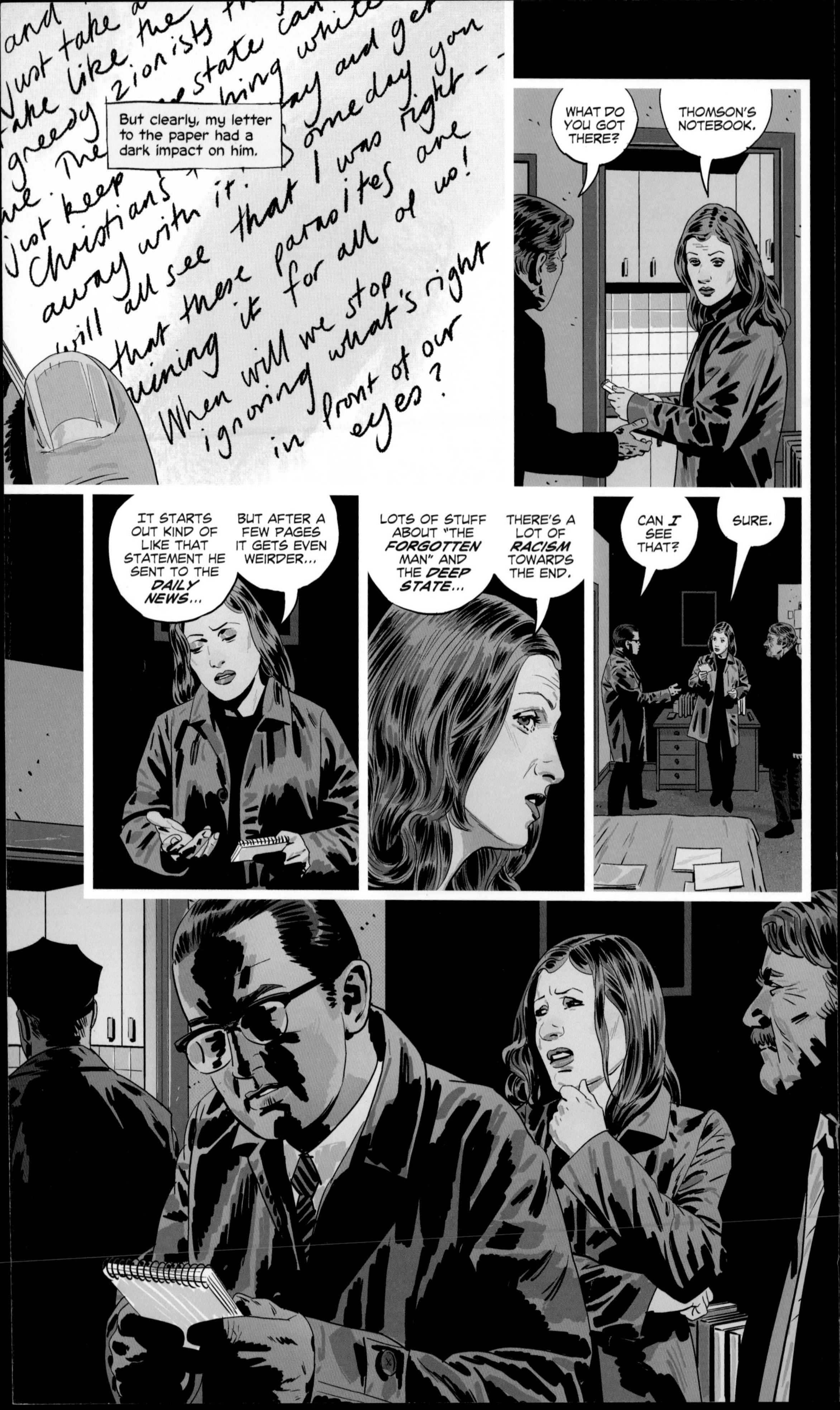

But clearly, my letter to the paper had a dark impact on him.
WHAT DO YOU GOT THERE?
THOMSON'S NOTEBOOK.
IT STARTS OUT KIND OF LIKE THAT STATEMENT HE SENT TO THE DAILY NEWS...
BUT AFTER A FEW PAGES IT GETS EVEN WEIRDER...
LOTS OF STUFF ABOUT "THE FORGOTTEN MAN" AND THE DEEP STATE...
THERE'S A LOT OF RACISM TOWARDS THE END.
CAN I SEE THAT?
SURE.

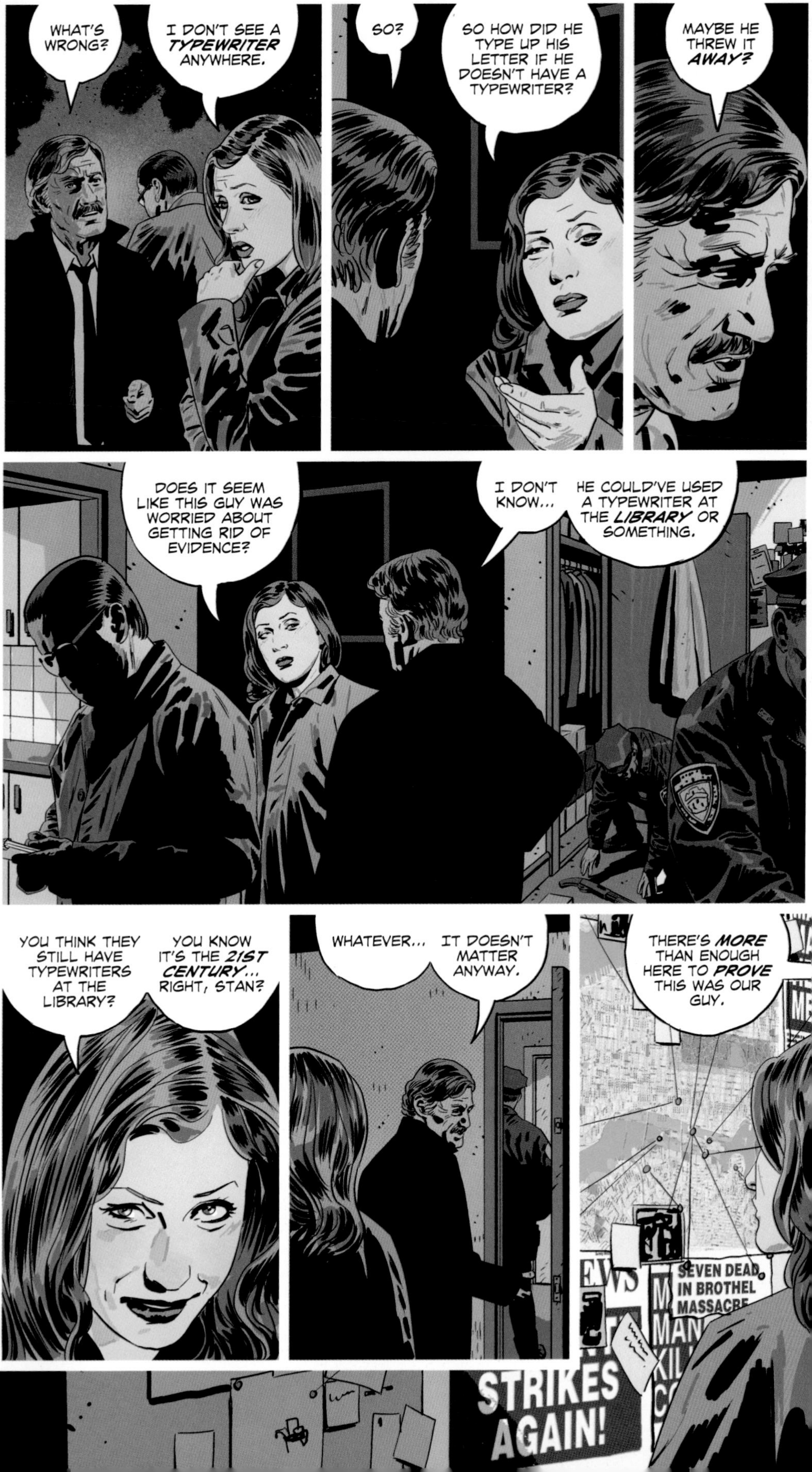
WHAT'S WRONG?
I DON'T SEE A TYPEWRITER ANYWHERE.
SO?
SO HOW DID HE TYPE UP HIS LETTER IF HE DOESN'T HAVE A TYPEWRITER?
MAYBE HE THREW IT AWAY?
DOES IT SEEM LIKE THIS GUY WAS WORRIED ABOUT GETTING RID OF EVIDENCE?
I DON'T KNOW...
HE COULD'VE USED A TYPEWRITER AT THE LIBRARY OR SOMETHING.
YOU THINK THEY STILL HAVE TYPEWRITERS AT THE LIBRARY?
YOU KNOW IT'S THE 21ST CENTURY... RIGHT, STAN?
WHATEVER...
IT DOESN'T MATTER ANYWAY.
THERE'S MORE THAN ENOUGH HERE TO PROVE THIS WAS OUR GUY.
SEVEN DEAD IN BROTHEL MASSACRE
STRIKES AGAIN!

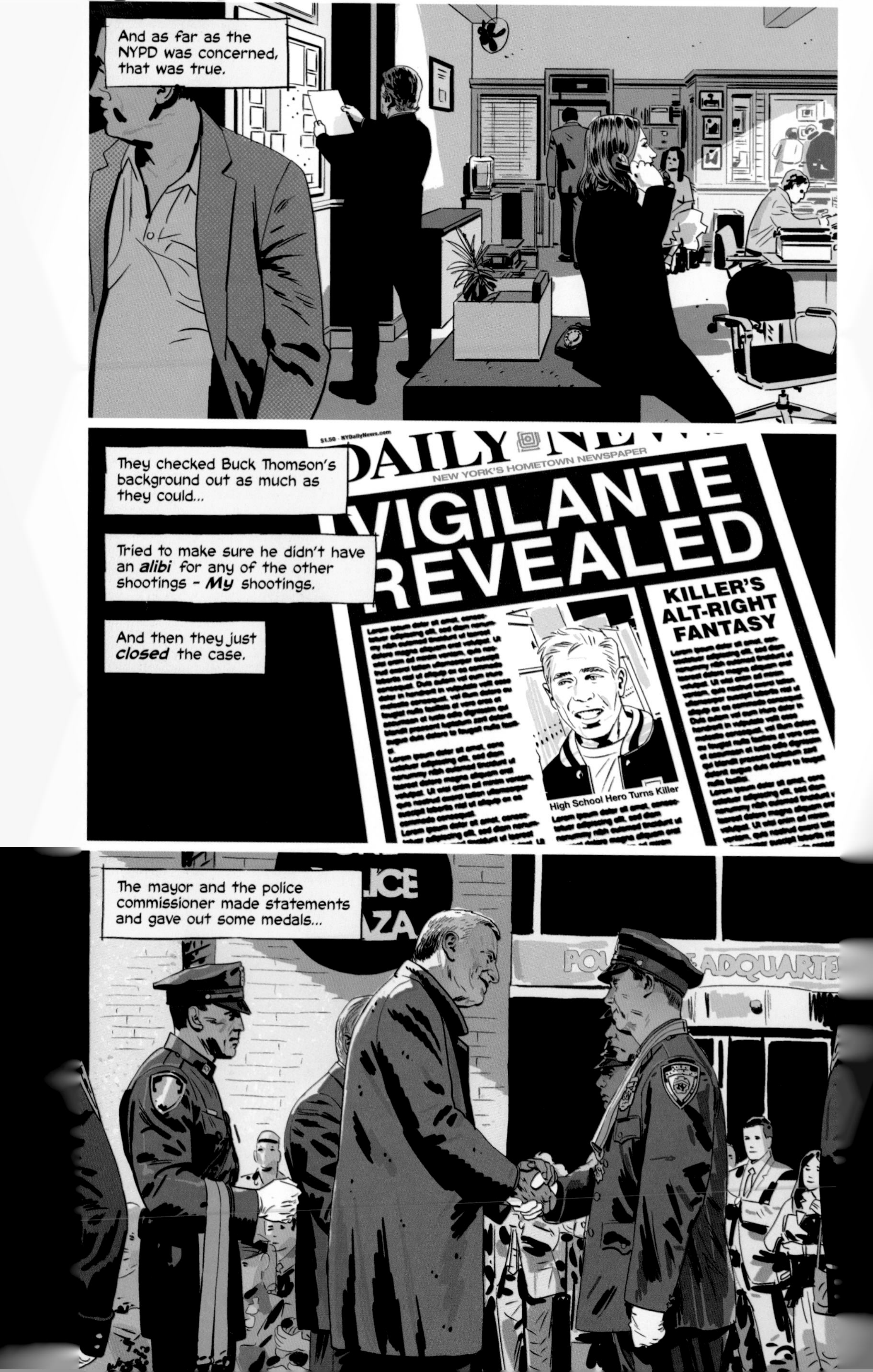
And as far as the NYPD was concerned, that was true.
They checked Buck Thomson's background out as much as they could...
Tried to make sure he didn't have an *alibi* for any of the other shootings – *My* shootings.
And then they just *closed* the case.
$1.50 · NYDailyNews.com
NEW YORK'S HOMETOWN NEWSPAPER
VIGILANTE REVEALED
KILLER'S ALT-RIGHT FANTASY
High School Hero Turns Killer
The mayor and the police commissioner made statements and gave out some medals...

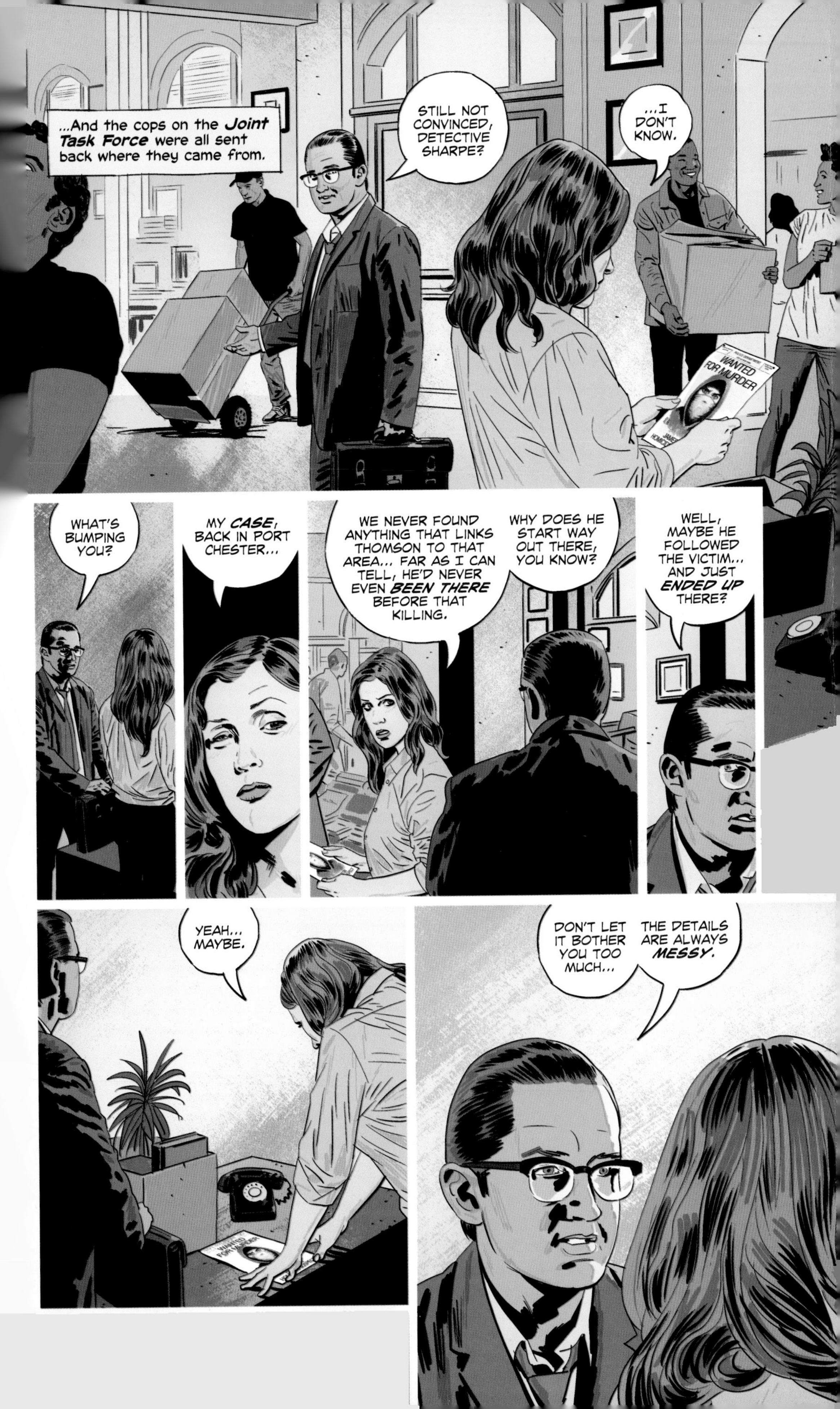

...And the cops on the *Joint Task Force* were all sent back where they came from.
STILL NOT CONVINCED, DETECTIVE SHARPE?
...I DON'T KNOW.
WANTED FOR MURDER
WHAT'S BUMPING YOU?
MY *CASE*, BACK IN PORT CHESTER...
WE NEVER FOUND ANYTHING THAT LINKS THOMSON TO THAT AREA... FAR AS I CAN TELL, HE'D NEVER EVEN *BEEN THERE* BEFORE THAT KILLING.
WHY DOES HE START WAY OUT THERE, YOU KNOW?
WELL, MAYBE HE FOLLOWED THE VICTIM... AND JUST *ENDED UP* THERE?
YEAH... MAYBE.
DON'T LET IT BOTHER YOU TOO MUCH...
THE DETAILS ARE ALWAYS *MESSY*.

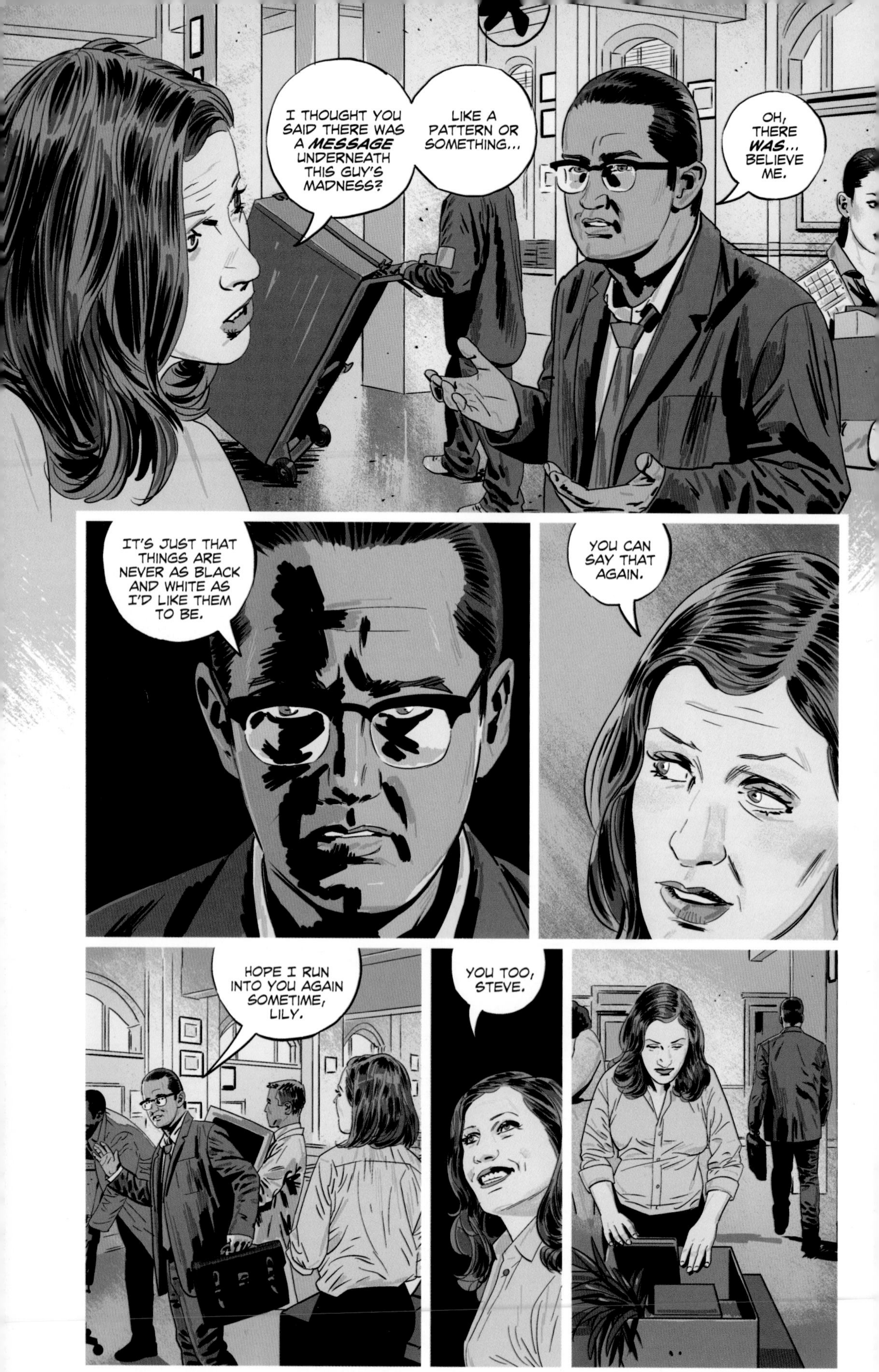
I THOUGHT YOU SAID THERE WAS A ***MESSAGE*** UNDERNEATH THIS GUY'S MADNESS?
LIKE A PATTERN OR SOMETHING...
OH, THERE ***WAS***... BELIEVE ME.
IT'S JUST THAT THINGS ARE NEVER AS BLACK AND WHITE AS I'D LIKE THEM TO BE.
YOU CAN SAY THAT AGAIN.
HOPE I RUN INTO YOU AGAIN SOMETIME, LILY.
YOU TOO, STEVE.

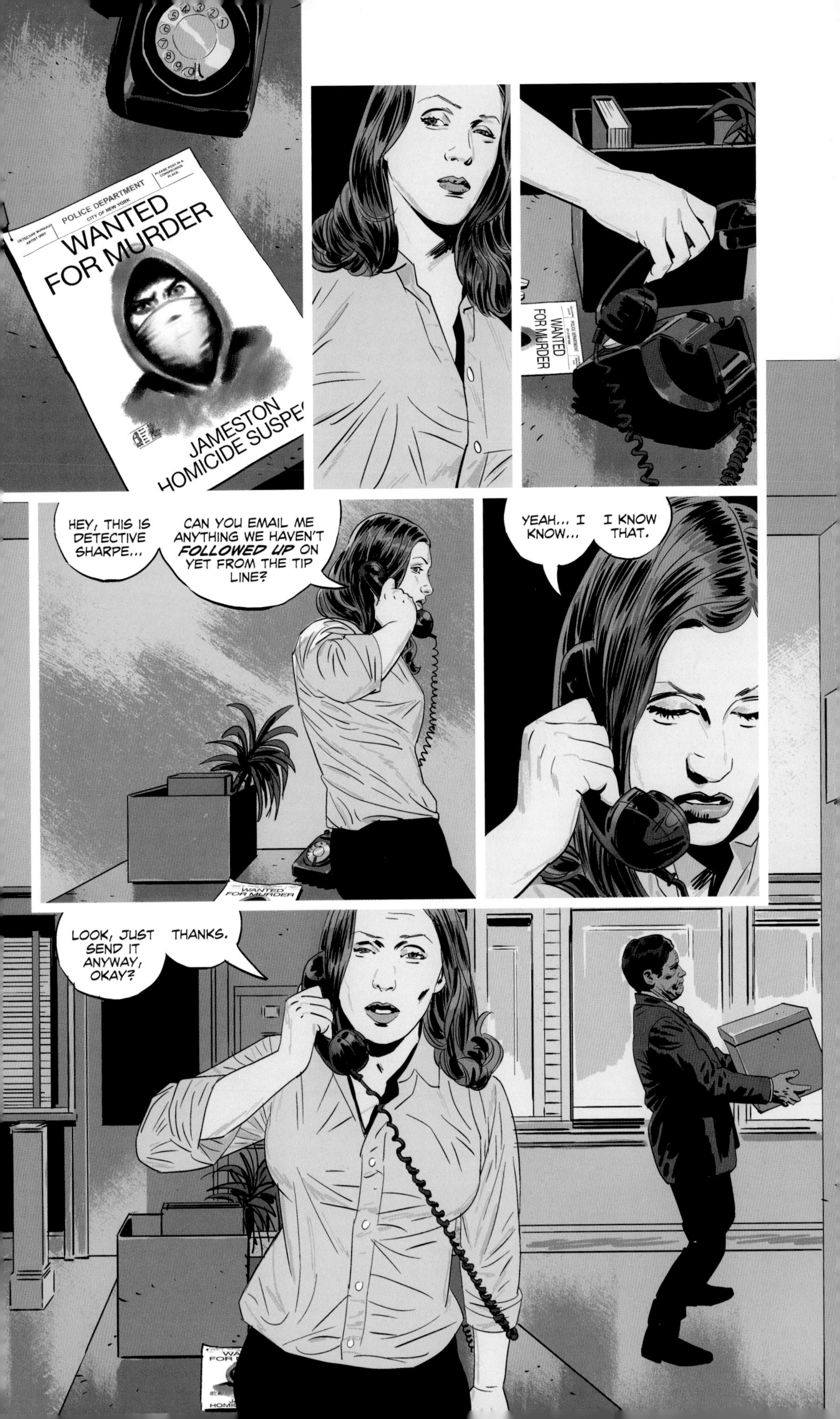
POLICE DEPARTMENT
CITY OF NEW YORK
WANTED FOR MURDER
JAMESTON
HEY, THIS IS DETECTIVE SHARPE...
CAN YOU EMAIL ME ANYTHING WE HAVEN'T *FOLLOWED UP* ON YET FROM THE TIP LINE?
YEAH... I KNOW...
I KNOW THAT.
LOOK, JUST SEND IT ANYWAY, OKAY?
THANKS.

So you can see where this is going, right?

Even after they send her back to her detective squad in ***Port Chester***... Lily doesn't give up.

It's a closed case, but she just can't let it go.

Buck Thomson doesn't feel like the killer that she was looking for all these months.

She's not even sure ***why*** she thinks that... but she does.

So she spends the next week checking into tips people had called in.

People hoping for rewards.

It's tedious work, like most of what the police do.

Phone calls to strangers, trying to discern if they're crazy... or if they're trying to scam ***money*** from the government...

Or if they're serious...

People actually trying to do the ***right thing***.

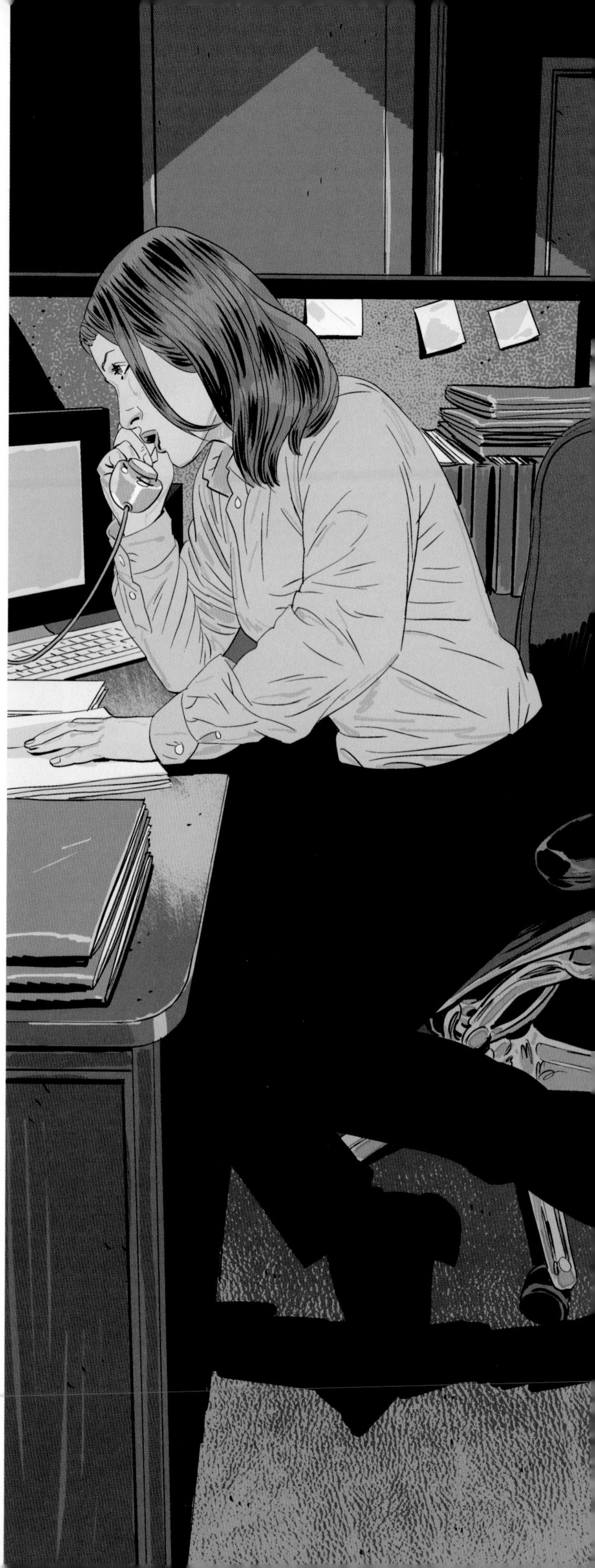

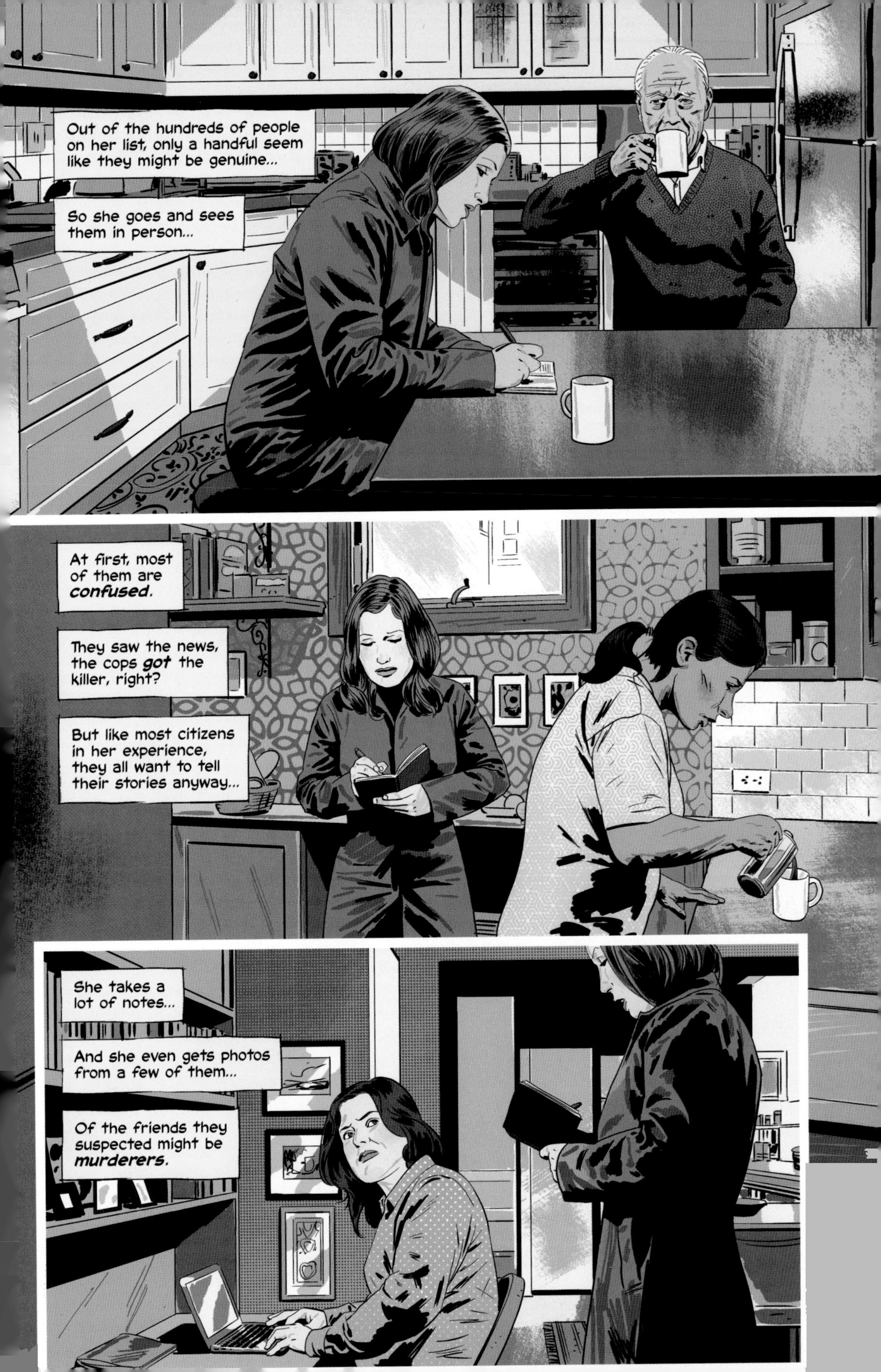

Out of the hundreds of people on her list, only a handful seem like they might be genuine...
So she goes and sees them in person...
At first, most of them are ***confused***.
They saw the news, the cops ***got*** the killer, right?
But like most citizens in her experience, they all want to tell their stories anyway...
She takes a lot of notes...
And she even gets photos from a few of them...
Of the friends they suspected might be ***murderers***.

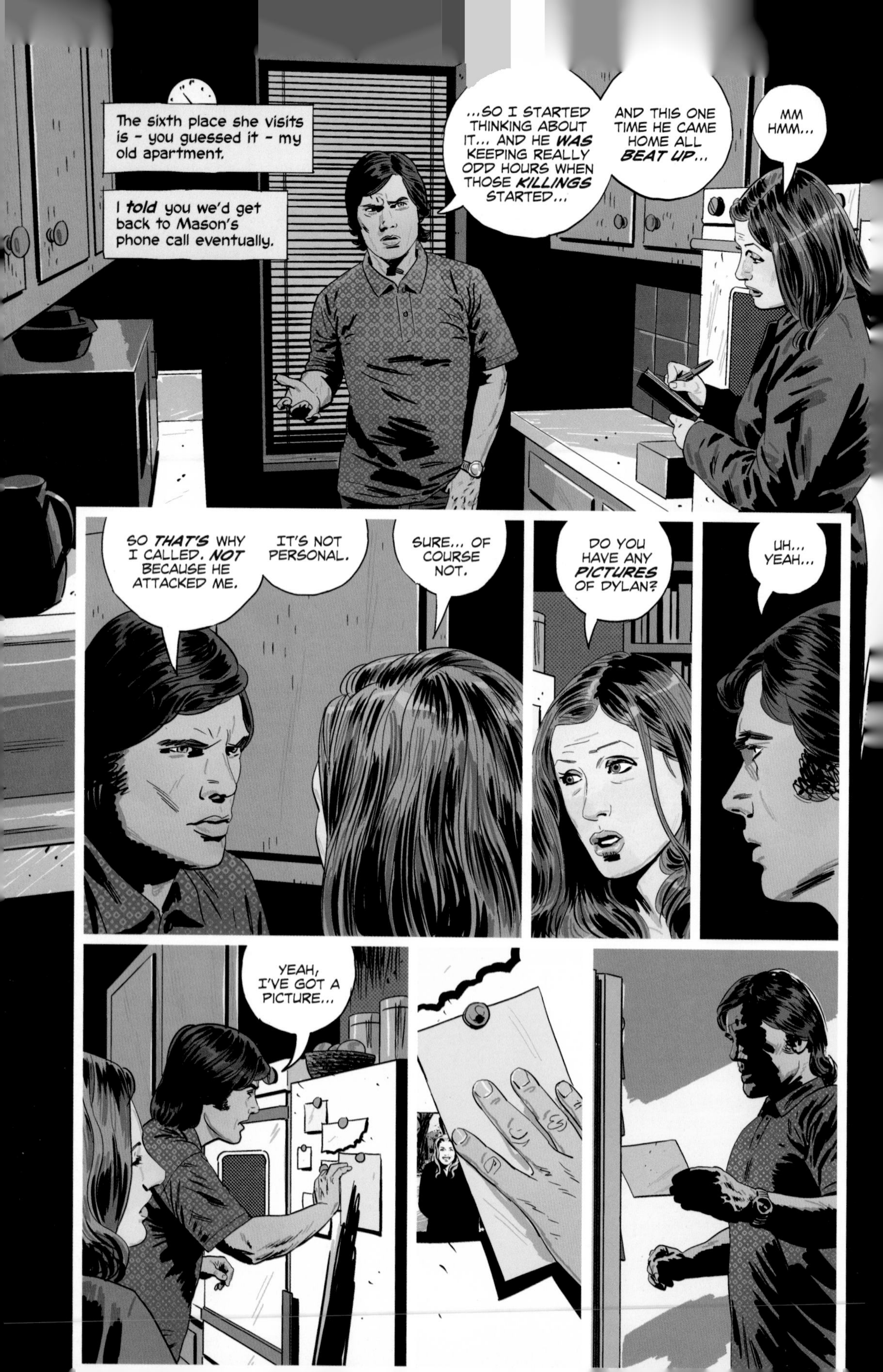
The sixth place she visits is - you guessed it - my old apartment.
I *told* you we'd get back to Mason's phone call eventually.
...SO I STARTED THINKING ABOUT IT... AND HE *WAS* KEEPING REALLY ODD HOURS WHEN THOSE *KILLINGS* STARTED...
AND THIS ONE TIME HE CAME HOME ALL *BEAT UP*...
MM HMM...
SO *THAT'S* WHY I CALLED. *NOT* BECAUSE HE ATTACKED ME.
IT'S NOT PERSONAL.
SURE... OF COURSE NOT.
DO YOU HAVE ANY *PICTURES* OF DYLAN?
UH... YEAH...
YEAH, I'VE GOT A PICTURE...

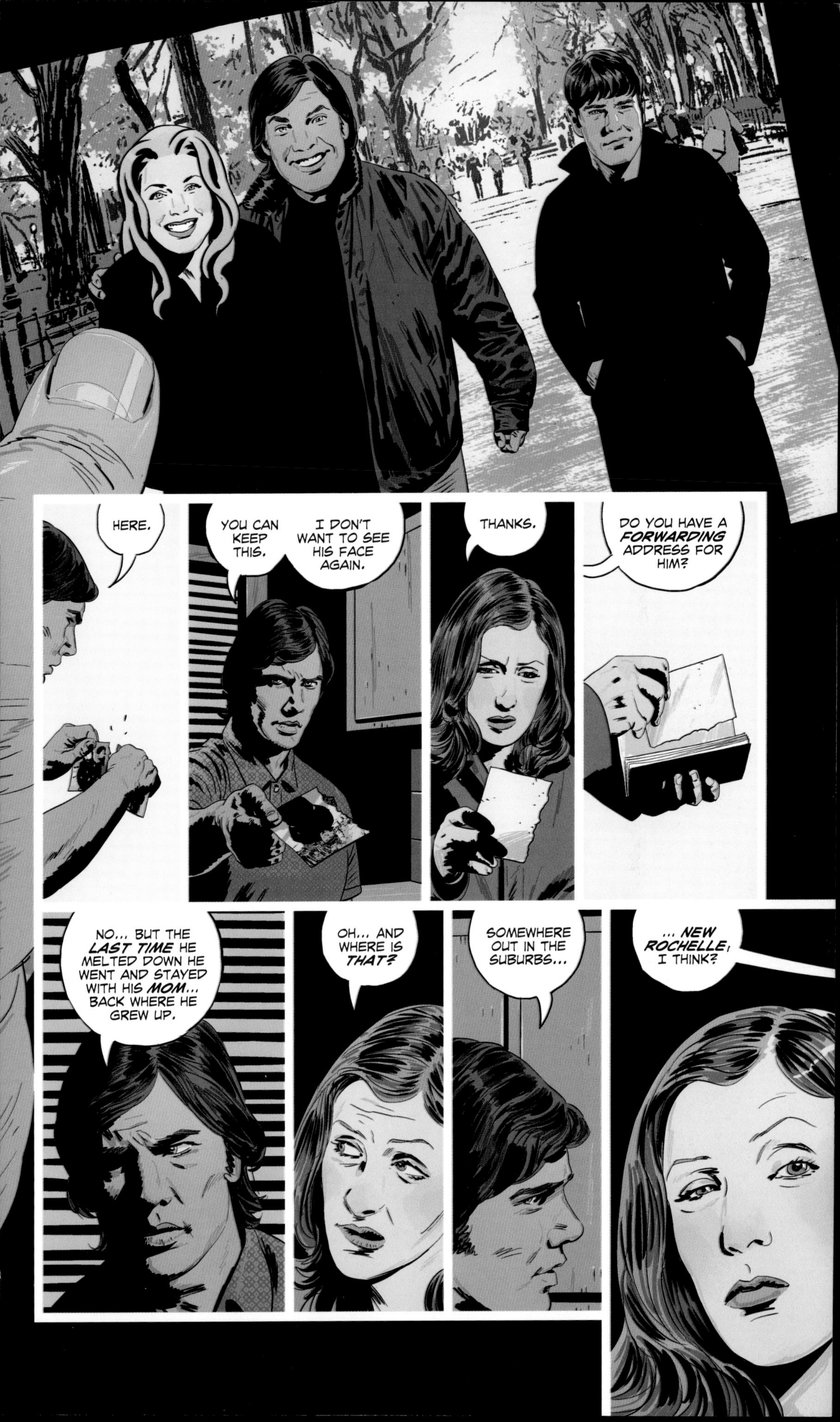
HERE.
YOU CAN KEEP THIS.
I DON'T WANT TO SEE HIS FACE AGAIN.
THANKS.
DO YOU HAVE A *FORWARDING* ADDRESS FOR HIM?
NO... BUT THE *LAST TIME* HE MELTED DOWN HE WENT AND STAYED WITH HIS *MOM*... BACK WHERE HE GREW UP.
OH... AND WHERE IS *THAT?*
SOMEWHERE OUT IN THE SUBURBS...
... *NEW ROCHELLE*, I THINK?

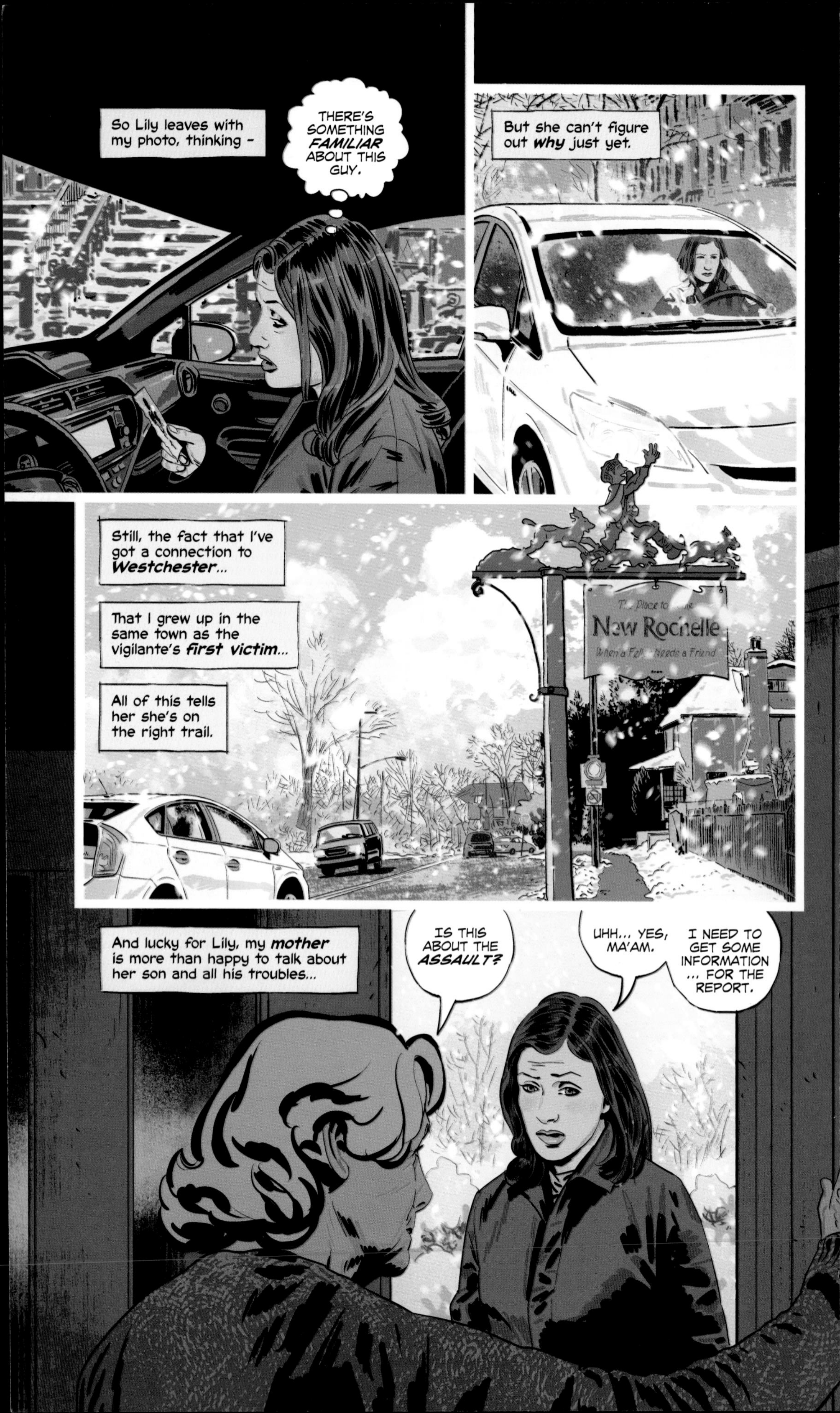
So Lily leaves with my photo, thinking -
THERE'S SOMETHING FAMILIAR ABOUT THIS GUY.
But she can't figure out why just yet.
Still, the fact that I've got a connection to Westchester...
That I grew up in the same town as the vigilante's first victim...
All of this tells her she's on the right trail.
New Rochelle
And lucky for Lily, my mother is more than happy to talk about her son and all his troubles...
IS THIS ABOUT THE ASSAULT?
UHH... YES, MA'AM.
I NEED TO GET SOME INFORMATION ... FOR THE REPORT.

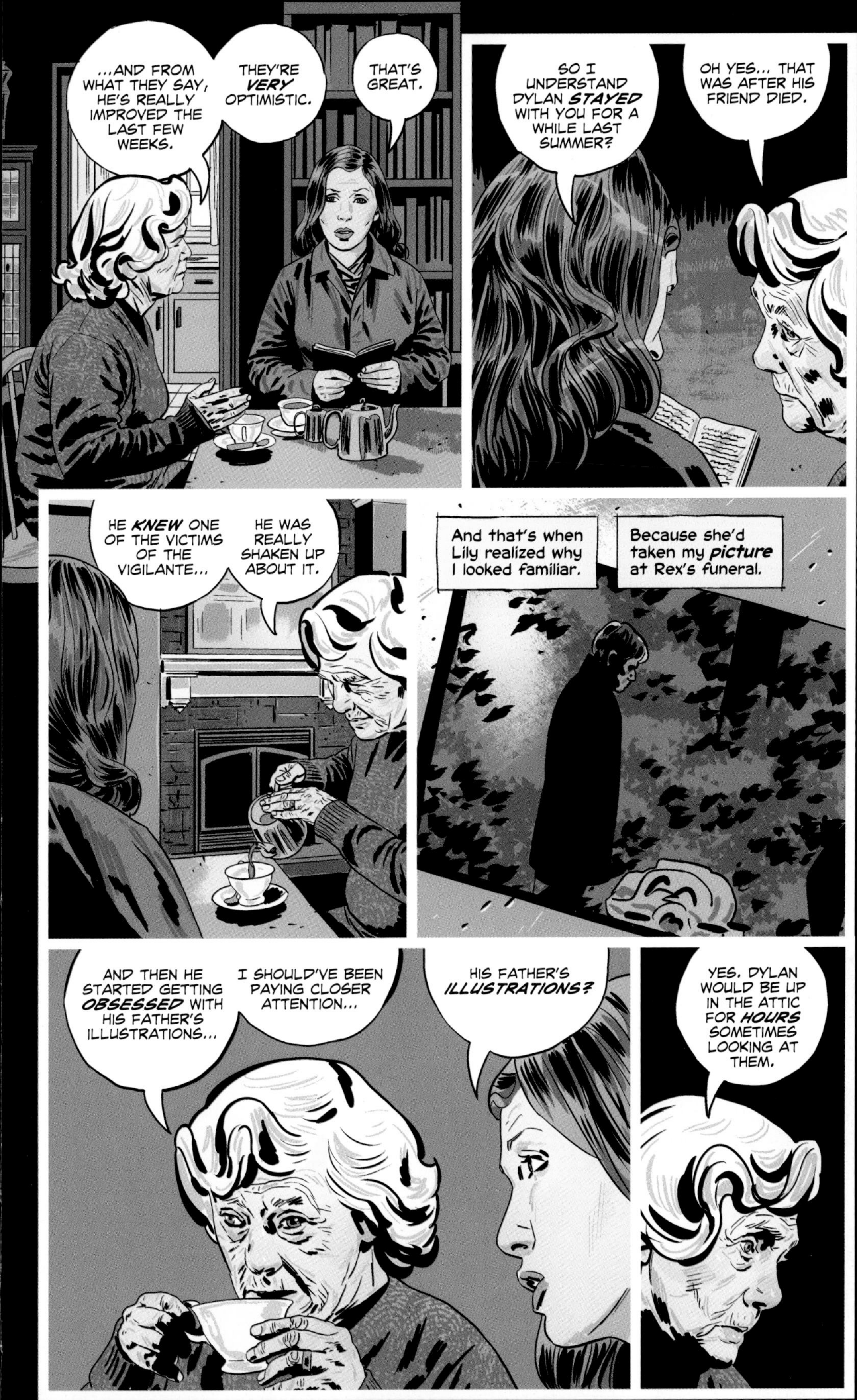
...AND FROM WHAT THEY SAY, HE'S REALLY IMPROVED THE LAST FEW WEEKS.
THEY'RE VERY OPTIMISTIC.
THAT'S GREAT.
SO I UNDERSTAND DYLAN STAYED WITH YOU FOR A WHILE LAST SUMMER?
OH YES... THAT WAS AFTER HIS FRIEND DIED.
HE KNEW ONE OF THE VICTIMS OF THE VIGILANTE...
HE WAS REALLY SHAKEN UP ABOUT IT.
And that's when Lily realized why I looked familiar.
Because she'd taken my picture at Rex's funeral.
AND THEN HE STARTED GETTING OBSESSED WITH HIS FATHER'S ILLUSTRATIONS...
I SHOULD'VE BEEN PAYING CLOSER ATTENTION...
HIS FATHER'S ILLUSTRATIONS?
YES. DYLAN WOULD BE UP IN THE ATTIC FOR HOURS SOMETIMES LOOKING AT THEM.

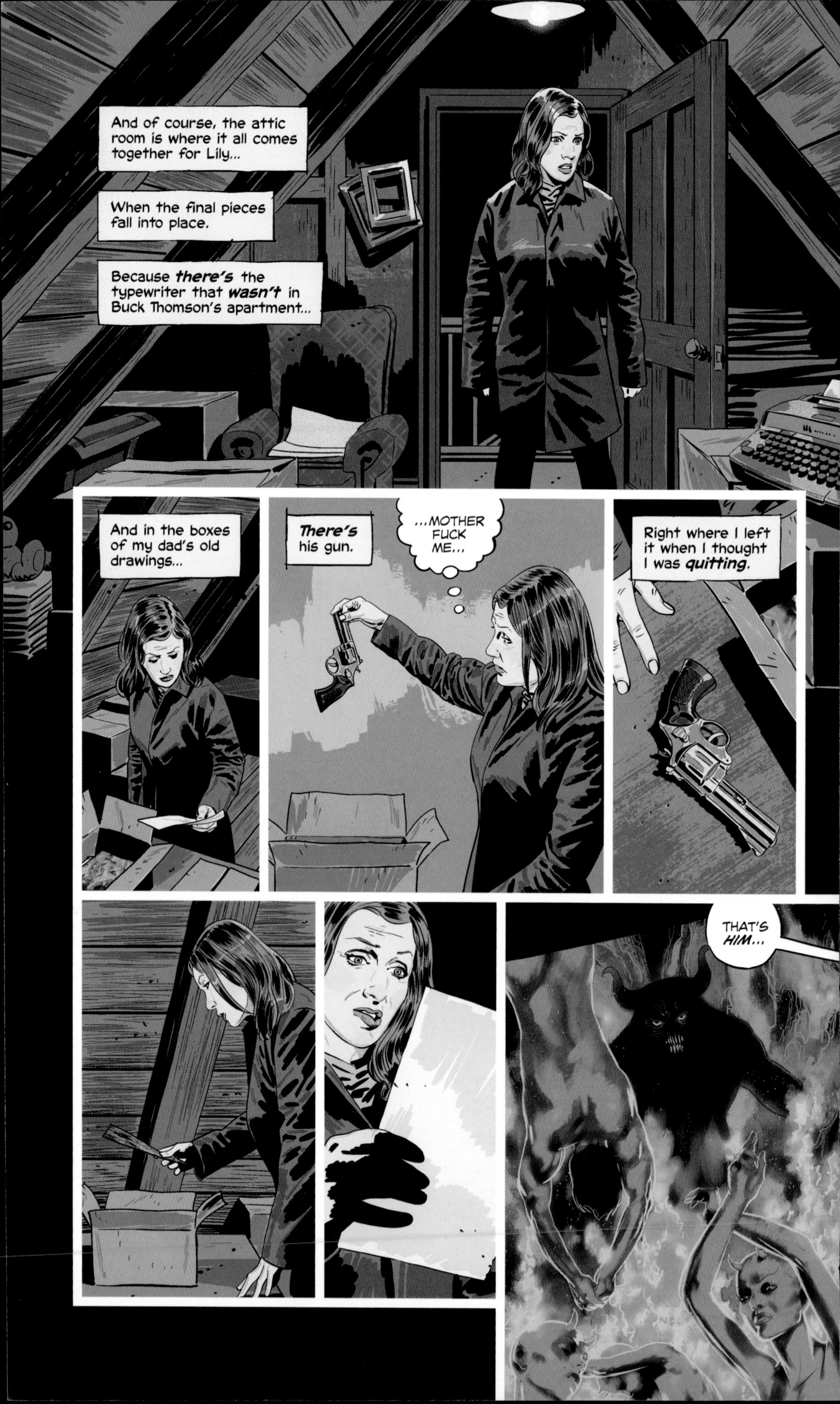

And of course, the attic room is where it all comes together for Lily...
When the final pieces fall into place.
Because ***there's*** the typewriter that ***wasn't*** in Buck Thomson's apartment...
And in the boxes of my dad's old drawings...
There's his gun.
...MOTHER FUCK ME...
Right where I left it when I thought I was ***quitting***.
THAT'S ***HIM***...

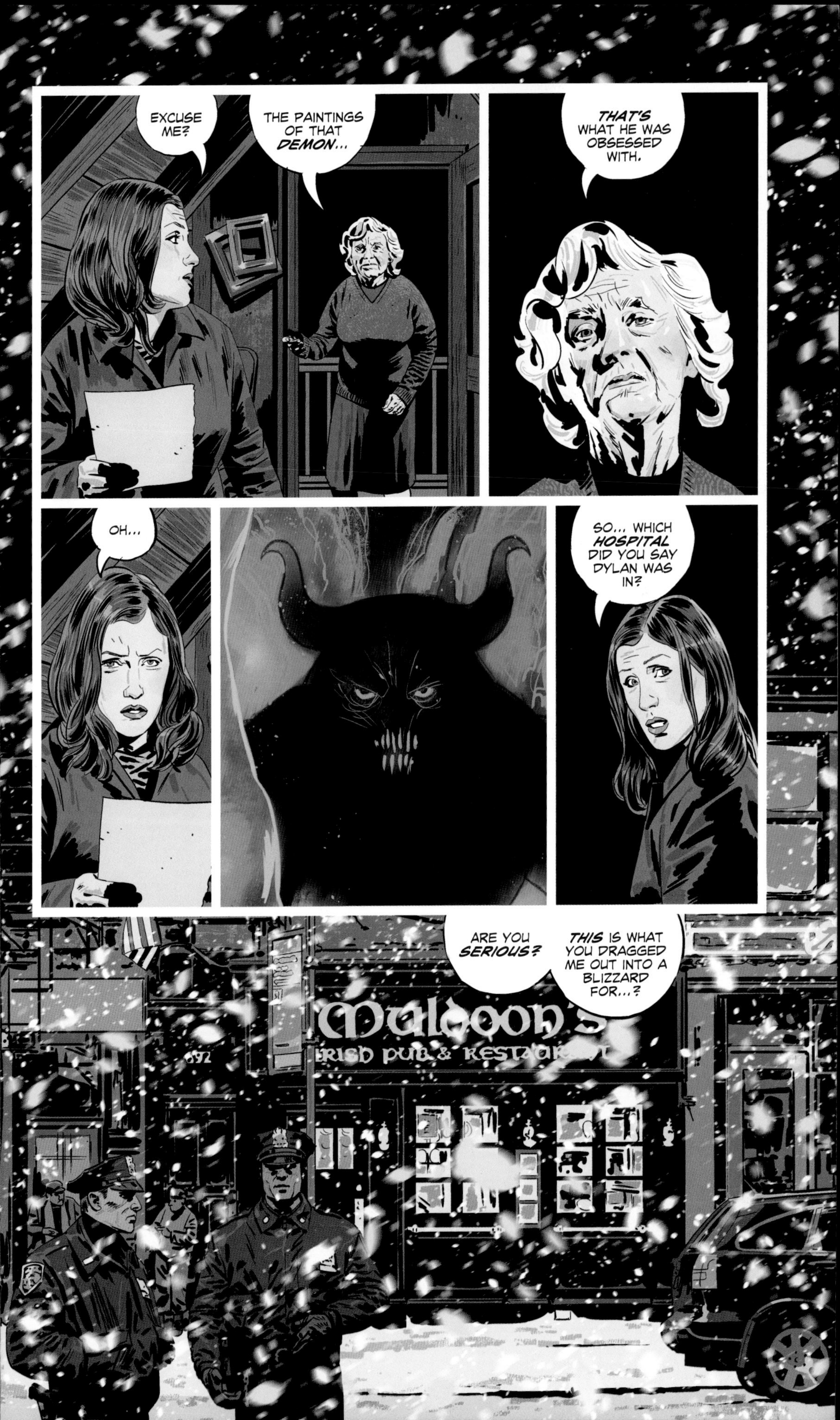
EXCUSE ME?
THE PAINTINGS OF THAT DEMON...
THAT'S WHAT HE WAS OBSESSED WITH.
OH...
SO... WHICH HOSPITAL DID YOU SAY DYLAN WAS IN?
ARE YOU SERIOUS?
THIS IS WHAT YOU DRAGGED ME OUT INTO A BLIZZARD FOR...?
MULDOON'S
IRISH PUB & RESTAURANT

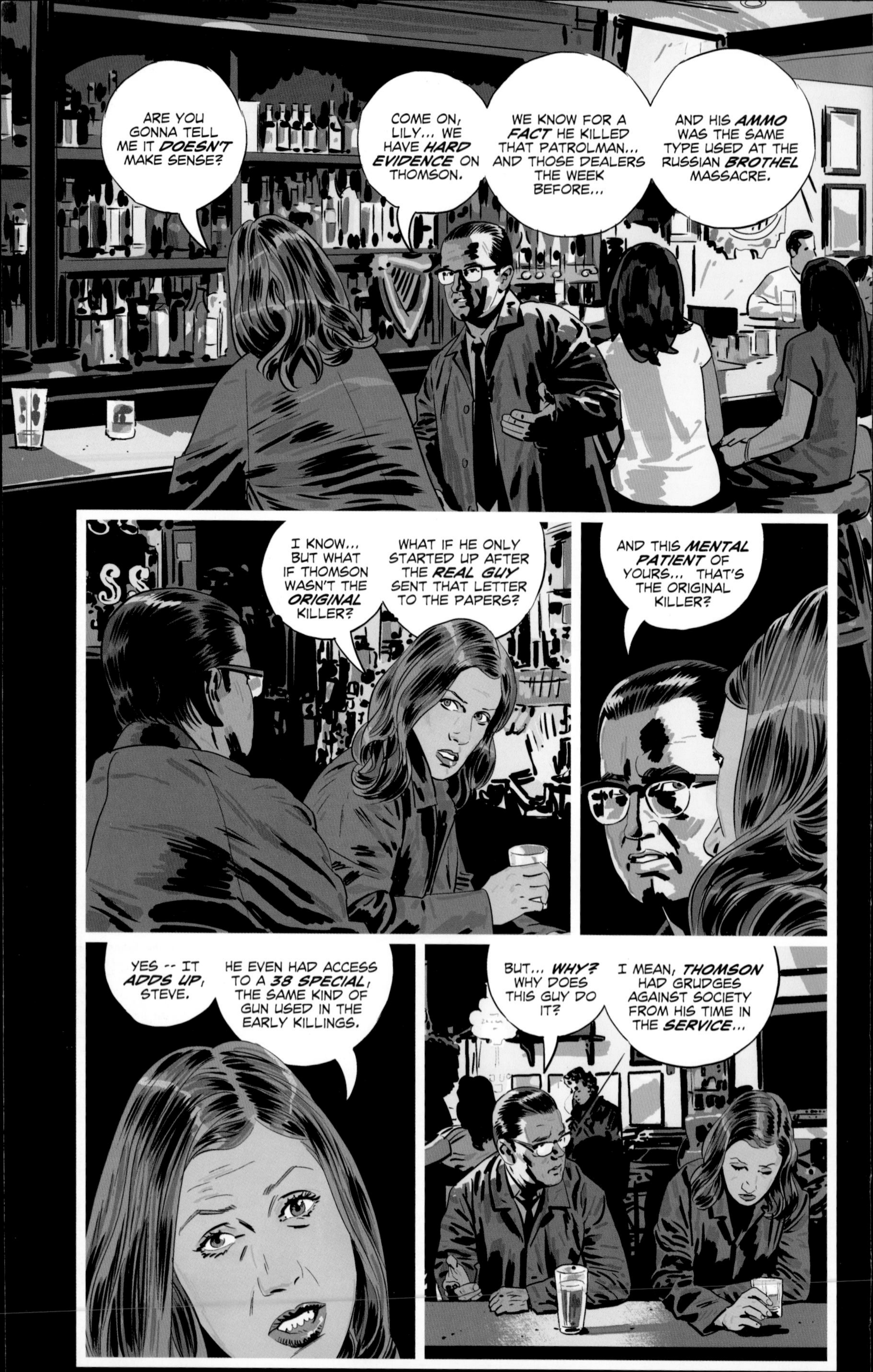
ARE YOU GONNA TELL ME IT DOESN'T MAKE SENSE?
COME ON, LILY... WE HAVE HARD EVIDENCE ON THOMSON.
WE KNOW FOR A FACT HE KILLED THAT PATROLMAN... AND THOSE DEALERS THE WEEK BEFORE...
AND HIS AMMO WAS THE SAME TYPE USED AT THE RUSSIAN BROTHEL MASSACRE.
I KNOW... BUT WHAT IF THOMSON WASN'T THE ORIGINAL KILLER?
WHAT IF HE ONLY STARTED UP AFTER THE REAL GUY SENT THAT LETTER TO THE PAPERS?
AND THIS MENTAL PATIENT OF YOURS... THAT'S THE ORIGINAL KILLER?
YES -- IT ADDS UP, STEVE.
HE EVEN HAD ACCESS TO A 38 SPECIAL, THE SAME KIND OF GUN USED IN THE EARLY KILLINGS.
BUT... WHY? WHY DOES THIS GUY DO IT?
I MEAN, THOMSON HAD GRUDGES AGAINST SOCIETY FROM HIS TIME IN THE SERVICE...

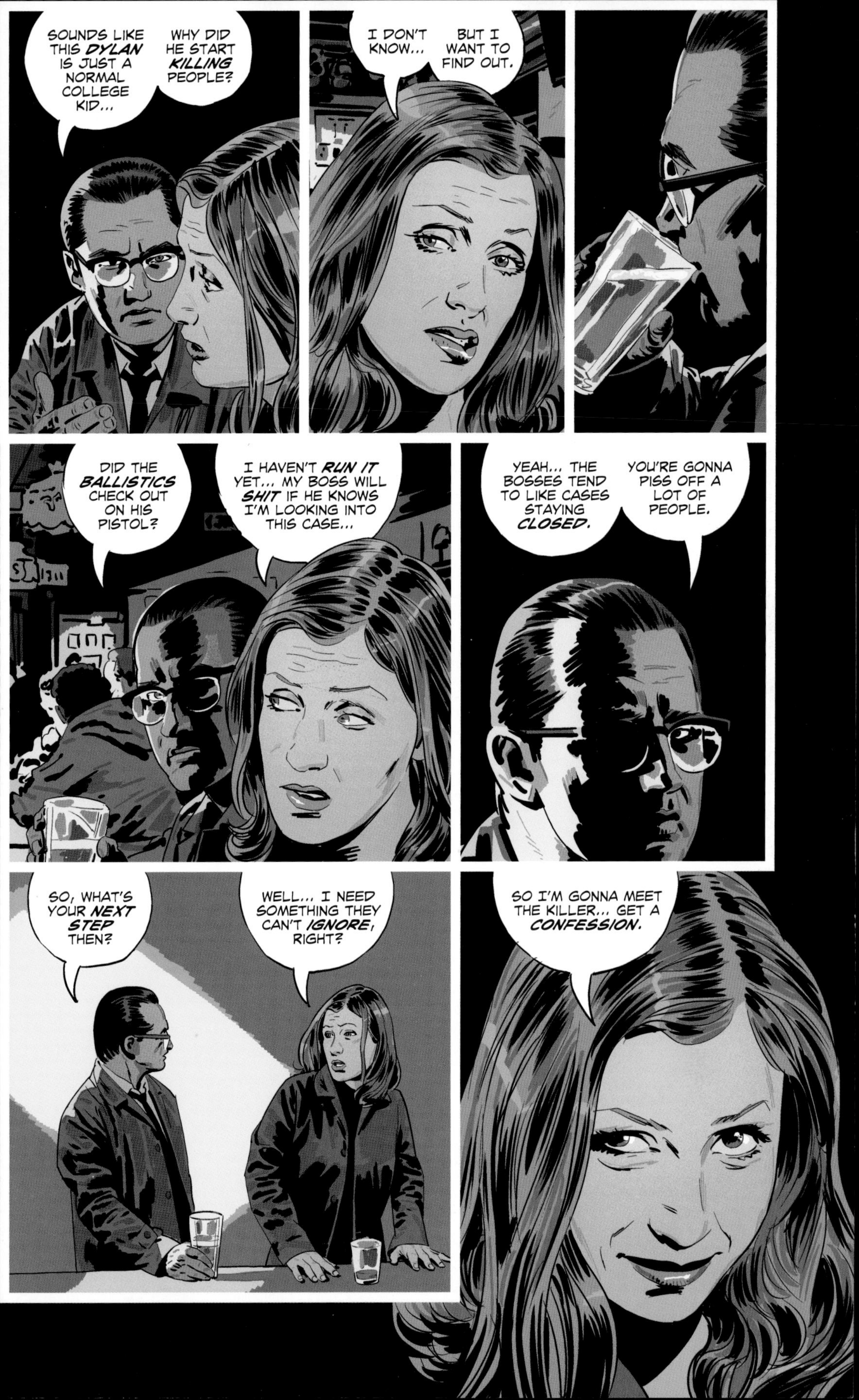
SOUNDS LIKE THIS *DYLAN* IS JUST A NORMAL COLLEGE KID...
WHY DID HE START *KILLING* PEOPLE?
I DON'T KNOW...
BUT I WANT TO FIND OUT.
DID THE *BALLISTICS* CHECK OUT ON HIS PISTOL?
I HAVEN'T *RUN IT* YET... MY BOSS WILL *SHIT* IF HE KNOWS I'M LOOKING INTO THIS CASE...
YEAH... THE BOSSES TEND TO LIKE CASES STAYING *CLOSED*.
YOU'RE GONNA PISS OFF A LOT OF PEOPLE.
SO, WHAT'S YOUR *NEXT STEP* THEN?
WELL... I NEED SOMETHING THEY CAN'T *IGNORE*, RIGHT?
SO I'M GONNA MEET THE KILLER... GET A *CONFESSION*.

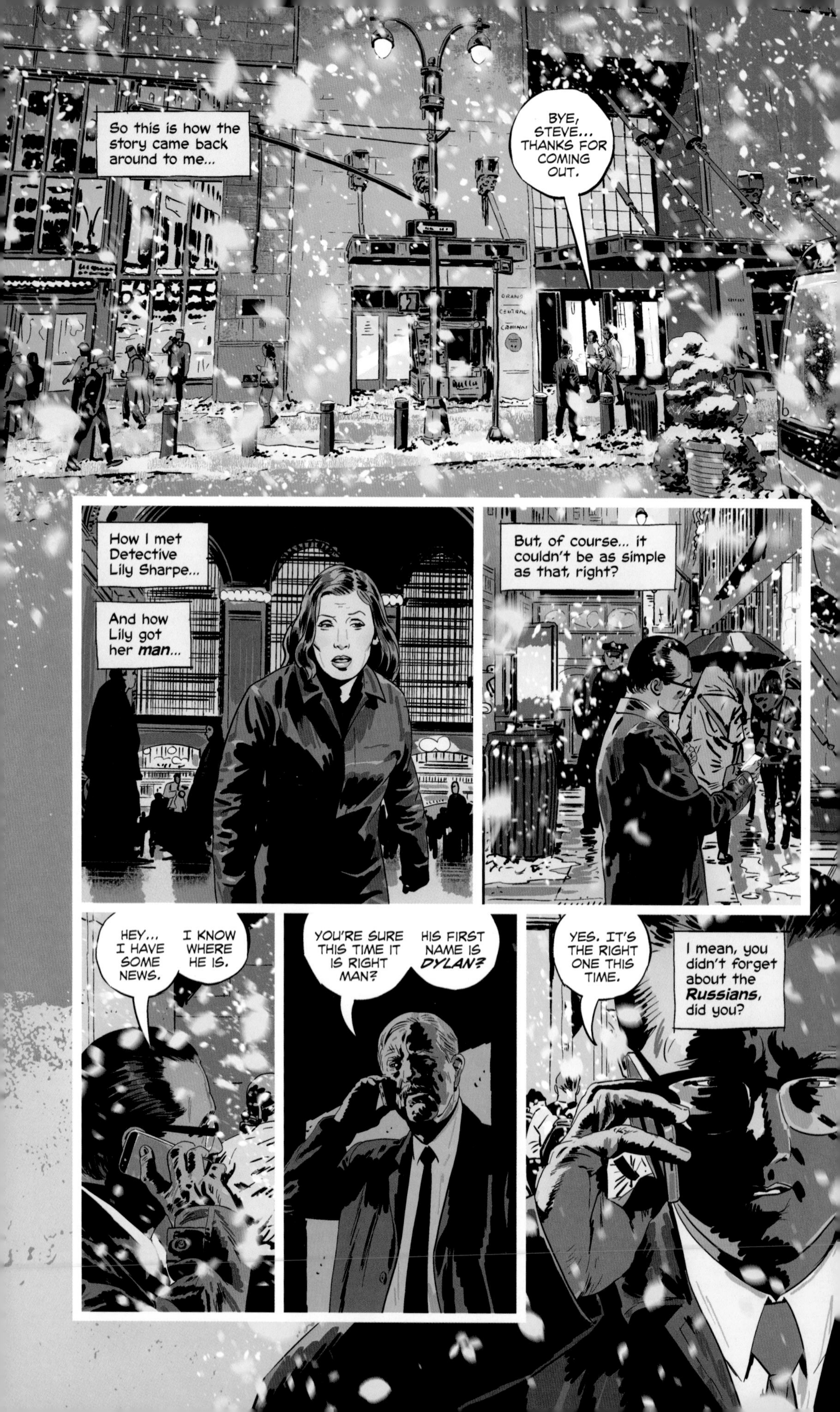
So this is how the story came back around to me...
BYE, STEVE... THANKS FOR COMING OUT.
How I met Detective Lily Sharpe...
And how Lily got her *man*...
But, of course... it couldn't be as simple as that, right?
HEY... I HAVE SOME NEWS.
I KNOW WHERE HE IS.
YOU'RE SURE THIS TIME IT IS RIGHT MAN?
HIS FIRST NAME IS *DYLAN?*
YES. IT'S THE RIGHT ONE THIS TIME.
I mean, you didn't forget about the *Russians*, did you?

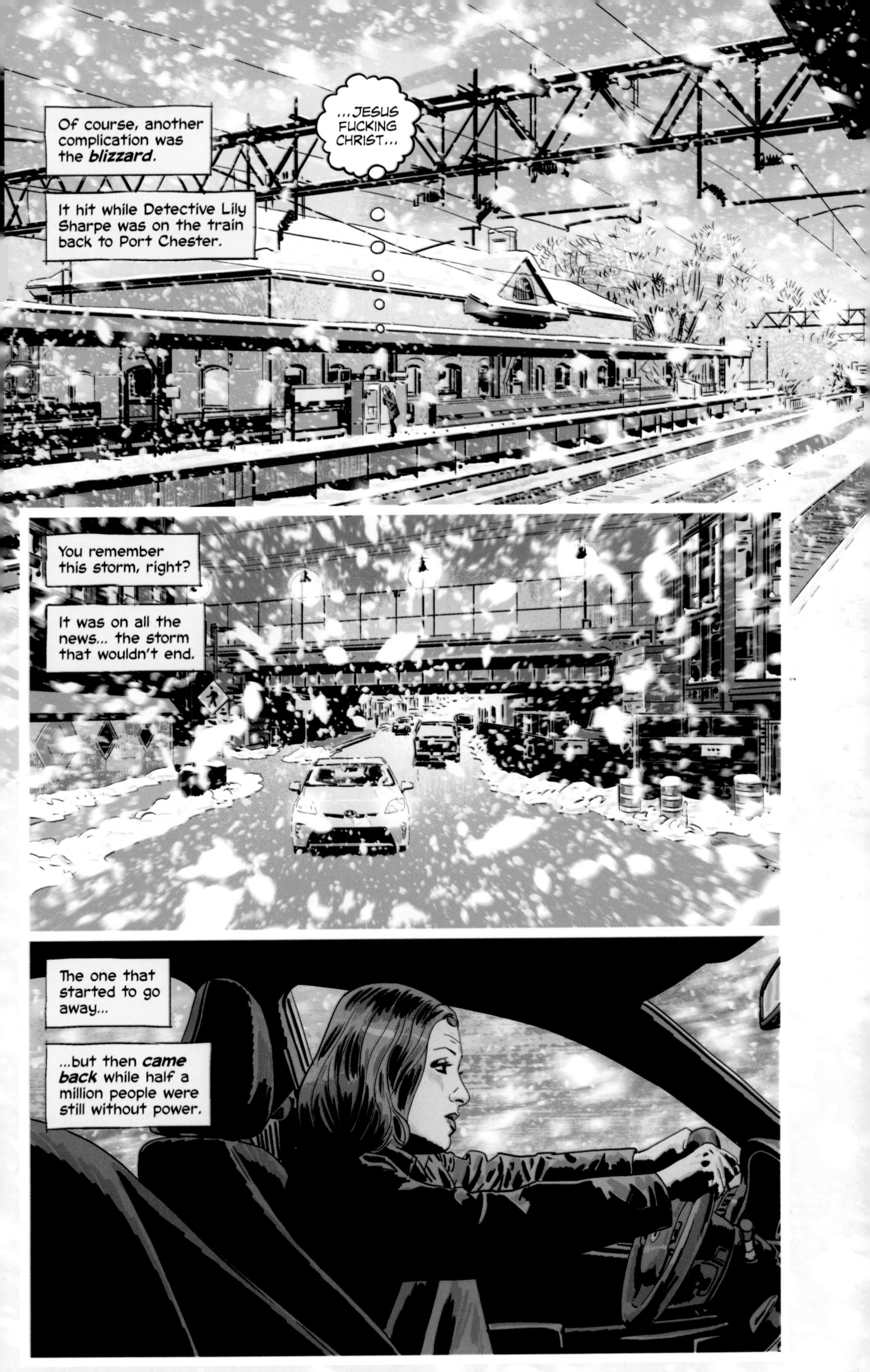
Of course, another complication was the blizzard.
...JESUS FUCKING CHRIST...
It hit while Detective Lily Sharpe was on the train back to Port Chester.
You remember this storm, right?
It was on all the news... the storm that wouldn't end.
The one that started to go away...
...but then came back while half a million people were still without power.

It's global warming, obviously... or climate change, whatever you want to call it.

They used to say it wasn't going to affect us for another thirty years... but no such luck, right?

And don't expect it to get better. Not with humanity in charge.

No, instead of trying to fix things, we've got idiots ripping up regulations and selling off coastal waters for more drilling.

It's the same broken system as everything else.

The public screams for what they want and the politicians do nothing.

Because they work for the other side.

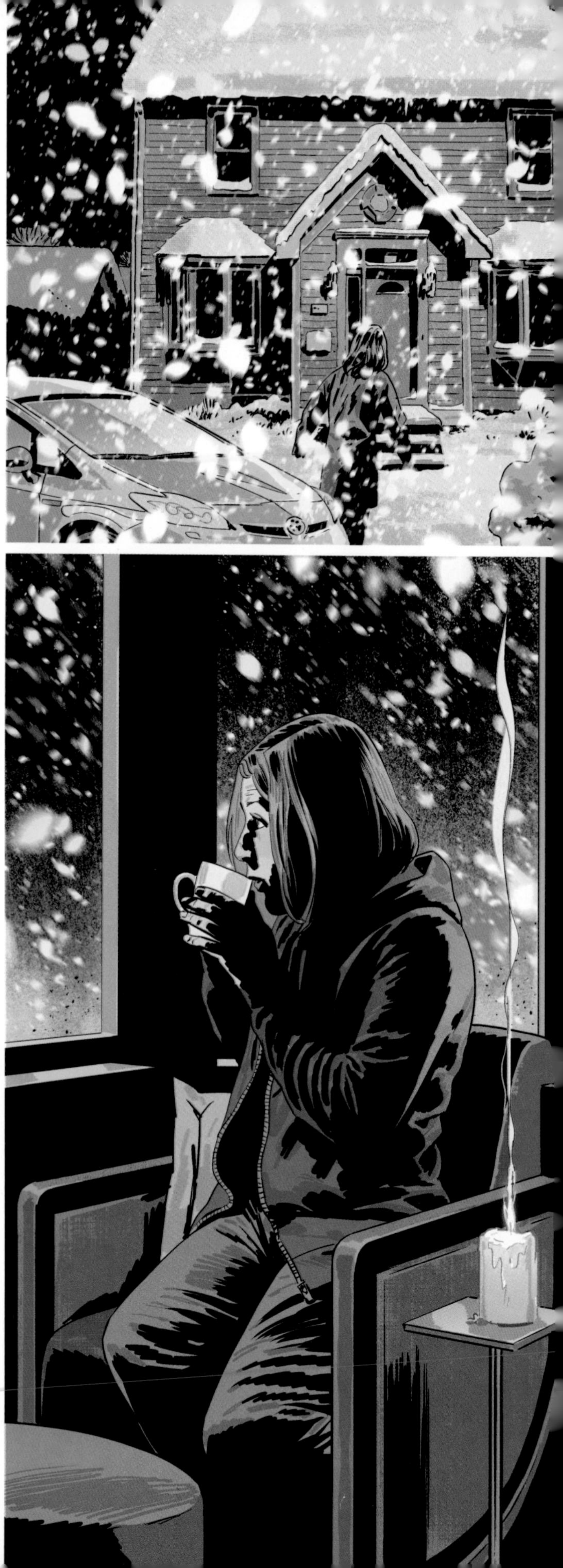

See, the real war - the one that's already being fought - isn't a war between countries... or liberals versus conservatives...

No, that stuff is just a way to stop us from seeing the forest and the trees... as they're burning down all around us.

The real war is between ***wealth*** and ***accountability*** and it's been going since civilization began.

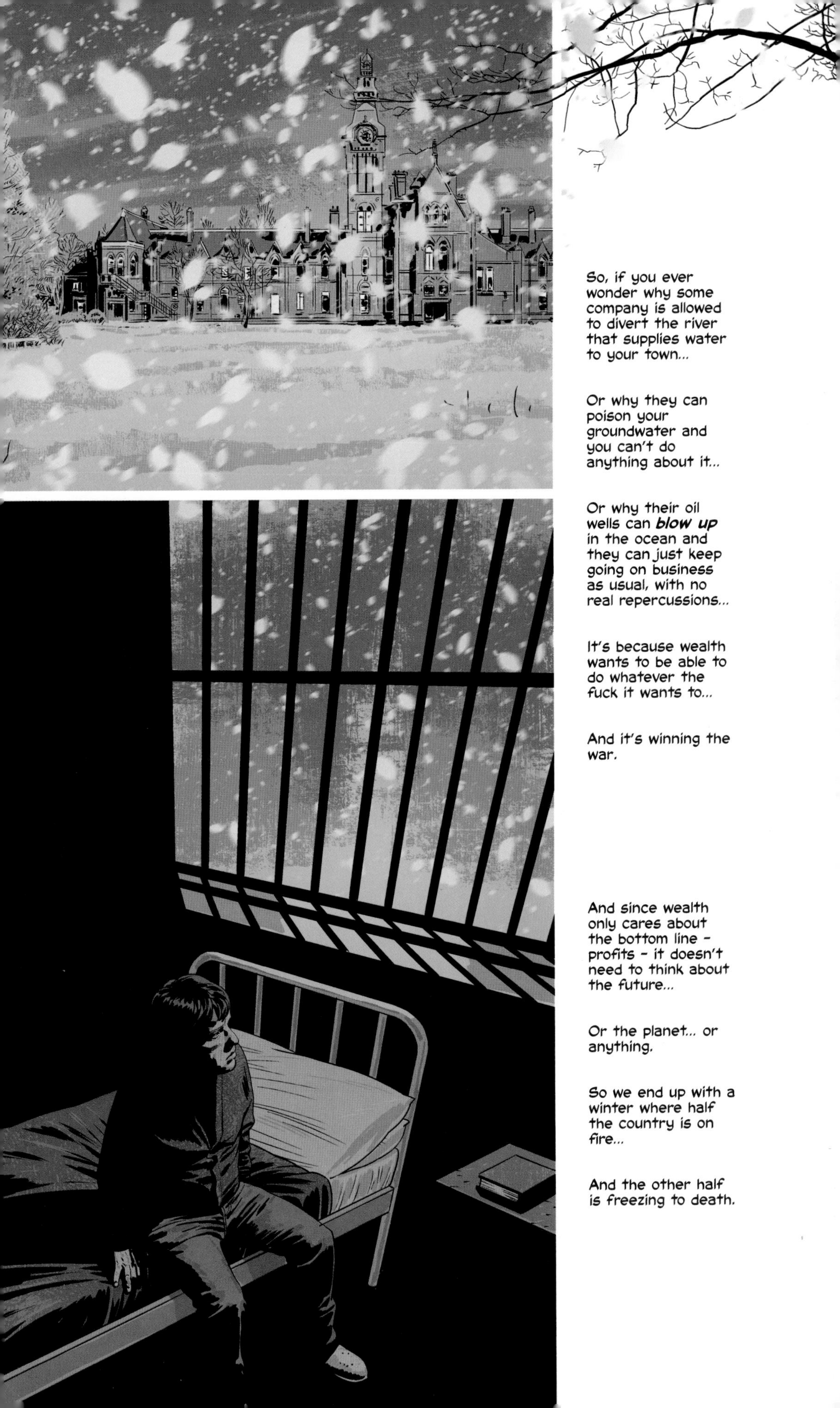
So, if you ever wonder why some company is allowed to divert the river that supplies water to your town...
Or why they can poison your groundwater and you can't do anything about it...
Or why their oil wells can ***blow up*** in the ocean and they can just keep going on business as usual, with no real repercussions...
It's because wealth wants to be able to do whatever the fuck it wants to...
And it's winning the war.
And since wealth only cares about the bottom line - profits - it doesn't need to think about the future...
Or the planet... or anything.
So we end up with a winter where half the country is on fire...
And the other half is freezing to death.

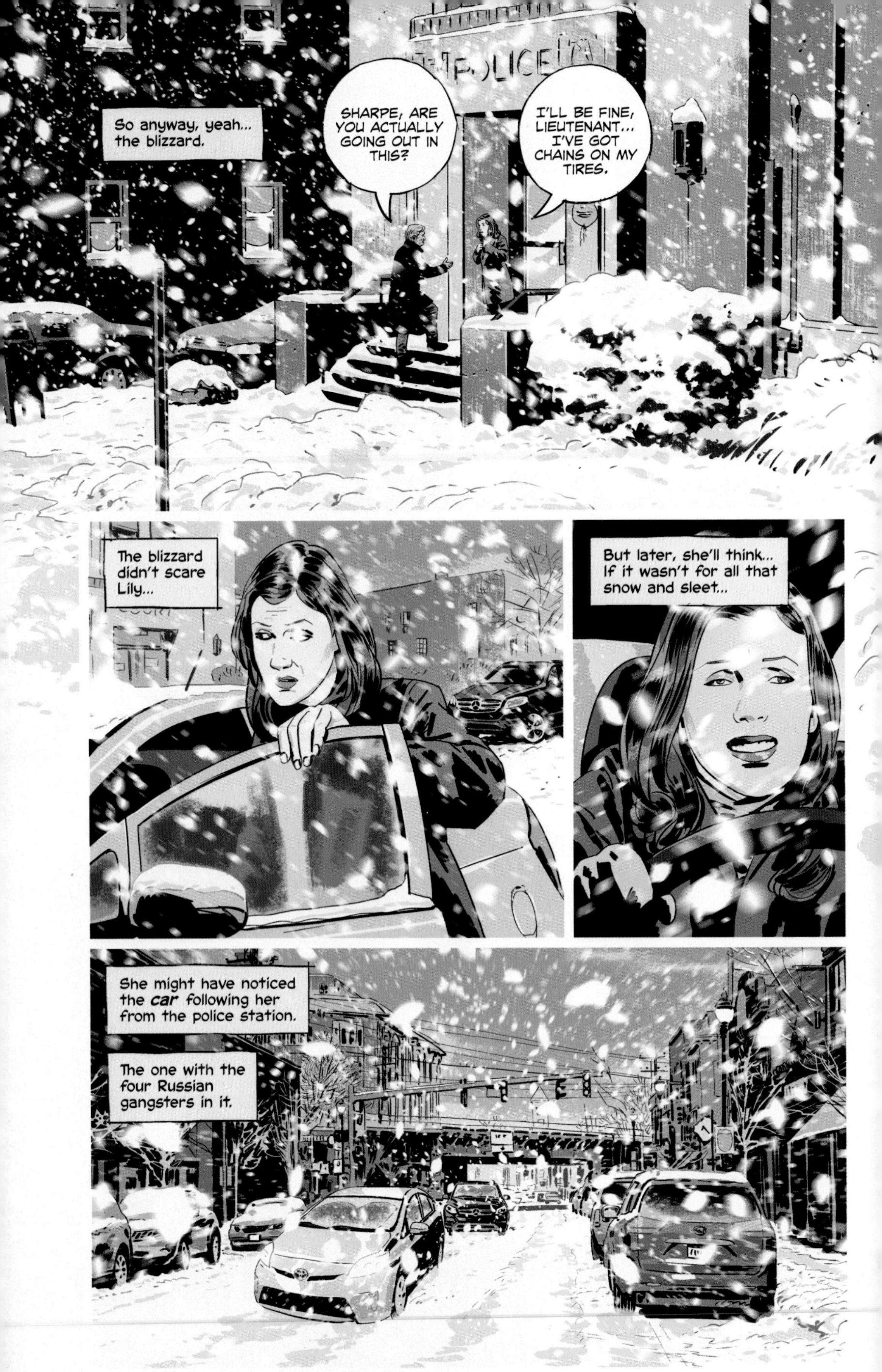

So anyway, yeah... the blizzard.
SHARPE, ARE YOU ACTUALLY GOING OUT IN THIS?
I'LL BE FINE, LIEUTENANT... I'VE GOT CHAINS ON MY TIRES.
The blizzard didn't scare Lily...
But later, she'll think... If it wasn't for all that snow and sleet...
She might have noticed the *car* following her from the police station.
The one with the four Russian gangsters in it.

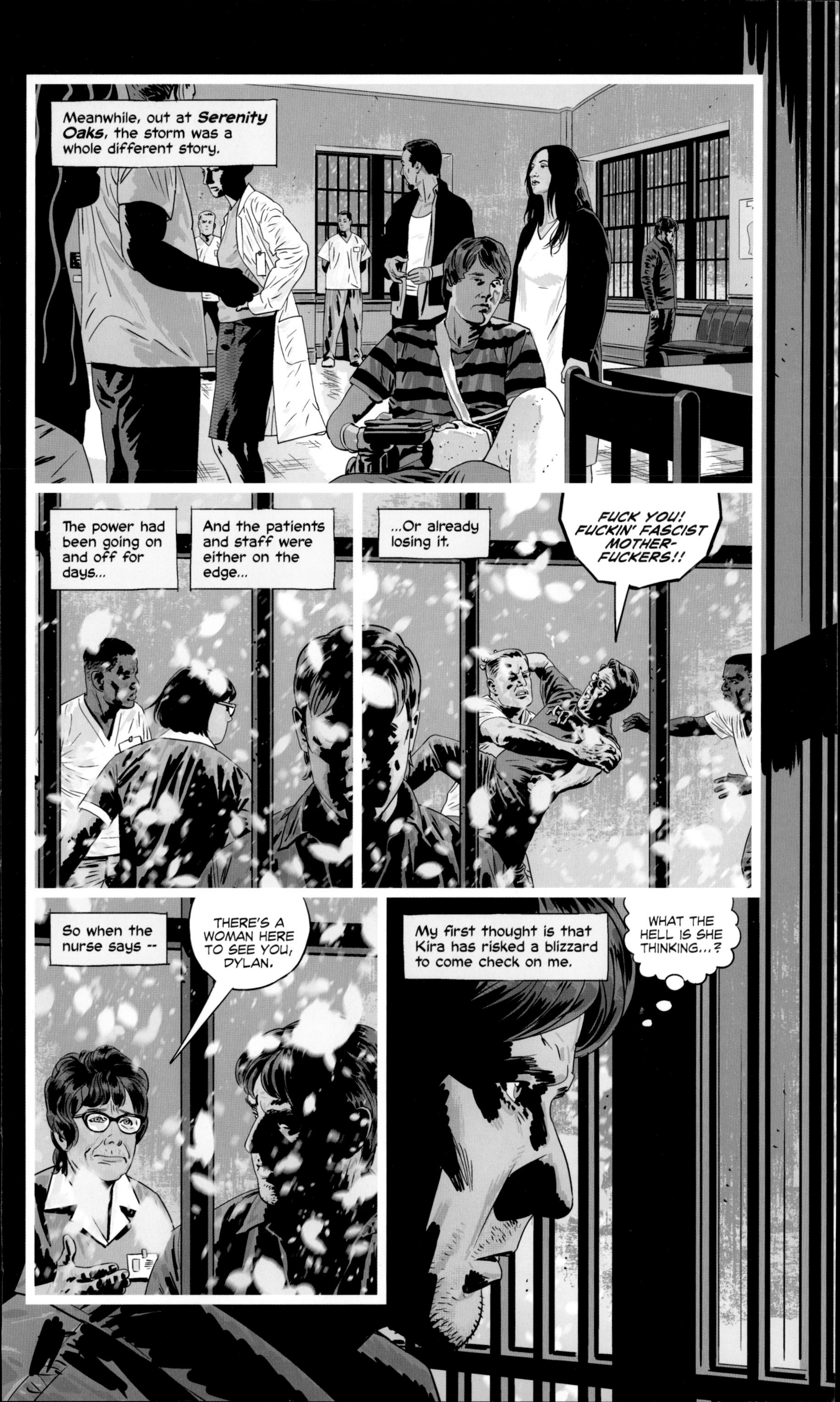
Meanwhile, out at ***Serenity Oaks***, the storm was a whole different story.
The power had been going on and off for days...
And the patients and staff were either on the edge...
...Or already losing it.
FUCK YOU! FUCKIN' FASCIST MOTHER-FUCKERS!!
So when the nurse says --
THERE'S A WOMAN HERE TO SEE YOU, DYLAN.
My first thought is that Kira has risked a blizzard to come check on me.
WHAT THE HELL IS SHE THINKING...?

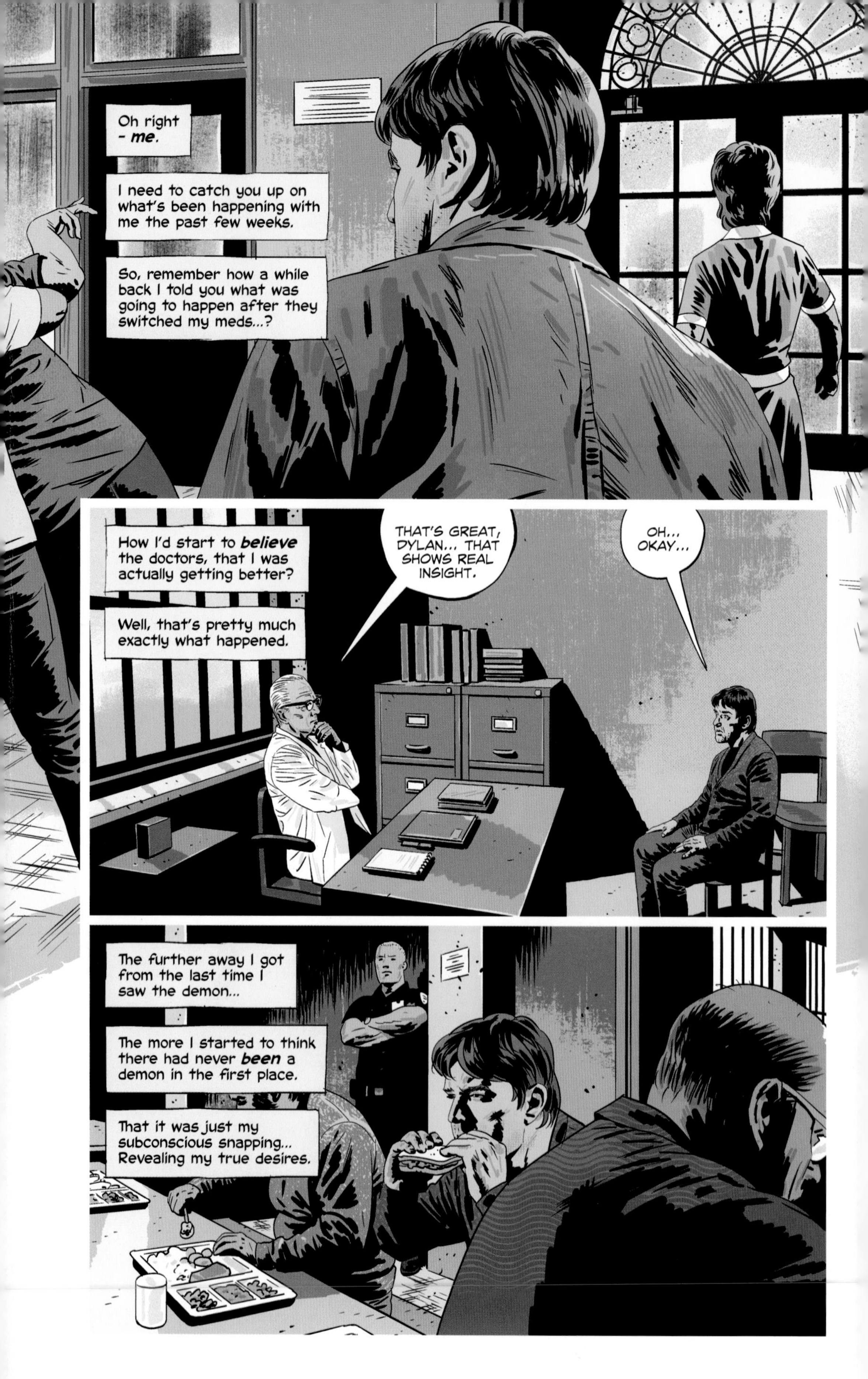

Oh right - *me*.
I need to catch you up on what's been happening with me the past few weeks.
So, remember how a while back I told you what was going to happen after they switched my meds...?
How I'd start to *believe* the doctors, that I was actually getting better?
Well, that's pretty much exactly what happened.
THAT'S GREAT, DYLAN... THAT SHOWS REAL INSIGHT.
OH... OKAY...
The further away I got from the last time I saw the demon...
The more I started to think there had never *been* a demon in the first place.
That it was just my subconscious snapping... Revealing my true desires.

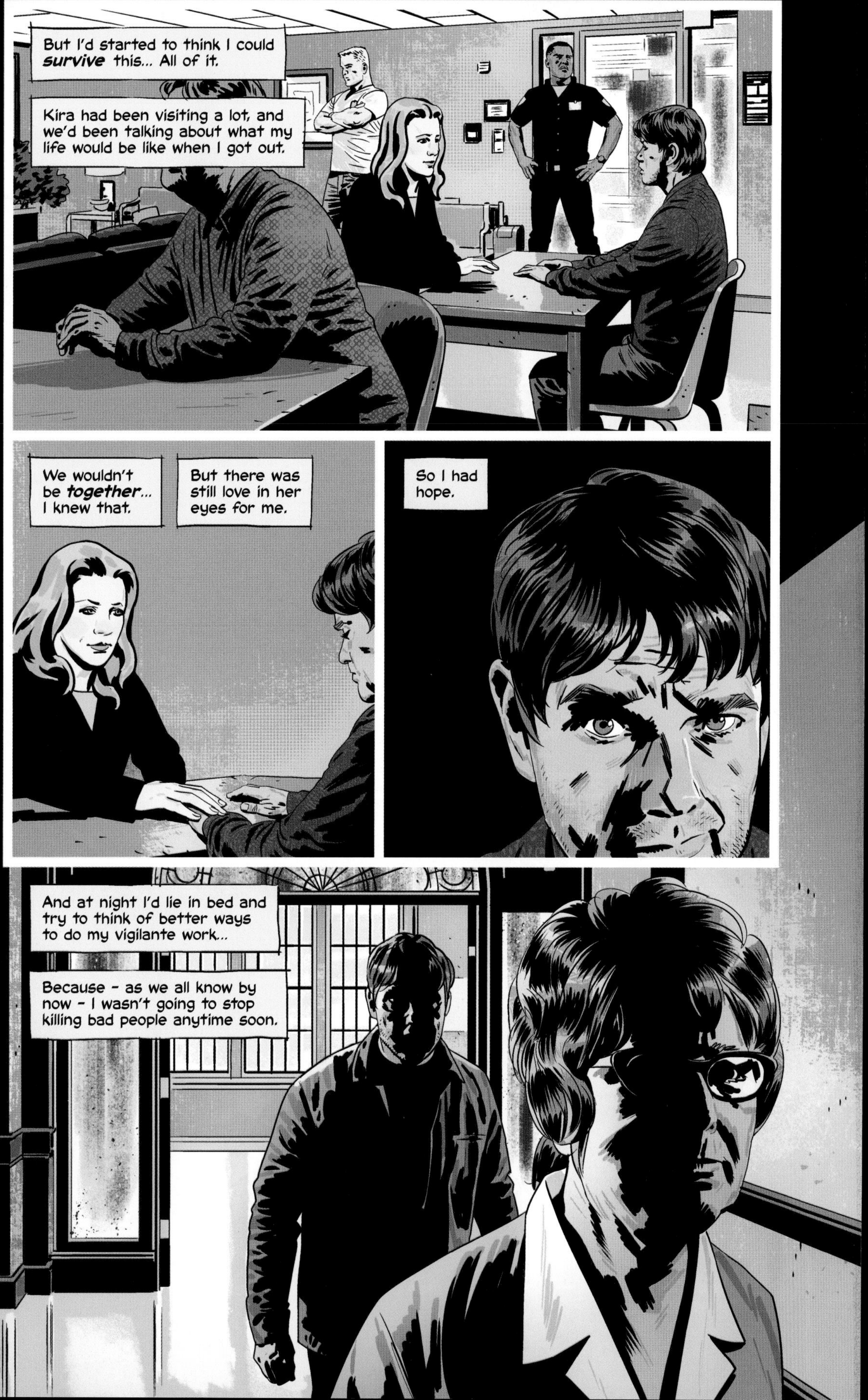

But I'd started to think I could *survive* this... All of it.
Kira had been visiting a lot, and we'd been talking about what my life would be like when I got out.
We wouldn't be *together*... I knew that.
But there was still love in her eyes for me.
So I had hope.
And at night I'd lie in bed and try to think of better ways to do my vigilante work...
Because – as we all know by now – I wasn't going to stop killing bad people anytime soon.

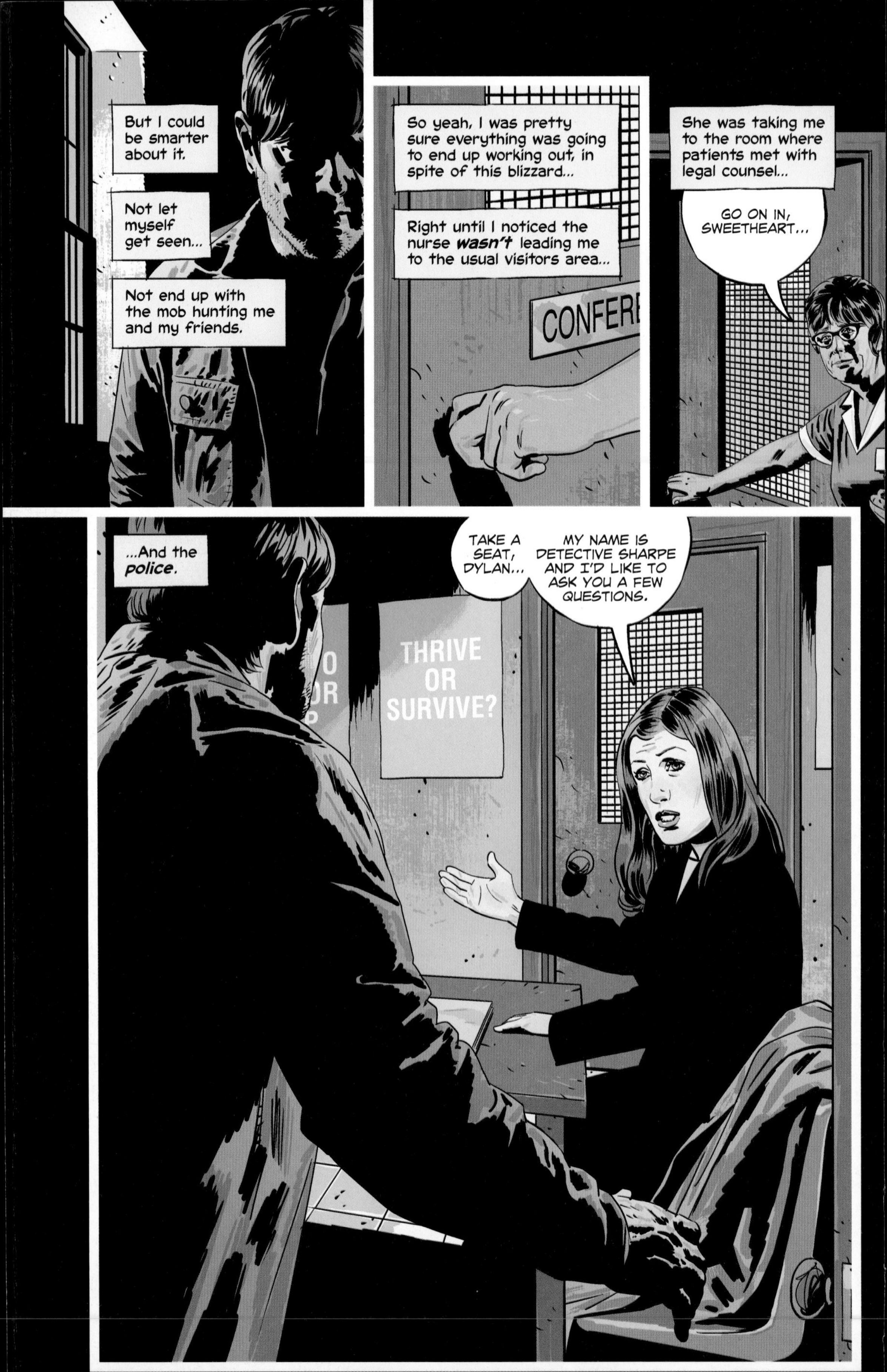
But I could be smarter about it.
Not let myself get seen...
Not end up with the mob hunting me and my friends.
So yeah, I was pretty sure everything was going to end up working out, in spite of this blizzard...
Right until I noticed the nurse *wasn't* leading me to the usual visitors area...
CONFERE
She was taking me to the room where patients met with legal counsel...
GO ON IN, SWEETHEART...
...And the *police*.
TAKE A SEAT, DYLAN...
MY NAME IS DETECTIVE SHARPE AND I'D LIKE TO ASK YOU A FEW QUESTIONS.
THRIVE OR SURVIVE?

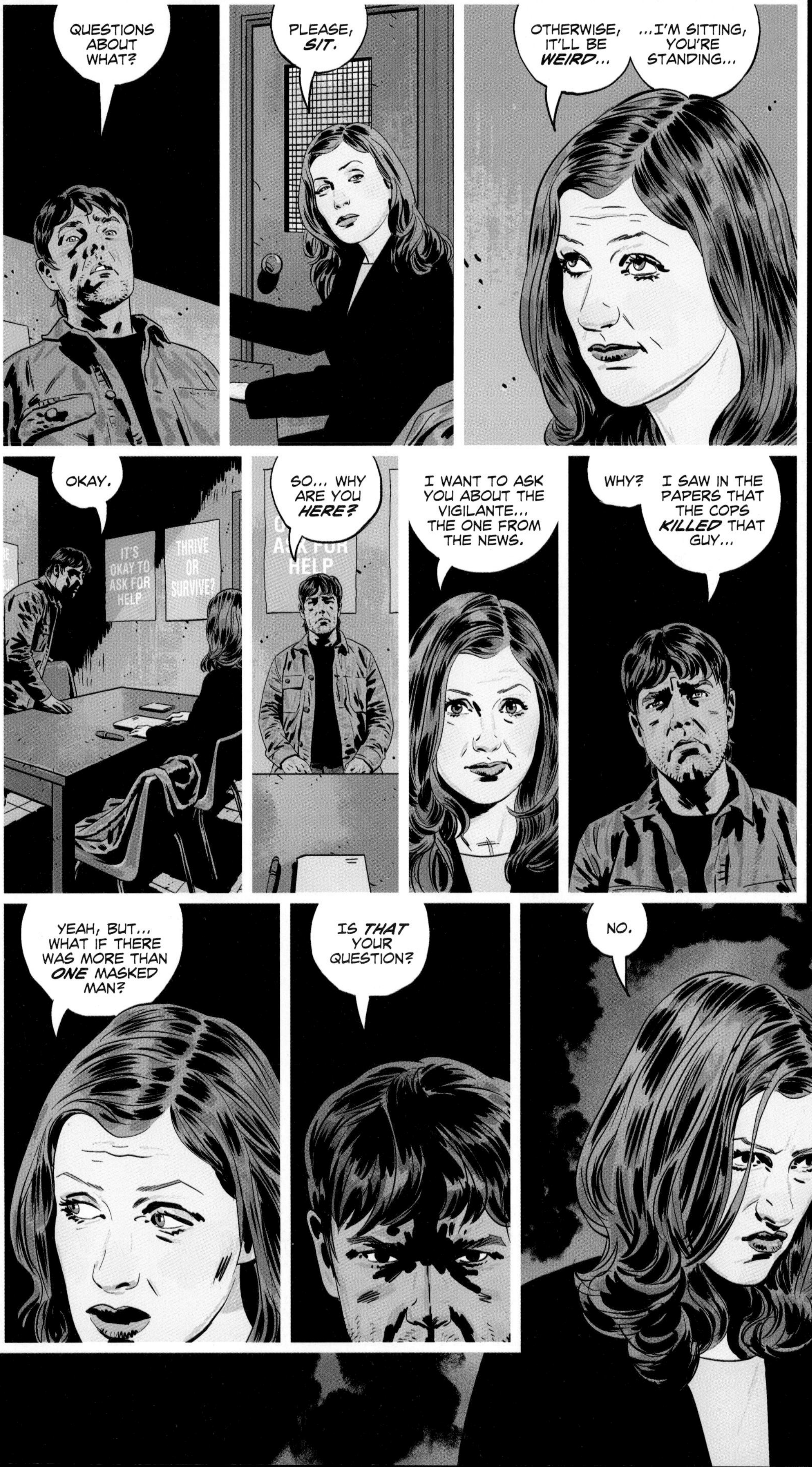
QUESTIONS ABOUT WHAT?
PLEASE, SIT.
OTHERWISE, IT'LL BE WEIRD...
...I'M SITTING, YOU'RE STANDING...
OKAY.
IT'S OKAY TO ASK FOR HELP
THRIVE OR SURVIVE?
SO... WHY ARE YOU HERE?
I WANT TO ASK YOU ABOUT THE VIGILANTE... THE ONE FROM THE NEWS.
WHY?
I SAW IN THE PAPERS THAT THE COPS KILLED THAT GUY...
YEAH, BUT... WHAT IF THERE WAS MORE THAN ONE MASKED MAN?
IS THAT YOUR QUESTION?
NO.

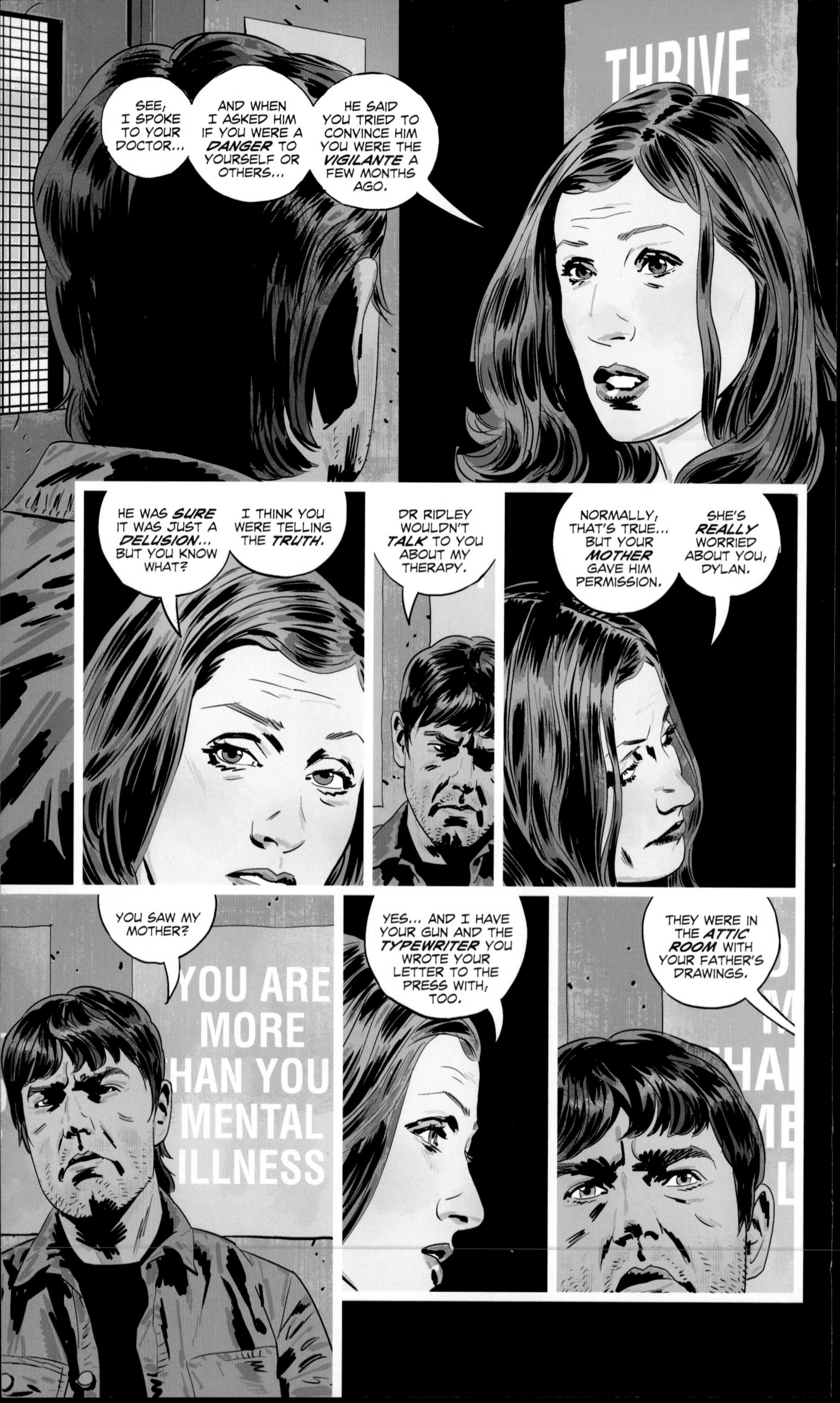
THRIVE
SEE, I SPOKE TO YOUR DOCTOR...
AND WHEN I ASKED HIM IF YOU WERE A DANGER TO YOURSELF OR OTHERS...
HE SAID YOU TRIED TO CONVINCE HIM YOU WERE THE VIGILANTE A FEW MONTHS AGO.
HE WAS SURE IT WAS JUST A DELUSION... BUT YOU KNOW WHAT?
I THINK YOU WERE TELLING THE TRUTH.
DR RIDLEY WOULDN'T TALK TO YOU ABOUT MY THERAPY.
NORMALLY, THAT'S TRUE... BUT YOUR MOTHER GAVE HIM PERMISSION.
SHE'S REALLY WORRIED ABOUT YOU, DYLAN.
YOU SAW MY MOTHER?
YOU ARE MORE THAN YOU MENTAL ILLNESS
YES... AND I HAVE YOUR GUN AND THE TYPEWRITER YOU WROTE YOUR LETTER TO THE PRESS WITH, TOO.
THEY WERE IN THE ATTIC ROOM WITH YOUR FATHER'S DRAWINGS.

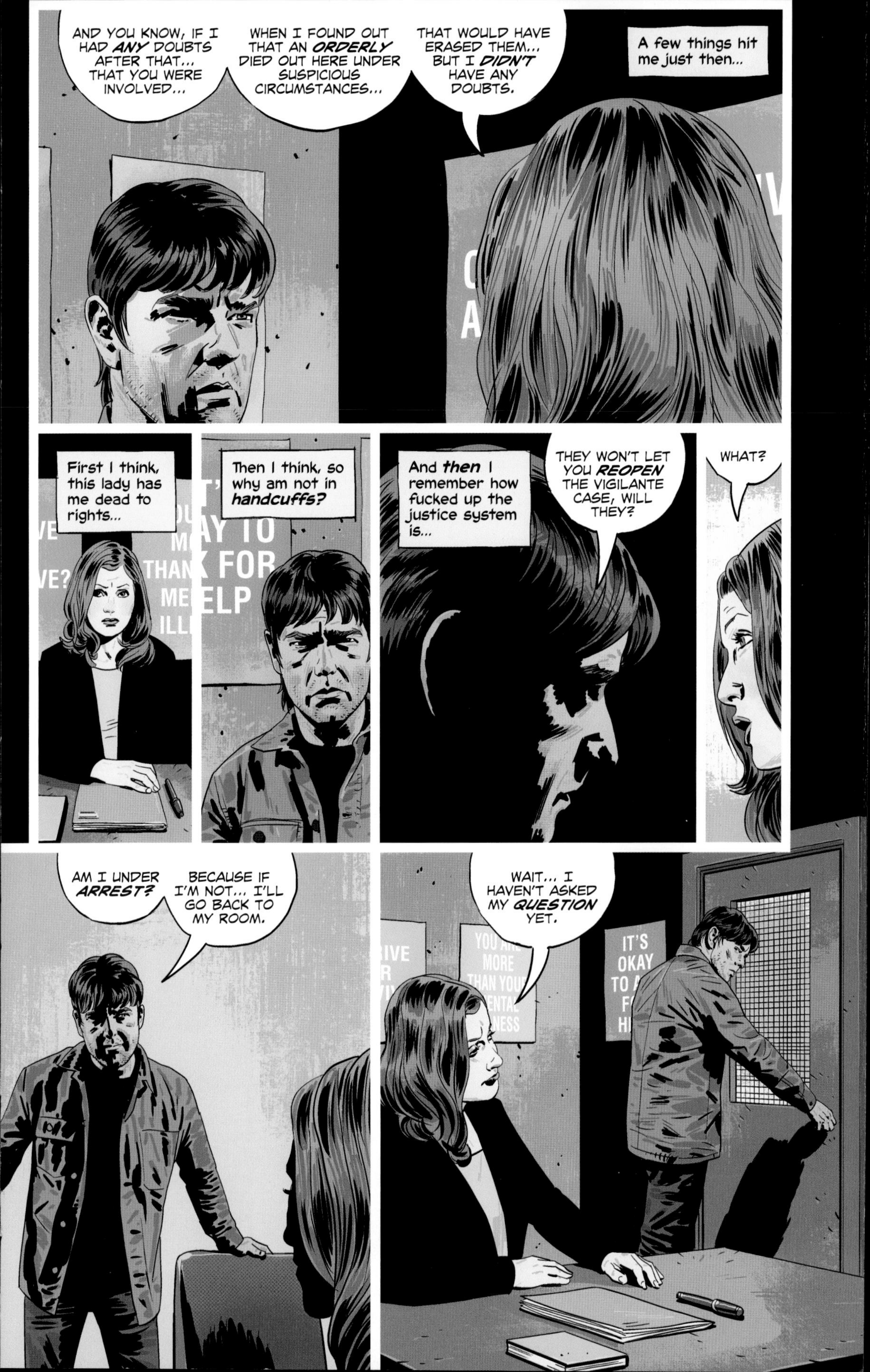
AND YOU KNOW, IF I HAD ANY DOUBTS AFTER THAT... THAT YOU WERE INVOLVED...
WHEN I FOUND OUT THAT AN ORDERLY DIED OUT HERE UNDER SUSPICIOUS CIRCUMSTANCES...
THAT WOULD HAVE ERASED THEM... BUT I DIDN'T HAVE ANY DOUBTS.
A few things hit me just then...
First I think, this lady has me dead to rights...
Then I think, so why am not in handcuffs?
And then I remember how fucked up the justice system is...
THEY WON'T LET YOU REOPEN THE VIGILANTE CASE, WILL THEY?
WHAT?
AM I UNDER ARREST?
BECAUSE IF I'M NOT... I'LL GO BACK TO MY ROOM.
WAIT... I HAVEN'T ASKED MY QUESTION YET.
IT'S OKAY

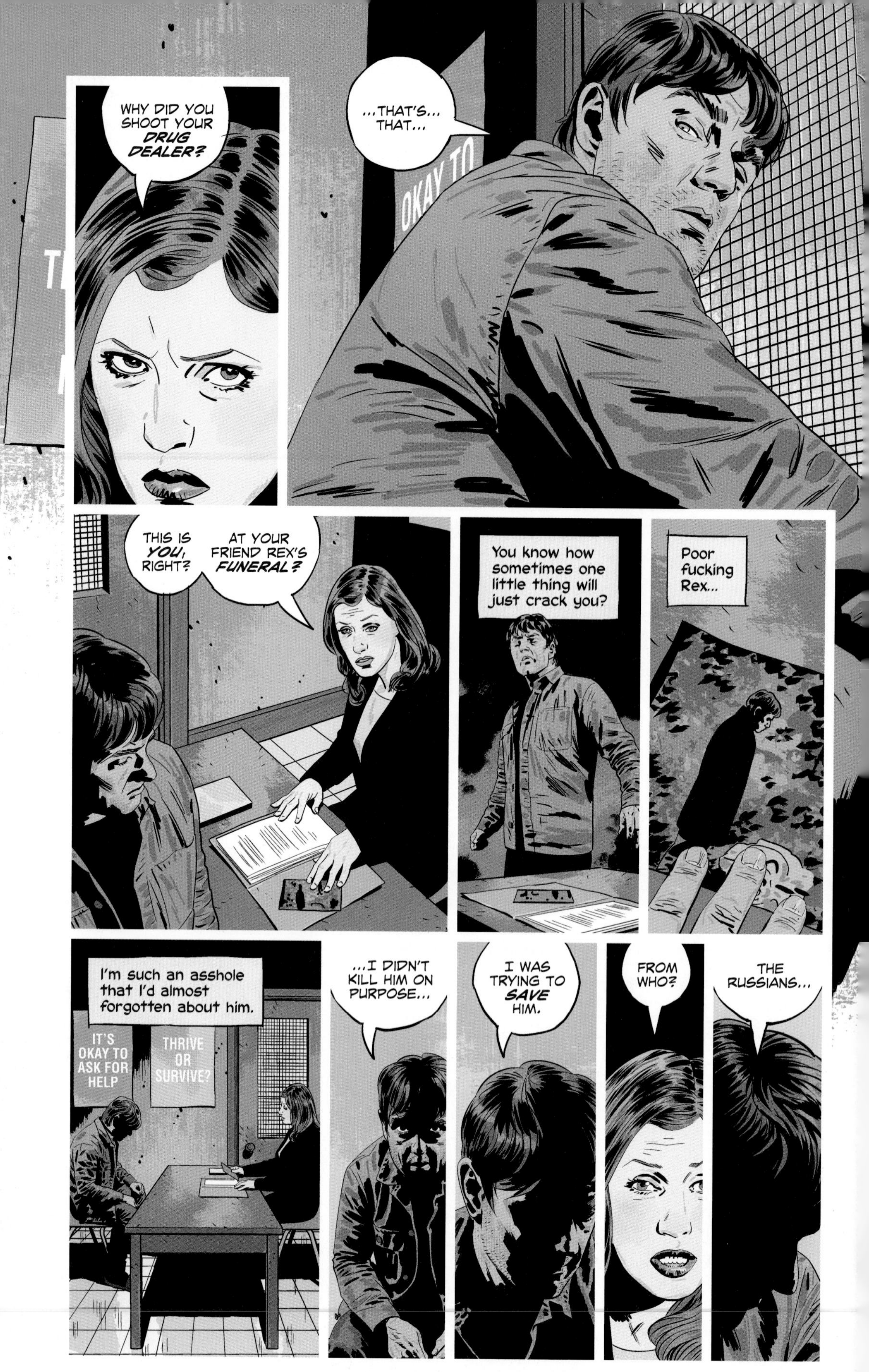
WHY DID YOU SHOOT YOUR DRUG DEALER?
...THAT'S... THAT...
OKAY TO
THIS IS YOU, RIGHT?
AT YOUR FRIEND REX'S FUNERAL?
You know how sometimes one little thing will just crack you?
Poor fucking Rex...
I'm such an asshole that I'd almost forgotten about him.
IT'S OKAY TO ASK FOR HELP
THRIVE OR SURVIVE?
...I DIDN'T KILL HIM ON PURPOSE...
I WAS TRYING TO SAVE HIM.
FROM WHO?
THE RUSSIANS...

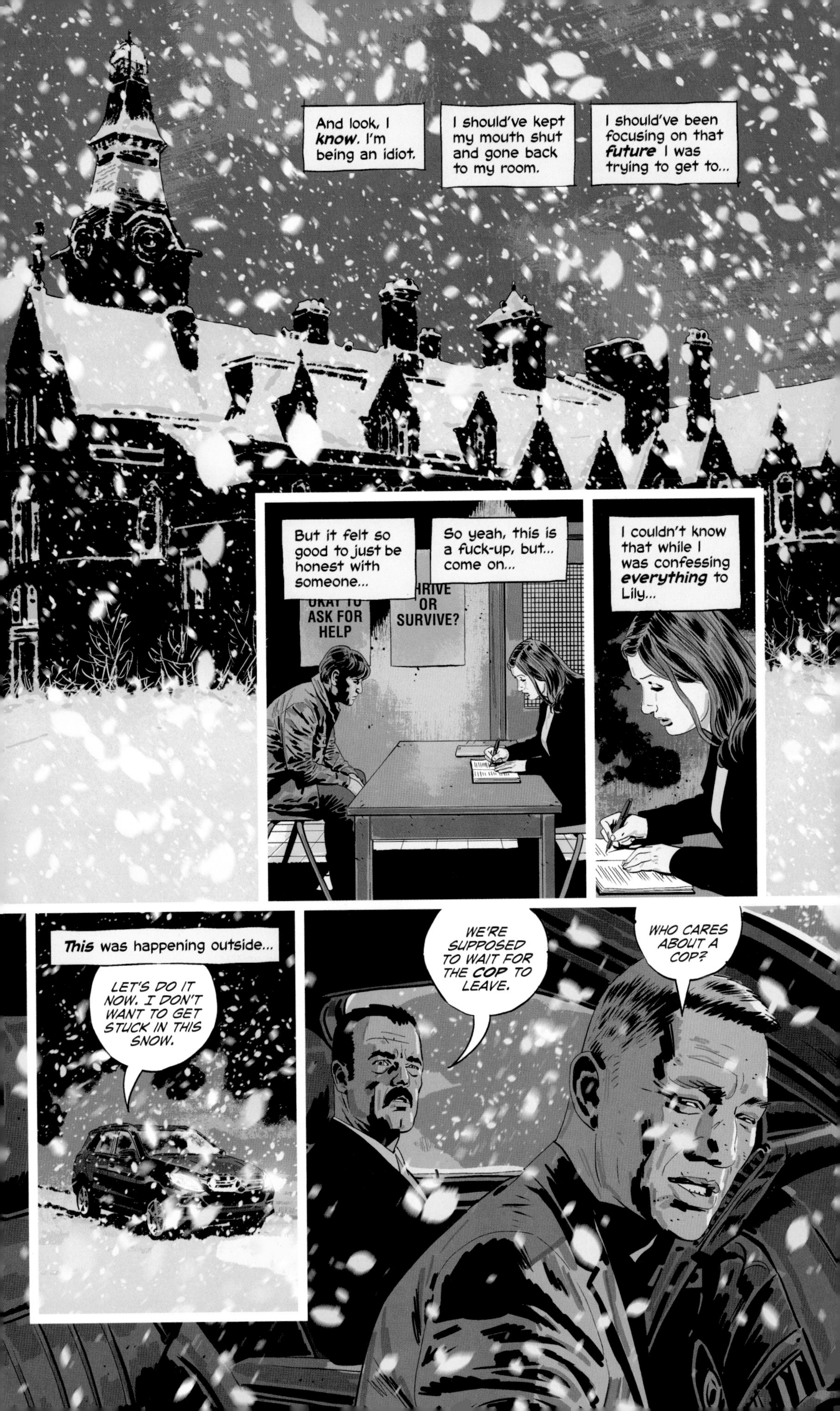

And look, I know. I'm being an idiot.
I should've kept my mouth shut and gone back to my room.
I should've been focusing on that future I was trying to get to...
But it felt so good to just be honest with someone...
So yeah, this is a fuck-up, but... come on...
ASK FOR HELP
OR SURVIVE?
I couldn't know that while I was confessing everything to Lily...
This was happening outside...
LET'S DO IT NOW. I DON'T WANT TO GET STUCK IN THIS SNOW.
WE'RE SUPPOSED TO WAIT FOR THE COP TO LEAVE.
WHO CARES ABOUT A COP?

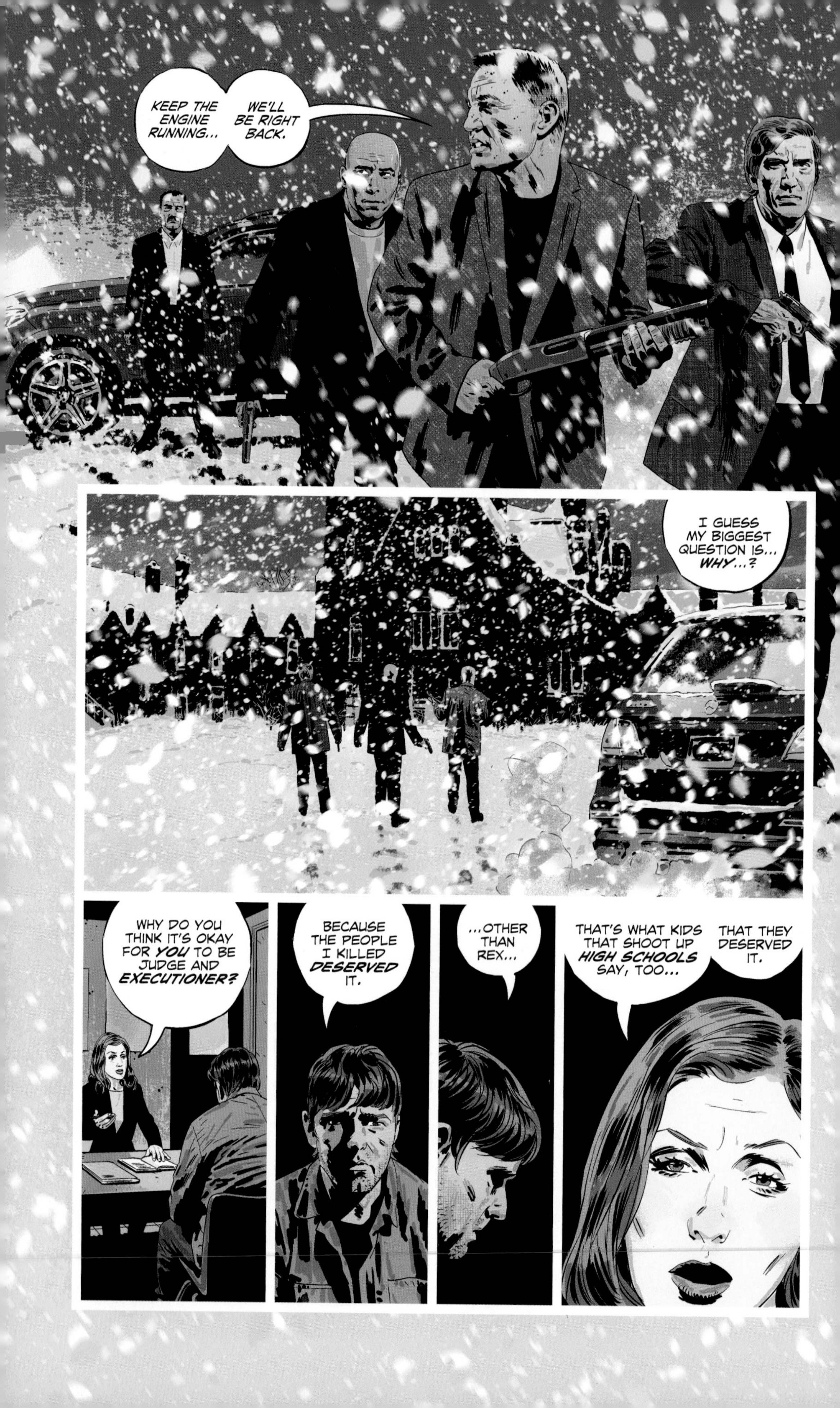
KEEP THE ENGINE RUNNING...
WE'LL BE RIGHT BACK.
I GUESS MY BIGGEST QUESTION IS... WHY...?
WHY DO YOU THINK IT'S OKAY FOR YOU TO BE JUDGE AND EXECUTIONER?
BECAUSE THE PEOPLE I KILLED DESERVED IT.
...OTHER THAN REX...
THAT'S WHAT KIDS THAT SHOOT UP HIGH SCHOOLS SAY, TOO...
THAT THEY DESERVED IT.

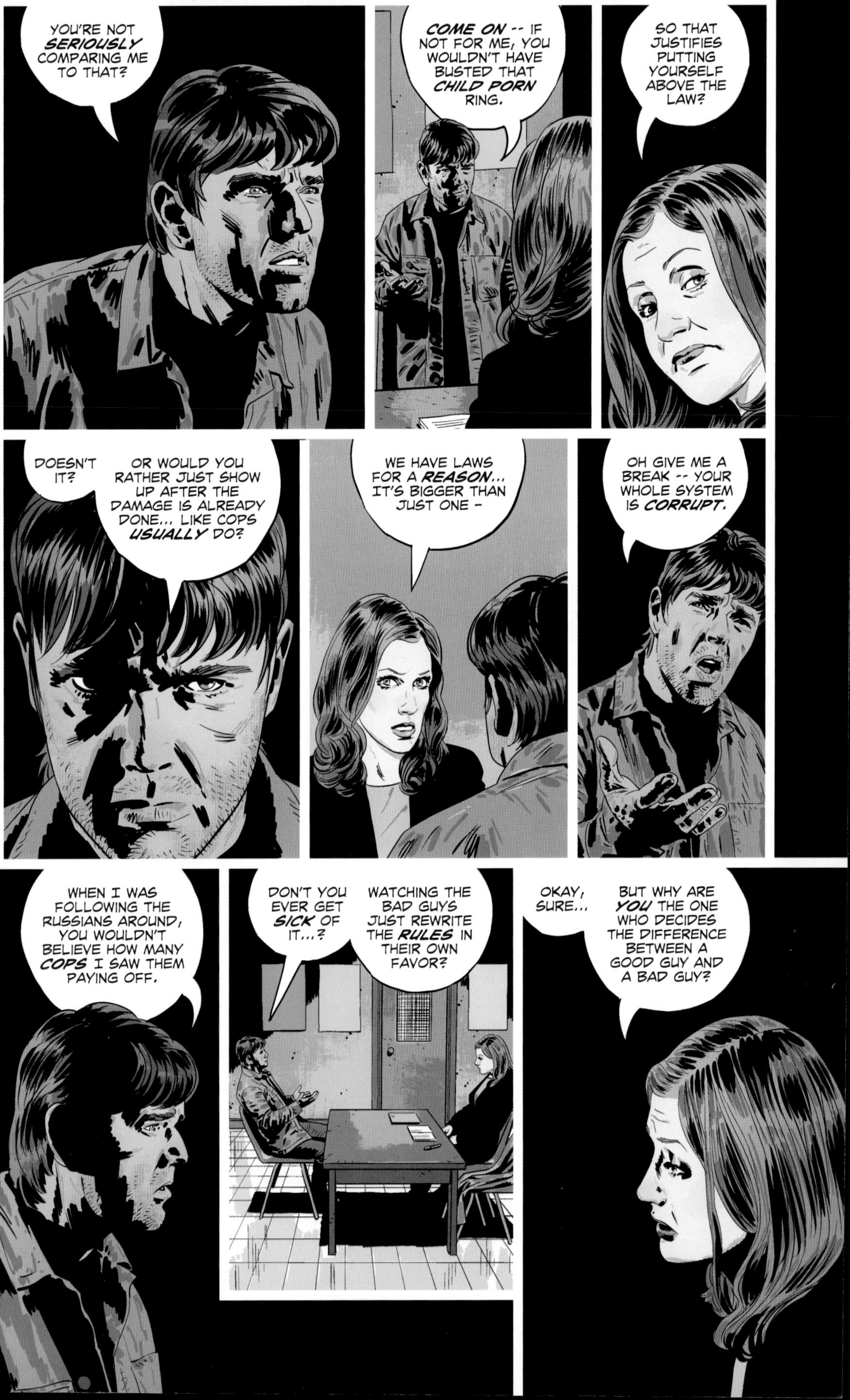
YOU'RE NOT SERIOUSLY COMPARING ME TO THAT?
COME ON -- IF NOT FOR ME, YOU WOULDN'T HAVE BUSTED THAT CHILD PORN RING.
SO THAT JUSTIFIES PUTTING YOURSELF ABOVE THE LAW?
DOESN'T IT?
OR WOULD YOU RATHER JUST SHOW UP AFTER THE DAMAGE IS ALREADY DONE... LIKE COPS USUALLY DO?
WE HAVE LAWS FOR A REASON... IT'S BIGGER THAN JUST ONE –
OH GIVE ME A BREAK -- YOUR WHOLE SYSTEM IS CORRUPT.
WHEN I WAS FOLLOWING THE RUSSIANS AROUND, YOU WOULDN'T BELIEVE HOW MANY COPS I SAW THEM PAYING OFF.
DON'T YOU EVER GET SICK OF IT...?
WATCHING THE BAD GUYS JUST REWRITE THE RULES IN THEIR OWN FAVOR?
OKAY, SURE...
BUT WHY ARE YOU THE ONE WHO DECIDES THE DIFFERENCE BETWEEN A GOOD GUY AND A BAD GUY?

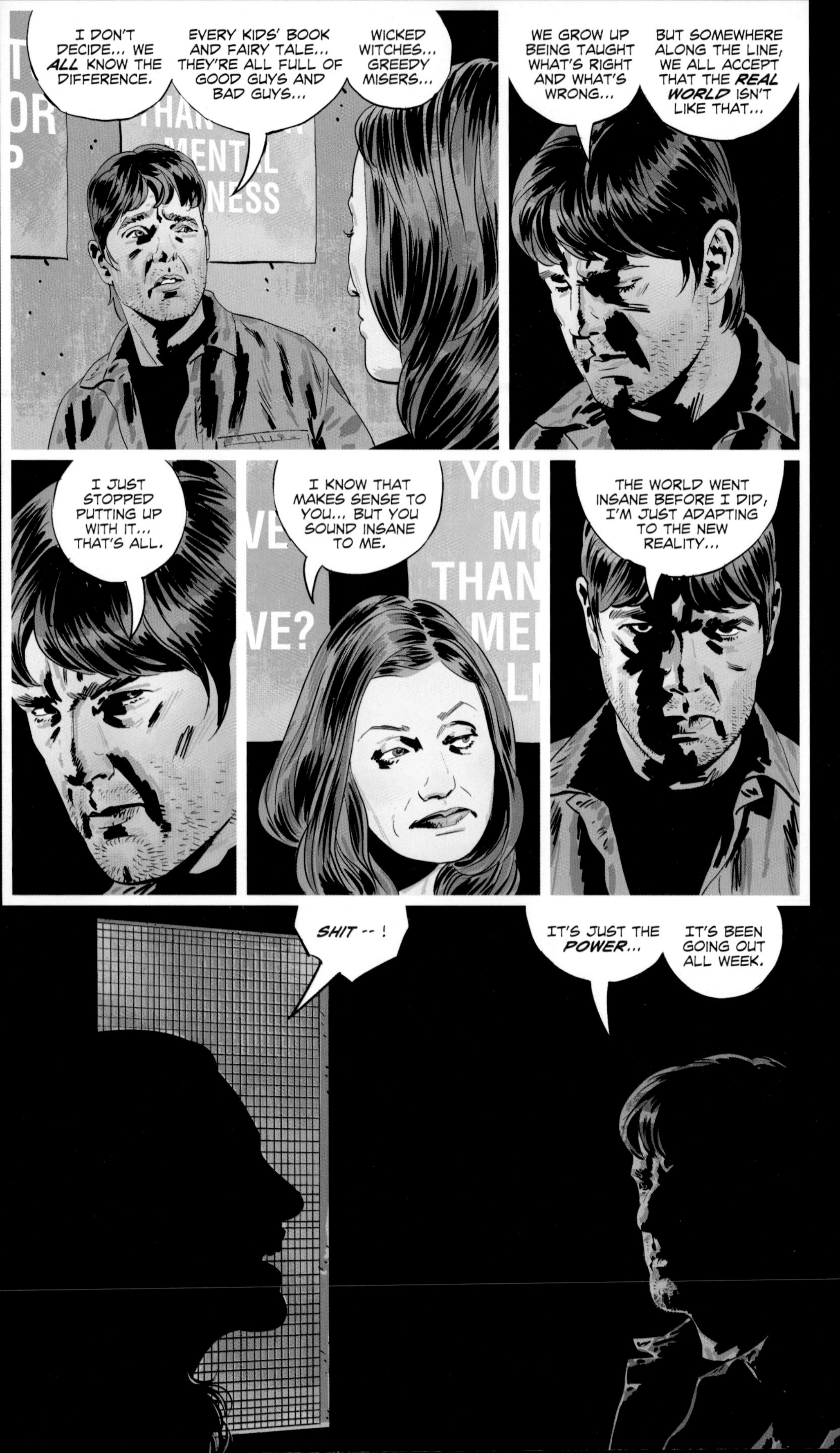
I DON'T DECIDE... WE ALL KNOW THE DIFFERENCE.
EVERY KIDS' BOOK AND FAIRY TALE... THEY'RE ALL FULL OF GOOD GUYS AND BAD GUYS...
WICKED WITCHES... GREEDY MISERS...
WE GROW UP BEING TAUGHT WHAT'S RIGHT AND WHAT'S WRONG...
BUT SOMEWHERE ALONG THE LINE, WE ALL ACCEPT THAT THE REAL WORLD ISN'T LIKE THAT...
I JUST STOPPED PUTTING UP WITH IT... THAT'S ALL.
I KNOW THAT MAKES SENSE TO YOU... BUT YOU SOUND INSANE TO ME.
THE WORLD WENT INSANE BEFORE I DID, I'M JUST ADAPTING TO THE NEW REALITY...
SHIT -- !
IT'S JUST THE POWER...
IT'S BEEN GOING OUT ALL WEEK.

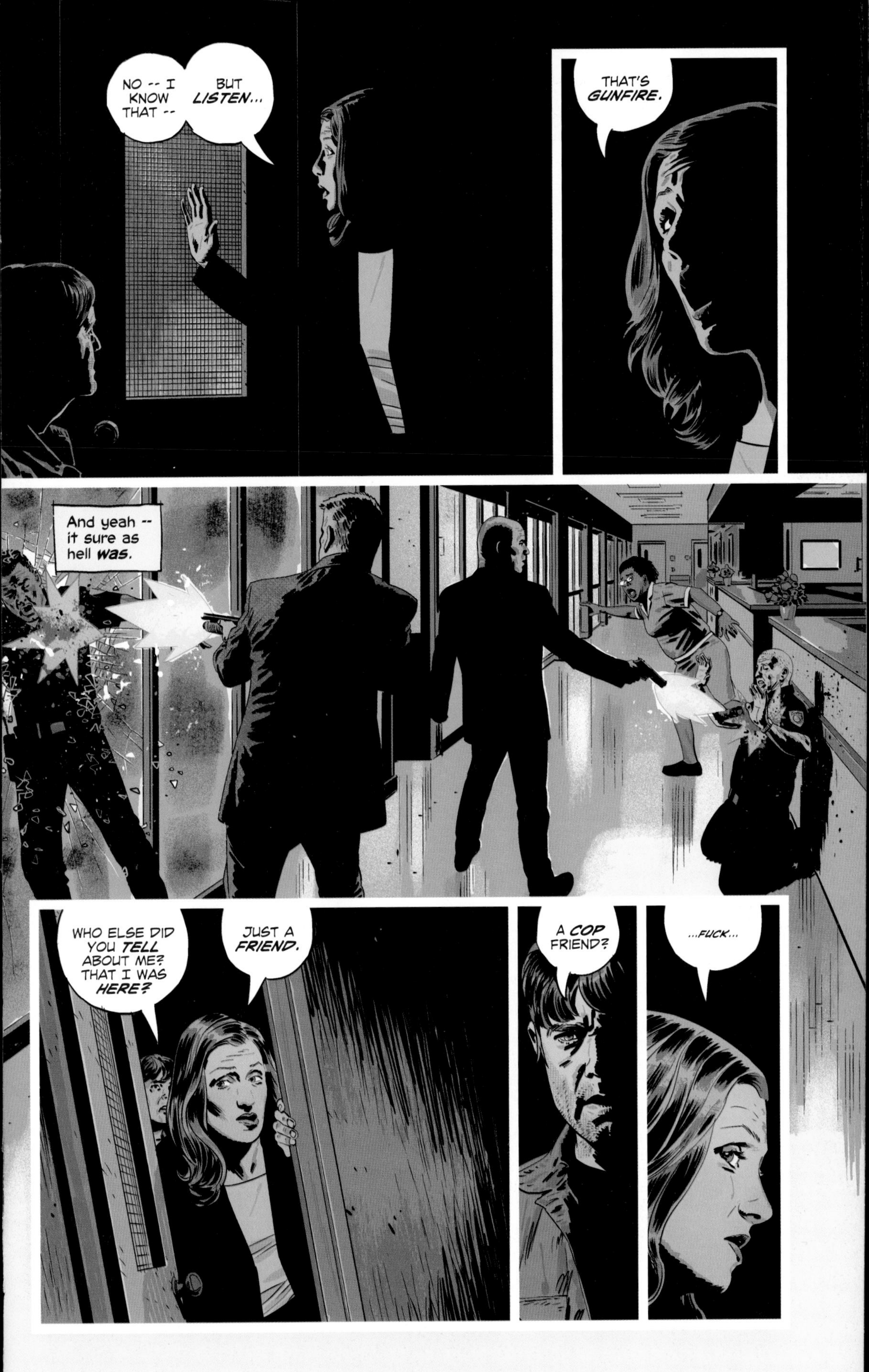
NO -- I KNOW THAT --
BUT LISTEN...
THAT'S GUNFIRE.
And yeah -- it sure as hell was.
WHO ELSE DID YOU TELL ABOUT ME? THAT I WAS HERE?
JUST A FRIEND.
A COP FRIEND?
...FUCK...

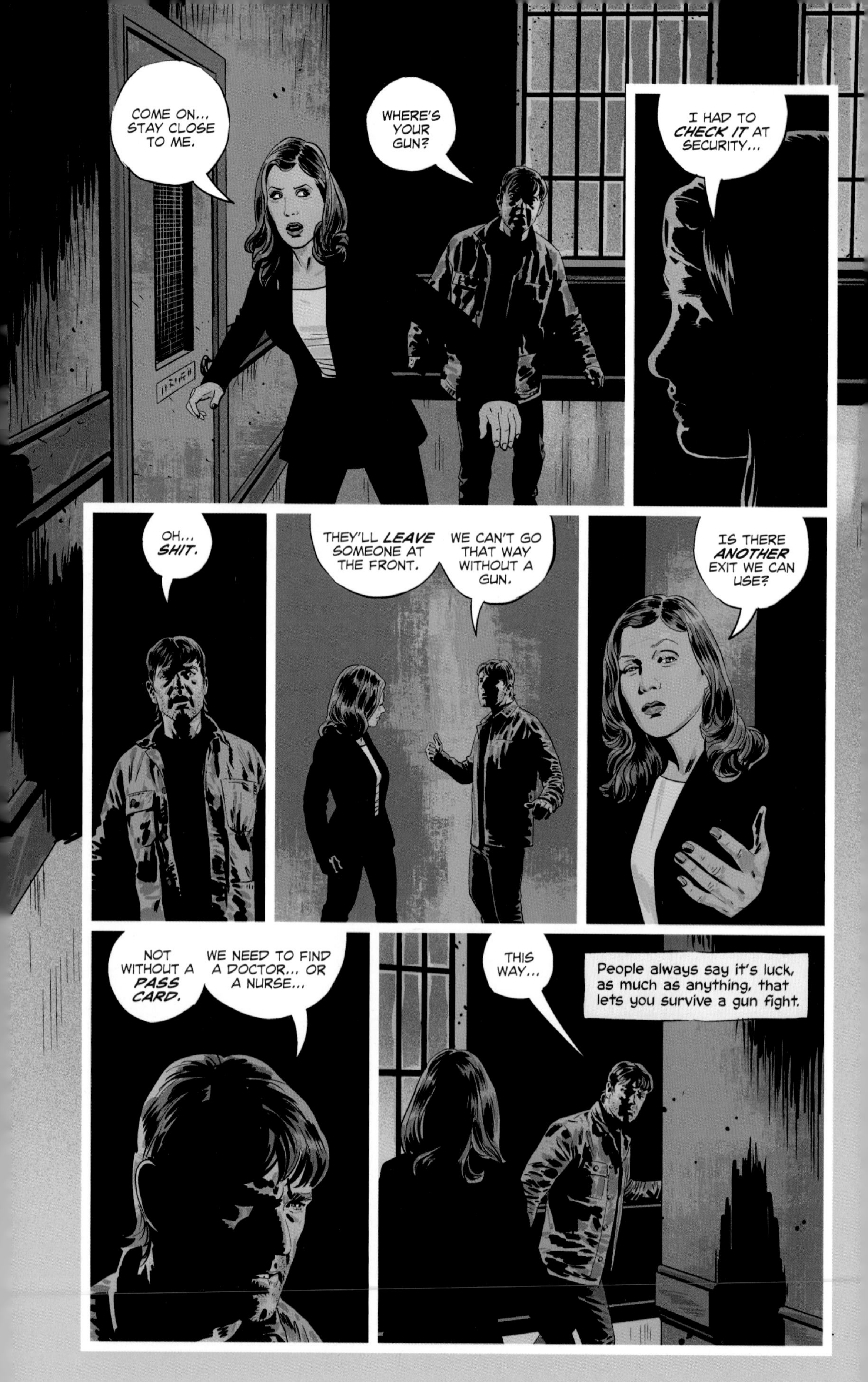
COME ON... STAY CLOSE TO ME.
WHERE'S YOUR GUN?
I HAD TO *CHECK IT* AT SECURITY...
OH... *SHIT.*
THEY'LL *LEAVE* SOMEONE AT THE FRONT.
WE CAN'T GO THAT WAY WITHOUT A GUN.
IS THERE *ANOTHER* EXIT WE CAN USE?
NOT WITHOUT A *PASS CARD.*
WE NEED TO FIND A DOCTOR... OR A NURSE...
THIS WAY...
People always say it's luck, as much as anything, that lets you survive a gun fight.

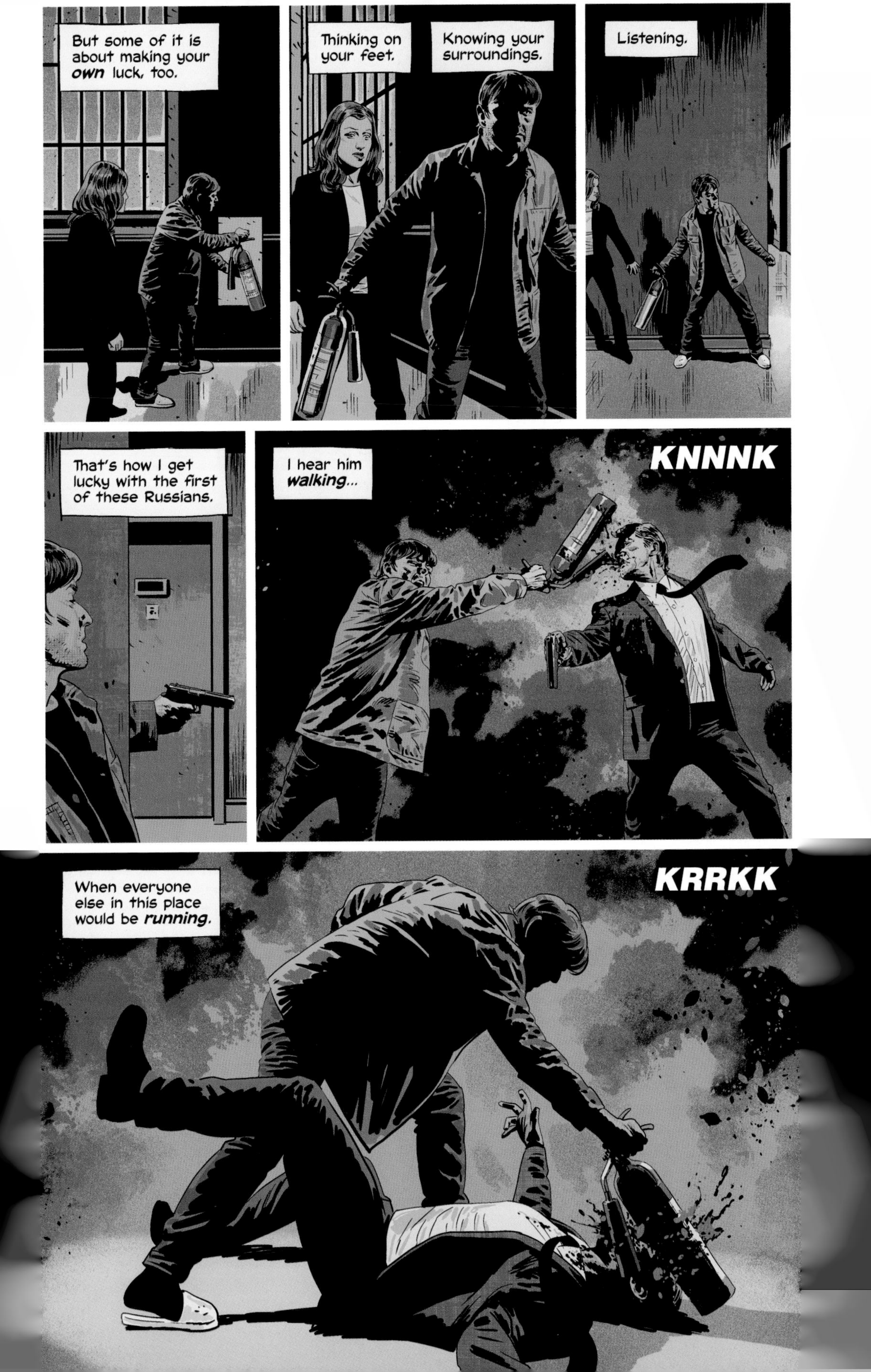
But some of it is about making your *own* luck, too.
Thinking on your feet.
Knowing your surroundings.
Listening.
That's how I get lucky with the first of these Russians.
I hear him *walking*...
KNNNK
When everyone else in this place would be *running*.
KRRKK

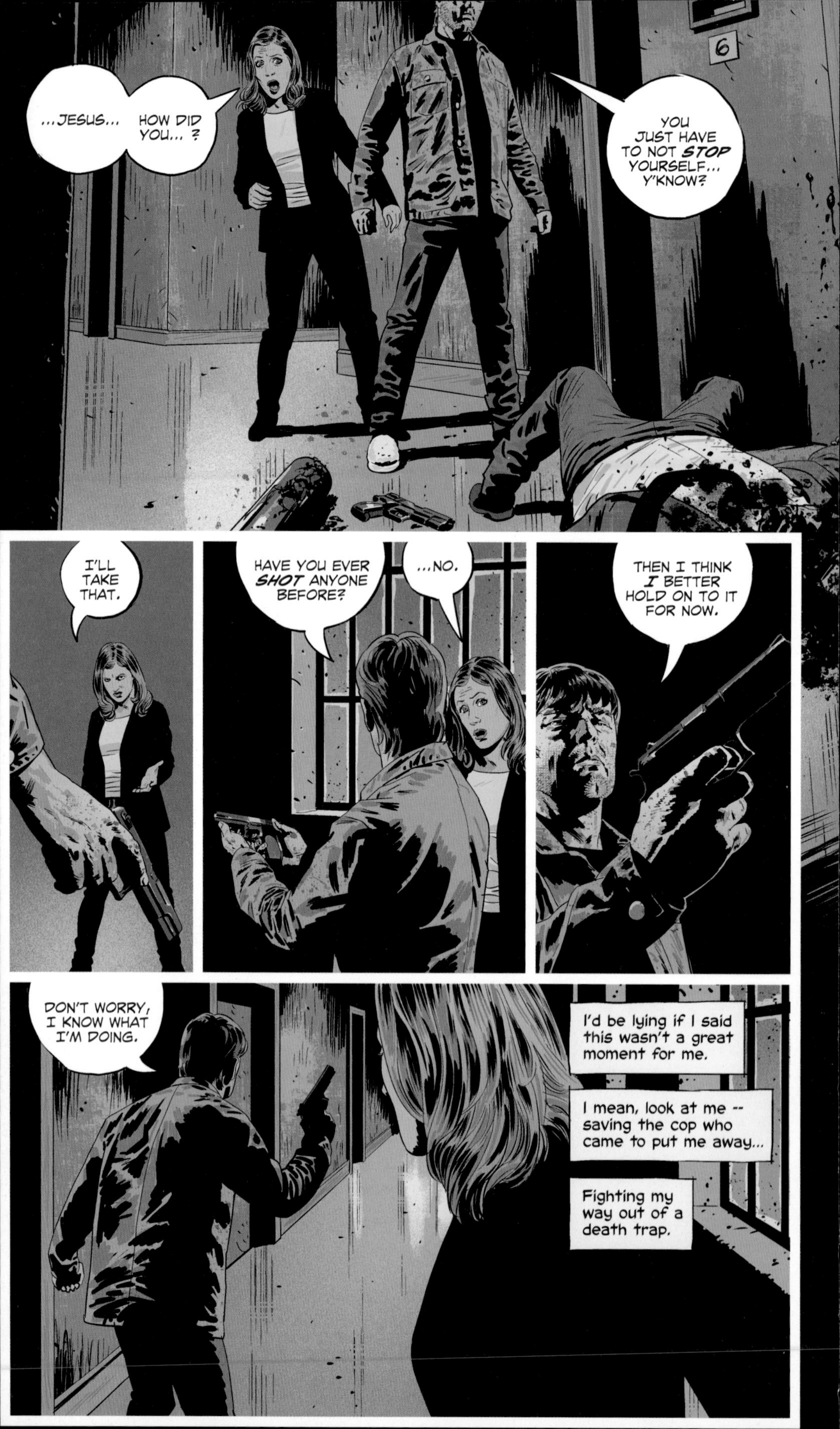
...JESUS...
HOW DID YOU... ?
YOU JUST HAVE TO NOT STOP YOURSELF... Y'KNOW?
I'LL TAKE THAT.
HAVE YOU EVER SHOT ANYONE BEFORE?
...NO.
THEN I THINK I BETTER HOLD ON TO IT FOR NOW.
DON'T WORRY, I KNOW WHAT I'M DOING.
I'd be lying if I said this wasn't a great moment for me.
I mean, look at me -- saving the cop who came to put me away...
Fighting my way out of a death trap.

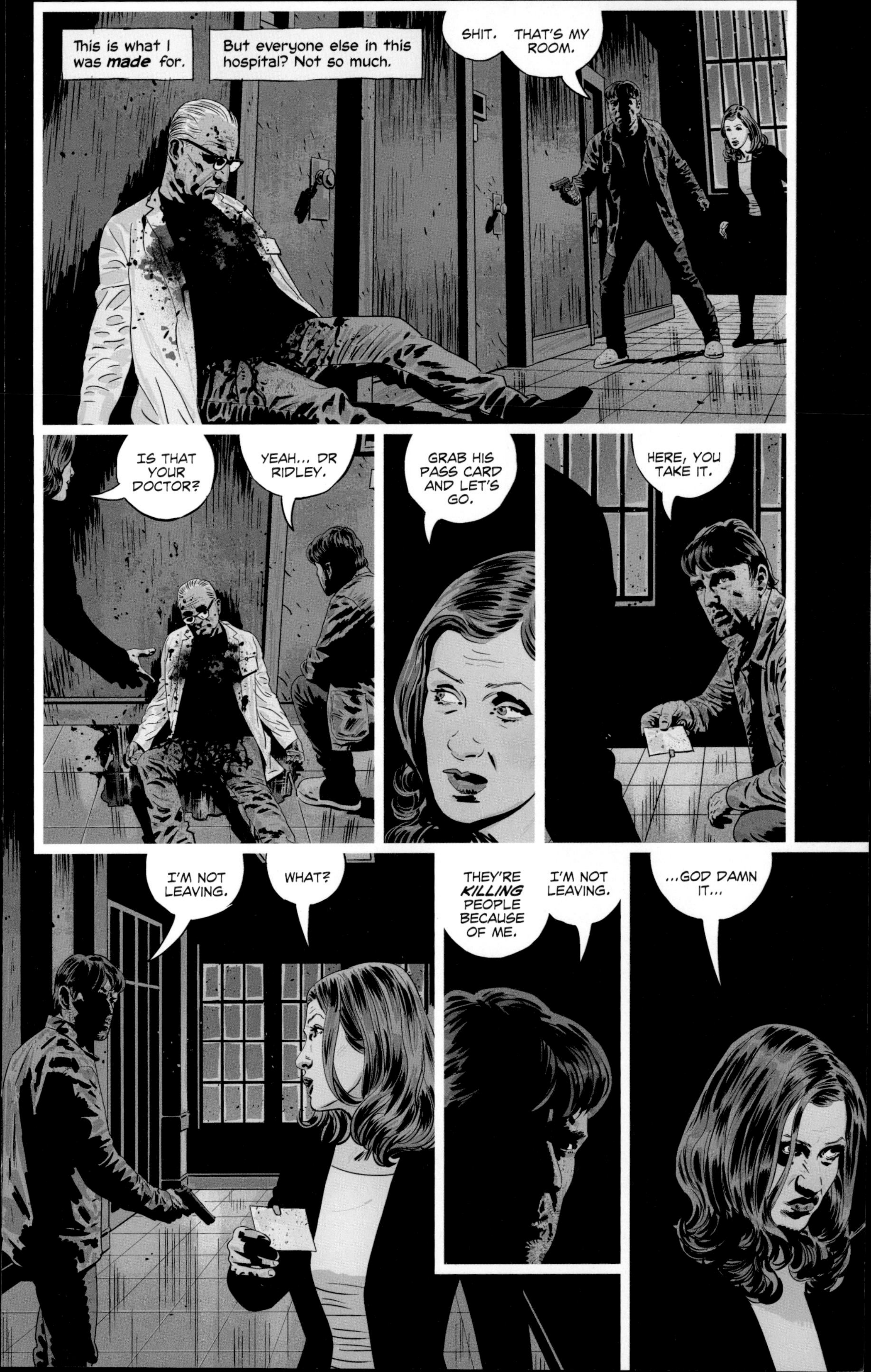
This is what I was *made* for.
But everyone else in this hospital? Not so much.
SHIT. THAT'S MY ROOM.
IS THAT YOUR DOCTOR?
YEAH... DR RIDLEY.
GRAB HIS PASS CARD AND LET'S GO.
HERE, YOU TAKE IT.
I'M NOT LEAVING.
WHAT?
THEY'RE *KILLING* PEOPLE BECAUSE OF ME.
I'M NOT LEAVING.
...GOD DAMN IT...

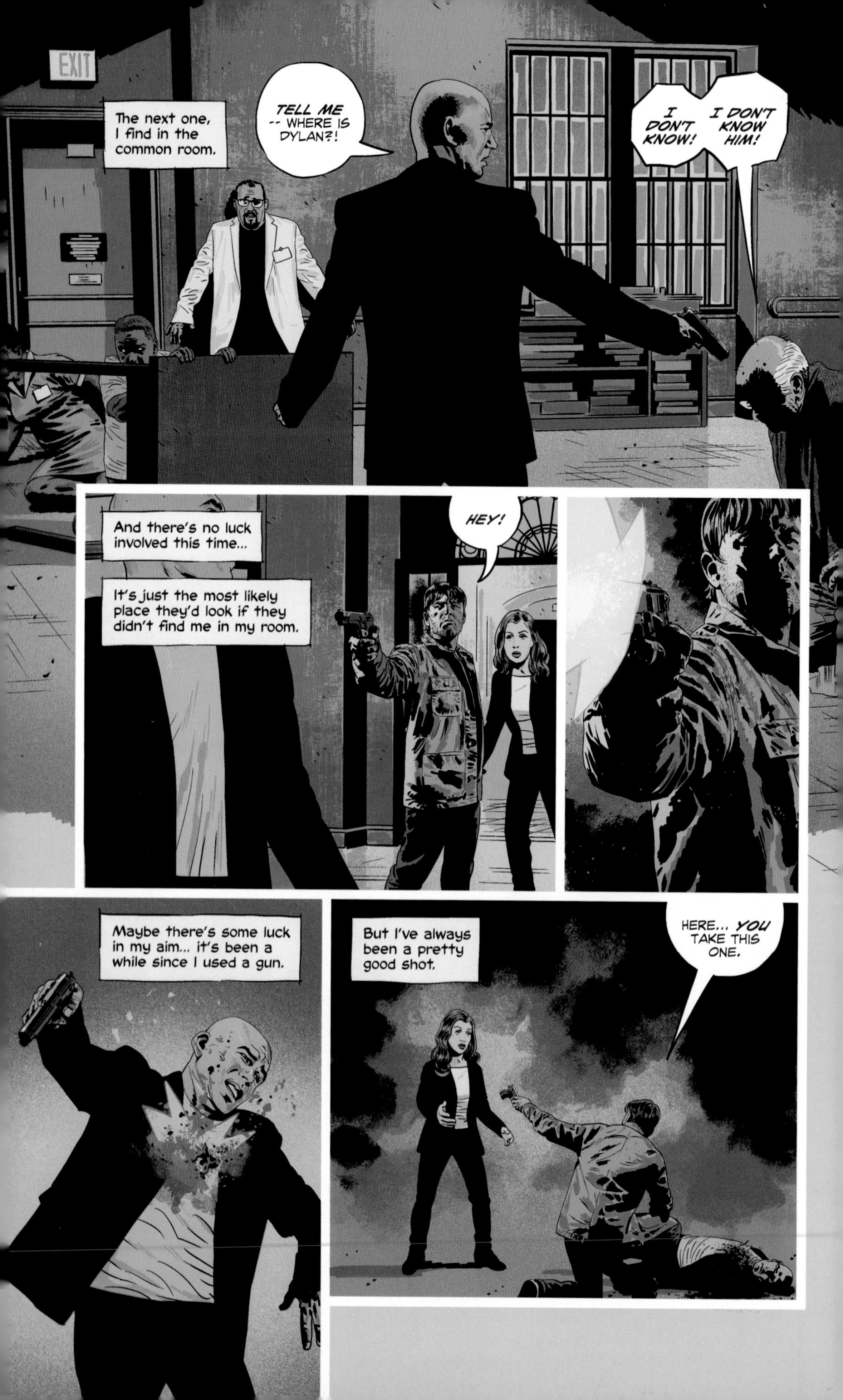
EXIT
The next one, I find in the common room.
TELL ME -- WHERE IS DYLAN?!
I DON'T KNOW!
I DON'T KNOW HIM!
And there's no luck involved this time...
It's just the most likely place they'd look if they didn't find me in my room.
HEY!
Maybe there's some luck in my aim... it's been a while since I used a gun.
But I've always been a pretty good shot.
HERE... YOU TAKE THIS ONE.

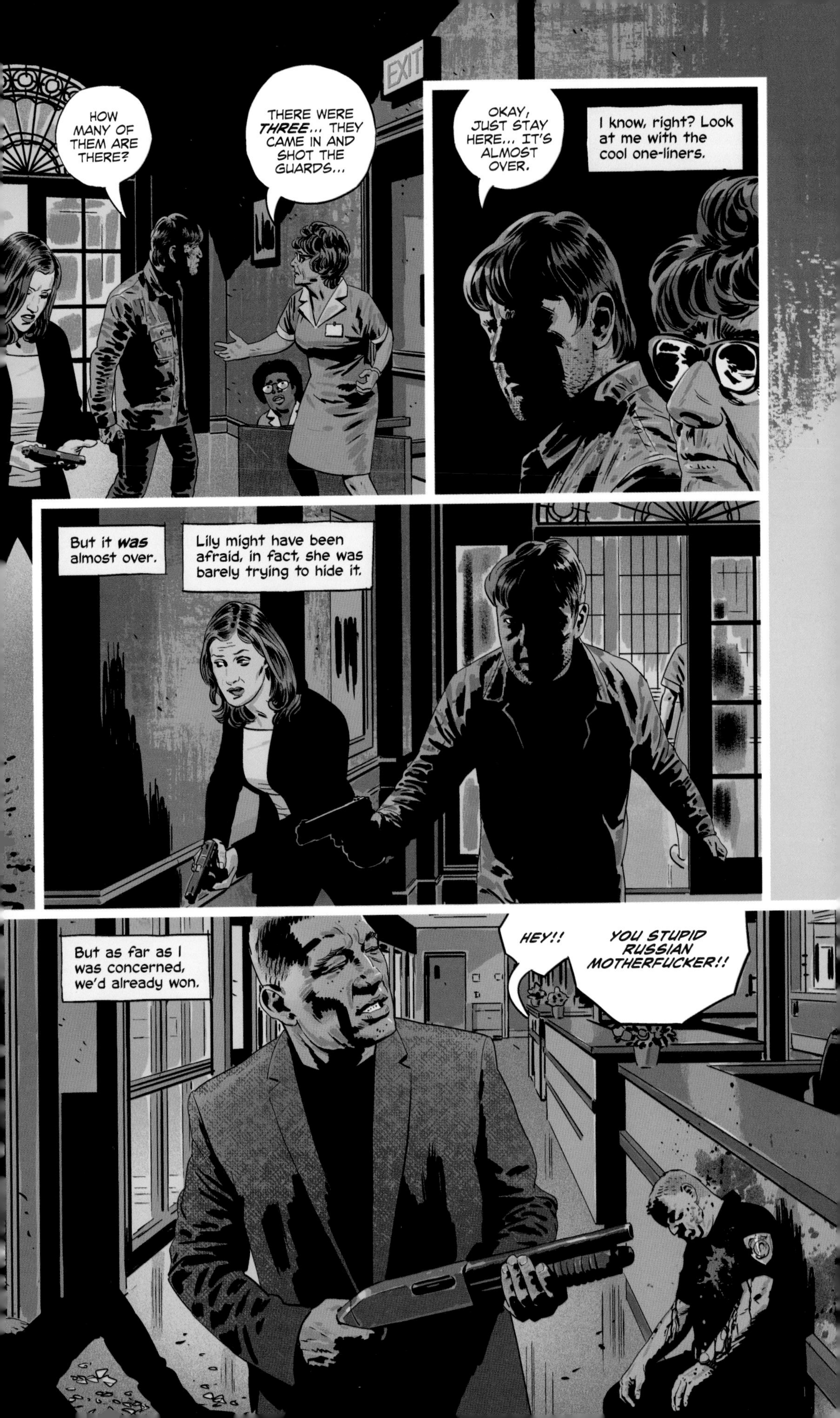
HOW MANY OF THEM ARE THERE?
THERE WERE *THREE*... THEY CAME IN AND SHOT THE GUARDS...
OKAY, JUST STAY HERE... IT'S ALMOST OVER.
I know, right? Look at me with the cool one-liners.
But it *was* almost over.
Lily might have been afraid, in fact, she was barely trying to hide it.
But as far as I was concerned, we'd already won.
HEY!!
YOU STUPID RUSSIAN MOTHERFUCKER!!
EXIT

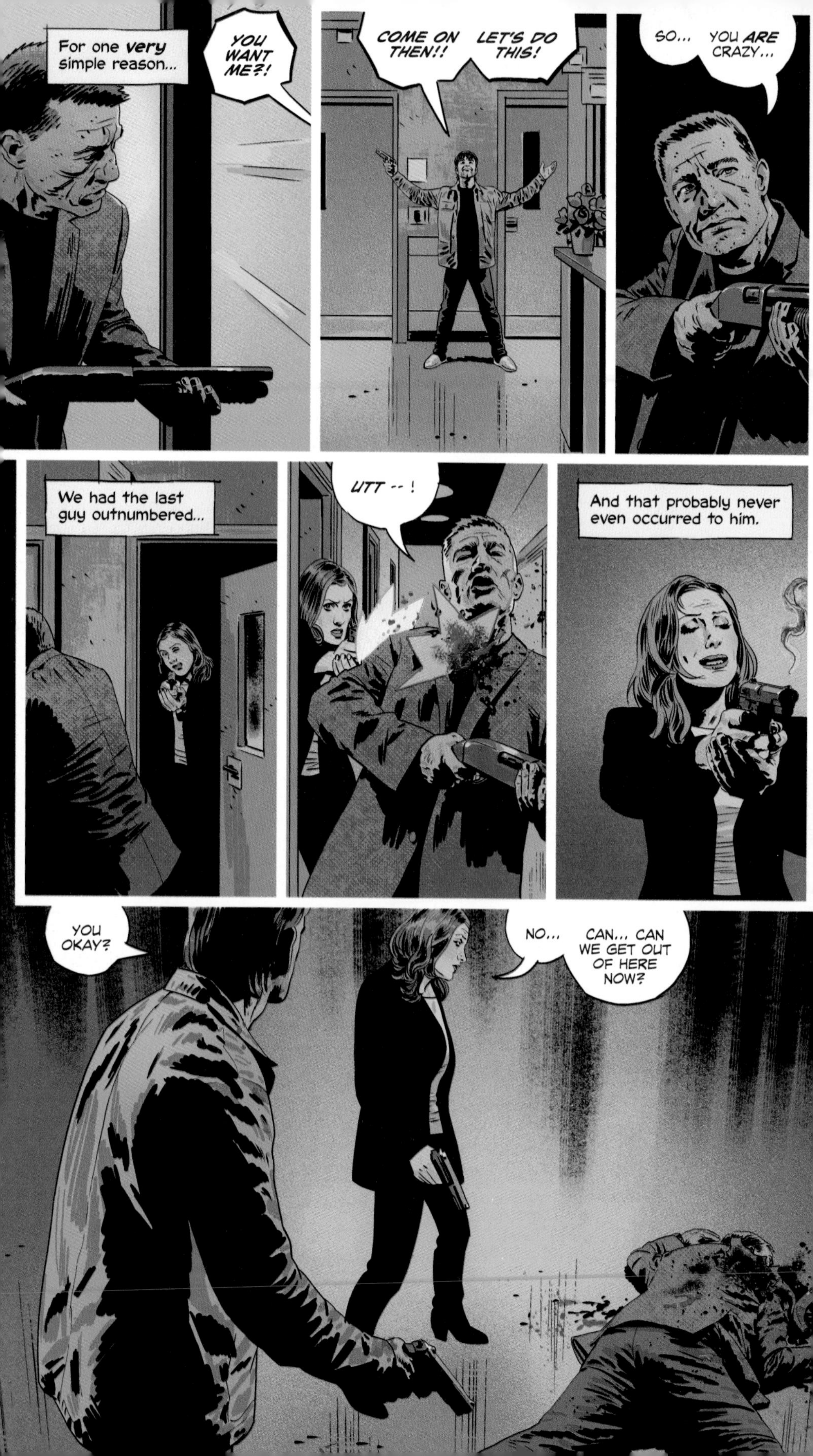
For one very simple reason...
YOU WANT ME?!
COME ON THEN!!
LET'S DO THIS!
SO... YOU ARE CRAZY...
We had the last guy outnumbered...
UTT -- !
And that probably never even occurred to him.
YOU OKAY?
NO...
CAN... CAN WE GET OUT OF HERE NOW?

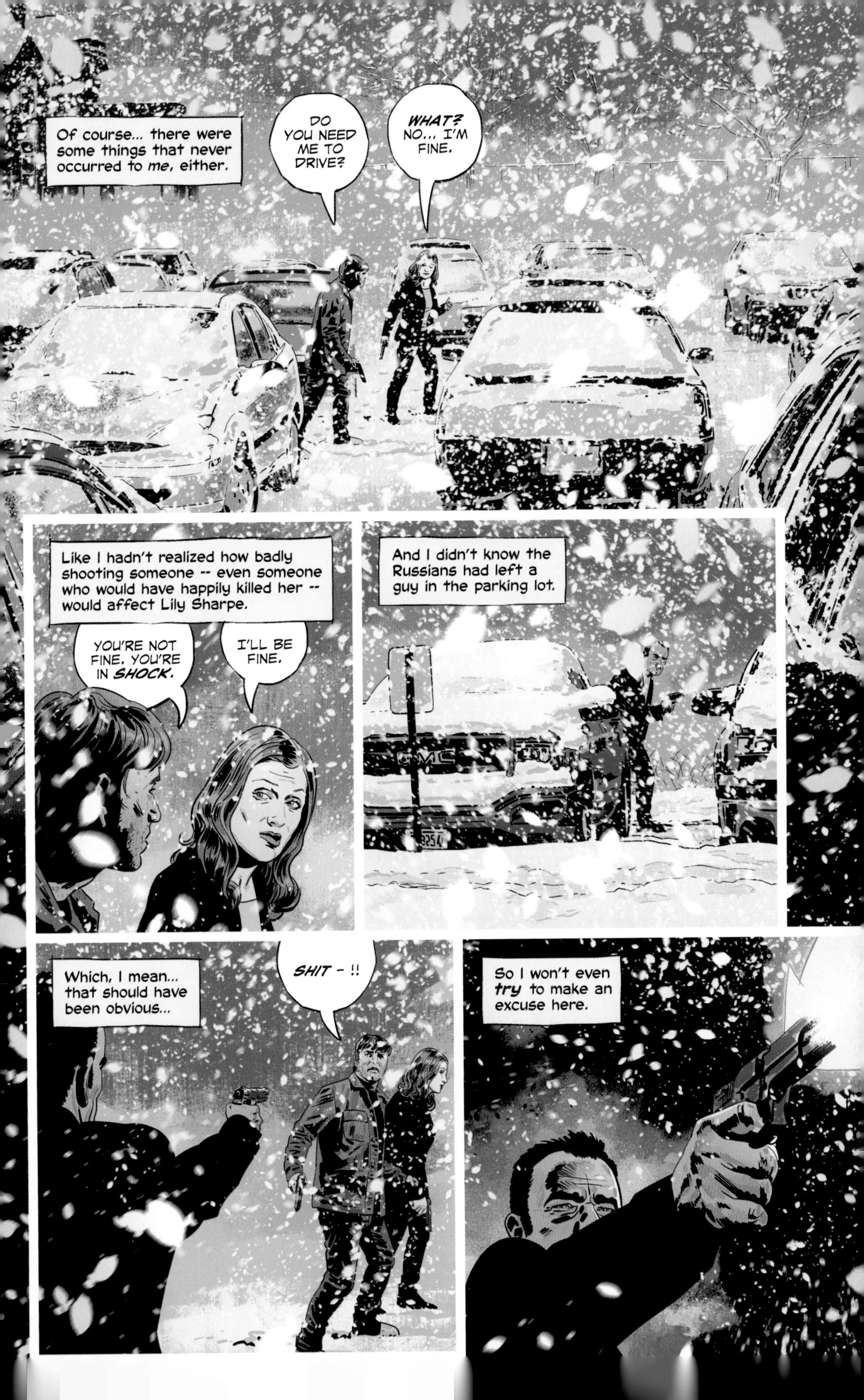
Of course... there were some things that never occurred to *me*, either.
DO YOU NEED ME TO DRIVE?
WHAT? NO... I'M FINE.
Like I hadn't realized how badly shooting someone -- even someone who would have happily killed her -- would affect Lily Sharpe.
YOU'RE NOT FINE. YOU'RE IN *SHOCK*.
I'LL BE FINE.
And I didn't know the Russians had left a guy in the parking lot.
Which, I mean... that should have been obvious...
SHIT - !!
So I won't even *try* to make an excuse here.

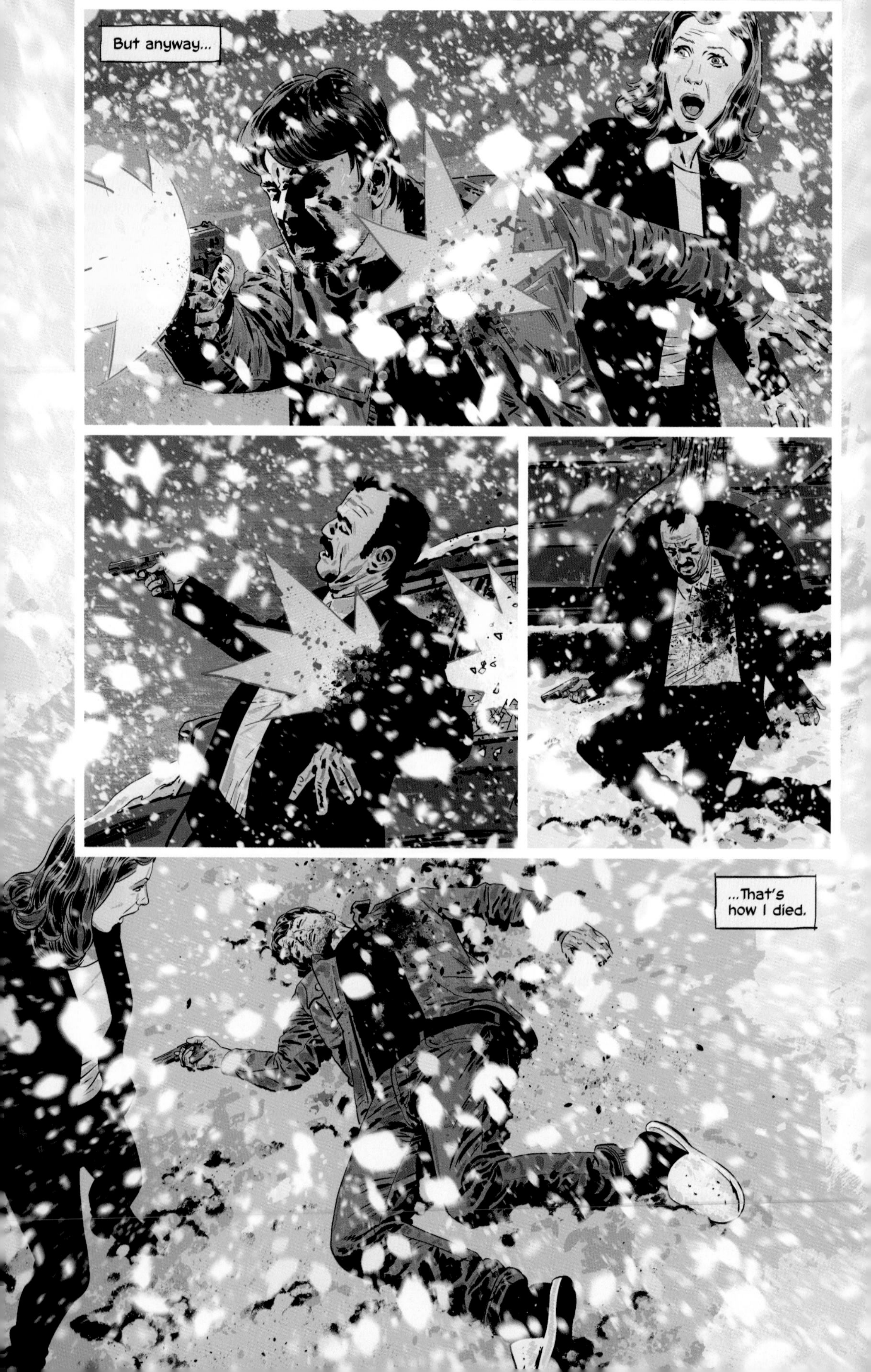
But anyway...
...That's how I died.

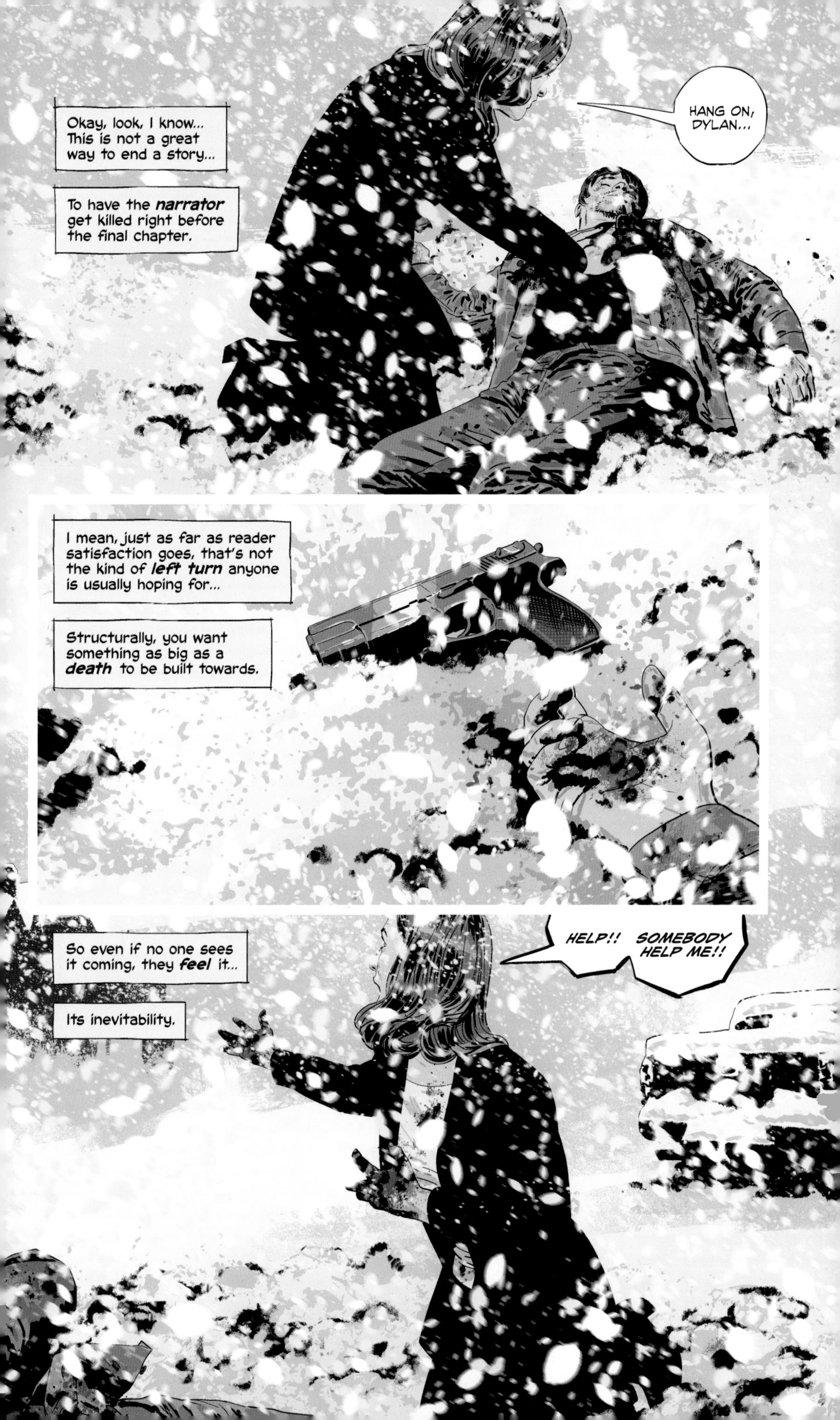
Okay, look, I know... This is not a great way to end a story...
To have the *narrator* get killed right before the final chapter.
HANG ON, DYLAN...
I mean, just as far as reader satisfaction goes, that's not the kind of *left turn* anyone is usually hoping for...
Structurally, you want something as big as a *death* to be built towards.
So even if no one sees it coming, they *feel* it...
Its inevitability.
HELP!! SOMEBODY HELP ME!!

But the thing is, life doesn't have a narrative structure.

Stuff just happens when it happens... and we just keep moving on.

Any shape your life has, you've added later... Trying to make sense of the chaos you spend your days inside of.

Like, 9-11 might feel like the culmination of something now.

Looking back, our minds turn it into a story -- into thousands of them, really.

And after almost twenty years of that, we forget what that day was really like... But I don't.

It was like, you know that scene in a movie when the heroes are driving along and everything seems fine...

And then a big fucking truck ***slams in*** from off camera?

It's a total cliché now, but that's what it felt like that day...

Like all of ***reality*** got hit by a Mack truck that we never saw coming.

That's what life - and especially death - is like.

Senseless and sudden.

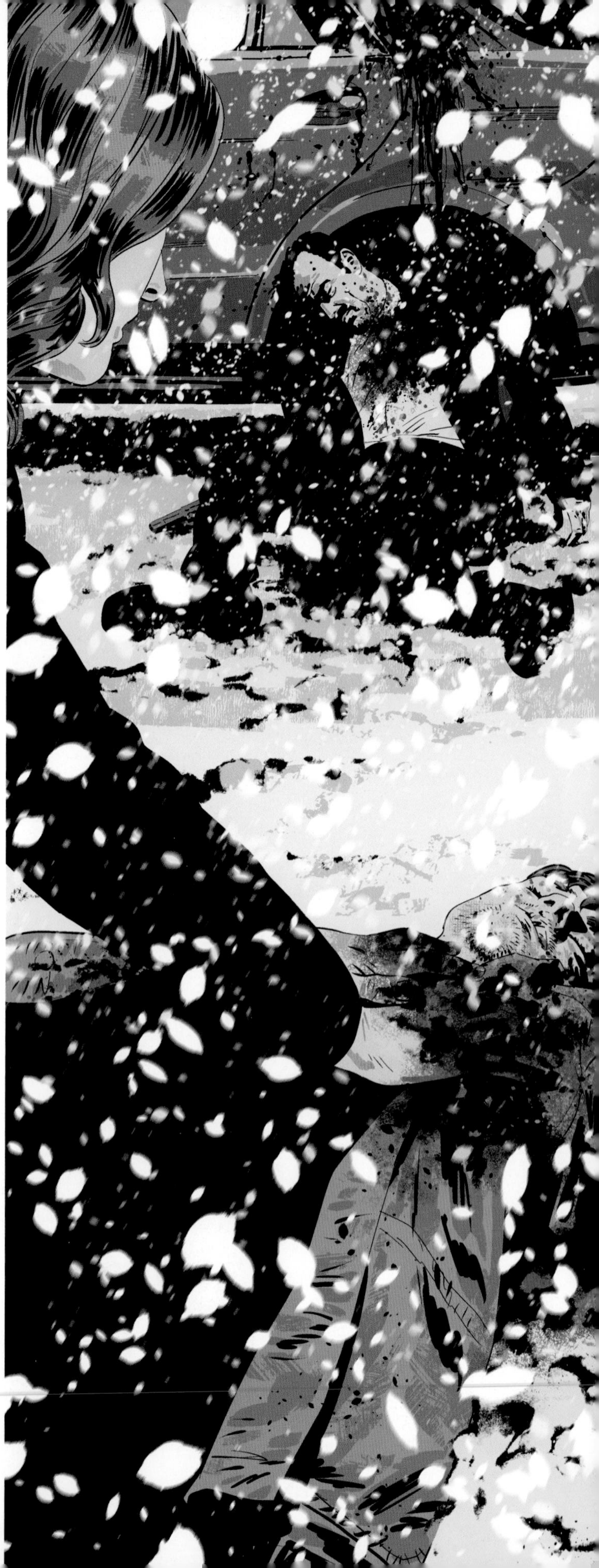

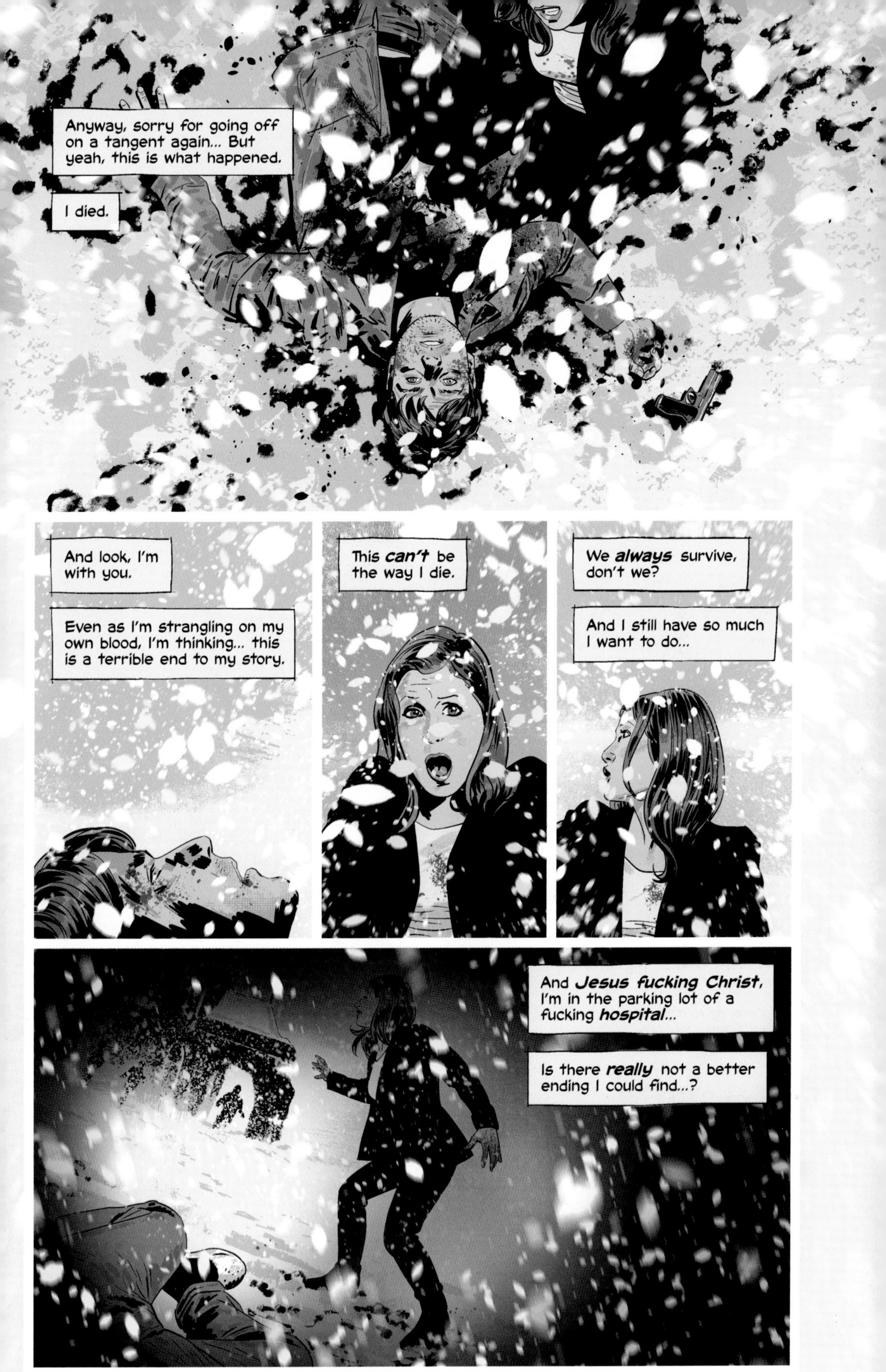
Anyway, sorry for going off on a tangent again... But yeah, this is what happened.
I died.
And look, I'm with you.
Even as I'm strangling on my own blood, I'm thinking... this is a terrible end to my story.
This *can't* be the way I die.
We *always* survive, don't we?
And I still have so much I want to do...
And *Jesus fucking Christ*, I'm in the parking lot of a fucking *hospital*...
Is there *really* not a better ending I could find...?

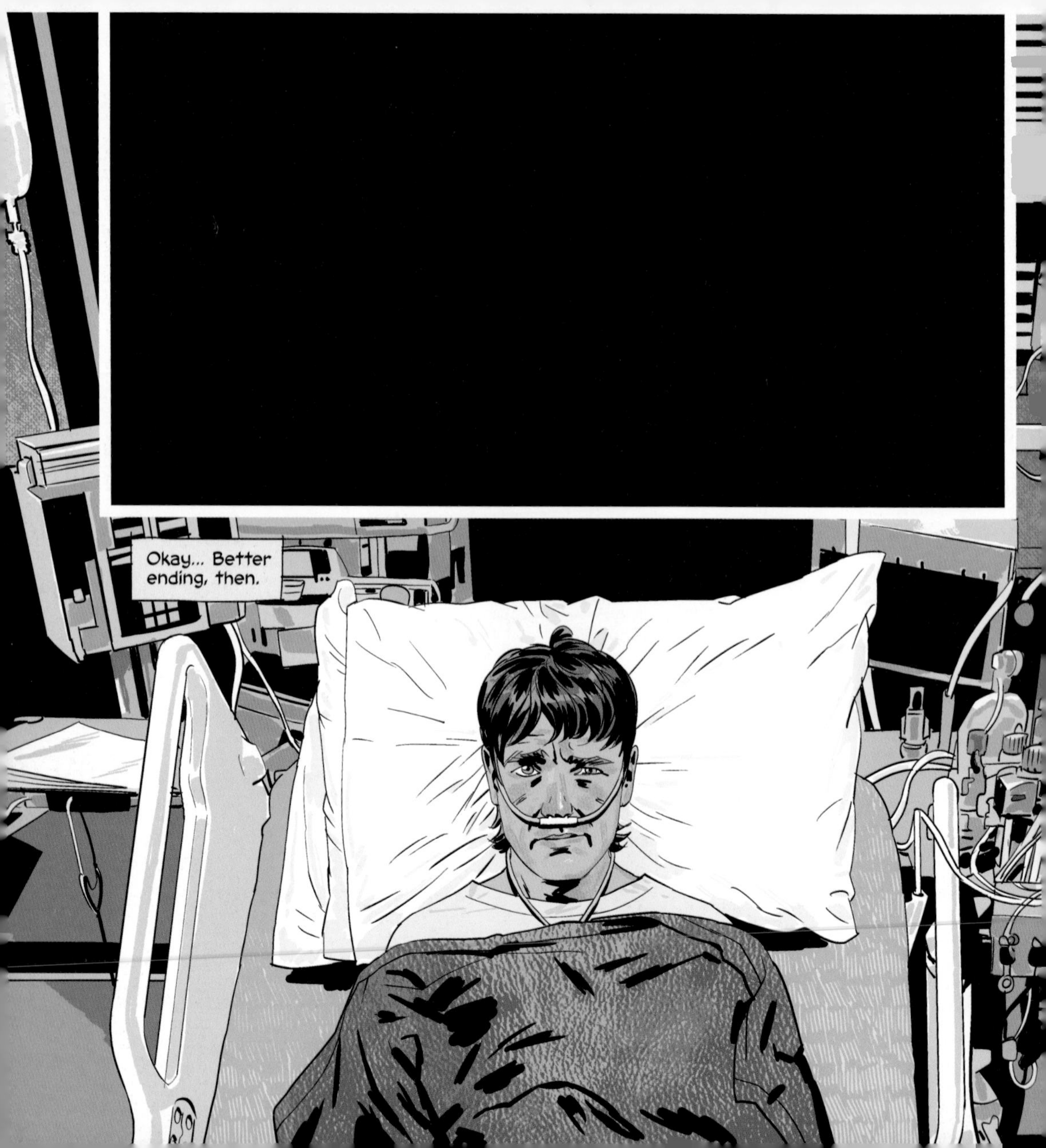
Okay... Better ending, then.

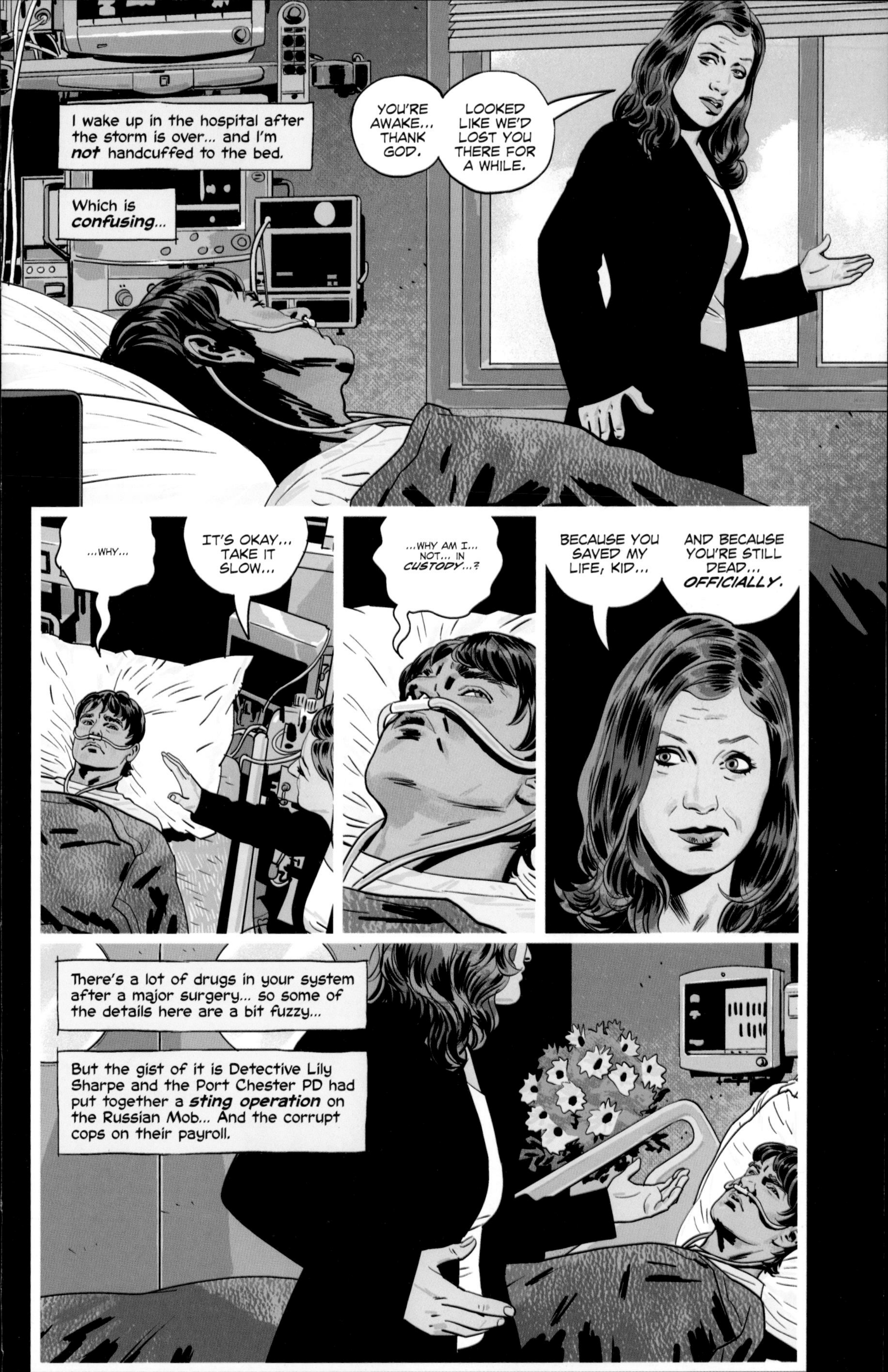
I wake up in the hospital after the storm is over... and I'm **not** handcuffed to the bed.
Which is **confusing**...
YOU'RE AWAKE... THANK GOD.
LOOKED LIKE WE'D LOST YOU THERE FOR A WHILE.
...WHY...
IT'S OKAY... TAKE IT SLOW...
...WHY AM I... NOT... IN **CUSTODY**...?
BECAUSE YOU SAVED MY LIFE, KID...
AND BECAUSE YOU'RE STILL DEAD... **OFFICIALLY.**
There's a lot of drugs in your system after a major surgery... so some of the details here are a bit fuzzy...
But the gist of it is Detective Lily Sharpe and the Port Chester PD had put together a **sting operation** on the Russian Mob... And the corrupt cops on their payroll.

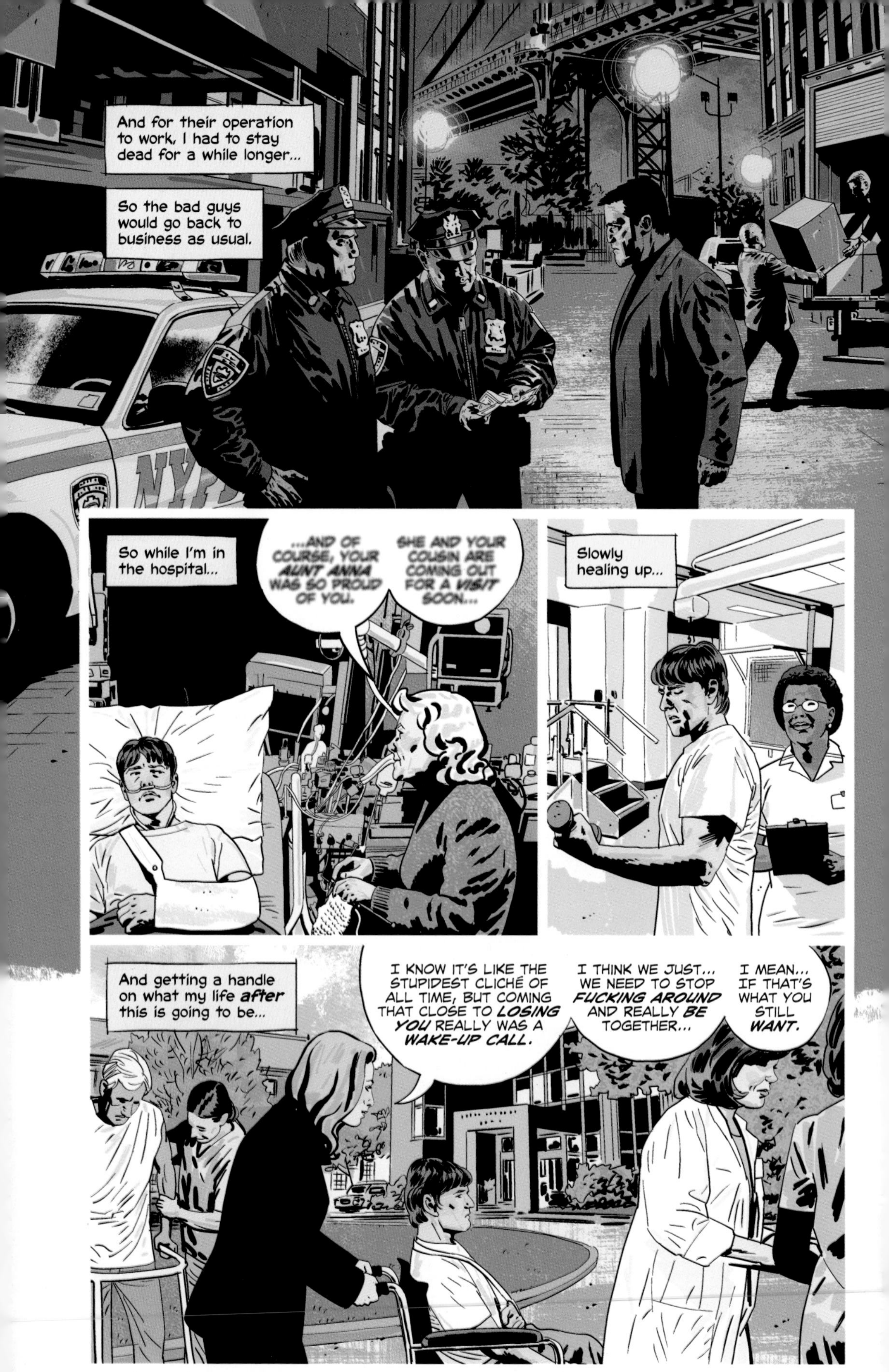

And for their operation to work, I had to stay dead for a while longer...
So the bad guys would go back to business as usual.
NYPD
So while I'm in the hospital...
...AND OF COURSE, YOUR AUNT ANNA WAS SO PROUD OF YOU.
SHE AND YOUR COUSIN ARE COMING OUT FOR A VISIT SOON...
Slowly healing up...
And getting a handle on what my life *after* this is going to be...
I KNOW IT'S LIKE THE STUPIDEST CLICHÉ OF ALL TIME, BUT COMING THAT CLOSE TO *LOSING YOU* REALLY WAS A *WAKE-UP CALL.*
I THINK WE JUST... WE NEED TO STOP *FUCKING AROUND* AND REALLY *BE* TOGETHER...
I MEAN... IF THAT'S WHAT YOU STILL *WANT.*

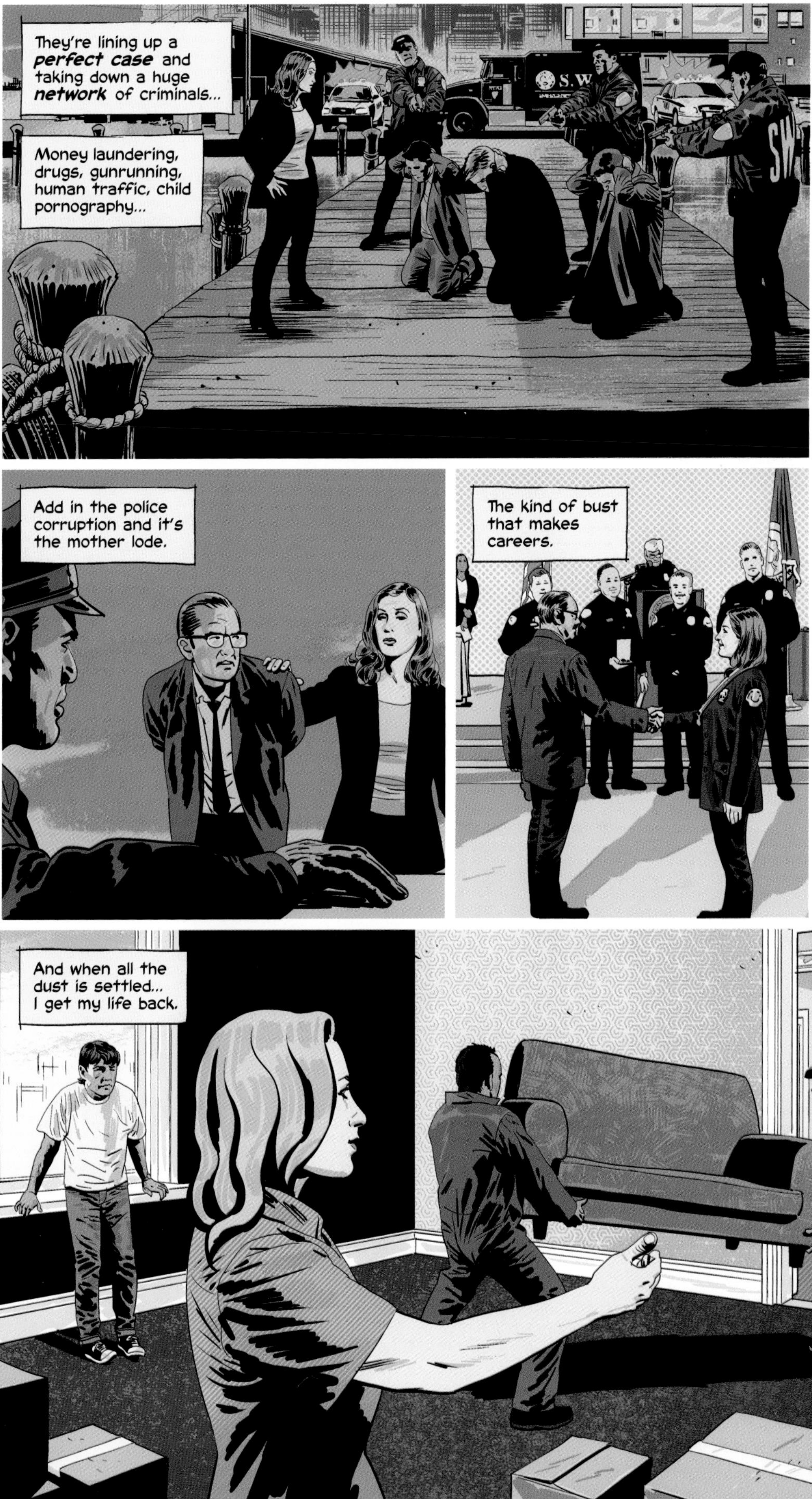
They're lining up a *perfect case* and taking down a huge *network* of criminals...
Money laundering, drugs, gunrunning, human traffic, child pornography...
Add in the police corruption and it's the mother lode.
The kind of bust that makes careers.
And when all the dust is settled... I get my life back.

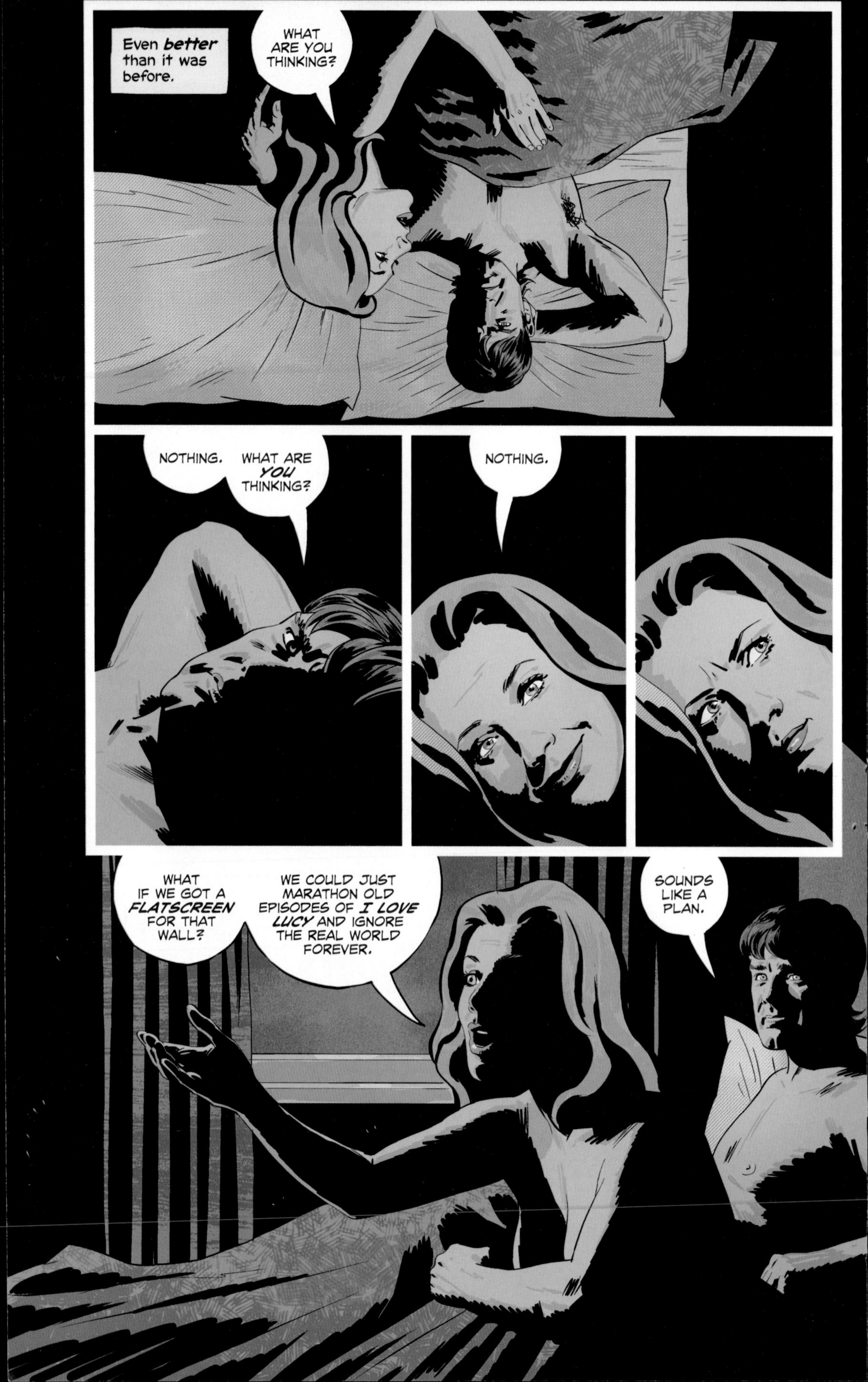
Even better than it was before.
WHAT ARE YOU THINKING?
NOTHING.
WHAT ARE YOU THINKING?
NOTHING.
WHAT IF WE GOT A FLATSCREEN FOR THAT WALL?
WE COULD JUST MARATHON OLD EPISODES OF I LOVE LUCY AND IGNORE THE REAL WORLD FOREVER.
SOUNDS LIKE A PLAN.

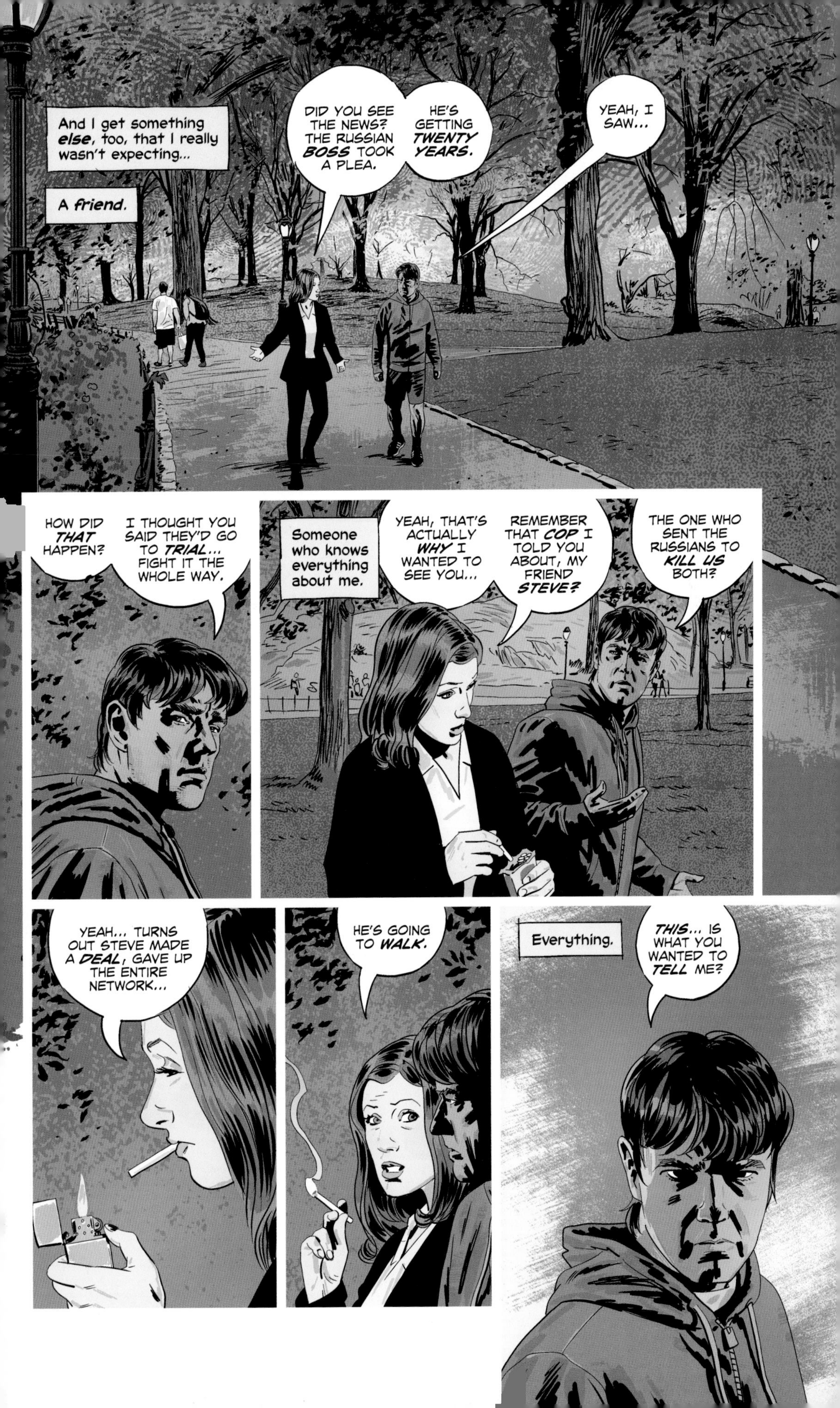
And I get something else, too, that I really wasn't expecting...
A friend.
DID YOU SEE THE NEWS? THE RUSSIAN BOSS TOOK A PLEA.
HE'S GETTING TWENTY YEARS.
YEAH, I SAW...
HOW DID THAT HAPPEN?
I THOUGHT YOU SAID THEY'D GO TO TRIAL... FIGHT IT THE WHOLE WAY.
Someone who knows everything about me.
YEAH, THAT'S ACTUALLY WHY I WANTED TO SEE YOU...
REMEMBER THAT COP I TOLD YOU ABOUT, MY FRIEND STEVE?
THE ONE WHO SENT THE RUSSIANS TO KILL US BOTH?
YEAH... TURNS OUT STEVE MADE A DEAL, GAVE UP THE ENTIRE NETWORK...
HE'S GOING TO WALK.
Everything.
THIS... IS WHAT YOU WANTED TO TELL ME?

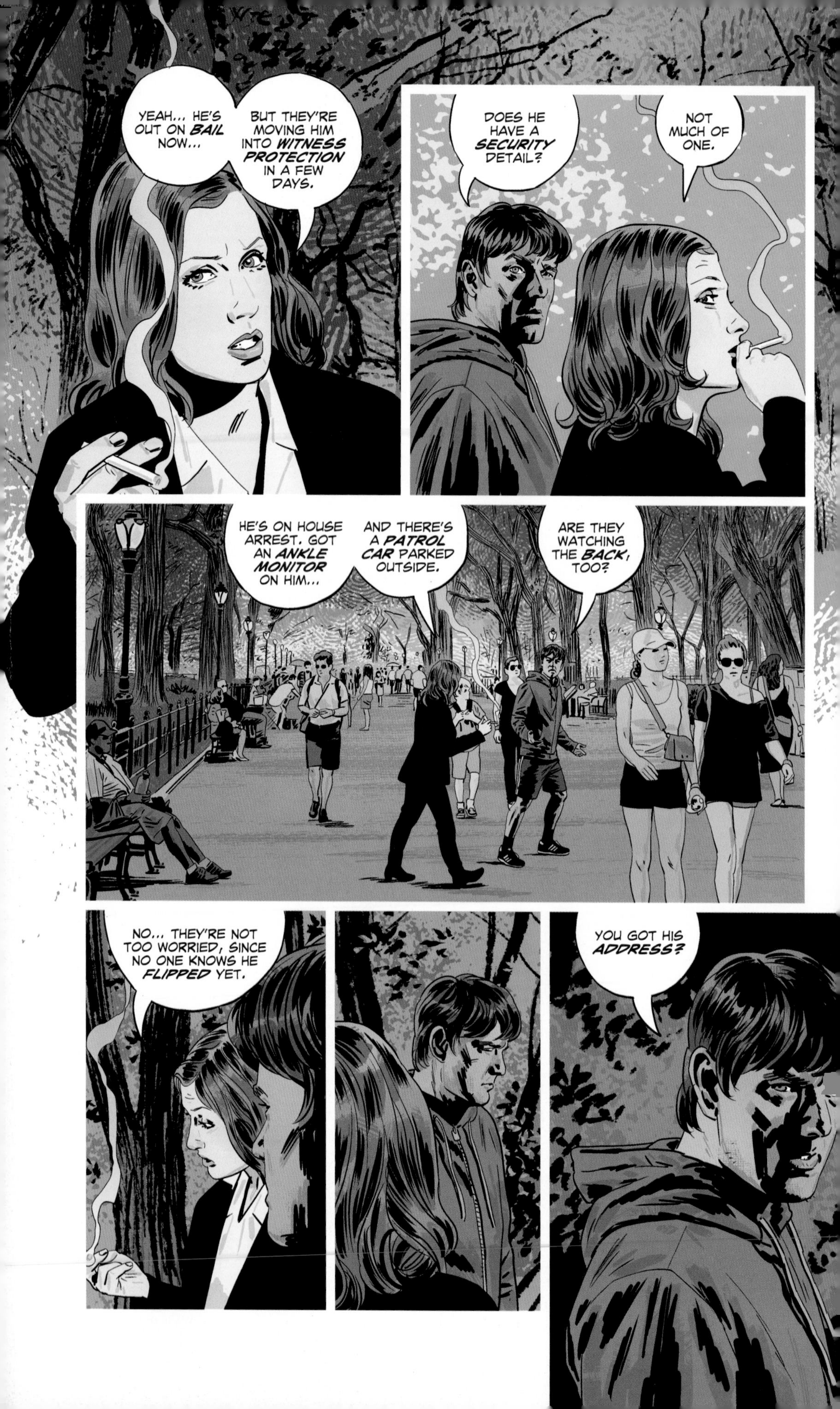
YEAH... HE'S OUT ON BAIL NOW...
BUT THEY'RE MOVING HIM INTO WITNESS PROTECTION IN A FEW DAYS.
DOES HE HAVE A SECURITY DETAIL?
NOT MUCH OF ONE.
HE'S ON HOUSE ARREST. GOT AN ANKLE MONITOR ON HIM...
AND THERE'S A PATROL CAR PARKED OUTSIDE.
ARE THEY WATCHING THE BACK, TOO?
NO... THEY'RE NOT TOO WORRIED, SINCE NO ONE KNOWS HE FLIPPED YET.
YOU GOT HIS ADDRESS?

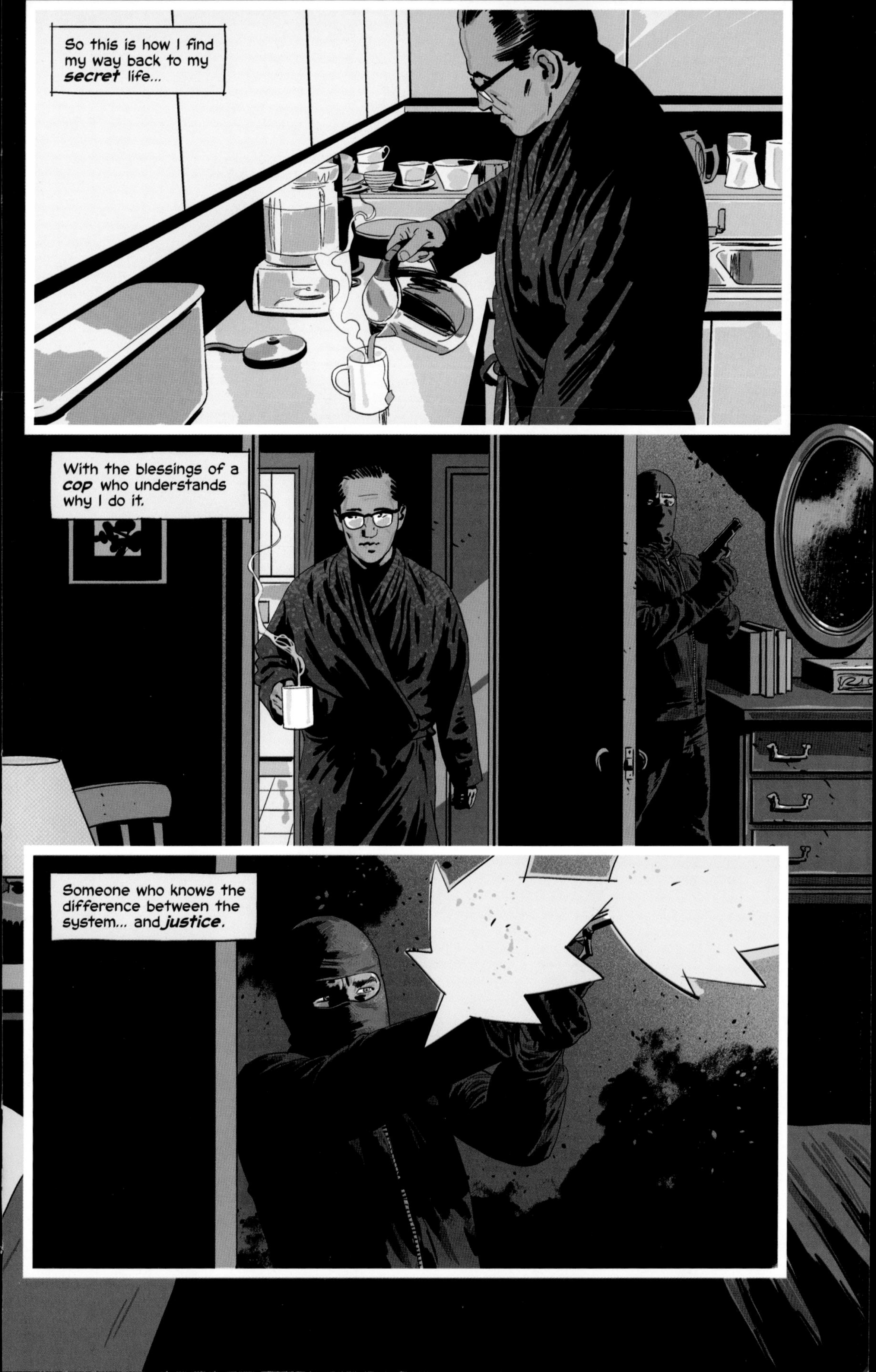
So this is how I find my way back to my *secret* life...
With the blessings of a *cop* who understands why I do it.
Someone who knows the difference between the system... and *justice*.

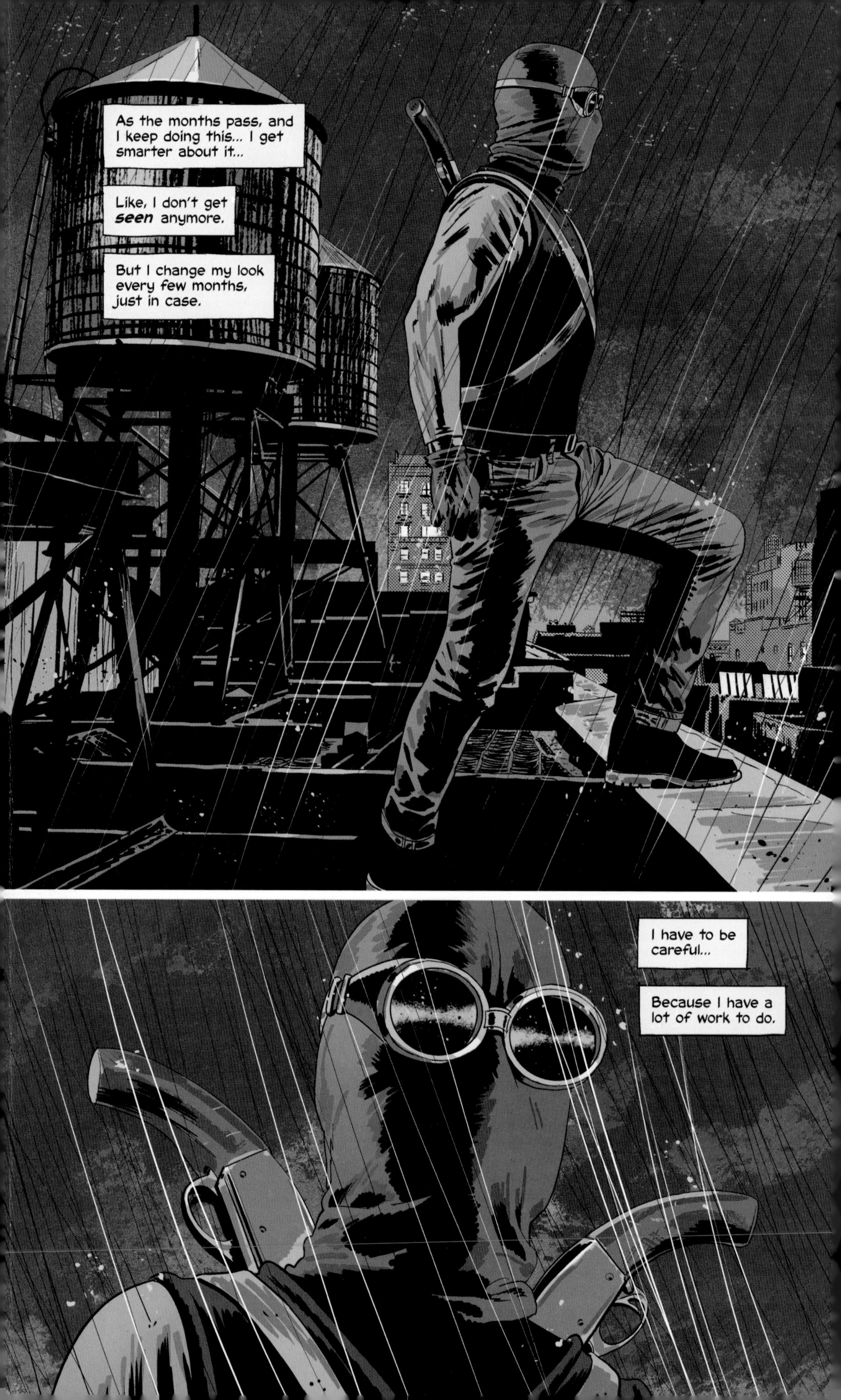
As the months pass, and I keep doing this... I get smarter about it...
Like, I don't get ***seen*** anymore.
But I change my look every few months, just in case.
I have to be careful...
Because I have a lot of work to do.

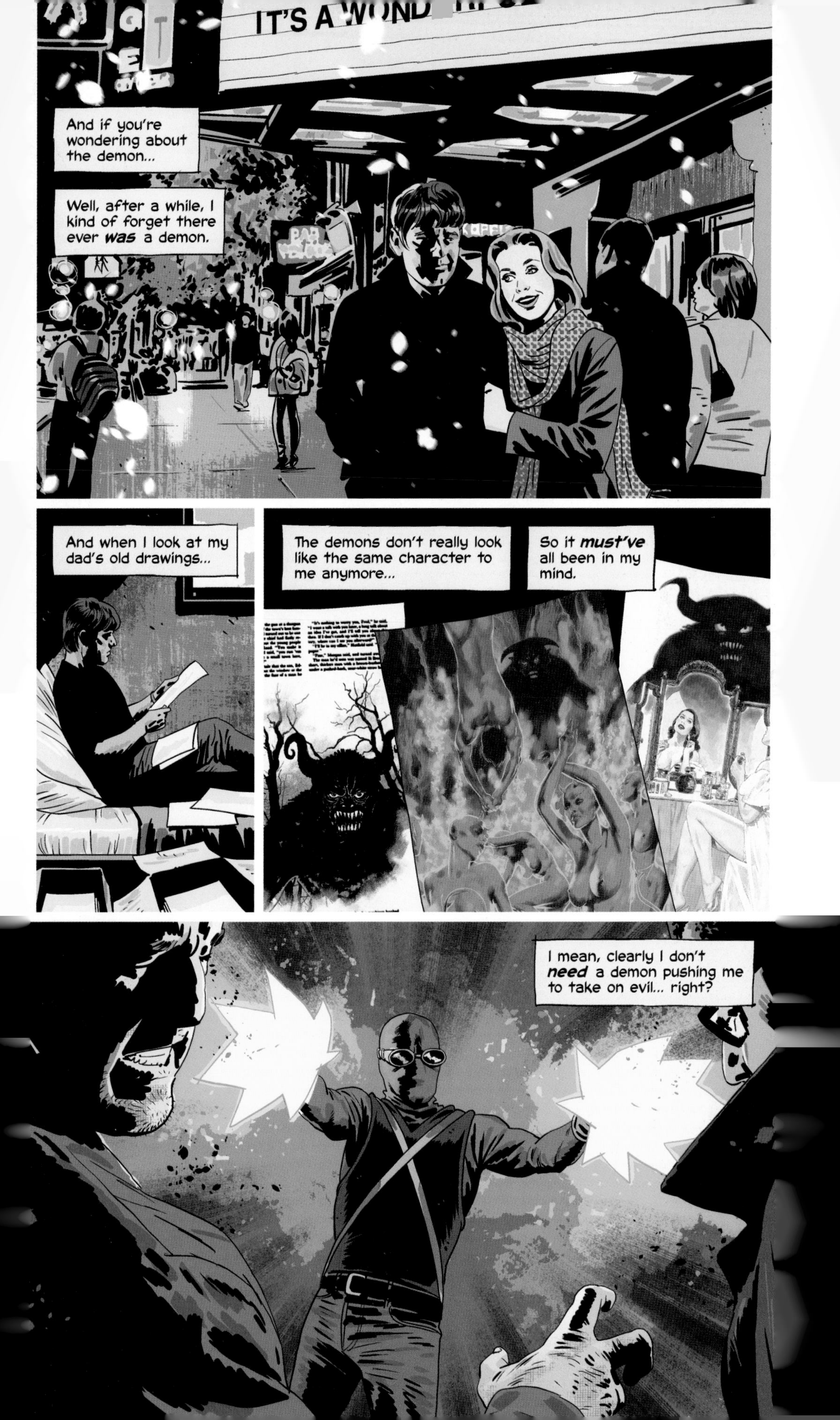
IT'S A WOND
And if you're wondering about the demon...
Well, after a while, I kind of forget there ever ***was*** a demon.
And when I look at my dad's old drawings...
The demons don't really look like the same character to me anymore...
So it ***must've*** all been in my mind.
I mean, clearly I don't ***need*** a demon pushing me to take on evil... right?

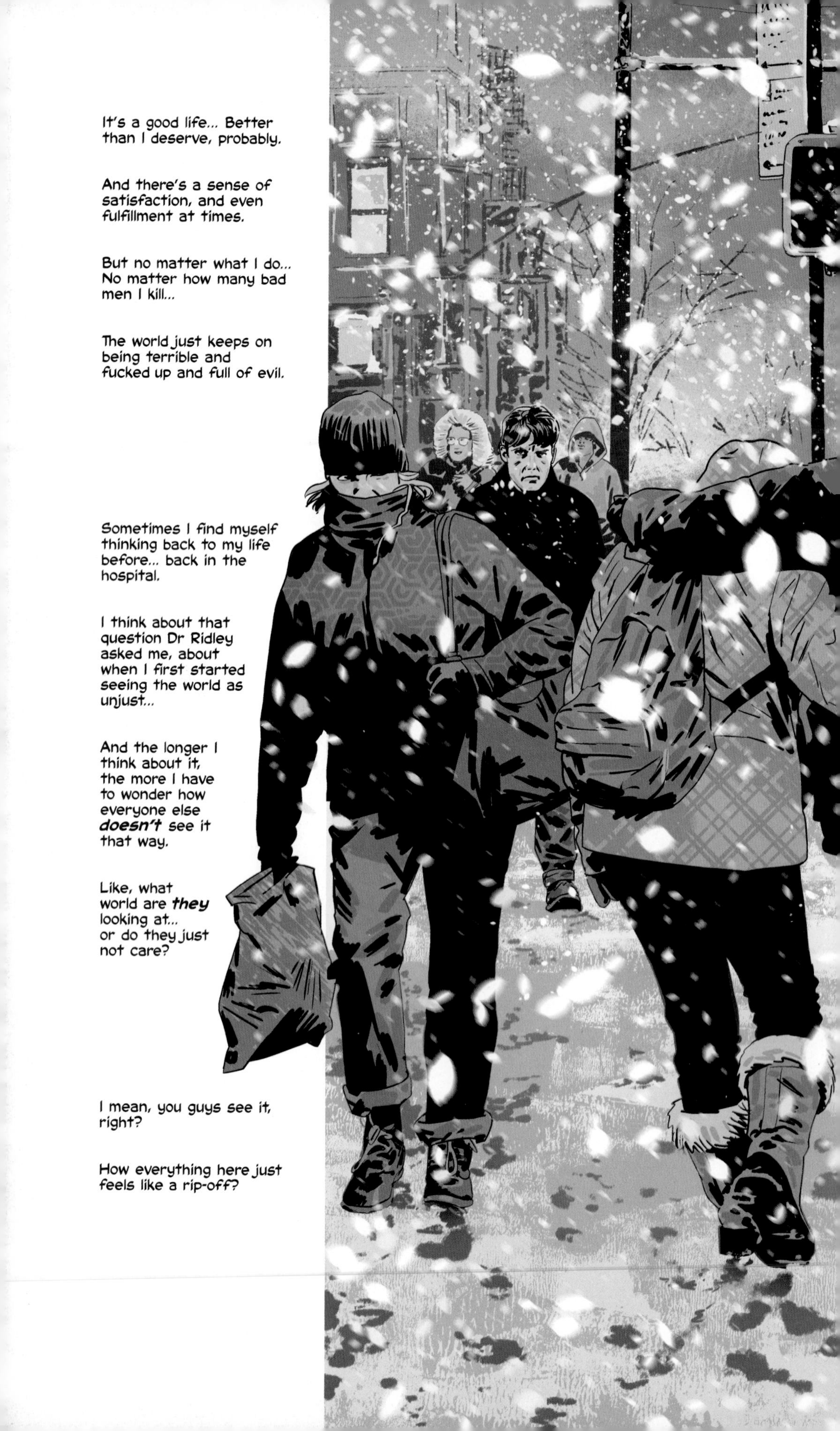
It's a good life... Better than I deserve, probably.
And there's a sense of satisfaction, and even fulfillment at times.
But no matter what I do... No matter how many bad men I kill...
The world just keeps on being terrible and fucked up and full of evil.
Sometimes I find myself thinking back to my life before... back in the hospital.
I think about that question Dr Ridley asked me, about when I first started seeing the world as unjust...
And the longer I think about it, the more I have to wonder how everyone else ***doesn't*** see it that way.
Like, what world are ***they*** looking at... or do they just not care?
I mean, you guys see it, right?
How everything here just feels like a rip-off?

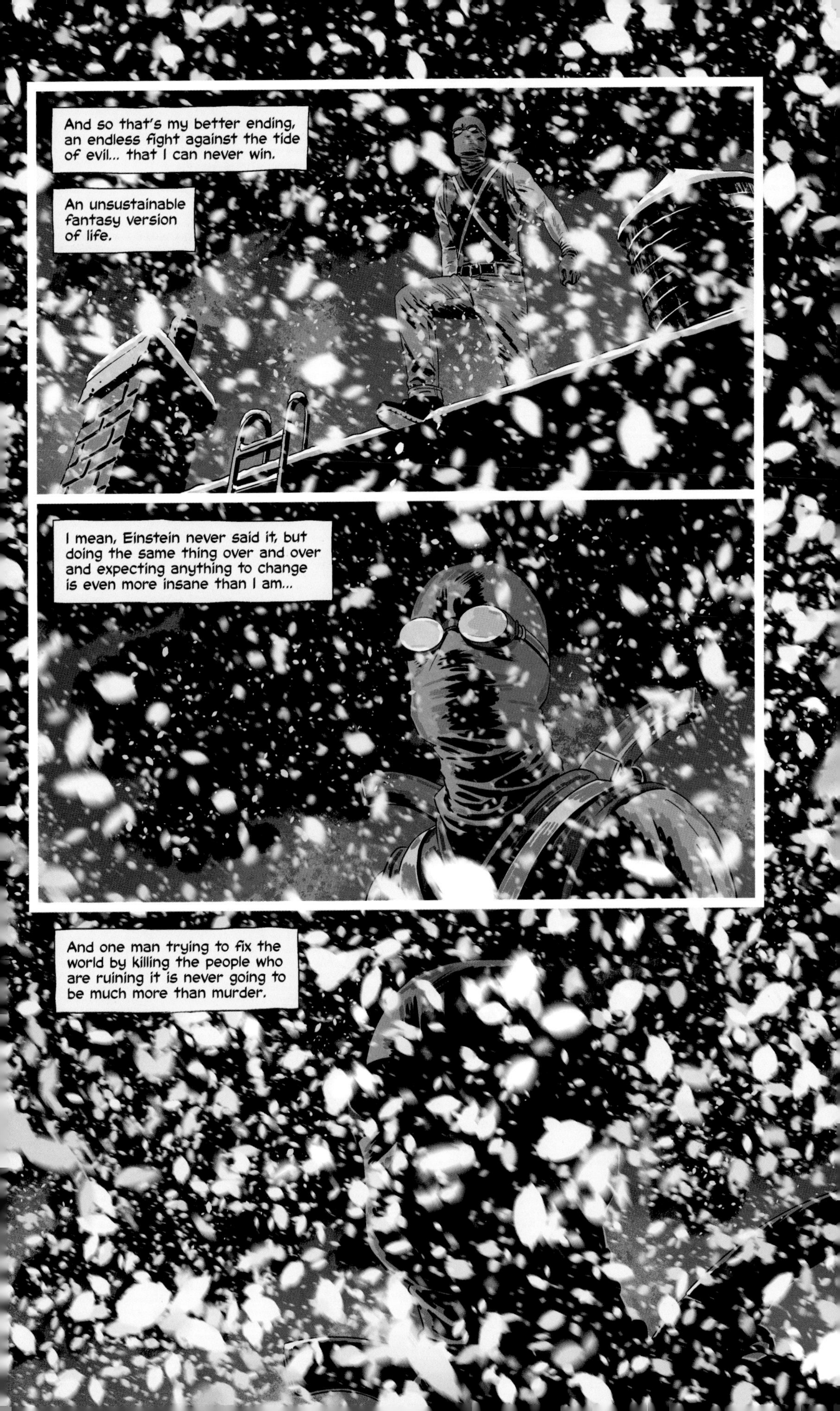
And so that's my better ending, an endless fight against the tide of evil... that I can never win.
An unsustainable fantasy version of life.
I mean, Einstein never said it, but doing the same thing over and over and expecting anything to change is even more insane than I am...
And one man trying to fix the world by killing the people who are ruining it is never going to be much more than murder.

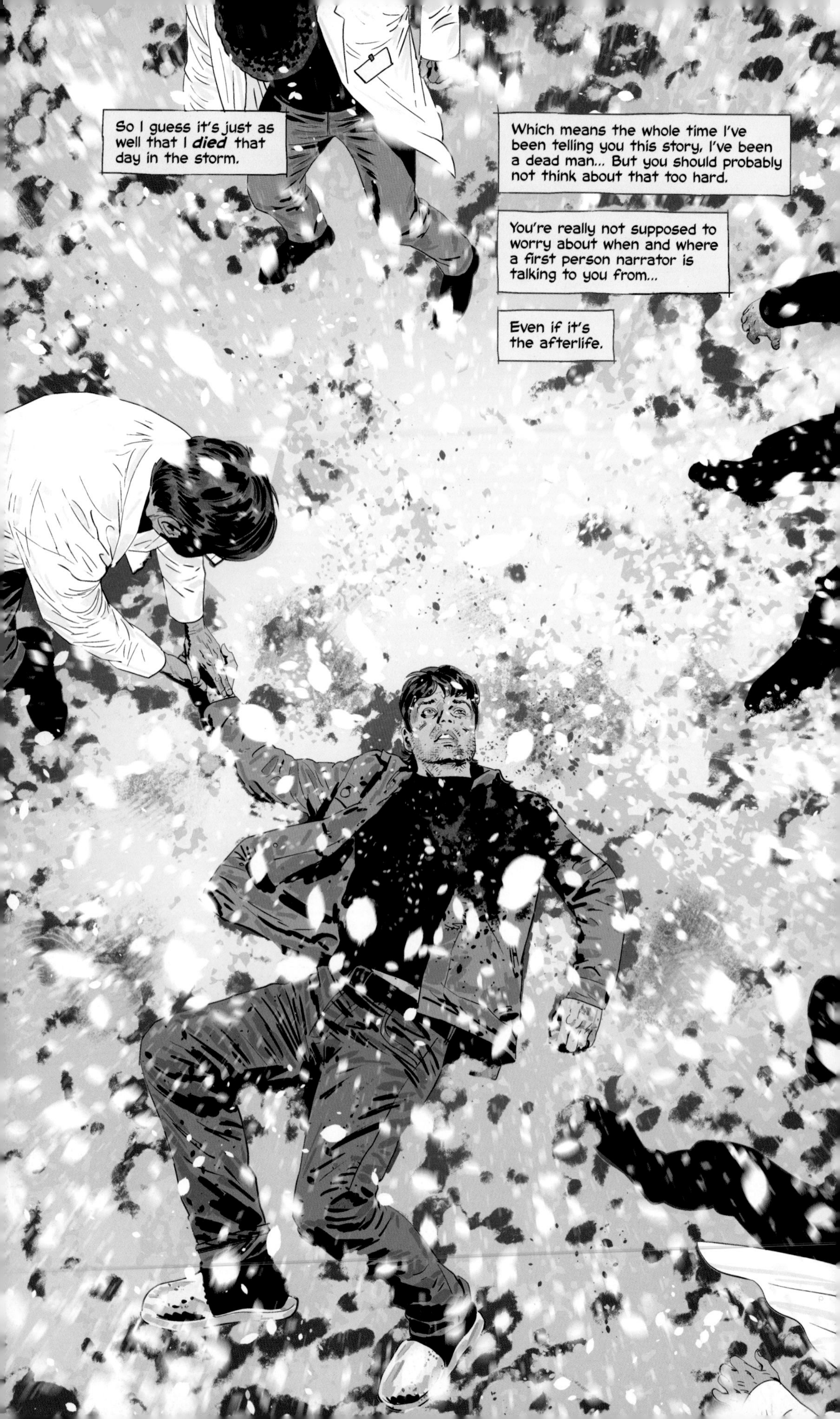
So I guess it's just as well that I *died* that day in the storm.
Which means the whole time I've been telling you this story, I've been a dead man... But you should probably not think about that too hard.
You're really not supposed to worry about when and where a first person narrator is talking to you from...
Even if it's the afterlife.

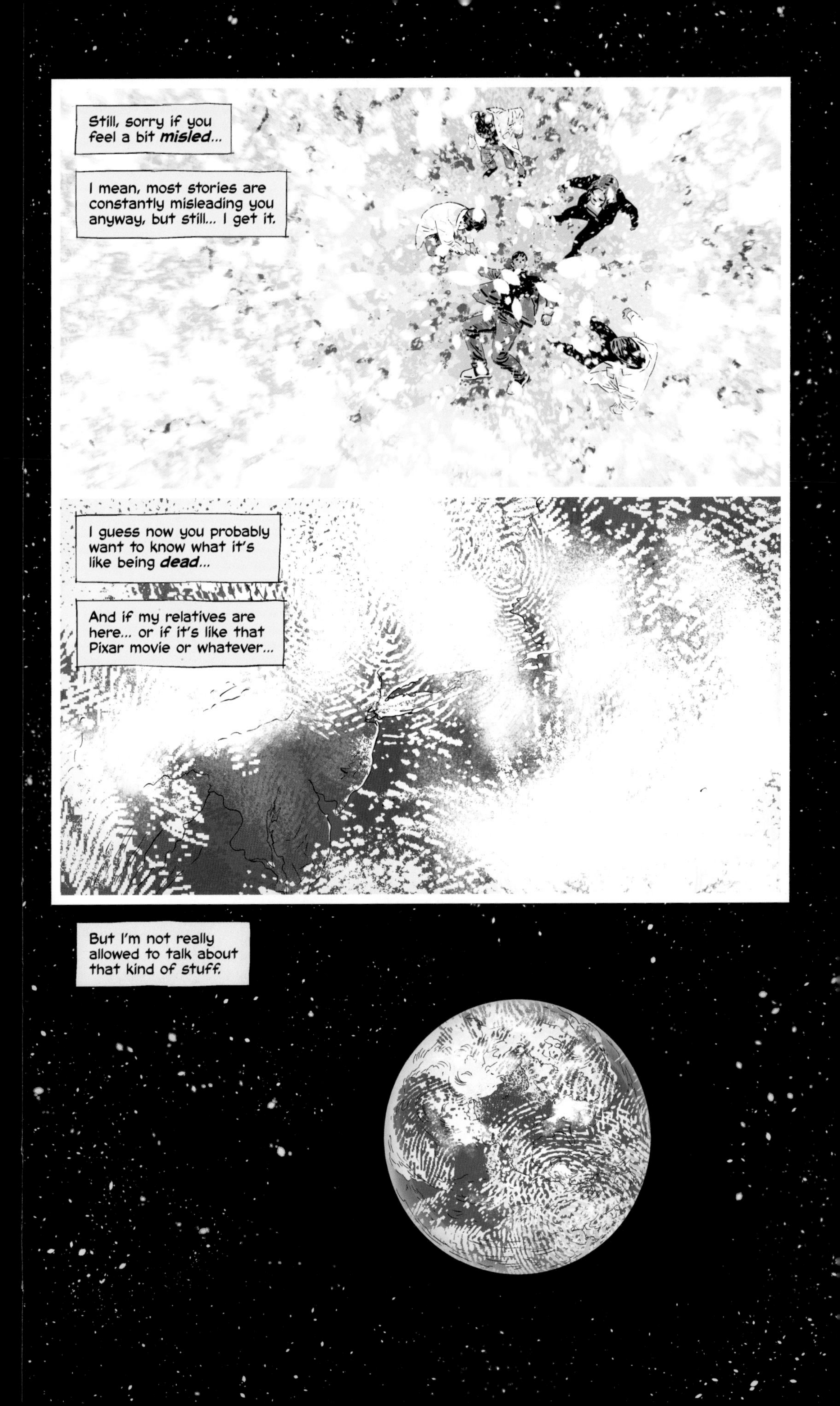
Still, sorry if you feel a bit misled...
I mean, most stories are constantly misleading you anyway, but still... I get it.
I guess now you probably want to know what it's like being dead...
And if my relatives are here... or if it's like that Pixar movie or whatever...
But I'm not really allowed to talk about that kind of stuff.

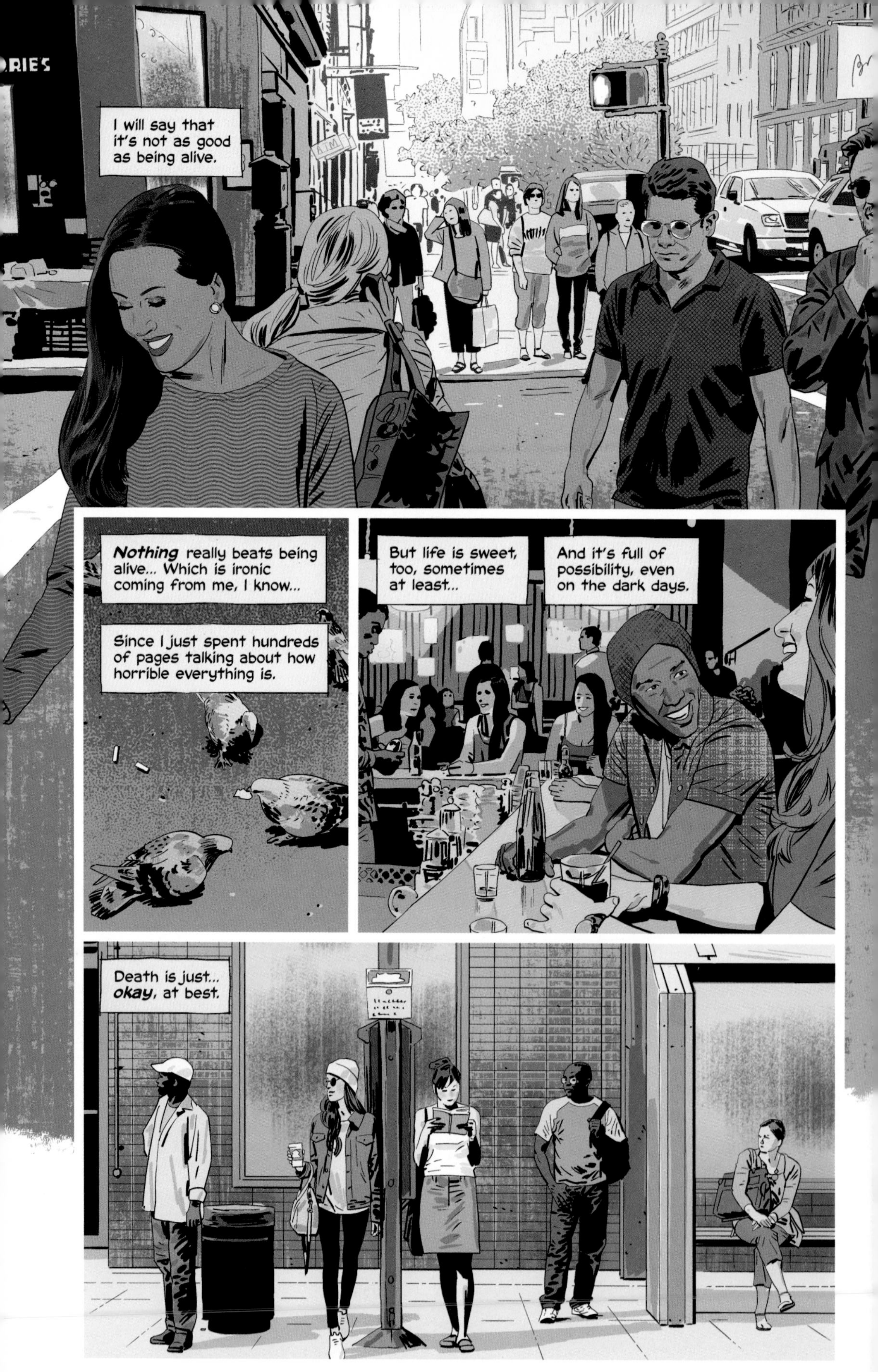
RIES
I will say that it's not as good as being alive.
Nothing really beats being alive... Which is ironic coming from me, I know...
Since I just spent hundreds of pages talking about how horrible everything is.
But life is sweet, too, sometimes at least...
And it's full of possibility, even on the dark days.
Death is just... *okay*, at best.

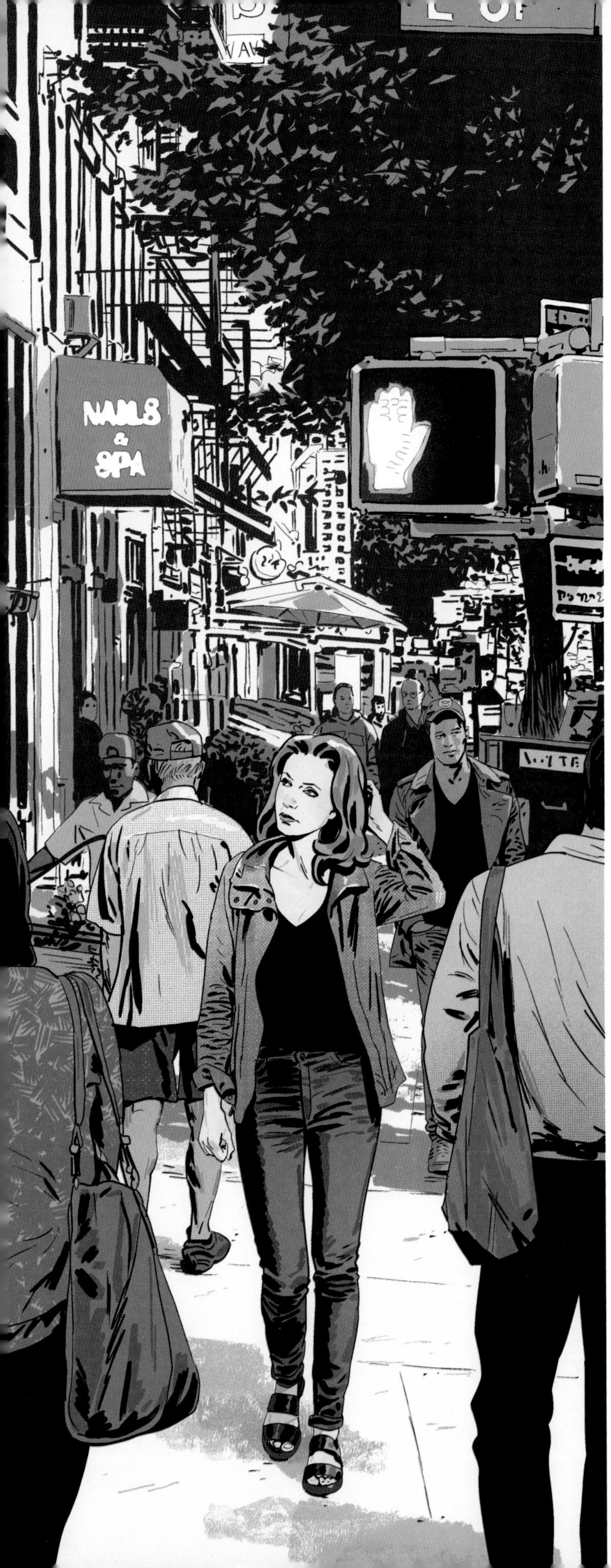
NAILS
&
SPA

I'll probably get in trouble for telling you that, and for talking about all that other stuff...

The vigilante thing and my mental issues.

I'm not just breaking narrative rules here, like I said, there are afterlife rules, too.

But I was never good at rules...

And really, I just wanted to talk about everything again.

I thought it would make me feel better to tell someone, but it didn't...

It just made me miss everybody.

Kira... Mom and Dad... Rex, my friends from school... Even that asshole Mason, kind of.

And I miss the world, too... the one I thought it was going to be, before I realized how fucked it was.

Man, it could've been such a great place, you know?

I guess that's all I wanted to say.

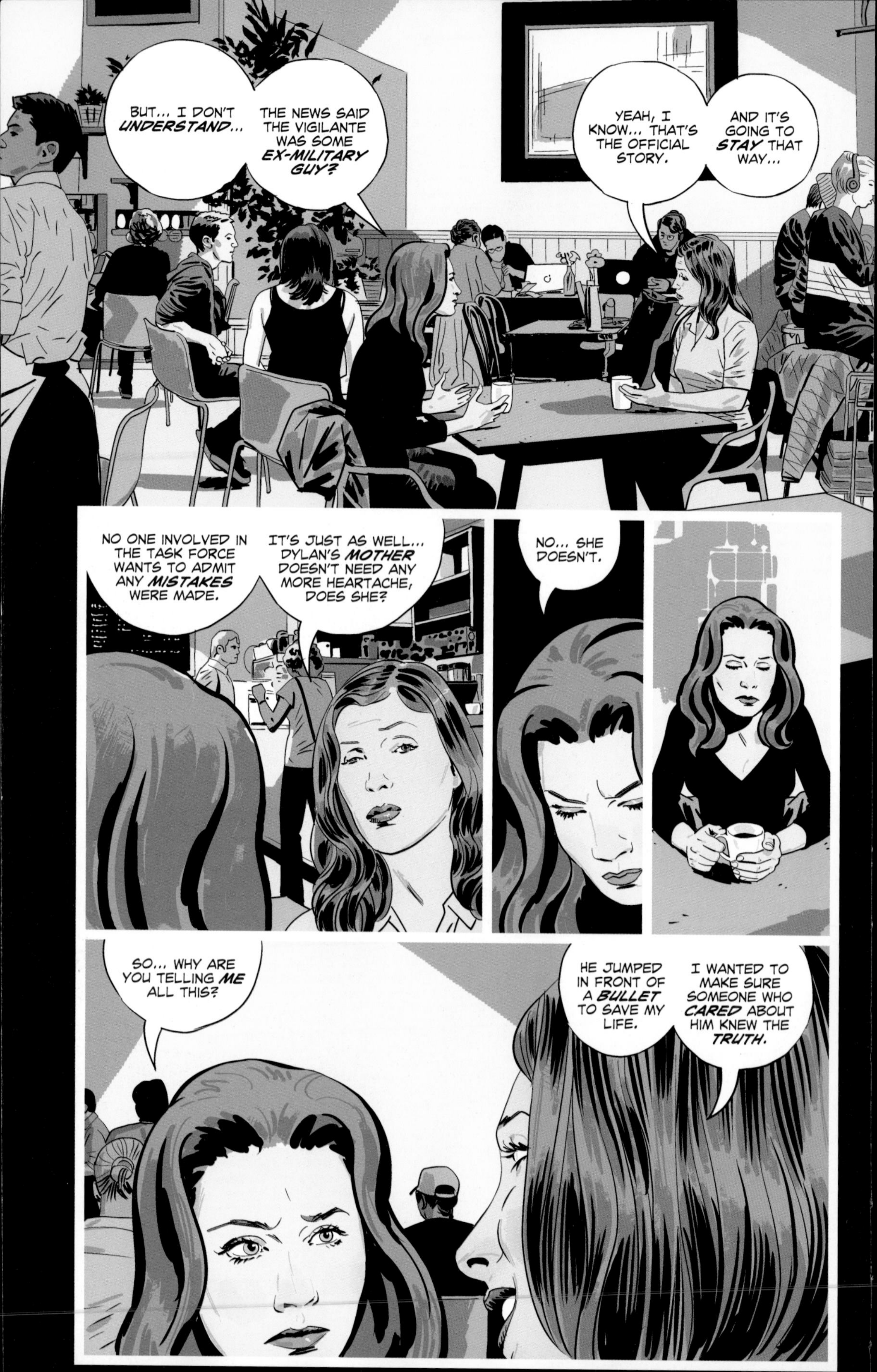
BUT... I DON'T UNDERSTAND...
THE NEWS SAID THE VIGILANTE WAS SOME EX-MILITARY GUY?
YEAH, I KNOW... THAT'S THE OFFICIAL STORY.
AND IT'S GOING TO STAY THAT WAY...
NO ONE INVOLVED IN THE TASK FORCE WANTS TO ADMIT ANY MISTAKES WERE MADE.
IT'S JUST AS WELL... DYLAN'S MOTHER DOESN'T NEED ANY MORE HEARTACHE, DOES SHE?
NO... SHE DOESN'T.
SO... WHY ARE YOU TELLING ME ALL THIS?
HE JUMPED IN FRONT OF A BULLET TO SAVE MY LIFE.
I WANTED TO MAKE SURE SOMEONE WHO CARED ABOUT HIM KNEW THE TRUTH.

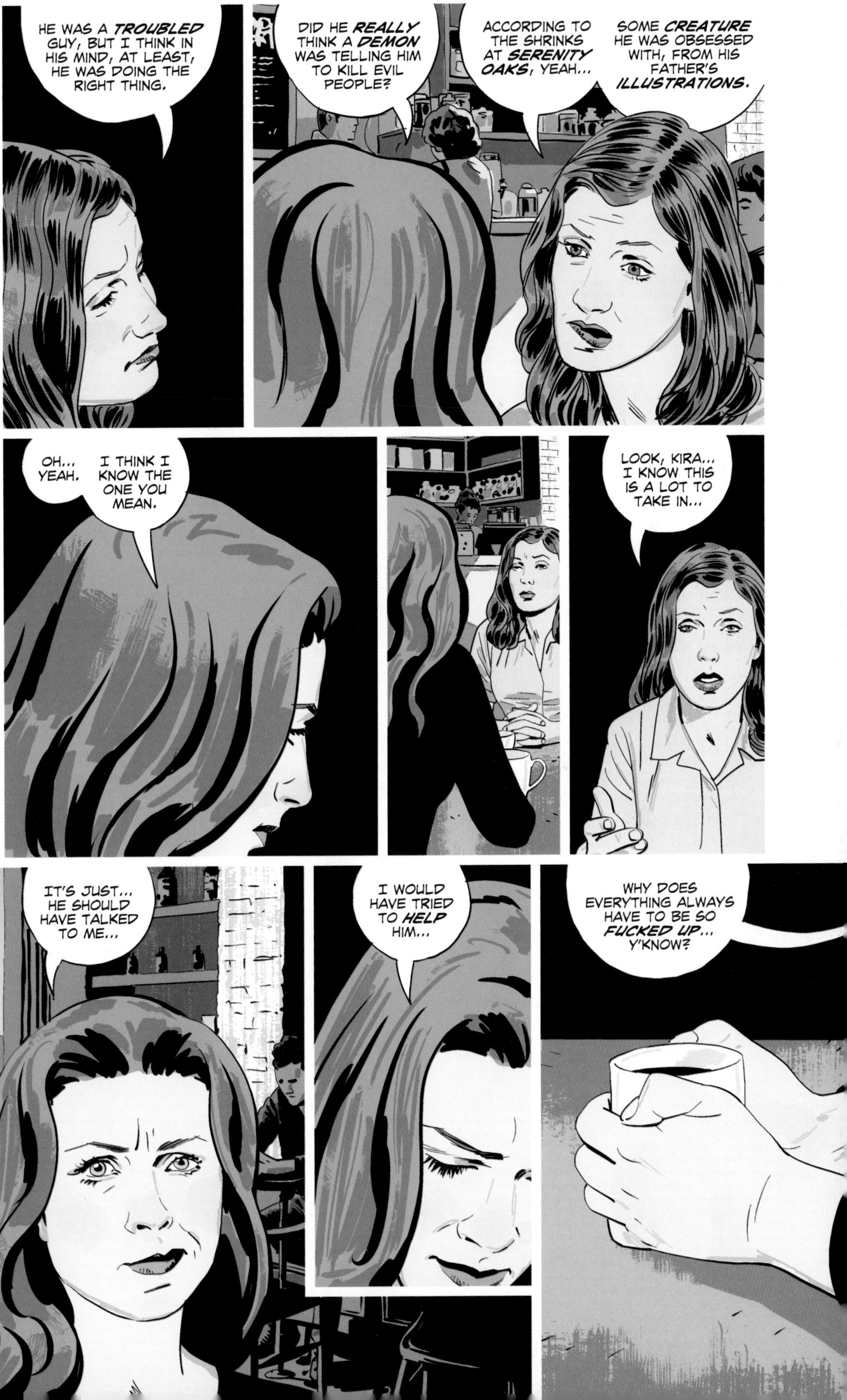
HE WAS A TROUBLED GUY, BUT I THINK IN HIS MIND, AT LEAST, HE WAS DOING THE RIGHT THING.
DID HE REALLY THINK A DEMON WAS TELLING HIM TO KILL EVIL PEOPLE?
ACCORDING TO THE SHRINKS AT SERENITY OAKS, YEAH...
SOME CREATURE HE WAS OBSESSED WITH, FROM HIS FATHER'S ILLUSTRATIONS.
OH... YEAH.
I THINK I KNOW THE ONE YOU MEAN.
LOOK, KIRA... I KNOW THIS IS A LOT TO TAKE IN...
IT'S JUST... HE SHOULD HAVE TALKED TO ME...
I WOULD HAVE TRIED TO HELP HIM...
WHY DOES EVERYTHING ALWAYS HAVE TO BE SO FUCKED UP... Y'KNOW?

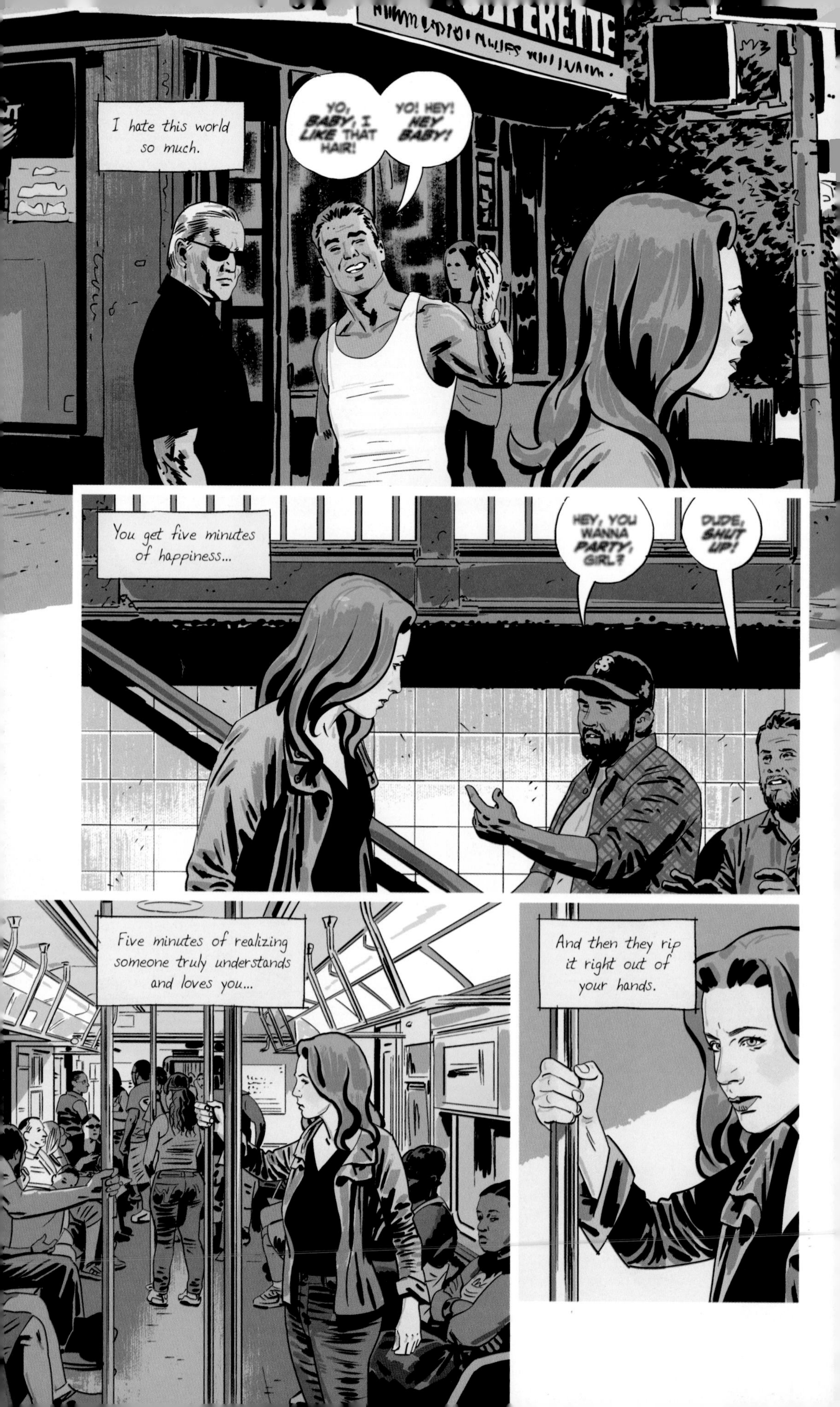
I hate this world so much.
YO, BABY, I LIKE THAT HAIR!
YO! HEY! HEY BABY!
You get five minutes of happiness...
HEY, YOU WANNA PARTY, GIRL?
DUDE, SHUT UP!
Five minutes of realizing someone truly understands and loves you...
And then they rip it right out of your hands.

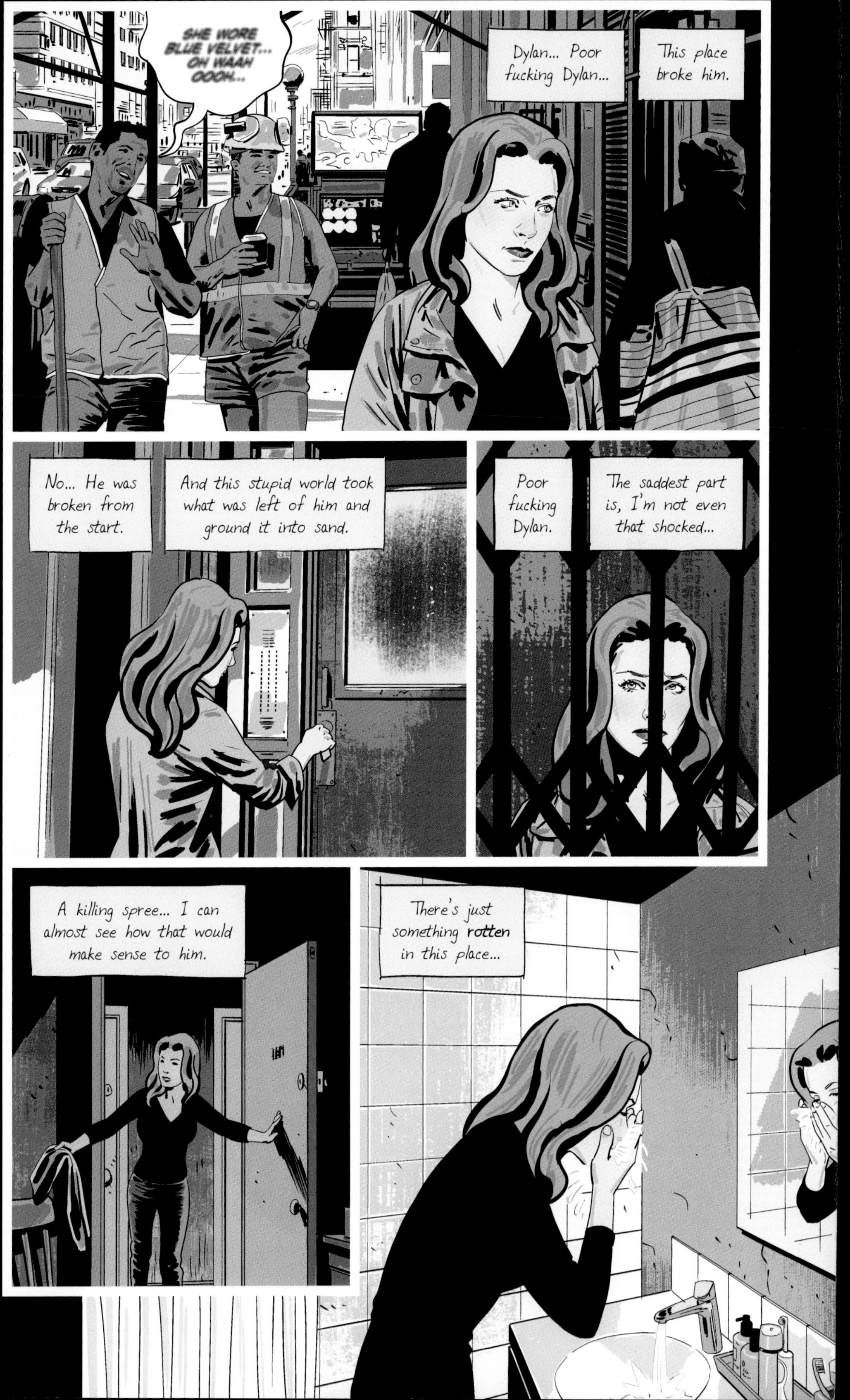
SHE WORE BLUE VELVET... OH WAAH OOOH...
Dylan... Poor fucking Dylan...
This place broke him.
No... He was broken from the start.
And this stupid world took what was left of him and ground it into sand.
Poor fucking Dylan.
The saddest part is, I'm not even that shocked...
A killing spree... I can almost see how that would make sense to him.
There's just something **rotten** in this place...

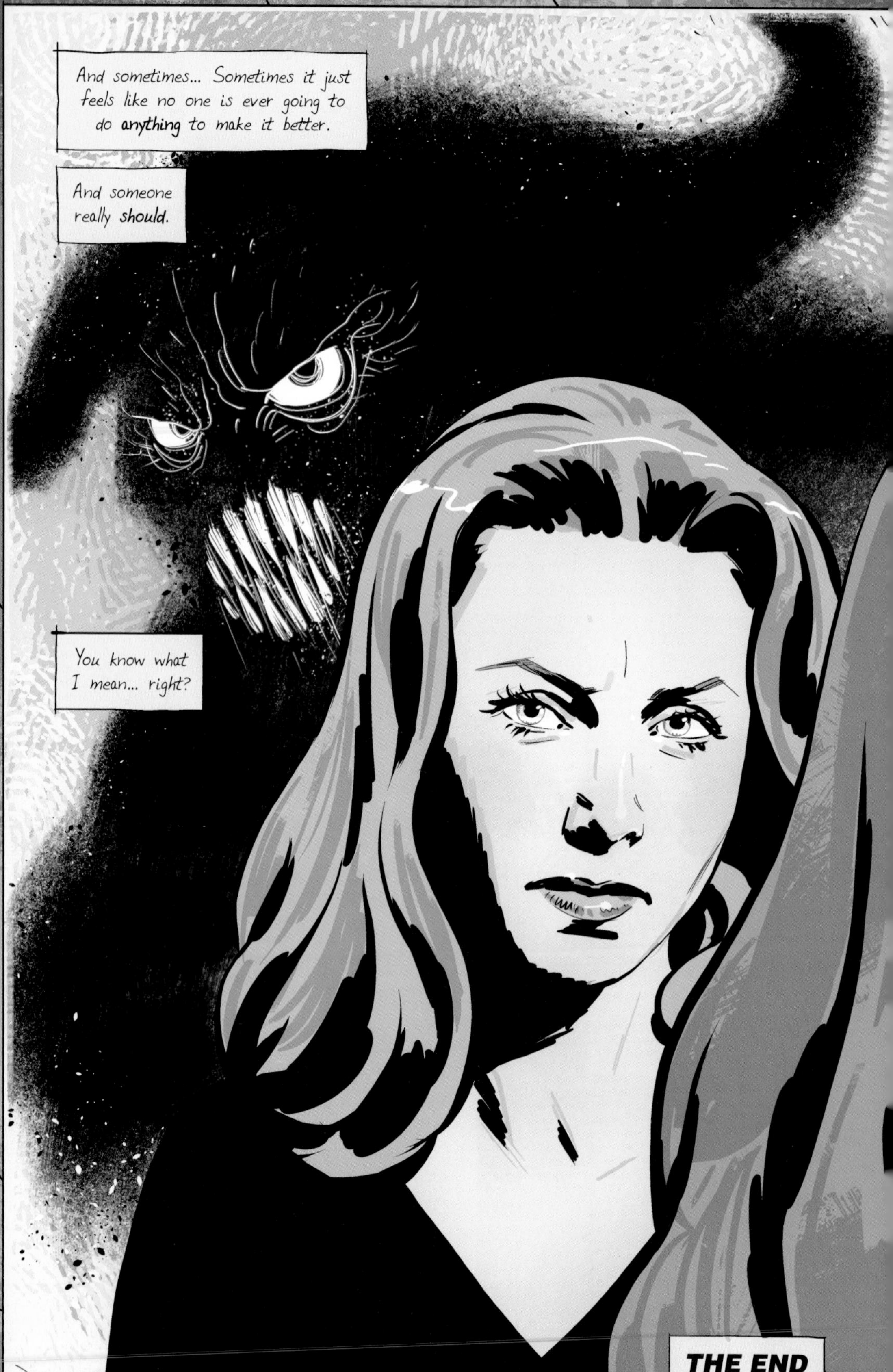

And sometimes... Sometimes it just feels like no one is ever going to do **anything** to make it better.
And someone really **should**.
You know what I mean... right?
THE END

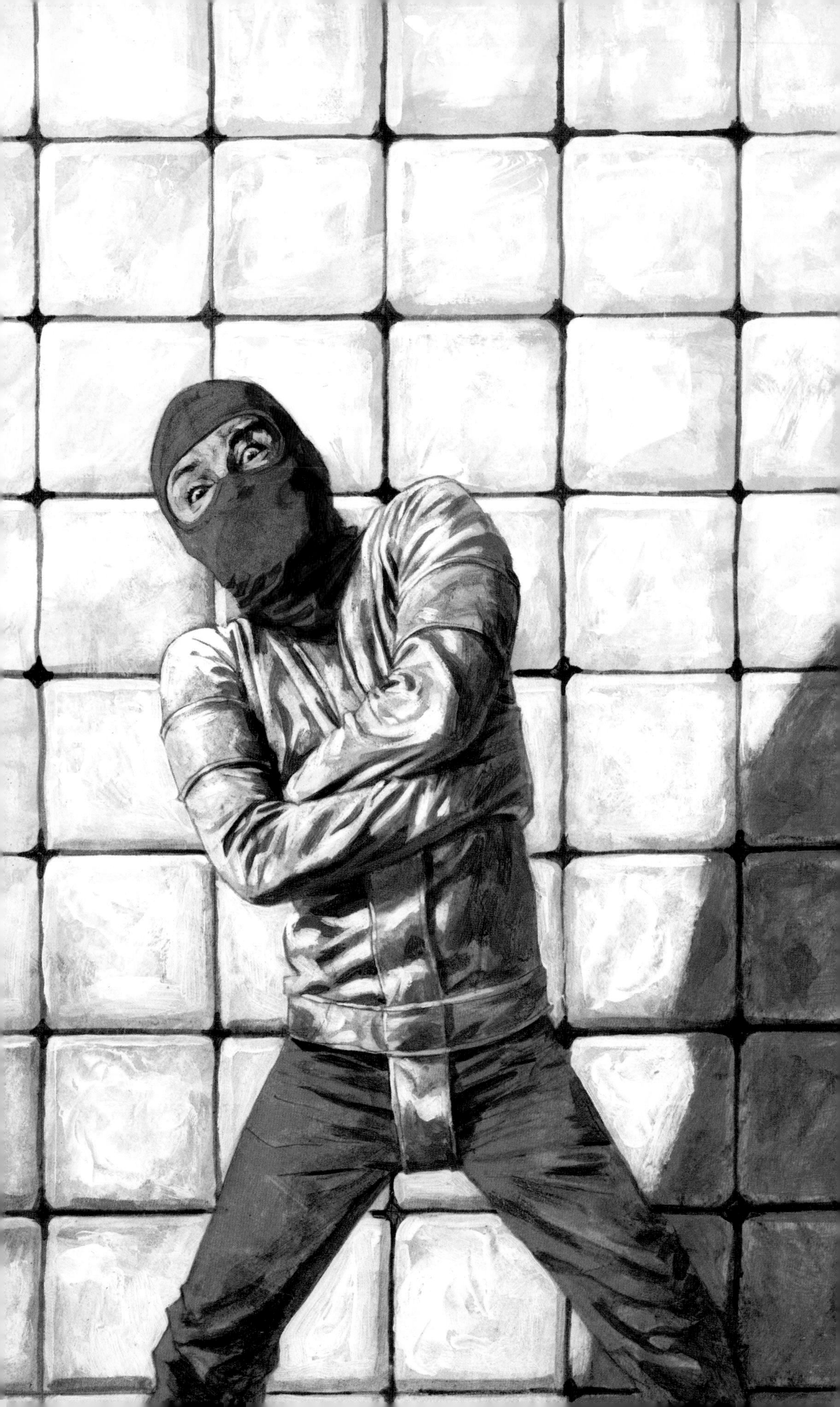

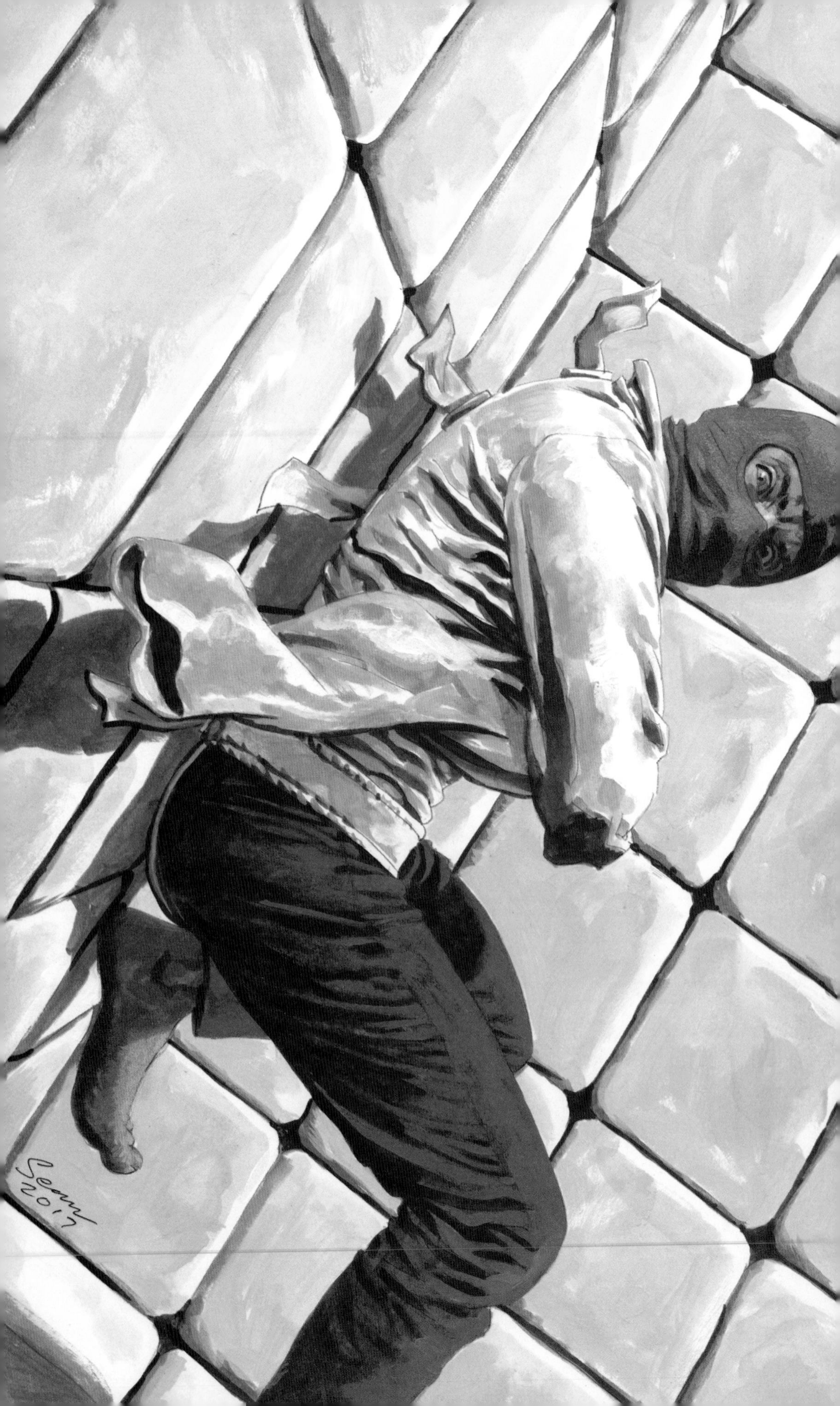

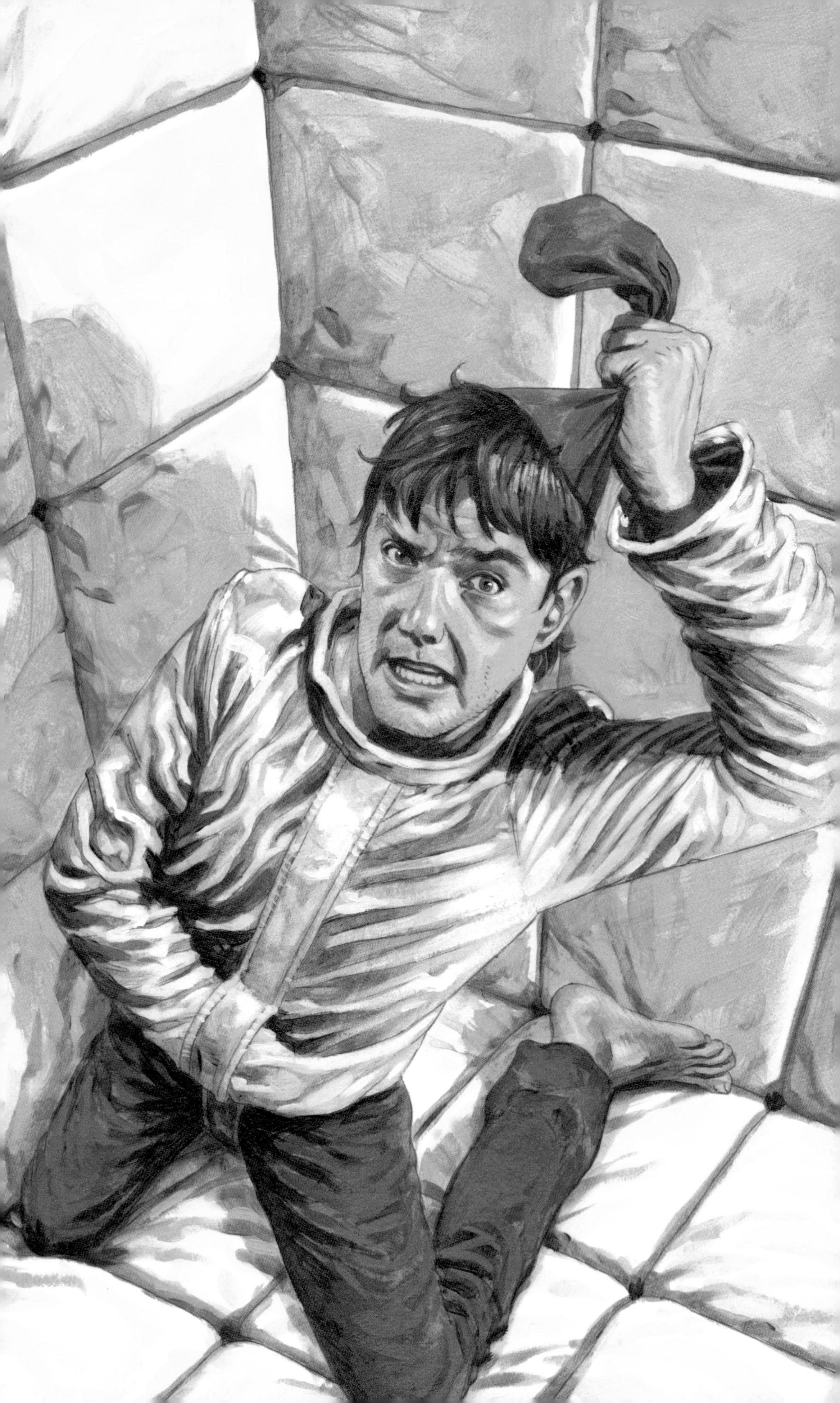

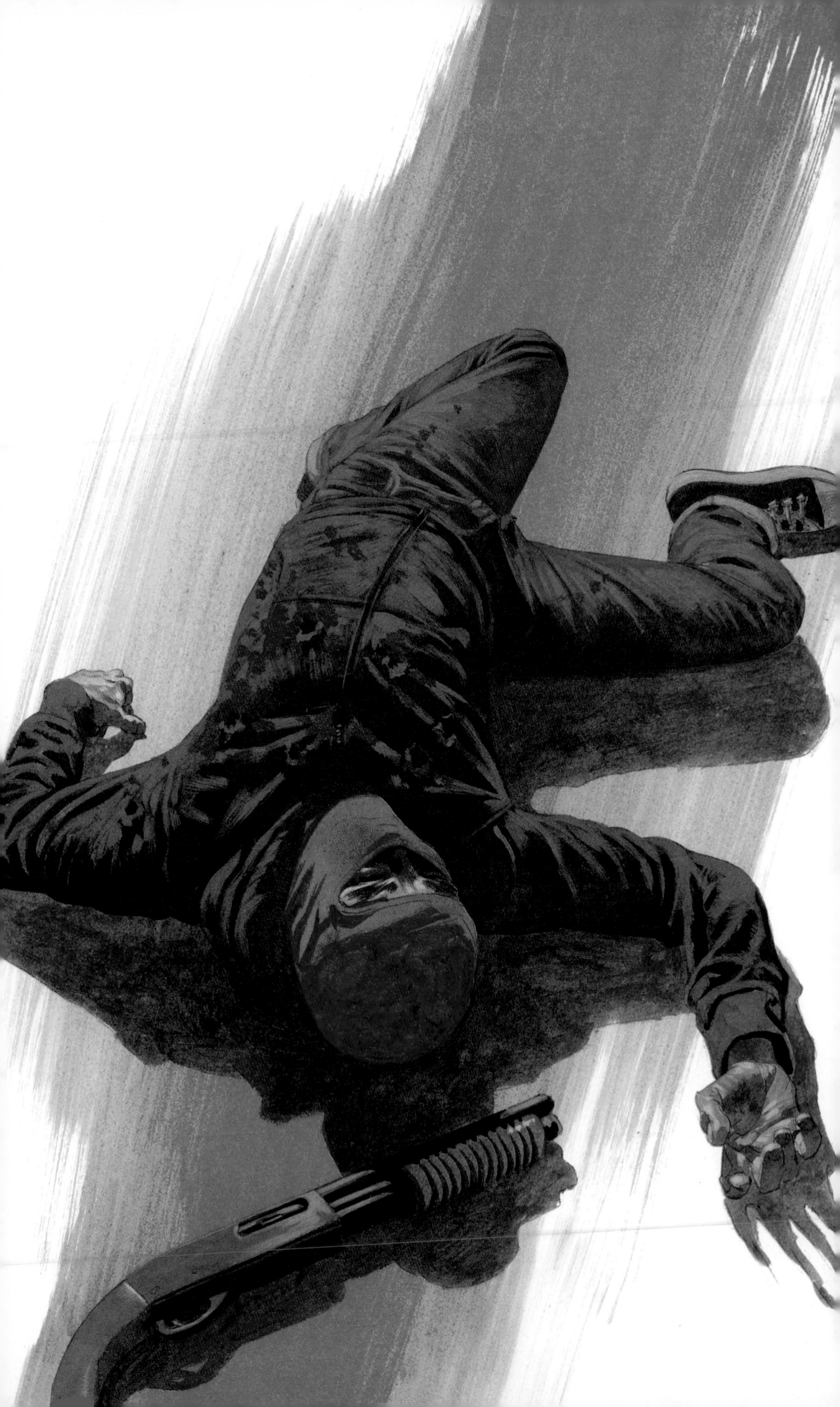

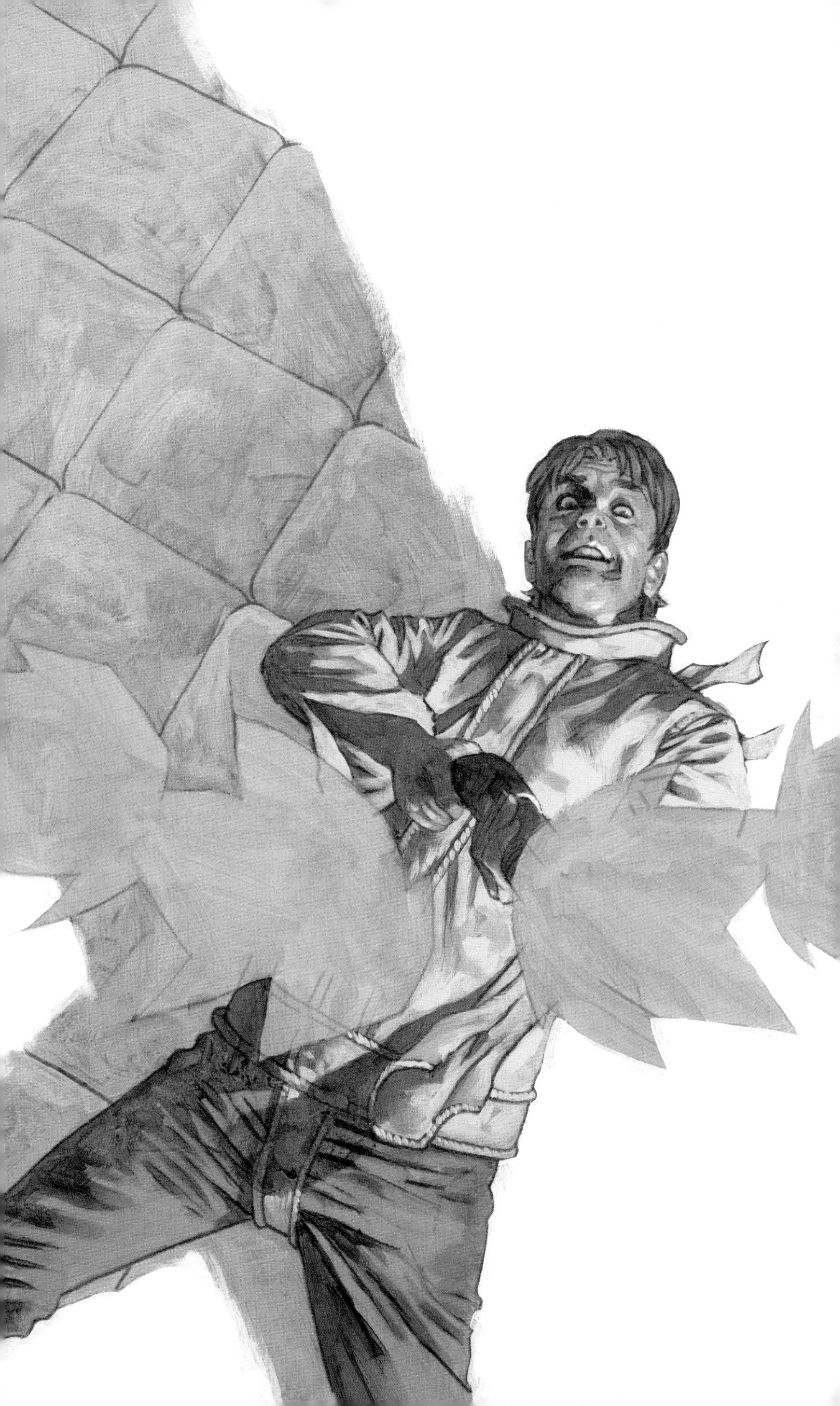

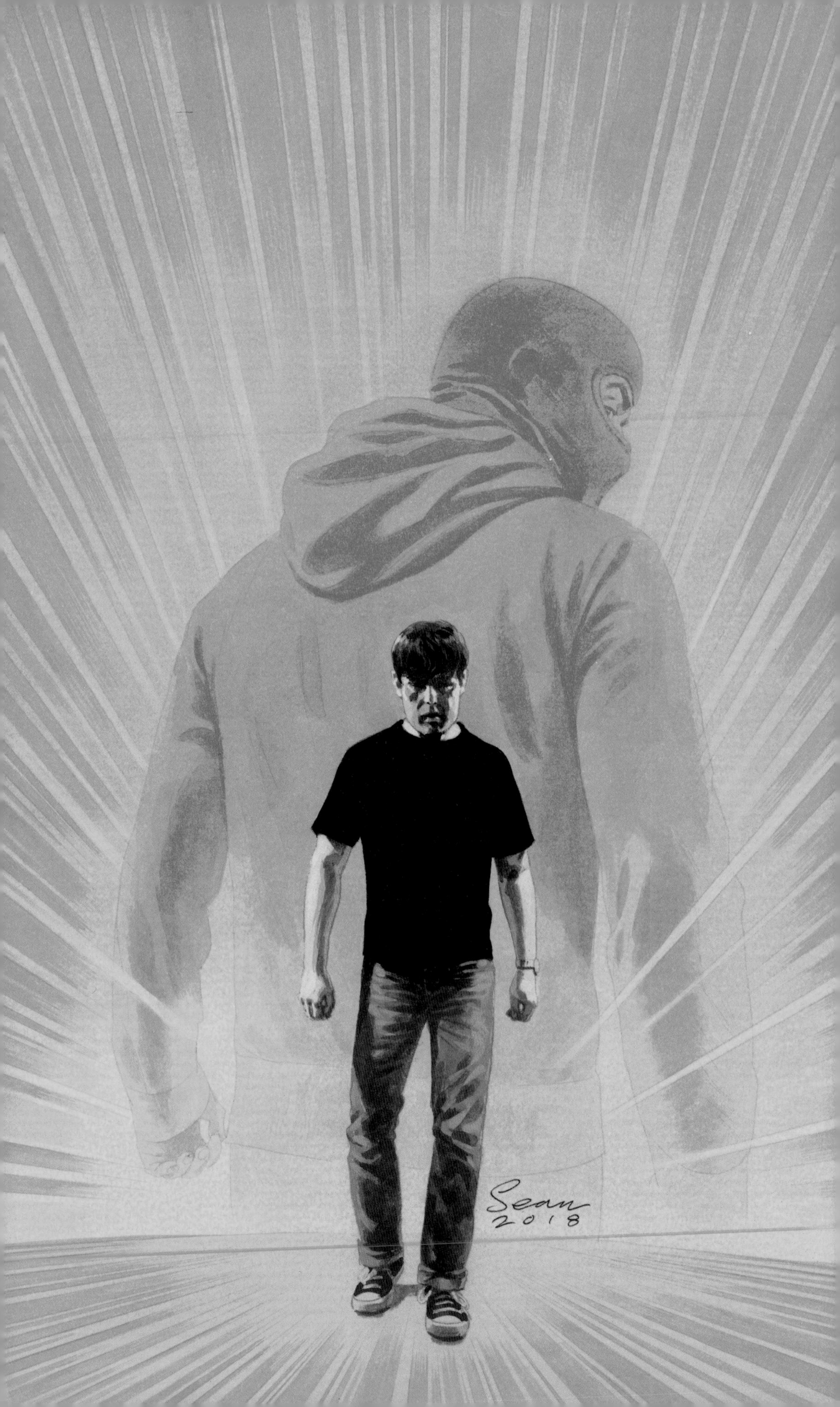
Sean
2018

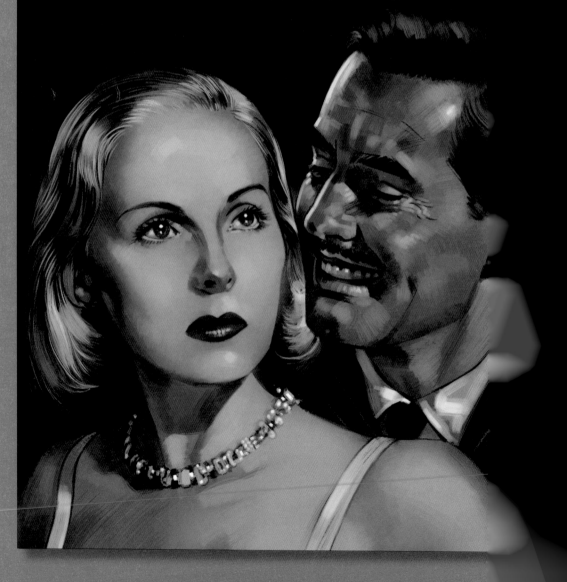

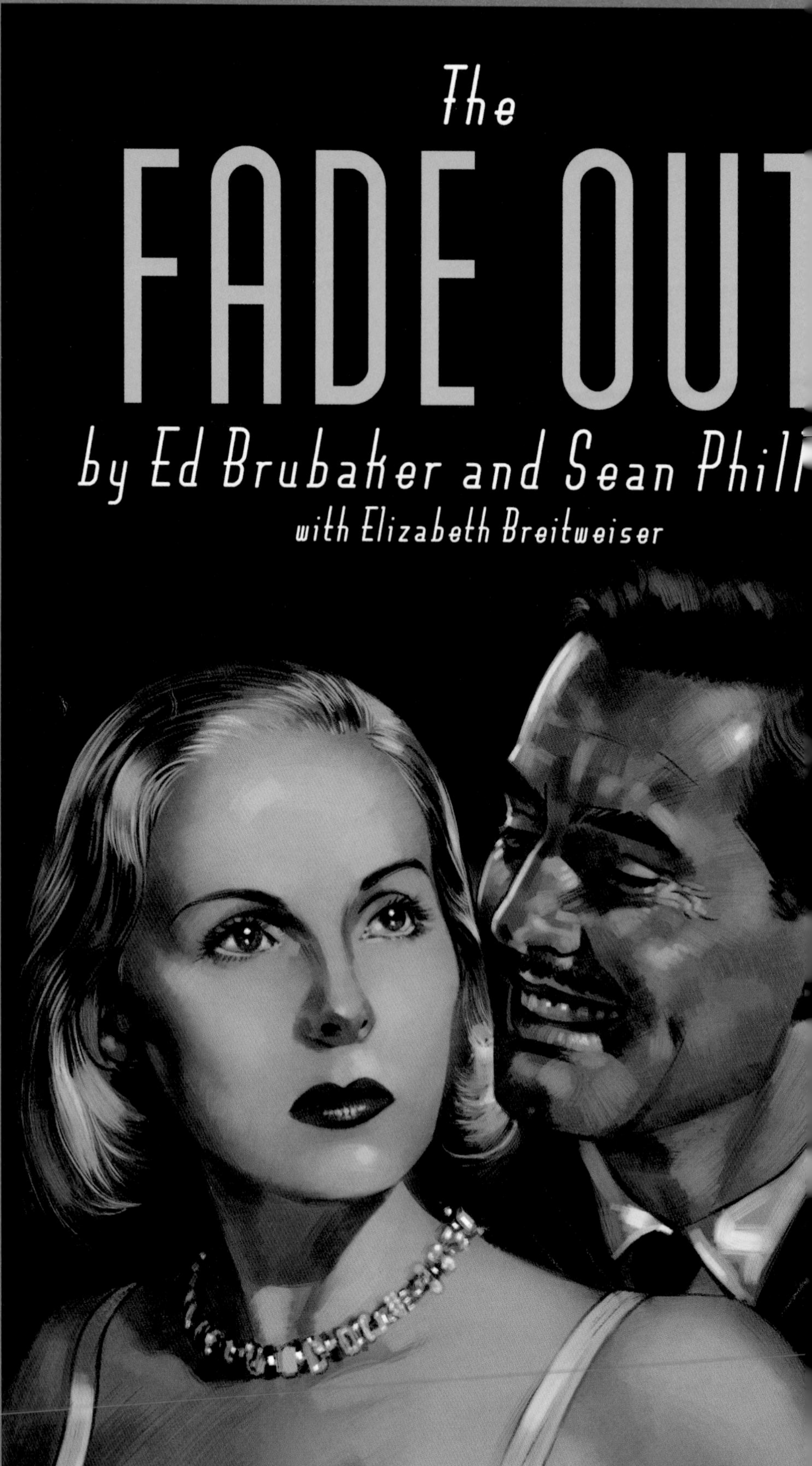
The
FADE OUT
by Ed Brubaker and Sean Phill
with Elizabeth Breitweiser

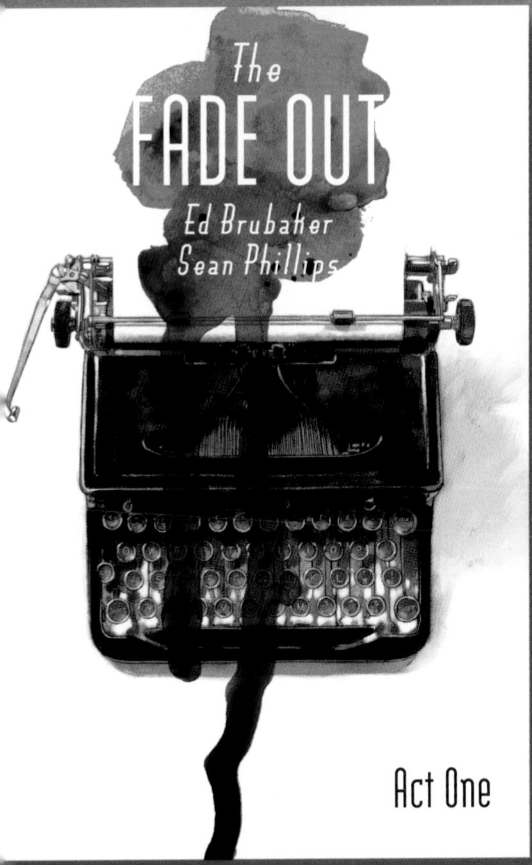
The
FADE OUT
Ed Brubaker
Sean Phillips
Act One

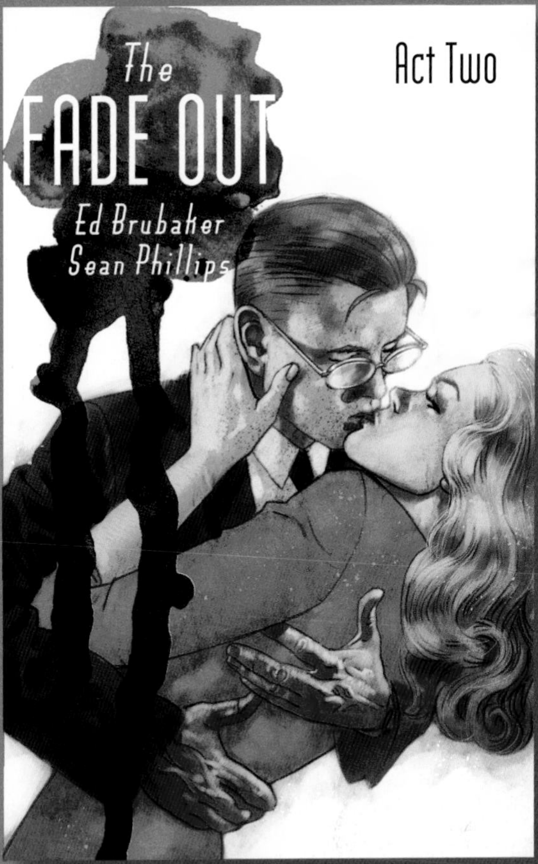
The
FADE OUT
Act Two
Ed Brubaker
Sean Phillips

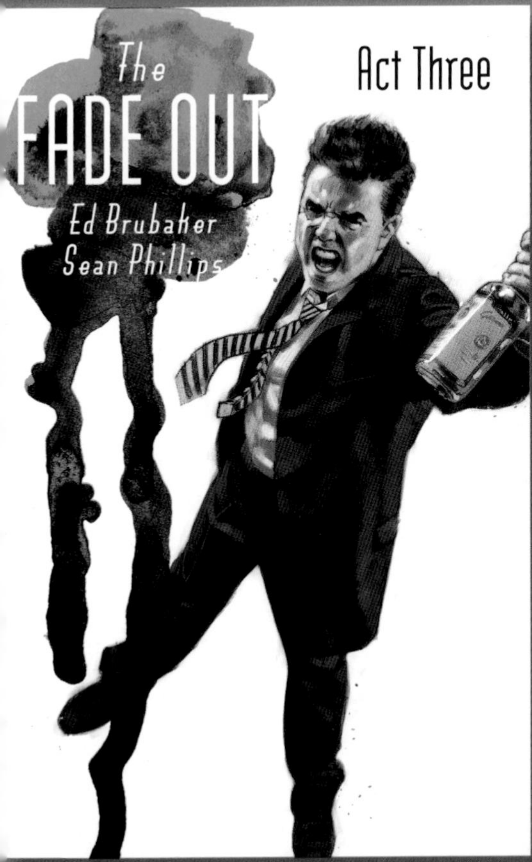
The
FADE OUT
Act Three
Ed Brubaker
Sean Phillips

"One of comics dream teams delivers their best story yet in ***THE FADE OUT****, an old Hollywood murder mystery draped against HUAC and the Red Scare."*

*- **New York Magazine***

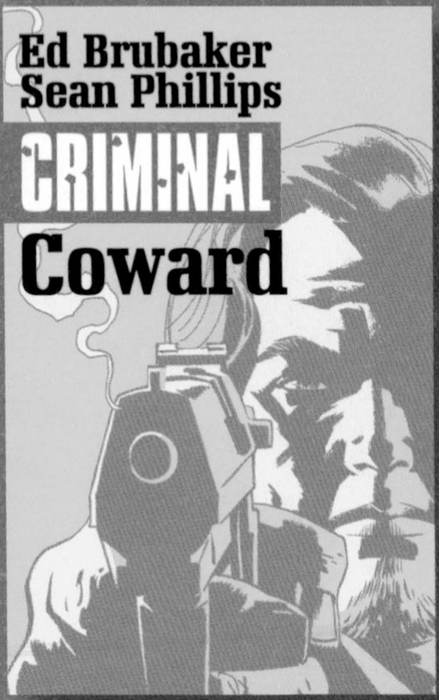
Ed Brubaker
Sean Phillips
CRIMINAL
Coward

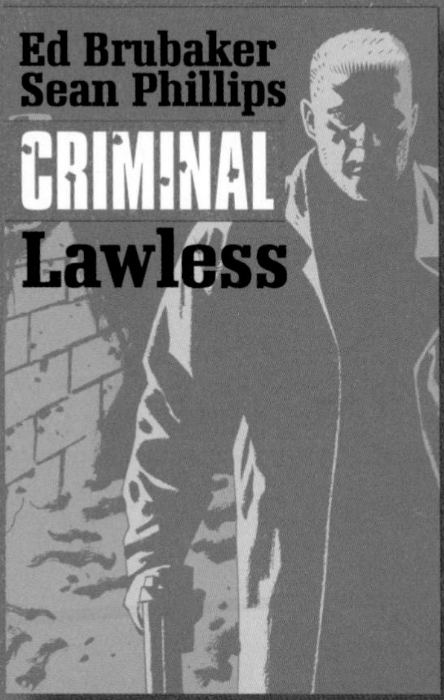
Ed Brubaker
Sean Phillips
CRIMINAL
Lawless

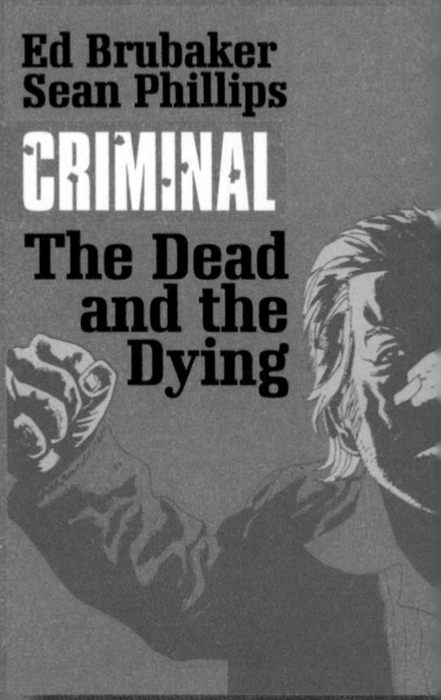
Ed Brubaker
Sean Phillips
CRIMINAL
The Dead and the Dying

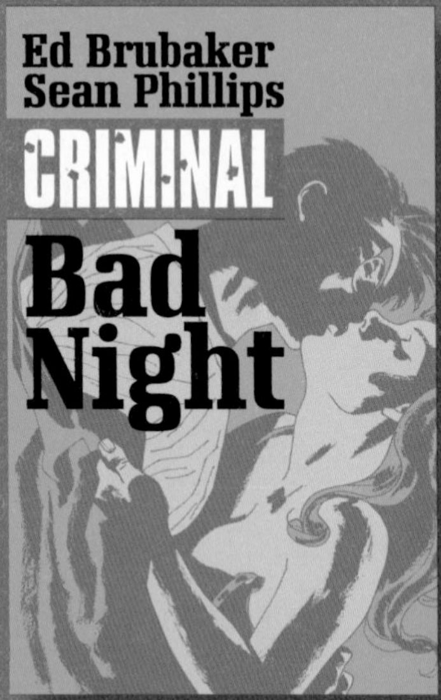
Ed Brubaker
Sean Phillips
CRIMINAL
Bad Night

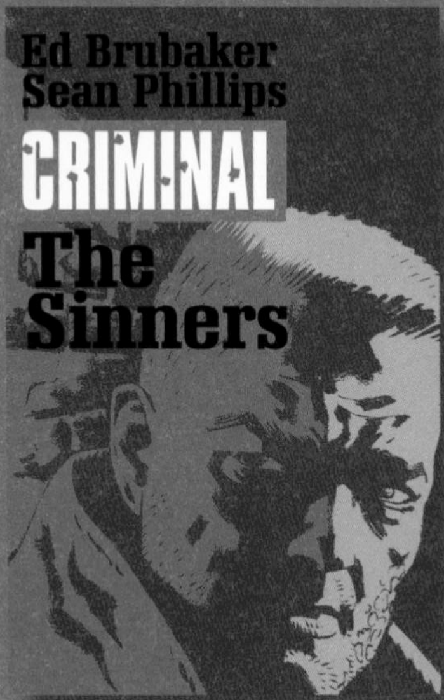
Ed Brubaker
Sean Phillips
CRIMINAL
The Sinners

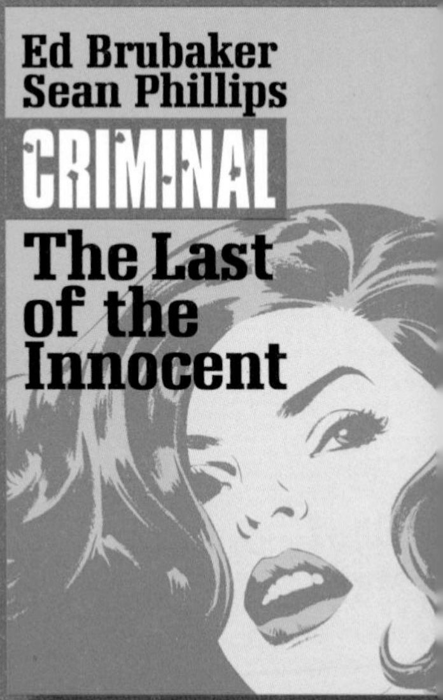
Ed Brubaker
Sean Phillips
CRIMINAL
The Last of the Innocent

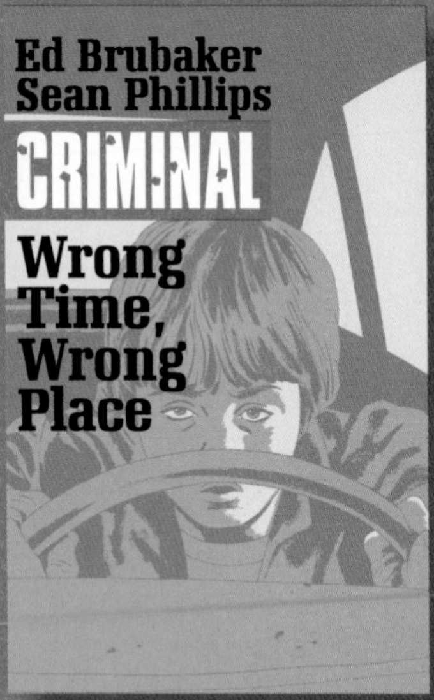
Ed Brubaker
Sean Phillips
CRIMINAL
Wrong Time, Wrong Place

"***CRIMINAL*** *is equal parts John Woo's* ***THE KILLER*** *Stanley Kubrick's* ***THE KILLING****, and Francis Ford Coppola's* ***THE GODFATHER.***"

- ***Playboy Magazine***